No Further Questions

GILLIAN McALLISTER

PENGUIN BOOKS

PENGUIN BOOKS

UK | USA | Canada | Ireland | Australia
India | New Zealand | South Africa

Penguin Books is part of the Penguin Random House group of companies
whose addresses can be found at global.penguinrandomhouse.com.

Published in Penguin Books 2018
001

Set in 12.5/14.75 pt Garamond MT Std
Typeset by Jouve (UK), Milton Keynes
Printed and bound in Great Britain by Clays Ltd, Elcograf S.p.A.

A CIP catalogue record for this book is available from the British Library

ISBN: 978–1–405–93460–2

www.greenpenguin.co.uk

For Tom, who taught me how to do voice
in a single summer

I

Martha

Somebody is lying in this courtroom. I don't know who, yet, but somebody is: the defence or the prosecution. They cannot both be telling the truth.

The legal jargon seems to swirl around me as I listen to expert after expert being examined, cross-examined, and then re-examined by the barristers. Most of the time, I'm following it. Most of the time, I understand what's happening.

But sometimes, like right now, I can't see how we ended up here.

Last August, I gave birth to Layla in the middle of the night. It was dark outside and we were sequestered away in a side room at the hospital, Scott sitting on the end of the bed. I don't remember when they finally handed her to me, but I remember her afterwards: a warm weight in my arms, her hand curling surprisingly around my own.

I'd texted my sister Becky, and only Becky, between contractions, though I hardly remember what I said. When she came to visit, she brought the late summer night-time chill in with her; I could feel her cold cheek against mine as she hugged me. 'You did it! Oh, you did it!' she said, celebrating me, and not the baby. It was exactly what I needed at that moment.

My sister.

The woman who used to WhatsApp me first thing, every single day, without fail. The woman whose eyebrows I plucked on the eve of her wedding, both of us laughing as they became more and more uneven. The woman who painted my living room with me one Easter weekend. We didn't stop chatting for the entire four days.

My sister. My best friend, Becky.

And now: here we are.

Cot death, the defence says – unexplained.

Murder, the prosecution says.

I look across at my sister in the dock.

The woman accused of murdering my child.

2

Becky

I can't resist them. My hands shake as I open my handbag and find the packet of cigarettes; their shiny, inviting inner foil unbroken and beautiful.

My breathing has already slowed as I bring the cigarette to my mouth for the first drag in weeks. I blow the clouds of smoke out into the night air and look at the sky above Dalston. I close my eyes in relief as the smoke hits my lungs. Sweet. Jesus. Poisonous joy.

There are no stars, but the moon is slung low and sepia-toned. I stare at it for a few minutes as I smoke and try not to cry. I'm not very good at not crying – classic drama queen – so my cheeks are wet with tears within seconds.

The television people I dress sets for would like a Dalmatian-print chesterfield armchair, and they want it by 9.00 a.m. This is the fourth time this has happened this week: a last-minute request, to be sorted out by me, and only me.

This wasn't how it was supposed to end up. I was going to be an Interior Designer. My obsession started with

Changing Rooms – God bless those leopard-print walls – but it endured beyond that. I dropped out of design school when I had Xander, my nine-year-old, and spent my twenties languishing on Pinterest, staring at copper lamps and furry throws. I thought set-dressing would give me an in, but instead it's just a dead end, like everything. *One day*, I tell myself.

My manager, Sandra, pokes her head out of the side door of the studio I am standing next to. 'On it?' she says. She is tall and slim and believes – very seriously, and very *vociferously* – in angels.

'Well, yes,' I say. 'But there aren't any. I've tried Gumtree, eBay and Etsy.'

'No chairs at all?'

'No.'

She sighs, her thin hand tightening on the metal door-handle. As I take my last puff and exhale, the smoke blurs her. 'How's it going to look, if we don't have that chair, Bex?'

Bex. I hate Bex. 'Bad,' I say petulantly.

'Have you exhausted every avenue?'

'I thought so.'

'Have another think,' she says, then goes back inside. The door sticks, and she doesn't pull it to like you're supposed to. I inch it shut with the toe of my shoe. I look back up at the old paper moon, and find my sister Martha's number in my phone: she will know what to do.

'Get a chair and some print then,' she says immediately. She has always been this way: clear-sighted and firm. 'It'll be easy,' she adds nicely. This must be the tenth work problem in a row that I have called her about this week.

4

Inflatable furniture, paddling pools, pug-printed duvet sets. Anything. Everything. She always helps, willingly and immediately.

'What – and cover it?' I say.

'Yes.' I can hear Layla crying in the background. Martha has her plate full, too, failing to take any maternity leave at all from her job – a charity that she set up herself – but here she is, answering my calls over a Dalmatian-print chair.

'Never mind,' I say. 'God. Don't worry about this stuff.'

'It's fine, Beck,' she says. 'Honestly.'

'A chair and print,' I repeat. 'I'll report back.'

We hang up, and I take to Google again. I ring four haberdasheries to see if they can help me, but they don't answer; they're closed.

Luckily, there is extortionate Dalmatian-print fabric on eBay, sold for mad people. I send one of the sellers a desperate message, and she responds almost immediately, the app ringing in my hand as I light up my second cigarette. I can get it from Islington before eleven tonight. *Great*, I think sullenly.

I get the Tube straight there, using the excellent new Tube WiFi to search for a chair on the way. There is an armchair in Balham on Gumtree. The seller's username is 'ILoveHarryStyles' and I think: *Well, don't we all?* I arrange to get it at 11.30 p.m.

The fabric is easy. The woman – short, plump, with a Bristolian accent – hands it to me wordlessly outside the front door of her ground-floor flat. I thank her profusely, and pay her on the eBay app while she watches over my shoulder. She doesn't move as I put my Verified by Visa account details in – no doubt I will get robbed soon – and then I send a photograph of it to Martha, captioned: *One down!* She sends a string of applauding hands back, and my mood lifts.

The chair lives ten minutes from Balham Tube station, at 193a Ravenslea Road. I gather the roll of fabric as the Tube pulls in. On the way up the escalator, a man complains at me for blocking the way – calls me a 'silly bint' – and I stand the roll of fabric on the stair in front of me and move out of his way. 'Don't bother to thank me,' I say to his back as he strides upwards. He turns to look at me.

'I'm sorry,' he says in a broad Essex accent. 'I was in a hurry.'

I walk past him in the foyer as he calls for a taxi. He comes out after me, and I let the door slam on his arm on my way out. He shouts something, but I march onwards. Twat.

A woman wearing an actual negligee answers the door in Balham. I blink as I take in the black fabric, the thin straps across her shoulders, then follow her in anyway. The chair is faded and green, standing in the corner of the room underneath a reading lamp. Behind it are leather-bound classics. It looks like the set of a Victorian murder novel. Well, at least I will die doing what I love.

I pay her fifty pounds for the chair, the rolled notes dry and papery in my fingers as I part with them. Her brown eyes linger over the fabric I'm holding, but I don't explain. She doesn't help me with the chair, and it thuds clumsily against my leg, squeaking along the wood, as I half-lift, half-drag it across her hallway and down the steps. She stands just inside her living room, arms wrapped around her body, silently watching me, then closes the door.

I'm already out of breath, having moved both items

only a few feet, and I stop and survey the dark street. Two men are walking on the other side of the road towards me, and I stare at them as they move past. I could ask for help. But this is London.

I have a small rest instead, thinking about interior design school, and where I might be by now if I'd finished. I think about bloody perfect Martha, juggling being CEO of a charity, having a newborn, and dealing with her errant sister's search for Dalmatian-print fabric.

At least I have a seat. I perch on it for a few moments, watching the world go by: a madwoman in a green chair on the street in Balham.

I hail a black cab and the chair sits next to me inside it like an obedient, silent animal. I don't look at it as I try to recall where I last stored my fabric stapler at the house.

As the taxi departs London at just after midnight, I text Martha and ask if she is up.

Of course I am – providing a round-the-clock service to a constantly crying baby she replies immediately.

I call her and say, 'I can't do this any more,' as soon as she picks up. My voice sounds thick and self-pitying. I stare at the taxi driver. He's also working late. *Think about it: he's got to drive you to Brighton, then drive back to London*, Martha would admonish me. There is always somebody worse off, so she says. She is nice like this. I am not. I have always wanted to be more like her, though not enough to actually try, of course.

'You can,' Martha says. 'Staple-gun the fabric. It'll only take twenty minutes. Then bed.'

'And up at six. For another insane request,' I say.

'Is Xander with Marc? After school?'

'Yes. It won't be long. This job is only a week,' I say.

Martha makes her sympathy noise. A low *mmhmmm*. 'It's rubbish, Beck,' she says. 'It's so rubbish.' She means it. She must mean it. But I think of *her* life, caring for always-crying Layla, and juggling work, too, and wonder how she can mean it.

'How's your To Do list looking, anyway?' I say.

'Oh – it's just impossible. The phone's ringing off the hook.'

Martha set up a charity the previous year, and hasn't *quite* relinquished control. She never does.

'Layla's crying all the time while I'm trying to bloody hire people.'

'Oh, oh no,' I say.

'I interviewed two childminders but they were rubbish. One didn't know what baby-led weaning was.'

'You should just get a nanny,' I say. 'You need *staff*, not help.'

'I don't even have time to hire anybody. That's how bad it is.'

'I see.'

We don't say anything for a few seconds.

Until I say, 'I want to quit.'

To her credit, she doesn't sigh.

'I don't even like dressing sets,' I add.

'Quit, if you want to,' she says. 'Life's too short to staple dead Dalmatians to chairs for ever.'

We laugh at that, for a long time, on the way home.

The next day, she makes a proposition, and I hand my notice in on the spot.

Monday

Prosecution

3

Martha

My hair has been falling out since it happened. Long, wet strands in the shower. I don't mind, really. There is more to life than hair.

I stare out into the public gallery. Mum, Dad, my husband, Scott, my brother, Ethan.

Ethan, a lawyer, looks relaxed amongst the wigs and the robes. I remember when he used to shake with laughter at juvenile jokes around the dining-room table. Becky used to say he changed, that he let life and its mundane struggles overcome him.

'You're like a grumpy old man,' she once hissed at him. It was at the meet-and-greet at my and Scott's wedding, and Becky hung back, downing her prosecco. I didn't say anything to either of them, fussing instead with my gown. She was tipsy. Ethan was reserved, preferring one-on-ones instead. It was a microcosm of our family dynamic, my wedding. I don't remember it fondly. Becky had accused me of being a bridezilla the night before. 'She's just organized,' Mum had said kindly.

Since Becky was charged, Ethan has been stoic; uncompromisingly uninvolved, refusing to speculate, to answer questions on procedure. 'Not my area of law,' he has said, interrupting us mid-question.

Scott catches my eye and nods, just once, his eyebrows raised ever so slightly, an encouraging expression on his face. 'You can do it,' he said to me last night, the night before the first day of the trial. 'You can, you can. *We* can.'

Becky is led into the courtroom.

I swallow. I haven't seen her for months and months.

She has become thin. Her ribs are a birdcage, her hands oversized compared to her arms. I want to reach out and hold those bony shoulders of hers. She was always tall, and broad, which she hated but I loved; I thought she seemed somehow full of life. But today she is diminished.

She has the same walk. I shouldn't be pleased to see it, but I am. You expect people will change utterly since *the night of*, but they don't. It has been nine and a half months since it happened, and nine months since we last saw each other. We were prohibited from speaking from the moment she was charged. We became opposing witnesses. Me for the prosecution and she for the defence. Two sisters, carved in two by the justice system.

But here it is, months on: her beautiful walk, in the flesh, as if no time has passed at all. You can't change a walk like that. She has always bounded, like an overly friendly Labrador, and she is no different today, standing at the door to the dock, somehow, in an extroverted manner. Loud, without being so.

Becky always worked hard at being cool. It was important to her. The right sort of bands and nail varnish and movies – 'No, Marth, the rips must be *across* the knees,' she said last year when I tried on a pair of incorrectly torn jeans – and always the thick layer of liquid eyeliner, the pink blusher. But her walk gave her away; her eager walk that I once loved so much. Still do, I suppose.

I am sworn in and take the secular oath. My voice is clear and loud in the courtroom, which surprises me. I was a geography teacher for years, though. I was used to performing through winter colds and extreme end-of-term fatigue. I pretend the public gallery is a classroom of bright-eyed children, for a moment, and it helps.

Some water has been placed in front of me in a white plastic cup with ridges around its sides.

And here we are: I am in the witness box and Becky is in the dock. She is staring straight at me, her head turned to the left, like a very pretty zoo animal. A deer, maybe, or a giraffe. Her eyelashes, they were always so beautiful. So long and curved, like a Disney princess's. Our eyes meet. *I am only going to say what I know*, I try to tell her. Afterwards, I'll join the public gallery, and watch. And, at the end of it, I will know the truth. For Layla.

Was it only a year ago when she came to the hospital right after Layla was born? I can't believe it. It feels not just years ago, but as though it happened to some other family; someone I know well, whose movements I've known all my life, like cousins or family friends we had over for dinner regularly. But not to us.

I avert my eyes from hers, and look at the jury instead. Eleven women. One man. None of them looks nervous, or as if they bear the weight of responsibility. One woman has a cat on her jumper, its black ears made of sequins. Becky would want to know what kind of selection process could lead to someone wearing a cat jumper to a murder trial. 'That is quite the statement,' she would say.

The prosecution barrister stands up. She tells me her name is Ms Ellen Hendry, even though we have already met briefly. It is all a performance, to her. She has an upper-class, raspy voice, like you would expect of a strict violin teacher or a housemistress at a private school.

'And you are Martha Blackwater. You are Layla's mum,' she says.

I almost double over on the stand. The present tense.

'Yes,' I say softly.

She regards me seriously over her glasses.

My hand shakes as I reach to push my hair back behind my ear. Scott used to do this, just occasionally. I would close my eyes and relax into his touch, like a contented animal. He doesn't do it any more, doesn't venture his hands within a few feet of my body; it's as if I am surrounded by a force field.

'Now, Martha, I know this is going to be *incredibly* difficult for you,' she says.

I don't say anything back: what is there to say? Becky always accuses me of favouring silence when things get awkward, and I suppose she's right, but anything I could say would be useless; trite, maybe.

'Why don't you tell us a little bit about baby Layla, her history.' She turns away from me, so I can only see the back of her wig, the crimped pattern on the back of her robes. The jury's eyes trace her hand as it reaches to straighten her wig like they are watching a famous actor in a play.

I am *Mum* and Layla is *Baby Layla*, and I see that, to her, we are merely proper nouns, legal constructs. Perhaps she must distance herself in this way, but to me it is distasteful. I would usually exchange a glance with Becky at a moment like this. She would raise her eyebrows, and say, 'And the barrister speaks like Winston fucking Churchill.'

My cheeks heat up just like they did at school whenever I was asked to speak.

I flounder for a few moments, thinking. I knew she'd ask this – and yet. The world tilts around me. How can I possibly explain it all, here, now?

'She wasn't an easy baby,' I say. 'She had reflux.'

In the distance of the courtroom, in the dock, I see Becky's head drop. I have condemned her.

'How bad?'

'She would writhe around after feeds. She cried – well . . .' I give a sad laugh. 'She is – was, she *was* – my first baby. So I don't know how normal any of it was. But she seemed to cry –' I stop, unable to continue. Those little tears of hers would break my heart for ever.

I close my eyes, just for a second. Her peach-fuzz skin. I can't open my eyes. Her tiny feet, those warm feet that would fit in the palm of my hand.

'She cried an awful lot,' I finish, returning to reality and looking at the barrister.

'How many hours out of every twenty-four?'

I throw up a hand. 'I don't know.'

The barrister says nothing, merely looks down again at her notes. 'Can you give us a rough guess?'

'It felt, to me, like she was crying whenever she was awake.'

'Whenever she was awake.'

'Yes, sometimes.'

'Thank you. And did she ever have fits? Was she ever unwell?'

'No,' I say, my voice sounding thick and coated. 'She was perfectly healthy, save for the reflux.'

'Nothing further,' she says. She pushes her glasses up her nose with a large hand. I catch a glimpse of her ring finger. Bare. Married to the job, maybe. Prosecuting on behalf of other broken families, instead of having her own.

The defence barrister rises as gracefully as a ballerina. 'Ms Blackwater, my name is Harriet. I act for the defence.'

This, here, must be the most important person in Becky's current life. She has neat, straight dark hair – pulled back in a bun underneath her wig – slim hips and a boyish waist. She is inscrutable, neither smiling nor frowning, her eyes cold as they meet mine.

'You arranged for the defendant, Rebecca, to become your baby's *nanny*, did you not?'

I draw my lips tight. 'Yes,' I say shortly, not looking at Becky, though I can feel her gaze on me. 'She was both her aunt and her nanny, for a while.'

'And did money change hands?'

'Yes. Of course. She left her job so I . . . so I could have the childcare that I needed.'

'And that was why she was Layla's nanny?'

'Yes. Becky – Rebecca – she had this job that – where she – that she didn't—'

'Why did you specifically appoint *Rebecca* to be Layla's nanny?'

'I – she loved her. And I trusted her.'

'Absolutely?'

'Yes.'

'And you never would have believed anything would happen to Layla in her care?'

'Never. I trusted her one hundred per cent,' I say. I can't look across at Becky, or over at my family in the public gallery. I don't look at anybody. Just down at the untouched cup of water on the edge of the witness stand, its clear surface trembling.

I remember when I hurriedly said goodbye to Layla for the last time. I don't recall her milk and lavender smell, or the weight of her. Instead, I see it from her point of view, watch myself retreating gradually away from her. Was she scared? Did she miss me in the primal way I missed her? Life had always been about so many things before her – reading novels and brunches out and mowing the lawn and my job – and then she came along: the linchpin. My large hand, so like my mother's, against her small back. I became fully adult the day I had her.

'One hundred per cent. Nothing further,' Harriet says quietly.

The lawyers want to address the judge at his bench, so everybody files out after my evidence. Mum joins me and we sit together in a side corridor. The others have stayed in the foyer. To give us space, I guess.

A man across from us is struggling to bring a shaking hand to his lips, his cup of tea taking a precarious route to his mouth.

Mum leans her head backwards. 'How are you feeling?'

'I'm okay.' I look across at her and wonder how this is for her. Her grandchild. Her daughters on opposing sides of a criminal case. Sometimes, when I call her up, her voice is hoarse and strangled, as though she has been crying. But she's stoic. She won't show her grief to me because, she would reason, mine is greater.

'You were good. Dispassionate and clear. They didn't trip you up.'

'They didn't ask me why I left her,' I say.

'And why would they?' She turns to me in surprise. She has a line of white roots at the top of her hair, dyed dark every few weeks by her long-time hairdresser, Anwar. She rests her leg against mine, and I could become a puddle of tears right here.

When Becky was first charged, Mum and Dad told me everything. The evidence against her, the charge, her defence, what the prosecution were alleging. They never said outright whether they thought she was guilty or not. They couldn't seem to and, soon after, not having said either way became an obvious omission. Taboo. Only Ethan has spoken out about his belief in her innocence. Mum and Dad prevaricate, and avoid the issue, caught between us.

And then, when the cogs of the justice system began to turn, Mum and Dad withdrew, telling me less and less. 'Leave it to the experts,' Dad would mutter, while Mum stared at the floor. I can't blame them: they didn't know what to do. Becky and I are opposing witnesses in a trial, after all. Unwilling participants in the theatre of the justice system.

I stopped hearing about her defence. About her side of it. What her medical experts said. Who was going to testify that she hadn't done it. It made them uncomfortable, I suppose, to be facilitating the exchange of dangerous information between two opposing sides. It was contraband. I was – in all but law – the victim. She was the accused. In the end, I couldn't take their guilty, shifty expressions, their anguish, and so I stopped asking.

'You were a funny child,' she says. 'Really funny. Do you know?'

'A bit,' I say.

'So thoughtful, and sensitive. It was *wonderful*. You thought about how the daffodils felt and whether a day seemed like an entire year to a woodlouse – all sorts of things.'

'It started with the homeless people,' I say with a shy smile. It's a well-worn family story, just like the old ragged towels Mum still has in her airing cupboard with their seventies prints. Becky hates those towels – she brings her own when she visits – but I love them, and still like to put my finger through their familiar holes, like to feel their threadbare fabric against my skin after a shower.

'It did. I never, ever thought I would have a six-year-old worrying about homeless people. And then asking and asking!' She reaches over and takes my hand.

The tears begin a waterfall in my chest and I let a few drops out before I resolutely turn the tap off again.

I am not sure whether I remember the moment itself, or a retelling of it. Mum used to let me have any ice cream I wanted, on the day she did the food shopping. We always collected the ice cream – always mint chocolate chip, in winter and in summer – and then went to Sainsbury's, where it dripped as I trailed around each aisle. On the way to the ice cream parlour, there was a homeless man in one of the Lanes in Brighton. He had bare feet, exposed to the cold air. My glimpse of him was only fleeting, but as Mum led me away, and we headed to Sainsbury's, I kept seeing those feet, those toes, the dirt of the streets set into the grooves of his flesh.

'Mummy, why was that man outside like that?' I asked.

Mum said something comforting. That some people weren't as fortunate as we all were. I liked that, repeated it to myself. But then, they were everywhere – the homeless men and women. The one on the pink blanket outside Woolworths, the one with the bull terrier, the one who sat on the seafront holding her empty coffee cup. More and more of them. I would lie awake in my bed and try to recite their descriptions. Pink blanket man. Dog man. Seafront woman. If I could name them all – if *I* knew them – then perhaps they would be okay. Maybe, I thought often, I was the only one who could really see them, and it was up to me to do something about them. I asked Mum about them so often that she agreed I could buy one of them a hot drink per day. Eventually, I had too many homeless people on my weekly list, and I was allowed two per day.

'It must have been weird,' I say now, with just an iota of parenting experience. 'How do you explain all of that to a child?'

'I couldn't. Not to a child with a social conscience stronger than mine,' Mum says with a smile. 'And, anyway – look where it led you.'

Stop Gap. My refugee charity.

'True,' I say, my feelings mixed, a happy-sad feeling inside me.

Maybe Layla would have been similar to me, in adulthood: cautious, too empathetic, neurotically organized. I could see that. She arrived on her due date; right on time. Or maybe she would have been more like Becky. Dramatic, sarcastic. Hilarious. *We'll never know*, I think, my eyes wet again.

'Does Becky talk about it?' I say without thinking.

The air stills around us as Mum digests what I have asked her, what I have resisted asking for months.

'She says she's innocent. That is all she ever says.'

'I see.' My own view on Becky's innocence seems to change with the tides.

One morning I am sure of it: she didn't do it. She is experiencing a miscarriage of justice, a catastrophe. Of course she didn't do it, my fun-loving but caustic younger sister. By that evening, I am convinced she is guilty. Of course she is. She always had a fiery temper. We all knew it. My baby was in her sole care for the entire evening preceding her death. It is obvious.

The rest of the time, the jury is out, in my mind. She's nothing. Neither innocent nor guilty. Play is suspended until I know. I have always been able to do this, to reserve judgement. To see things from all sides. Becky was useless at it – said I was a pushover – but it always came naturally to me. I never experienced staffroom politics or clashes with the head teacher. I could always understand why people did the things they did. 'People are complicated,' I once said to Becky, to which she replied, 'People are dickheads.'

But sometimes, now, late at night, when the toil of another day is over, I look at myself in the bathroom mirror, and admit it to myself: I *want* to believe her. I want her to be innocent so badly, I can't trust my own judgement.

'She doesn't want to discuss it beyond that,' Mum says. 'She says she doesn't know what happened. She doesn't know.'

She makes a kind of moue with her mouth. Her skin creases either side of it. What used to be dimples are now wrinkles, and I wish I could reach out and stop time from marching on. Instead, we sit there outside the courtroom, her hand in mine.

I take my position in the public gallery. There is a shifting as the journalists let me in. Some of them stare at me. I try not to judge them. They are only doing their jobs, I tell myself. *Stop being such a saint*, Becky's voice says in my head. *They're morbid. They're making money off this stuff.*

The prosecution's second witness is a nurse called Bryony. She has dark hair and freckles, rimless glasses and a stoic pragmatism to her, as if she might often say, 'We are where we are. Now, let's sort it out.'

I have never met her. She did not treat my daughter after it happened. She did not call a time of death. She did not take me into a side room, sit with me, make me a cup of hot, sweet tea.

She met Becky, six weeks before it happened, in an incident that began its life separately from Layla's but became sinister in its connection to it.

She swears in, confirms her name and her profession, and then the prosecution lawyer turns to her and says, 'Tell me what happened.'

'It was a Tuesday afternoon in A&E,' Bryony says. She has a thick northern accent.

I sit back, watching her. Listening to her story.

4

Bryony Riles

Every year, the student nurses got obsessed with that bloody red telephone. Bryony could see two newbies standing next to it now, waiting for it to ring. It signalled trauma, and the juniors hated that.

The two student nurses moved out of her way as she brushed past them, ready to deal with her next patient.

The boy's face was young-looking – plump-featured and sheepish – but his body was more like eleven or twelve. Tall, like the buxom woman standing in the bay next to him, and muscular, too, across the shoulders. He was holding himself cagily. His shoulder, she guessed. She checked the clipboard. Xander Burrows. His mother: Becky.

'He's hurt his shoulder,' Becky said.

Dislocated shoulder, was scrawled on the notes. *Nine-year-old boy. Mother pulled him out of traffic. Relocation, reset with intranasal diamorph.*

It would need strapping. 'Okay,' Bryony said. 'Won't take long.'

Xander hadn't said a word yet. Bryony silently noted it. She had started attending further study courses a couple of years ago, when everyone she had trained with started going on endless, back-to-back maternity leaves. It gave her something to do to pass the time while her friends were off. They were full of extra-keen people, but she liked the day away from the hospital and the cups of tea. First was the advanced ulcer prevention course. But after that was the safeguarding course – now, that really *had* been interesting – and she was soon promoted to be the safeguarding nurse, tasked with referring suspicious admissions upwards. As with everything, though, it hadn't exactly turned out as planned, and she now spent her days spotting paedophiles and abusers and drug addicts and filling in forms about them.

She looked down at the notes again. *Mother pulled boy out of oncoming traffic.*

'Traffic, then?' she said.

'Nightmare,' the mother said.

The boy still hadn't said anything. He was staring down at the floor, chin almost on his chest. He had thick dark hair, black eyelashes and blue eyes.

'You really look like my nephew. Though he's not as big a lad as you.'

'Right,' Xander said.

'What are you – ten?' She knew his age from the notes, of course, but she wanted to flatter him. To put him at ease.

'Nine.'

'Big school next year?' she said.

'Year after.'

Xander darted a nervous look at his mum, then flicked his eyes back down to the floor. Bryony watched, waiting for it again.

A man arrived in the bay behind her, drawing the curtain back. 'Sorry,' he said. 'Xander's dad.' He looked youthful, with blond, boyish hair, tanned skin and Xander's blue eyes.

'Alright,' he said, more to Becky than to Xander.

She started strapping Xander's shoulder. 'This will pull a bit,' she said. She didn't like to bullshit. 'But it'll be worth it for feeling better.' He met her eyes and she smiled. 'My nephew comes over every Wednesday evening,' she said as she tightened the strapping and he winced. 'He likes my rabbits.'

'Rabbits?' Xander said shyly.

He was coming out of his shell, she could tell. Very slowly.

'I've got two. House rabbits – giant.'

'Wow,' he said. He smiled. Two dimples, either side of his mouth.

'Yep. They like to sleep by the fire.'

'I need to call Martha,' Becky said to Xander's father, rising from her perch beside her son on the bed. 'I was supposed to be meeting her and Layla in the park, and I've dashed off.'

Becky had that artfully messy hair the new nurses were sporting. It drifted around her shoulders as she walked out the door.

'See you,' the man said easily, sitting down so heavily that Xander bounced on the bed and set his mouth in a grim, straight line. But he didn't cry out.

That was unusual, too.

She concentrated on the strapping. The tape was rough underneath her fingertips. She liked doing a tight, deft strap. This was all nursing used to be. Not a risk assessment form in sight.

Xander seemed happy enough, sitting on the bed, studying the bedsheets. Not in too much pain if he was still.

'So you're Dad,' she said, looking across at the father.

He was staring at Xander.

'Marc, yes,' he said. 'Pleasure.' He nodded at her.

'Your son will be right as rain in no time,' she assured him.

Marc turned to Xander as though she wasn't there. 'So, mate. Climbing frame? A bit of rough and tumble?'

Xander frowned at him, confused, while Bryony watched.

So he didn't know. *Oh.* They were divorced, separated, maybe. 'Almost done,' she said to Xander, noticing he hadn't answered Marc yet.

The boy lifted his right arm and raked his hair back. 'No,' he said to his dad eventually.

'What then?' There was just the slightest edge to Marc's tone.

Xander was quiet.

'Nothing,' he said after a few moments.

Bryony's hands stilled. Xander was staring fixedly at the curtain, as though he was concerned it would be slid across at any moment.

To Bryony's annoyance, the father didn't push him. She carried on strapping, the under/over motion as rhythmical and as natural to her as walking or swimming. Under and then over. Pull it tighter. Under and then over.

Marc evidently knew his son better than Bryony thought because, eventually, Xander spoke. 'She just yanked me,' he said.

'Mum?' the man said, his blue eyes suddenly even wider.

Goosebumps appeared all over Bryony's body.

Okay. This wasn't courses. This wasn't paperwork. This was real.

A *woman*. It was never a woman. It was almost always the man, they said on the course. She had nodded, feeling vindicated in her single status.

She finished strapping.

'Yeah. In the kitchen,' Xander said.

The hairs on her arms stood up. He was contradicting his mother's story. One of them was lying.

She ought to stop and report, refer up to Social Services. Perhaps even direct it to the police. But she couldn't help herself. She felt a fizzing in her veins, the way lay people would never understand. Rare cancers, abuse, interesting blood work. They got all the medics going. She had forgotten. She had forgotten how it felt.

'The kitchen, you say?' she said, trying to make her voice sound friendly but detached. 'Our kitchen growing up was full of dangerous things.'

Xander looked away, then, not saying anything more.

She was putting the final piece of tape down when Becky reappeared. Xander's expression dropped, turning sullen.

Marc looked at Becky. 'Alright?' he said to her.

Becky met his eyes and held his gaze for just a moment longer than was usual. 'Yeah,' she said.

That was interesting, too. So they were divorced or separated, but he didn't accuse her. Still looked at her with warmth, and just a dash of wariness. But no accusation.

Marc brought his hand across his face and rubbed at his stubble.

27

Bryony turned to leave them. 'All done,' she said to Becky. She couldn't let her know. That was one of the rules. Act naturally, then refer. Don't arouse suspicions.

She couldn't help but sneak a look at Becky. Green eyes, nice make-up. Cagey-looking, if she were being critical. Becky's eyes flicked down towards the corridor, then back to meet Bryony's gaze again. *I know you*, Bryony thought. You might be middle class, in a thigh-length camel-coloured cardigan. You might not be typical. But your son is frightened of you.

She reported it immediately.

'Yes, that's suspicious,' the social worker agreed. 'Very. We'll take it from here.'

The words rang in her ears just like the red telephone. Trauma. Abuse. *Poor kid.*

5

Martha

'Thank you,' Ellen, the prosecution barrister, says to Bryony. She is the barrister for the State, trying to prove Becky's guilt. Bryony nods back, not saying anything. 'And so your suspicion – during the A&E visit – was raised by what, exactly?'

'Differing accounts of an injury are always a red flag,' Bryony says. 'And the way Xander looked at his mother was – it was nervous. He looked nervous.'

Nervous. Was Xander nervous of Becky? I didn't think so. He was more likely to be nervous of Marc. Marc had been quite a strict parent, a disciplinarian, which had surprised me. 'Oh, Marc has a steely core,' Becky once said when I raised my eyebrows after Marc shouted at Xander at a family barbecue. Later, Xander was sneaking a piece of meringue in the kitchen and said, very seriously to me, 'Please don't tell Dad.' I'd laughed it off, but Xander had simply said it again, his blue eyes holding mine. 'Please don't tell Dad.'

'And what did you suspect?' Ellen says now.

'That she had caused the injury.'

'Thank you,' Ellen says.

Bryony appears to brace herself as the defence barrister stands up.

Harriet, Becky's defence lawyer, looks ready, her mouth

drawn in a thin, grim line. Her eyes track Ellen as she sits down and shuffles some papers, and then she stands, looks directly at Bryony, and tilts her head to one side.

'So, let's talk this through,' she says to Bryony. 'You immediately made this *urgent* report to your colleague, a social worker, didn't you?' she says. I am surprised by the sarcasm she has imbued her question with. Like a fierce animal protecting her brood.

'Yes. That day. She took it over.'

'And we have the report, here, which has been admitted as agreed evidence. It says—'

She reaches down to the desk and picks up two pieces of paper. She then picks up the white plastic cup and takes a sip, seemingly not caring who waits for her. I almost smile: she must get on well with Becky, as that's just the sort of thing my sister would do. The theatre of it. I admire it.

'Paragraph 5.3: "After a one-to-one meeting with me on 21 September, Xander retracted what he told Ms Riles in Accident and Emergency on 12 September. He had walked into traffic the week before, and his father, Marc, had admonished him. He'd told him he was on his last warning. So, in front of his father, he had fabricated something else. After a long talk, he confirmed the account of the kitchen was fiction, and that his mother had been telling the truth." Paragraph 9: "During my meeting with Xander, I saw no evidence at all that he was frightened of either parent, beyond what might reasonably be expected, or that he told lies about their treatment of him. His home with Rebecca Blackwater seemed stable and loving and his relationship with both parents healthy and functional." Paragraph 19: "I therefore closed my file on 28 September, having fully investigated matters and having satisfied myself that nothing was amiss." Have you read that report?'

'I – yes,' Bryony says.

'So, really, not only had the defendant been telling the truth, she had also rescued her son from traffic. Thus making her a good parent. Rather than a bad one.'

'I only told you what I heard in A&E.'

'Nothing further.'

The prosecution lawyer is biting her bottom lip in an exaggerated way, looking thoughtful. How could they do this, day after day? A new case when ours finishes, next week. Another after that.

Ellen sits back in her chair, seeming to consider the situation. She rises, says, 'No re-examination from me,' and then sits again.

Bryony looks at the judge, who nods at her, and says, 'You're free to go, Ms Riles. Thank you for your time.'

Becky's eyes track her as she moves across the courtroom.

We finish at lunchtime. A witness isn't ready, and will come tomorrow instead. The judge turns to the jury, and says, 'Now, ladies and gentleman. Thank you for listening so carefully and attentively. In order that you should feel well rested, and not overworked, I would like to finish now and start afresh tomorrow morning at ten.'

I follow Mum, Dad, Scott and Ethan out into the heat. The day is sadly only half done. Hours and hours until I can call another day *over* and go to bed.

Becky remained in the courtroom, released from the

dock by an usher but lingering with her barrister and solicitor. She's on bail. The court said she wasn't a risk; that she wasn't likely to hurt anybody or try to flee the country. And so they bailed her. She is allowed to reside with Mum and Dad. It's only during the court hearing that she is imprisoned in the dock. It is a strange artifice.

Will she walk in through Mum and Dad's door later? What will they talk about?

The press are still clustered on the steps, a few spread out even further, on the street, and they swoop down on us as we emerge. 'You're in the public gallery, Martha. Are you supporting your sister or wanting to see justice for your child?'

I say nothing, but I turn and gape at the reporter asking. She has a mop of curly hair, smile lines around her mouth. Surely she eats breakfast, goes to the cinema, can't be bothered, maybe, to take her make-up off, late at night? And yet, here she is, a human being, asking me the most inhumane of questions. Does she have children? I look closer, for rudimentary evidence – a wedding ring, a tell-tale tiredness around the eyes, a certain sort of pear shape I've come to recognize – but my sight is momentarily blinded by tears. I blink, and our eyes meet, just for a second. She looks wounded.

Once we are out of the throng, I turn to Scott, and say, 'Did you know about the social worker?'

He shakes his head, looking solemnly back at me. 'No. It doesn't sound like it was—'

'No,' I say. I try not to think of what happened leading up to it, and after it. Had Xander really lied? He was withdrawn, sometimes. Thoughtful – he used to ask me the most profound questions, when he was four or five. And, yes, maybe slightly shifty at times, taking a biscuit and lying about it, despite the crumbs around his mouth. But weren't all children?

And besides, is it any wonder? I try to go through it logically. I think of Marc again at the barbecue. 'Xander, I'm going to count to five,' he had said. Xander had continued to kick his football against the side of the house. '*Xander*,' Marc had said, then he'd stood up, calling him into the house with him. He'd shut the patio door, and I didn't hear anything else. When I'd looked over at Becky, her cheeks had been flushed.

Unless . . . unless Xander hadn't been lying in A&E. Maybe he had lied to Social Services. Later. After Becky had spoken to him. I can see how it would play out, as though it is happening in front of me. 'It's for the best,' she would tell him. She could be so persuasive. Marc's temper might be quick to rouse, but Becky was charmingly manipulative. Sometimes.

No. I can't think it. The lawyers clearly aren't. Or, at least, they have never raised it.

I try to reverse my thoughts. They're traitorous. Would Becky be thinking these thoughts, if it was me in the dock, accused, and her in the public gallery? No, she would believe in me wholeheartedly. I know she would.

She would regard me as innocent until proven guilty, as is right. As is the way it should be.

Scott and I fall behind everybody else. His shoulders look tense; he is not good with stress. He is a developer for an IT firm who walks along the seafront when he has coding problems he cannot figure out. 'I know,' he will say, as he walks through the door, his hair blown back by the sea air. 'It's a segmentation fault. Of course.' But this problem, our life, has no solution.

He takes my hand now. He doesn't say anything, but he doesn't need to. Our hands remember how to hold each other: muscle memory that spans the length of our relationship.

Mum, Dad and Ethan are up ahead. They never look at Becky or speak to her while we are in the courthouse, I have noticed. Mum and Dad live with Becky but, publicly, they support me. I frown. Is that right? But then – what else could they do? It is an unprecedented situation. I try to imagine Becky, later, in their living room, in her casual guise. Shoes off. Legs tucked up underneath her on the sofa. A cup of tea in her hand. I can't see it. I haven't spoken to her for nine months. I think I can remember everything about her, but the truth is that I don't. Does she take sugar in her tea? I find I have to think twice before landing on the answer: yes, three. 'It's why I am so fat,' Becky had once said, poking her stomach. She was laughing, but there was a bitter edge to it, a mournful expression flitting across her features as she took in my slimmer frame.

'Bite to eat?' Mum turns and says kindly to me.

We stop walking. The ground underfoot is hot, and it warms my feet in my ballet flats. I've never known an August be this warm. Usually summer seems to die off quietly, like leaving a party without saying goodbye, with rain and blank white skies.

Dad lifts an arm in a wave to me, up ahead. 'Chin up,'

he says softly. His eyes linger on mine for a few seconds. 'Okay?'

I nod.

'I'll walk home,' he says. He walks everywhere, has to do twelve thousand steps per day. 'Even through murder trials, obsession prevails,' Becky would say drily to me. I can hear the wry comment as clearly as if she was standing here, right next to us.

'I need to go to the office,' Ethan says.

'Really?' Scott says. 'Aren't you off for the day?'

They have stopped a few metres in front of us. Scott is rhythmically rising up and down on his feet, his head bobbing. He was doing this the night we met, in the hallway of an acquaintance's house, though I didn't then know the significance of the blond man standing in the entranceway, unsure where to hang his coat. He was as insignificant as anybody on the street. I sometimes see that same Scott, these days, late at night. That shy, hesitant man.

Life cannot resume for us, since Layla's death. Not properly. Not the way it used to be: there are no conversations about work as the oven heats up. No shared showers, no sex. But, sometimes, something will appear on the fringes, as tentative as a wild deer stepping out into a clearing. Scott will stand on the landing, a T-shirt in his hand that he will throw into the laundry basket, and a lightness will come over me. We will be able – for ten seconds, for five minutes – to resume life. A shared smile. A small laugh. His warm touch on my shoulder. It never lasts, but every time, I hope it will.

'I've got stuff to do,' Ethan says to Scott now. 'I've said I'll work in the gaps, so I can see the whole trial.'

I wonder what sort of employer would make this arrangement with somebody whose niece has died, and whose sister is on trial for it, but I decide not to ask. It would be unkind. My family are at one remove from all of this. Of course their lives go on, full of work emails, social engagements and cars needing MOTs. It is only me, Becky and Scott whose lives have stopped completely, stuck in October last year.

'I'll get home, if you want,' Scott says, and I'm grateful for that. He gives a small, shy squeeze of my hand, and I nod, and say, 'I'll just pop out with Mum for a bit.'

He knows what I need; he always has. Right now, I need a bowl of pasta and my mother. I want to feel as though there is a whole line of mothers before me, and that there will be after me, too. While I have ceased to be a mother, I still have my own, and can still be comforted. Momentarily no longer a grieving parent, but a child once more.

With one last squeeze, Scott releases me. He waves as he begins the long walk back to our car, his back to us, his raised hand silhouetted against the sky.

'Just us then,' Mum says when we are alone. She smiles tentatively. All of her wrinkles have joined up, the smile lines and the laughter lines, and there is not a single smooth spot of skin on her face.

We head to an Italian in the Lanes. Outside, fairy lights zigzag across the blue sky. Mum wafts her hand in front of her face as she walks, and I see a cloud of tiny flies disperse.

We're seated at a table in the window on the first floor, looking down at the streets, and I wonder how we must look. Mother and daughter, out for lunchtime pizza. Nobody would believe what we have been doing today.

We all live within a mile of each other, and Mum, Dad, Ethan, Becky and I came here for dinner a year ago. It was nothing, really. An impromptu meal arranged over WhatsApp after we had all had a mediocre day. I was heavily pregnant. Scott was away, attending more and more developer conferences. Marc had annoyed Becky over childcare arrangements. Ethan had closed a big deal the week before and still hadn't caught up on sleep. And there we were, one Wednesday at nine o'clock, squabbling over dinner – Ethan had ordered a pizza with macaroni on that Becky said was disgusting, and she thought he ought to pay for it separately. Ethan said, 'Those were not the terms we agreed,' and Mum threw her head back and laughed, and said, 'We didn't realize we should have read the small print.'

On our way out, I excused myself and went to the bathroom. As I washed my hands, I looked at myself in the mirror, took a deep breath as my baby kicked inside me, and thought: *Here I am. Here we all are.* Our family was about to expand, and my baby would be part of all these in-jokes and impromptu pizzas with her aunt and uncle, her grandma and grandad. Those were the best times. In a posh toilet in a restaurant. In the garden at a New Year's Eve party. Temporarily alone, with the bubble of my family waiting just inside, in the next room, just over there. My eyes fill with tears now as I study the menu. Here we are now, down from five to two. From *six* to two.

'You should eat,' Mum says.

I order a sparkling water which arrives fast and sits,

untouched, in front of me, slices of lemon bobbing on its surface.

'The nurse was good,' Mum says. She drums her wrinkled fingers on the table.

'Yes.'

'Fair. Balanced,' Mum says. 'Sorry. Not good. I didn't mean good.' She leans down over the menu, her dark hair falling in front of her face.

'She didn't seem nervous at all,' I say.

'No.'

'They're trying to make Becky out as an abuser,' I say. 'Set her up, even. The A&E incident . . . it was nothing, in the end. Wasn't it?'

'It's their job, I suppose,' Mum says.

I push a lemon segment under the water with the end of my straw. A strand of my hair falls on to the table and I brush it on to the floor. I'll be bald by the end of the trial.

'Still falling out then?' Mum says.

'Yes.'

'I'm sorry,' she says.

I feel myself curl inwards. We are out for lunch, and so here it is. The me-time I craved when I had a newborn. Enjoy it, Martha.

It's always in the afternoons and evenings that the thoughts creep back in. The sun begins its descent down to the horizon, and the thoughts fire up. Am I still a mother? Is Scott still a father? I can't bear it otherwise. We are and always will be. Like non-practising doctors, like retired priests. What we were we are; we always will be.

'I was thinking the other day about when you were

little,' Mum says tentatively. 'When Dad stayed home with you for that year.'

'Oh, yes,' I say. I hardly recall it, but I do remember discussing it since. It's become family lore: the trips we took, the things we did when Dad was, briefly, the primary carer.

'Anyway. It's a joint thing, you know?' she goes on. 'Everyone in that court is focusing on you. But that's wrong. Scott went away too.'

'I know,' I whisper. 'But thank you for saying.'

She nods, then covers my hand with hers.

'Will you discuss the trial tonight, with her?' The question emerges unexpectedly out of me as if I were a pipe that's sprung a leak.

Mum pauses, pushes her glasses up her nose, then nods. She knows exactly who I mean. 'She's our daughter.' Her hand covers my own. 'As are you.' She is avoiding my question.

I wait.

'She might discuss it. But she only ever says the same thing: that she is innocent.'

'I see.'

Becky moved in with Mum and Dad right after it happened. They are to supervise her contact with Xander. Marc can't, Social Services say, because he believes too strongly that Becky is innocent. He wouldn't enforce the contact order that she doesn't see Xander alone. I don't know what that says about my parents. I used to ask them often, in the early days. Mum would try to placate me – 'We love you both' – and Dad would avoid, as he always has. In the end, we had several evening-long talks about it. We read articles about wrongful prosecutions.

At the end of one evening, I said, 'I just don't know what to think. Somebody tell me what to think.'

Mum turned to me, and said, 'Look. She's accused. Layla was our granddaughter. Becky is our daughter. What do you think I think?' The skin around her mouth was crumpled and puckering. 'We don't know, Martha! Nobody *bloody* knows! Now stop asking, for God's sake.'

She had apologized, the next day. She said the situation had got to her, and she had crossed a line. But I hadn't asked again after that. It wasn't fair to anybody. Nobody knew. Going over and over it wasn't helping anybody. We had to let the justice system decide for us.

'She watches true crime documentaries about people who were wrongly accused,' Mum says now.

'Does she?'

She nods. 'Tons of them. Late at night, mostly. She shows them to us, sometimes.'

Her tone is hesitant, slightly ashamed. She leaves long pauses in between her sentences. It makes me wince. I have embarrassed her, my kind mother, out for Italian food with me even though I am no company.

She stares back at me, and I don't say anything. Can't.

'I see,' I say softly. Some days, most days, I am just saturated with it, this situation, and the excess merely runs off me, as if I were a full glass of water with yet more liquid flooding in.

'Marc keeps trying to tell us . . . he keeps trying to tell us why she is innocent. He brings things over sometimes – medical articles.'

Of course Marc believes Becky, I find myself thinking. Even in separation they are a unit. Always have been. They are always looking at each other.

I remember the first time I met him. I'd gone to visit Becky in her student house. She was nineteen, and pregnant, and I was twenty-two.

'Come on then, Samuel,' he had said to her as we were leaving to go out.

'Samuel?' I mouthed.

'Long story,' she said, sharing a smile with him.

It was the first time I wasn't privy to something of hers. A joke just for the two of them.

A waitress approaches and Mum orders a Margherita pizza. I'm not hungry, but the GP said the hair loss could be because of weight loss, so I order the same.

'You get to see Xander, at least,' I say.

'Yes. That's lovely.'

'How is he?'

'He's fine. He's computer-game-obsessed,' she smiles. 'He's a bit – I don't know. Withdrawn, I guess, seeing Becky so much less, and living full-time with Marc. It's a big change. But we are all struggling . . .'

'Which computer game?' I say.

Xander and I used to play together, often. I had a little avatar on his Xbox One called Auntie Martha. It wore glasses, even though I don't. When I asked him why, Xander said simply, 'Because you're so not cool.' The next time we played, the glasses were gone. It was typically Xander: a desire to please, but not directly so. He was sweet like that. He has a PlayStation now. The Xbox stayed at Becky's, switched off. Marc upgraded him when

Xander went to live with him. As a treat, for all the *upheaval*, I guess.

'I'm not sure,' Mum says.

'She's got nobody,' I say. 'Becky.'

'She's got Marc. And her lawyers. And she does have us. It'll be . . .'

I stare out of the window, hoping to catch a glimpse of Becky, alone, away from her lawyers. Oh, to meet her in the street. 'Whatever happens,' Mum says, 'it'll be easier afterwards, when you're not a witness. You can go and see her. Talk to her.'

Go and see her. Not *meet up*. Not Becky coming to me. Prison. Surely. I look at my mother, sitting opposite me, staring into space, and wonder what she really thinks – deep down, beyond the unknowing. Whether she thinks her other daughter is guilty.

Mum wants to drop me home, but I don't let her. It's only six o'clock. It's not late enough. I need to be exhausted, so tired that I only have to walk up the stairs to my bed and fall asleep.

I wander back down to the Brighton seafront. The restaurants are busy, their lights illuminating the concrete outside them in a futuristic glow. Every single person in the window of a Chinese is on their smartphone. A baby sleeps in a car seat, placed on the floor in front of the window, and I can't help but drift towards it and stare in, until they see me looking.

I walk down through the marina, then loop back up into the headlands that overlook the sea. It was here that we spent much of our childhood, unknown to our parents. They thought we were only a few streets away, playing safely, but we were always here, miles from home. There is an expanse of green, a sea view, and a bat house, standing tall and wooden against the sky. We were obsessed with the bat house. It was like a tree house on stilts. We used to sit on the grass underneath it and try and catch glimpses of them. Our bedtime was whenever it got dark, and so we never quite managed it. Becky liked the gothic quality of it; of being surrounded – invisibly – by bats at night. I liked the science of it, would get home and research them. Later, when I was a teacher, I led an entire session on bats. Everyone had loved it, and I'd told them to go to the bat house with their parents. I saw it as passing the joy on.

I stay there, my arms becoming dry and salty as the sun sets, and I keep looking for her, even though I know she won't arrive.

We used to have all sorts of pretend games, here in these fields. We'd bring our bikes, sometimes, say that they were horses. I would always want to feed and water them, would often try to introduce the concept that the horses could talk. Becky was much more interested in pretending we were professional jockeys. She'd invent all sorts of politics about the other jockeys, which I found stressful. She liked the drama of it.

The bike. The memory seems to rise up in me before I can stop it, even though I don't want to look at such a horrible memory of Becky; such a troubling memory, like reading her diary or going through her pockets.

It was all about the recorder group in primary school. Becky had been begging for weeks to join. Mum and Dad paid up front for the term, and Becky bought a tenor recorder from the Music shop, with a load of sheet music she couldn't read. I found her fascinating; the *joie de vivre* with which she commenced her hobbies. It never seemed to cross her mind that she might be rubbish.

One night in November, Becky announced at dinner that she was going to leave the club, saying smilingly that she would take up art instead. Mum and Dad refused; it was all paid for, they said. The sweet and sour rice I was eating was clogging my throat as Becky's voice rose higher and higher.

She started crying during pudding: big, dramatic tears that upset me, too. When Dad tried to change the conversational topic – as he always did in these situations – she left the table, wrenched the back door open, grabbed her bike from the drive and pedalled it at full speed all the way down the path and into the side of Dad's car.

She didn't break anything. Her nose bled, her tooth was chipped – she had to get it fixed – but she didn't break anything. Dad's car was scratched. She was grounded for a month. The only extra-curricular thing she was allowed to attend was the recorder group, which she did silently, like a martyr.

Afterwards, Dad adopted *the recorder group* as synonymous with bad things. 'Don't do a recorder group,' he would say when Becky got stroppy.

I shiver as I recall it now. It wasn't the recklessness of it, or the switch from charming to tantrumming. It was the expression on her face as she did it. I was staring at her through the living room window, my palm pressed to the glass just as hers was pressed to the dock this morning.

It wasn't rage on her face, that evening on the bike, exactly – it was something more complicated. Some sort of self-sabotage, as if she didn't care what got damaged in the process of proving her point. Including herself.

Did she look at Layla that way when she did it? That menace? That sabotage? I think of Layla's injuries, and close my mind against them.

Scott is stacking the dishwasher when I get in. The flat feels menacing. It has ever since my return, after it happened. Everything is just the same – the stylish exposed-bulb lamp in the corner of the living room that I have always hated, the navy-blue feature wall. But something is off, as though the air we breathe is filled with dread.

Scott stops stacking as I arrive and looks at me with his hands on his hips.

'I'm just going out,' he says.

He's been going out more and more, lately. For longer and longer stretches. I didn't ask where, at first – I couldn't bring myself to – and now it's too late; his absences have become tolerated within our relationship. I would look hysterical if I asked too much, now.

I used to sleep with my cold feet against his shins. He didn't mind. He said he had enough warmth for the both of us, would scoop his arm right around my waist and draw me in. They were our private moments, in bed together. His naked form against mine. Sometimes, just lately, I can't remember the last time I looked him in the eye. Has it been several weeks? It feels like it. Is it just the isolation of grief, a measure of how inward-looking I have become? Or is it something more?

Where had he been that evening, a few days ago, when he didn't read my text message for hours? Maybe he's looking at places to live. Maybe he's taken up a new hobby, made new friends. Perhaps he needs space away from me, is preparing to leave me. I wouldn't be surprised, though it feels as though my heart turns over when I consider the possibility.

'Okay,' I say, woodenly, now. I reach for his hand.

It's a cursory gesture. Neither of us can speak to the other yet, not properly, but we can reach for each other's hands.

'I'm going to the land,' he says. He knows I want to know, that I don't feel I can ask.

This is what he calls it. He owns a tiny patch of land, donated by his grandfather, down in Hove, and on it he grows things.

Four summers ago, he brought me back a punnet of strawberries. I commented on their sharp, sweet taste, and, after that, the gifts began. Peaches, proffered every day for weeks, until something else came into season. 'We can have them with ice cream,' he had said happily.

I didn't have the heart to tell him I don't even like fruit that much. When it started to take over, and he was going all the time, I began to resent it.

Now, visiting his land seems especially pointless; pointless rearing.

Alone, I venture into what was Layla's room, though she never slept in it – she had still been in with us. But I promised her that I would go into her old room, once the trial had begun. To look at it. To acknowledge her. And to say goodbye.

46

Layla's room is untouched. It was never the crime scene. That was at Becky's house. They photographed her spare room – the makeshift nursery where Layla had been sleeping while Becky looked after her. They'd done it immediately, before suspicion was even raised. A Scenes of Crime Officer attended. I haven't seen the photographs yet; I'm not sure what they showed. Nothing, probably.

I ease open the door and flick the light on. Her cot is still there. White railings. It looks enormous. She never slept in it.

I think of the one-year-olds that I know. Fat feet. She'd have little fat feet, just like Xander did. Spongy bulges on the tops of his arches . . . and now, his are a bony child's feet, stuffed into football boots. New school shoes every term. The luck of it. To experience that. Does Becky know how lucky she is that he is still here with us?

There on the floor is Flappy – the cuddly toy Becky and I used to share – that Becky passed to Xander, that Xander passed to Layla. It's an unidentifiable animal: small, yellowing, with long soft brown, ears that flap.

Becky and I discovered it in the loft when Mum and Dad decided to sell our childhood home. They were downstairs. Becky had hit her head on one of the rafters in the hot loft and was sitting cross-legged, a hand held to the developing lump, when I found the box marked 'miscellaneous'.

'Look,' I said, pointing to the items spilling from the box.

'Oh, man!' she said, reaching for him. 'Shit, what was his name?'

'Flappy,' I said immediately.

I always had the better memory of the two of us. Becky remembers almost nothing of the past. Where I know

47

every date, every event and its relation to another, Becky seems to remember only the broad emotional tone of something, not who was there, or when it happened, not even the year. I wish I could forget things now, of course. Perhaps I will remember every moment of this trial for ever, whatever the result, and hold it against her for ever.

'Flappy. Of course.' She brought him close to her face and breathed in.

'Let's have him,' she said. She was in her early twenties. She already had Xander, who was two. 'My babies can have him, then yours.'

'Okay,' I said.

We binned the rest of the box, but we kept Flappy, emerging down the ladder with him. On the cooler upstairs landing, Becky passed the toy to me.

'I used to suck his ears,' she said.

'Gross,' I said, holding it carefully by its body.

'It'll have helped your immune system,' she said with a sage nod. 'So you're welcome.'

Becky put Flappy in the back pocket of her jeans and its ears moved as she walked. Marc was waiting downstairs for her.

'Look,' she said, showing him Flappy.

'Ah, a Blackwater relic,' he said, with no sense of irony at all. He took Flappy off her and turned it over in his hands. 'Let's put it on the mantelpiece,' he said, and she cracked up; evidently it was yet another inside joke between them.

He enfolded her into his arms, then, and I looked away. They were perfect together. Where could Scott and I find that secret language? I found myself thinking. I wished fervently I could purchase it, bottled.

48

It was a strange day, clearing out the family home all together. Mum removed a canvas photograph from the living-room wall that Becky had always hated and the wallpaper was fresh underneath it, a bright square surrounded by faded paper. I reached a finger out to touch it as we were leaving.

Standing now, in the room that Layla never got to sleep in, holding Flappy, I find myself thinking: *This cannot be right*. It cannot have been her. Becky cannot have done it. I feel it with a certainty, right in my stomach. I cannot help but notice, though, that I also have the other moments. When I remembered the recorder club, I was sure she had done it, too. They are both true and untrue, at the same time. Becky is suspended, Schrödinger's cat in the dock. And next week, we will know. Ethan keeps trying to tell me we might not. That the trial may run on, get adjourned, that it won't give me the answers I'm looking for, but I ignore him.

I'm going to make a list. In here. Of likely scenarios and outcomes. There must be another possibility besides murder.

There was no suspicion, at first, in A&E, just shock so intense I can't remember anything except images. A brick-coloured circle of a cup of tea on my knees. A medical tag around Layla's tiny grey wrist.

Becky came straight over when they charged her. She was still holding her charge sheet in her hands, on police bail. Marc brought her and sat in the car, the engine running, outside on the street. Layla had been dead for ten days, a sixth of the length of her life; something I knew to be a fact, but struggled to comprehend.

Becky was to attend the Magistrates' Court a couple of

days later. Scott was sitting on the sofa, staring at nothing. I was pretending, as I unthinkingly let my sister in, that Layla was with him, that he was winding her, that she was crying, not sleeping, being red and angry and *alive*.

'Nothing happened,' Becky said, as she stood in the centre of our hallway. 'I didn't do anything.'

I didn't say anything to her. I was poorly prepared, didn't know how to behave. My sister was accused. My baby was dead. What was the done thing?

When I hadn't spoken for a moment, she said, 'Please believe me.'

I didn't ask her to leave in order to be dramatic, or to make a point. That was just the first day that I had that glass-spilling-over feeling. I was at full capacity and had room for no more.

She raised her hands in a kind of surrender, and turned to leave, but just before she did, she jerked her head, trying to look into Layla's nursery, I thought. The door was closed.

As she walked down the corridor, I said I would be in touch. But I haven't been, because then the slow, creaking wheels of the justice system had begun to turn, and my relationship with Becky had ceased being about sisters discovering a childhood teddy, or sharing a takeaway together, or a series of jokey text messages. It had become something beyond itself, expanding from just us, and being invaded by bigger concepts: justice, evidence, guilt. We were no longer sisters, instead a witness and a defendant.

Contact was prohibited, and so that was the last time we spoke.

Please believe me. Would she say that if she were innocent?

Or guilty? I sit down on the floor next to the cot and pick up Flappy. I close my eyes. *Please believe me.* Why not *I'm so sorry, Martha?* Was it the shock of being under suspicion, or something more? It was all about Becky. That's the thing. The thing I try to forget. Things have always revolved around Becky. Especially now.

But being selfish doesn't mean she's guilty.

I reach up and take out the notepad and pen I kept by the breastfeeding chair. Those early days of motherhood felt like I had become the CEO of a vast, sprawling company with no training, and I had been for ever making lists of things to buy, and what needed to go in the washing with the muslin cloths, and how much tummy time I needed to start introducing.

I have always been hard-working, effortlessly organized. My binders at school and university were colour-coded, alphabetized by topic, practice papers printed out on the first day of term and filed in the back of a lever arch file, ready for exam season. Becky used to think it was hilarious, but then I became a teacher, and every single one of my colleagues was like it, too. I spent my summers reorganizing my classroom displays, and Becky helped sometimes. 'If you're going to be anal about it, you may as well make them look pretty,' she'd said once, joining me with sugar paper, glitter pens and glue.

But motherhood took even me by surprise. Owning a charity, having been a teacher for years . . . and yet nothing could have prepared me. Keeping a small human fed, clean and happy was the biggest undertaking of my life.

It's impossible to explain the juggernaut of motherhood to anybody who hasn't been there: the vast reorientation that takes place in the labour suite and never really rights itself again or, rather, doesn't need to. Even Scott, he didn't matter, not up against Layla. He was her co-creator, with me, but at her conception we ceased to matter. We passed the gauntlet to the next generation, but – and it was a surprise to me – it happened willingly, happily.

I remember the first night we had started trying. Scott had made a lasagne – I loved to watch him cook. He was methodical and calm, one saucepan discarded and placed in the waiting dishwasher immediately. His layers of pasta and sauce and Bolognese were careful and neat. I had looked around our flat, after we had eaten: half a bottle of wine left on the driftwood table, but nothing else. I looked at it and thought: *After all these years, I still love spending the evening with you.* His shirt was rolled up to the elbows, and I walked across to him. He immediately hugged me, as he always did, always would. Never moody, never highly strung, never petty. Always ready to hold me.

'Wouldn't it be nice if there was someone else here, just over there?' I had said lightly. 'Somebody to look after. Somebody to . . .' I didn't finish the sentence. *Somebody to bind us together.* It would have sounded wrong.

He didn't say anything, but his eyes were bright as he looked at me. 'Yes?' he said. 'Go on.'

'A tiny little someone,' I said softly.

And he'd nodded.

It was simple to him. He was following the formula to life. Buy a flat, get married, have a baby. It was all instinct, all correct – none of Marc and Becky's chaos – and there was nothing wrong with that. Perhaps it had been just right.

We threw the condoms away and made love while the dishwasher rumbled in the background. I went to get a glass of water in the kitchen, later, and looked at it, our tidy kitchen, our life together, the underfloor heating warm under my bare feet, and felt totally and completely safe. I wanted our baby to feel that way, too. I was ready for it. To bring someone else into our lives, and to make them feel safe. I hoped they would have Scott's calm manner, his still mind.

I draw a dark, navy-blue swirl across the top of the page now, in the nursery. I was always making lists at work, too. Lists that led me to leave Layla with Becky. What had I been thinking? How *could* I? Scott tried to talk to me about it, a few months ago. The circumstances were unusual, he said. My job at Stop Gap, the charity, hadn't been a normal one. I had stared silently into my dinner.

It won't bring her back, this list. But it might help *me*. I lean my head against the wall. I stare out of the window and look at the way the Brighton street lights flare up into the sky and I write at the top of the pad:

In order to recover, I need to understand it.

I google the definition of murder and write it out on the next, clean, smooth piece of paper:

Murder is committed where a person of sound mind and discretion unlawfully kills . . . with intent to kill or cause grievous bodily harm.

I stare at the piece of paper. I think the defence's case is that Layla's death is unexplained. Natural causes, or an accident. No murder, just tragedy.

On the left, I write:

An accident?

Underneath the list, I draw a line. On it, I write down Layla's bedtime. Only Becky, Scott and I know it, her routine. I start there. It's as good a place as any. It won't bring her back, but it might bring me peace.

Above the timeline, I write:

The night in question.

6

Judge Christopher Matthews, QC

Christopher lets himself into his seafront town house alone. It smells empty. Cold, too, despite the late summer heatwave. The cleaner has been – he has never met her, but he imagines her to be petite and ruthless – and the wooden floor gleams as he sets his red robing bag down on it. The dog walker has been, too, and Rumpole emerges, the sound of his claws on the tiles like clinking marbles.

'Alright,' Christopher says to him, as if he is a house-mate or child.

Rumpole stops and looks at him seriously, then turns his head to look sideways, pointedly, at his bowl.

For the first time in years, Christopher feels unsettled by a case. He shivers in his cold kitchen and rubs the dog's head.

It is a baby case. Is that why it feels eerie? He supposes so. An eight-week-old, found unresponsive in the morning. Of course that is chilling. Of course it is.

Not to mention the rest. Two sisters, ripped apart by the justice system. An ad hoc nannying arrangement, gone horribly wrong.

No, that isn't why, he realizes, as he looks out on to his back garden. That isn't why he feels spooked and strange.

It is the cause of death.

Smothering.

Even the word is sinister. The images it brings to mind. 'Horrible, isn't it, Rumpole?' he says.

Layla had been found unresponsive in the morning, and had been in the sole care of the defendant, Becky, for the entire previous evening. There had been no witnesses.

It is cut and dried, surely.

The experts were in agreement that the baby had died in the evening – between 8.00 p.m. and 9.30 p.m. The 999 call was made at eight o'clock the next morning. *The delay doesn't look good*, Christopher thinks.

That said, the police hadn't suspected murder for a whole week. Cot death, they'd thought, until the post-mortem showed smothering. No, not smothering, he corrects himself. Asphyxiation. There is a subtle difference. Often, asphyxiation means smothering, but not *always*. Sometimes, it is an accident. She could have rolled over. Become tangled up in her blankets. Something he hopes for. Natural causes. *The only possible defence*, he thinks.

'We'll have to see, won't we?' he says.

Rumpole looks back at him, cocking his head.

Sadie bought them the dog. Completely out of nowhere, when they were forty-five, and still in love, he supposes. He arrived home from a case about one prisoner encouraging another to hang himself, his gut still in knots from it, and there was Sadie, her slim ankles tucked up underneath her, her legs tanned from the summer, a Labrador sitting upright, primly, next to her as if they were in a waiting room.

'He was abandoned,' she said immediately. Apologetically, he thought.

He studied the dog. Blond fur, eyes rimmed with dark brown. The dog considered him, too.

'Oh, for God's sake,' he said to Sadie. A sentence he bitterly regrets.

He pours himself a glass of water now from a bottle in the fridge. He should read the submissions, later tonight. There is something in Becky Blackwater's past they want him to consider. He hopes it isn't something bad. Something even worse than what is playing out in front of him.

He's never seen an aunt accused before. Had Becky done it? He holds the glass up to the light and looks at its cloudy contents. It is a hard-water area. Sadie had always said it made her hair fluffy. He had never said it didn't. That her hair looked just fine. It was dark, no greys until she was in her late forties, and it shone with glimmers of light when she turned her head. Why hadn't he told her how beautiful she was?

Is Becky guilty? Hmm. She'd been the only person there that night. And eight-week-olds weren't mobile enough to have accidents. What other explanation can there be? He hopes for one, though. Some tragic explanation he can't quite think of at the moment.

Her lawyer is under pressure, though: he can tell. He sips the water again. Sometimes, the lawyers look tense like that when their clients are innocent, and they know it. But sometimes they just look like that when they've had a run of bad luck, tough cases. It's hard to tell.

Well, what will be will be, he tells himself. The jury will sort it. He reveres them, these lay people who are summonsed, who give up their time for justice, who listen carefully and – pretty much always – return the right result, even when faced with the most complex of legal concepts.

He finishes the glass and gets the file out of his brief-case. Rumpole places his head on his lap, and Christopher shifts comfortably; content.

Now. Yes. To Becky's history. He sets the papers on the arm of the sofa and begins to leaf through them. As he does, his hands still. He reads the words again and again.

Oh, God, he thinks to himself. Oh, God.

Now, that changes things.

Tuesday

7

Martha

I sometimes dream of Becky. Nothing much happens, I'm just watching her, as though my brain is trying to hang on to her features, to memorize her, so she doesn't slip away. Her arched eyebrows. Her bottom lip, slightly bigger than her top. The crooked incisors. Those Bambi lashes.

Pulling the laces of my trainers tight still gives me a kind of Pavlovian pleasure, even though all of my last three hundred morning runs have been bleak. It only takes five minutes to get down on to the seafront and the air seems to expand as I arrive. They are digging up the ground, near the marina, and I slow as I negotiate pedestrians on a temporary walkway, joining throngs of commuters in my leggings and T-shirt.

After a few minutes, I escape and run behind the beach huts.

Do they wonder how I could leave her? The lawyers didn't question me on it. Perhaps it is too delicate, or perhaps it is irrelevant. Either way, I appreciate it.

In a funny sort of way, it was a morning run just over two years ago that led me to leave her, though she wasn't born yet. Scott and I were in Kos, on an all-inclusive break during the school holidays, when I first saw the refugees, though such a word does not do them justice at all.

Nobody expected them. It was the very beginning of the crisis.

They arrived on the inflatable boats – as flimsy as our Li-lo that we used to float around on, drinking cocktails. Wet toddlers, their hair smeared against their scalps, curling and cow-licking like a newborn's. A boy with one trainer on, one trainer missing. A woman, baby at her breast, whimpering into a headscarf so that the baby wouldn't see. A life vest, bobbing in the water, its owner unknown.

We were there right as it happened, right as it hit the newspapers and social media. Scott held my hand when I got back to our hotel, and didn't complain when, out to dinner, my eyes strayed to the sea, to the beach, again and again.

'They must be exhausted,' I said to Scott over prawns.

'Of course,' he said, the subtext a sad but stoic: *What can you do?* It was his response to almost everything. During extreme turbulence, he would calmly say, 'Well, we can't do anything about it,' as though that made it less frightening. As though he was fine with disaster, with destruction, with death.

'What must your life be like – to get on a ship like that? No, not a ship . . . a raft, pretty much. You must have to be so . . . desperate.' Their bodies flitted into my mind. The life vest. The missing trainer, bobbing alone somewhere in the sea. It was too much.

'Can we go down? And help?' I said.

He nodded immediately, never minding how he spent his free time, wanting only – it seemed – to please me.

We helped out for the rest of our holiday, taking parcels from the Red Cross centre to a refugee camp. I handed over cheap fleece blankets, canned goods, plasters and bandages. I gave them to anybody who would take them. Scott didn't mind. He never once said he wanted to be back by the pool, eating unlimited food and reading books.

The Greek government put the refugees up in an old, abandoned airport. Anybody could go in, and I did, while Scott was showering one night. I sneaked over there, after an all-you-can-eat dinner at our hotel, a warm paper bag in my hand.

The noise and the heat of it struck me first. Worse than a dormitory. Strung-up sheets were makeshift curtains, held together with pink clothes pegs. The signs were still up: TERMINAL 1. TERMINAL 2. DUTY FREE. Plate-glass windows had shattered, leaving shards that somebody from the Red Cross was sweeping up. How could this be? How could we walk away from this and return to our sunloungers?

I sat on a wooden chair, not wanting to stand and stare any more, and then I saw it: a dark eye. It blinked, then locked on to mine. I smiled. Could he see both of my eyes, or just one? I crept closer to the curtain, the wooden chair squeaking on the floor.

A little hand emerged from between two curtains, the fingers curling around a pegged-up sheet. The hand retreated, after a second, leaving dirty marks behind it. I sat on a rickety wooden chair and watched. Then the brown eye again, peering out at me from between two grubby sheets.

He revealed himself, and there he was, a little boy, maybe two – he was so thin it was hard to tell. The other hand – dark with dirt, tidemarks of it across the back of his hand – was in his mouth, sucking on his index and third fingers. His feet were bare, slapping on the linoleum floor as he moved unsteadily towards me. Those brown eyes on me, on mine.

And then the thoughts came. I could leave here, leave Kos, finish my holiday, forget these children. I could read about them in the newspapers and donate to Save the Children and do all the right things – above and beyond the right things, even – that anyone might have expected of me. But that grubby hand in his mouth. His skinny little legs that should have been fat with rolls of flesh. Where were his parents? He was alone, behind that curtain, advancing towards a perfect stranger.

No. I couldn't. I couldn't buy *The Big Issue* and drink Fairtrade coffee and leave it at that. I couldn't. Those dark eyes. Those little hands. I could not leave them.

We played for a few minutes – peekaboo – until a woman in a headscarf came to collect him. Her arms were slim and toned and the veins on her hands stood out in the heat. She scooped him up and took him back behind their curtains. I saw as she disappeared behind the sheet that it contained a bench, an old airport bench. Exactly the sort Scott and I would sit on in a few days' time as we waited to board our flight home.

I left, making my way back to our hotel which sat at the top of a hill, away from the beaches and the life vests and the children. I arrived back at our hotel room half an hour later. Scott was asleep on the bed, in his towel.

I sat down carefully next to him. He opened his eyes immediately, a smile already on his face. That was one of the things I loved most about him: he was always – unfailingly – pleased to see me.

'You've been sleeping,' I said. 'I've been to see the children.'

'I was sleeping to forget them,' he said. He rolled over on to his side and pulled me towards him. 'How can we think about going home?'

'I know,' I murmured, lying next to him. I closed my eyes. Of all the people on the planet, here I was, lying next to the man who felt the same as me.

I returned just under seven weeks later, my registered charity set up. Scott paid for it with his bonus. 'My gift to you,' he said shyly over dinner one night. 'No. Not gift. My—' he stammered. 'Our joint venture. For the greater good.'

I clinked my glass against his and didn't think I could love him any more than I did then.

The local Greek authority let me have the old building the fish market used to operate from before the recession. They didn't seem to care who took it. It was cool, and dark, but the smell: oh my!

I scrubbed it. Cleaned the walls during the last week of the summer holidays. I would set something up – something helpful – and be home by September, I told myself. I returned a few months later, pregnant with Layla. Stop Gap had grown from a tiny start-up to an established charity with a budget and a business bank account. The children lined up every morning for lessons, for food, for a go on an iPad. We had to turn half of them away most days.

Those dark eyes; those little hands. So vulnerable, so desperate, that I forgot my own baby, in need of me at home.

I wonder if she missed me, if she wondered where I had

gone. If she knew that I would be back. That I was coming back to her as she died.

Scott and I ascend the court steps together.

'Ms Blackwater – what do you think happened?' Another morning, another microphone.

This time, I forcibly push it away: how would I know?

'Where were you, Ms Blackwater?' a male voice says.

I can't help but turn and look at him.

'That night?' he adds, like a prompt. Like I don't know what he's talking about.

My face is scalding, and I will it to cool down, even though it only makes it worse. Scott glances at me, just briefly, his eyes full of concern. He reaches for my hand and takes it in his: we were both missing that night, he is saying with his hand, as he has said to me a hundred times before. No matter what the court says, the media, other people. We were both missing.

I remember when I took Becky's call. It was only afterwards – after I had attended A&E and I had seen Layla for the final time – that her words had sunk in: 'Scott stayed an extra night.'

I closed my eyes to it. Surely not. I had been away for two nights, and Becky was supposed to have Layla for only one of them. Scott should have been back for the second.

But he hadn't come back. He had simply extended his stay.

I thought of all my preparations to leave Layla. All the things I put in place: making sure Becky was available, transferring the Moses basket over, expressing enough milk, washing enough muslin cloths, giving Becky the reflux medication, the sling, the pushchair. It had seemed like a military operation. Later, I learnt that Scott had just sent a text to Becky. One measly text. The conference was really useful: he wanted to stay an extra night. How easy it was for him.

I try to be fair: would I ever have done the same thing? Stayed another night, because I was enjoying myself, because it was useful? *No*, I think miserably. *I wouldn't have.*

But it started with me: I chose to go away. And I chose not to come back until the Friday, by which time it was too late. Scott's actions – to the media, to the lawyers, and so to me – seem incidental somehow to what happened to Layla.

I, the mother, left her baby. It began with me.

I look up at the building. It feels different on this, Day Two. Much like a house on the second viewing, things are coming to light that I hadn't noticed before. The sprinkling of cigarette butts just outside the doors in two distinct clusters.

I notice more about the lawyers, too, as I settle myself down at the very back of the public gallery. I eyeball Becky, first. She's not looking at me.

The prosecution and the defence are chatting as the courtroom fills up. The prosecutor has taken her glasses off, and she's leaning in towards the defence lawyer as if they were two women in a café or a bar. *Of course*, I think. Of course they know each other. Of course they have countless trials at Hove Court against each other. The prosecutor is tapping her pen against the desk, faster and faster, as they chat. Harriet, the defence barrister, lets out a tiny laugh, and they stop speaking.

I think of the timeline I made last night. It clarified

nothing. Only what we already know. That Becky had Layla all evening, and that Layla died, sometime around eight or nine. My brain can't make sense of it.

'The prosecution calls Carol Richards,' Ellen says, when the case has reopened.

A small, mousy woman about fifty years old is brought in by an usher. She confirms her name and is sworn in.

I settle back to listen but my eyes scan the jury, searching. What do they think? What do *they* think happened?

8

Carol Richards

Carol was preoccupied by the tea bags. Why did people find it so bloody difficult to clean up after themselves? She stared at those still-warm oozing tea bags, clustered like disgusting profiteroles on the little plate next to the staffroom kettle.

'Carol,' her colleague Alicia said, hurrying inside.

Carol turned around quickly. Perhaps she should not, as the head teacher, be pondering the tea bags so seriously. She ought to be thinking deeply about discipline policies or oppositional defiance disorder. But one tea bag was still steaming, like a fresh dog turd, right there on the counter.

'Hmm?' she said.

'Xander's mother isn't here again.'

'*Again?*' Carol said, before she could stop herself. Most unprofessional.

'Phone's off, too.'

Carol looked at her watch: 4.00 p.m. An hour late. 'Where's the dad?' she said with a sigh. What was his name? They were getting divorced, she knew, but his name escaped her.

'Away with work – near Oxford. He's coming in an hour, if she doesn't turn up.'

Carol looked out into the hallway. She could see Xander, a curious child, swinging his legs, the tips of his school shoes hitting the underside of the chair in front of him, jostling it slightly with each thump. Inch by inch, it moved away from him. He wasn't sullen, exactly. She thought he might simply be anxious, shy.

As if he could sense her looking, he darted a glance at the window to the staffroom, then looked quickly away again. He had his mother's elegant neck.

'Are you worried?' she said simply to Alicia.

'It's . . . she was very sorry the first few times. They were right after she'd split up with Marc,' Alicia said.

Marc, that was it.

Carol remembered the first occasion well. It had been spring, and Becky had rushed in, her cheeks flushed pink. Her expression was rueful, her words rushed and panicked, Carol had thought, while listening in, pretending to be looking at the timetable on the whiteboard out in the foyer. 'I'm so, so sorry,' Becky had said, dropping her usual cool exterior. Alicia had nodded, and Xander had gone to Becky.

Becky's head wasn't in a good place, Alicia had explained later, which Carol thought was pretty fair. Of course not. Carol remembered those post-divorce days. She'd lost her house keys twice in the same week. It was as though her brain had simply emptied itself of normal life.

Forgotten, Carol had said to Alicia. Becky's first indiscretion should be forgotten. It was a one-off. And Carol *had* forgotten, mostly. At parents' evening, she saw Becky across the room, wearing an artful scarf, not with Marc, yet so cordial towards him, which was interesting in itself – and recalled the incident again. But other than that, it had been forgotten, along with a handful of other parents' indiscretions. But then it had happened again. And again.

And now, Becky was missing for the fifth time in recent months. It couldn't go on. Carol had to intervene, as the head, though it pained her to do so.

'Next steps?' she said brusquely now to Alicia. She mustn't be too indecisive, get caught up in the politics of it all. She mustn't, either, be too sympathetic, let her own experience cloud her judgement.

The door opened, letting in a blast of cold air. And there she was. Becky, shaking raindrops off a yellow umbrella.

'I'm so, so sorry,' she said again, rushing over to Xander.

He stood up and stepped towards her, leaning into her as she embraced him, Carol noticed. Good. She didn't want to have to alert anyone. But she should. Her heart felt fat and full. *I'm sorry*, she thought. For making your single-parenting life harder. For making the burden heavier. Carol knew it well: the burden of the life led alone. Remembering to buy wrapping paper, and to get euros, and to buy rinse aid for the dishwasher . . . still, she got twenty-five per cent off her council tax, as an unhelpful friend once told her.

'I've been looking after my sister's baby, Layla, and my sister only just got back, and I didn't have a car seat and . . .' Becky was saying.

Carol caught a scent of something on her breath. She paused. Alcohol, was it? Surely not.

71

'Your phone was off,' Alicia said simply.

'I know – it died, and I was at my sister's flat and we don't have the same chargers, and she doesn't have a landline . . .'

Carol looked properly at Becky. There were myriads of solutions, it seemed to her. Borrow a neighbour's phone. Send an email. Send a text from a website. Becky's eyes were darting around the foyer.

'Becky,' Carol said. She tried to say it gently.

'Yes?' Becky said. She was fussing with her bag, but looked up and stilled, must have sensed Carol's tone.

Xander reached over and un-looped the strap. It was caught in her coat. Becky smiled at him gratefully, and he smiled back. A quick, genuine, broad smile. Carol was pleased to see that moment pass between them.

'I'm afraid – this is the fifth time . . .'

'I know. I do know.'

'. . . he's been left,' Carol finished, nodding discreetly to Xander.

'Yes, I know.' Becky turned to Xander and passed him a key. 'Go to the car,' she said, smiling widely, falsely.

Carol tried to suspend her judgement. Of course he would be fine in the car by himself. Perhaps Becky was trying to shield him from the conversation she knew was coming.

'Becky,' Carol said. 'If it did happen again . . .'

'Yes,' Becky said.

'We would have to arrange a home visit – to check everything is . . . well.'

Becky let out a gasp and Carol stepped back. A charged moment passed between them. Becky's eyes widened and she covered her mouth. Carol could tell that Becky knew she knew, that she could smell it. The alcohol.

'It was wine o'clock, this afternoon, before I went to pick up Layla,' she said. 'Happy hour with some of the other mums.'

'I see,' Carol said.

Becky's lips parted. Her whole face blushed, even her forehead. 'It's not like that – this isn't how it looks. There were a few of us, we went to a cocktail bar – God, that sounds seedy. It was someone's birthday, and it was rubbish weather and we just thought we'd go and have a drink and a giggle in the middle of the day. It'd been organized for ages. I only had one. It was hours ago. It's not – it's not how it seems. I wasn't – I wasn't drunk or anything, when I collected Layla. It was nothing. Just one drink.'

'This is the last warning,' Carol said.

9

Martha

'Thank you,' Ellen the prosecutor says when Carol finishes speaking. 'So tell me . . . you had to issue the defendant with that final warning – why?'

I stop looking at Carol and instead look down at my hands. I had no idea. I knew Becky had forgotten Xander a few times, but I didn't know about the most recent occasion. The sacrifices she made for me. Without telling me. That was true loyalty: suffering things without ever letting on.

But . . . *five* times? How could that be? I close my eyes and think of Layla. I would never have not known where she was. Not even when I was away from her. Not even then. But . . . I admit to myself. That's not true, is it? I hadn't texted to check in, the night she died. I didn't know.

Was Becky neglectful? I examine the thought, this way and that. Maybe. Maybe. She was young, and chaotic, and sometimes selfish, yes. Perhaps she hadn't bonded with Xander, as I worried I hadn't bonded with Layla in those early weeks. Perhaps there really *is* more to Becky than I know.

Nor did I know about the cocktail. Did I mind that she had been in charge of my daughter after a cocktail? God – did I? If this hadn't happened, I would have thought nothing of it. A couple of glasses of wine at a barbecue, mothers marching their children back home, their tread laughingly uneven on the way home . . . it was just life, wasn't it? Wine o'clock, a few too many gins, a bit of a tipsy lunch in the middle of the day. None of us are saints.

Looking across at Becky, I try to think the best. She's not an alcoholic. It didn't make her late. She is just a normal woman who, like many women, might occasionally have alcohol on her breath in the late afternoon. I remember that lunchtime cocktail occasion. Becky had been looking forward to it, and look what it has become: a shameful outing, paraded in a courtroom in support of a murder conviction.

But then . . . she had a cocktail, looked after my child, and forgot her own. She'd driven, too. Had she been over the limit? Why couldn't she just *abstain*? If she didn't have a problem?

I shake my head, trying to get rid of the over-analysis.

I picked Xander up from school myself, once, years ago. He must have been six or seven. I thought I was early, but he was still waiting for me, with a teacher – he was a conscientious sort of child; would always make sure he was where he said he would be – leaning against the lamp post outside the school. His hair had grown and lightened – it was late spring – and his limbs had lengthened and, as I pulled over and looked at him, I was struck by a thought: I was pushing thirty years old, childless, but, somewhere in the future, my children existed, as yet unknown to me. What would they look like? A loping, dark-haired, soulful child like Xander? A petite girl? I couldn't imagine them, yet they already existed, somewhere in the future of my life. I felt the knowledge, the certainty that they were out there, and almost missed them, my children. Xander got into the car a few seconds later. We were going to the cinema.

'Pick 'n' Mix?' he said hopefully.

'Oh, yes,' I said.

'The best thing about Pic 'n' Mix is there's *so much choice*,' he said gleefully. His enthusiasm was infectious; that childlike joy.

Would my future son say things that would make me smile just like that? Xander smelt of earthy, crisp summer air as he reached behind me to stash his backpack on the seat, and I breathed in deeply. Afterwards, we went to Becky's and played some computer game up in his room. I couldn't work out the puzzles to move us from room to room, but he could. We laughed about that, together.

I swallow hard now, in the courtroom; a mother, but childless once again, Layla's potential having evaporated into nothing. Tears prick my eyes. Not for Layla, and not for Xander, but for Becky. Her parenting, put on the stand up there. What would my own look like?

'Why did you sometimes sob when Layla cried,' they would ask me. 'And what led you to leave your child alone with Becky on so many occasions? Why did you prioritize other people's children over her?'

I wouldn't be able to answer that, now.

'It was a mistake,' I would say. 'It was a mistake because I believed they needed me more than she did. And it was a mistake because I believed that Layla would be safe.'

'I thought forgetting a child *five times* was a bit beyond disorganization,' Carol answers now, darting a look at Becky. 'I suppose – I thought that she had a child and perhaps didn't prioritize him.'

'Neglect,' Ellen says, her voice suddenly louder in the courtroom. 'Was there any other evidence of this, would you say?'

Other evidence. They were clever.

'Bits and bobs. Xander was subdued, sometimes. She was evasive. Ignored letters. Once, he cried when I shouted at him.'

I sit back in the public gallery. The chairs are hard and uncomfortable.

'I didn't get the impression he was hugely supervised, at home. He played a lot of computer games. Adult ones, I thought.'

I had heard Becky shouting, once, through an open window as I raised a fist to knock on her door.

'Give that back,' she said, as I stood outside. 'I can't bloody deal with you any more.' Her voice raised higher and higher in its pitch. '*Xander.*'

I stepped back. I'd been calling in when I was working long hours from home setting up Stop Gap. I'd been breaking up my day, on the way back from Sainsbury's. It was probably normal, I reasoned. A parent, during the Easter holidays, shouting at her then eight-year-old. I didn't knock on the door, but I didn't judge her, either. I thought hardly anything of it, until later, when I wanted to shout similarly at Layla. I got it, then. Now, I'm not so sure.

The two Beckies, innocent and guilty, stand before me, and I avoid the gaze of each one of them.

'Nothing further,' Ellen says.

Harriet stands up for the defence. I'm getting into the rhythm of it now, the rhythm of the trial investigating my daughter's death. The prosecution witness tells the story.

Then the defence obliterates it. In a few days, it'll switch, like a football team moving en masse towards the other end of the pitch to try for a goal after half-time. And with each moment that passes, we are closer to knowing.

'So the defendant didn't turn up at school a handful of times,' Harriet says. She studies her nails, then looks directly at Carol. 'Five times in . . . six months?'

'A little less. Roughly once a month.'

'How many other parents have done this?'

'Many do it once or twice,' Carol says. Her head doesn't move, but her eyes flick towards Becky.

Becky has more make-up on today. Her eyes look wide and dramatic, her cheeks pretty and pink, just like when she got married.

I can still picture her wedding day. She'd changed into a black jumpsuit after the ceremony. 'Why would I wear a stiff dress all day when I can wear something actually nice?' she had said. Marc was sitting alone at the edge of the room, eating two slices of cake off a napkin. Becky came from the dance floor and went over to him, dancing moves from 'Thriller' in front of him. Marc's face was creased with laughter. He waved her away, but continued to watch her dance, his eyes on her body.

'Many. I see,' Harriet says now.

'Yes.'

'And being forgetful is hardly neglect,' Harriet says. 'By your own admission, many parents have done it. Especially those going through marital issues, separations . . . working freelance, as the defendant was.'

'Yes. But it's indicative, isn't it? Five times in as many months.'

78

Harriet swallows and reaches to adjust her wig. 'I don't think it's for you to comment on whether the defendant did or did not care about her child,' she says icily. 'Your evidence is that she was late to collect her child several times. She had a lot going on on these occasions. A separation – and then looking after a newborn. We've all become forgetful at busy times in our lives – haven't we? When our minds are overloaded—'

'Is there a question here?' Ellen interjects, beginning to rise to her feet.

'Is your only evidence the forgetting?'

'Well – Xander, her child, also occasionally seemed a bit – I don't know. A bit meek and frightened, I suppose, which can indicate an overbearing parent . . . at home.'

A memory pops into my head. They come from nowhere, these days. Sometimes I find myself waiting for them, frightened of my own thoughts – what I might find in the back rooms of my mind. Becky and I were at her house, years ago, when Xander was only little, and would still sleep like a frog in his cot, his legs all tucked up. A car had sounded outside. One, two, three beeps of the horn. A pause, and then the same again. Xander was napping. It was a warm day, and the windows were open. On the tenth toot of the horn, Becky held a hand up to stop me speaking, stood up, and wrenched open her front door. 'Can you shut the fuck up?' she yelled. I had flinched. Xander had woken up – roused from sleep by his mother's voice, not the car horn. Afterwards, she sat back down like nothing had happened. *Volatile.* That's how she was. 'A loose cannon, is Becky!' Dad used to say.

'Are some children not more reserved – more timid – than others?'

'Yes, they are, that's true.'

'With no reason?'

'Yes.'

'So your only *evidence*, actually, is that the defendant was somewhat forgetful. Isn't it?' Harriet says now.

'Yes. I suppose so.'

'The mother, Martha, wasn't able to care for Layla, despite being on maternity leave. She needed Becky's help. Becky was trying to spin the plates that day she forgot Xander, but she dropped one. That's all. Did you have any other evidence?'

I am winded in the public gallery. People shift around me, embarrassed, or perhaps that's just my imagination. *Wasn't able to care for Layla.* Is that the truth? Surely not. Our private arrangement – our botch-job, our shambolic solution to an impossible situation – has the beam of the spotlight on it, now, in court. Our private life, made public.

Scott reaches to take my hand again. 'The mother. Always the mother,' he sighed a few weeks ago as he read about me in the newspaper. My eyes dampen now with the injustice of it.

'No other evidence,' Carol says.

'How sure were you that the defendant had alcohol on her breath?'

'Very sure.'

'Is this the first time you have smelt alcohol on a parent's breath?'

'No.'

'Would it concern you – usually?'

Carol pauses, looking at the floor, then up again. 'Not on its own. Not when it was just once.'

'Had you ever smelt alcohol on the defendant's breath before?'

'No.'

I swallow. Poor Becky. I can't help but sympathize with her. All of her flaws, all of her ill-judged decisions, things she has done privately – a cheeky cocktail in the afternoon, just *once* – discussed in open court for all to see. And to judge.

Harriet adds, 'Why did you issue the final warning?'

Carol pauses, seeming to think for a moment.

'Well – our handbook advises to issue a final warning before arranging a home visit if we . . . if we ever suspect any sort of neglect.'

'So not out of personal concern?'

'Well, the handbook—'

'Were you personally concerned for Xander? Did *you* think he was being neglected?'

'To tell you the truth,' Carol says after a few seconds, 'I've always had a bad feeling about Becky.'

'We're talking facts, not feelings,' Harriet says icily, but her cheeks redden, and she backs out of the questioning. 'Nothing further.'

Harriet turns around in her seat and tries to catch Becky's eye. Becky's body stiffens, but she doesn't look at Harriet. After a few moments, Harriet turns back to her papers, tapping her pen softly against them. Her angular eyebrows are drawn together. I see her shoulders rise as she inhales, and then sink as she breathes out: a long, sad exhalation. It could just be the toil of the job, the seemingly endless prosecution case, each witness raining pejorative facts down like gunfire. But as I stare at her rising and falling shoulders, I think it might be something else.

She is worried. Either because she thinks the prosecution's case is too strong, and her innocent client might get sent to prison.

Or because she is persuaded by their case. Forgetting Xander. Xander being withdrawn. Carol's clear expertise, and her *feeling* about Becky. The alcohol. They all add up to more than the sum of their parts.

They add up to guilt. That's how it seems. She thinks her client is guilty.

10

Becky

I am holding a bag of beansprouts so large that one of Martha's neighbours stares at me. '*What?*' I want to say. 'They were 89p for almost a kilogram. A *total* bargain, even if we bin almost all of them.'

It's eight o'clock at night when I knock on her door. She opens it and Layla is curled up in the crook of her arm.

'How's my niece?' I say. 'She's not crying.'

'It's a miracle. How's the Dalmatian chair?' Martha says drily.

'Used and abused. I expect they've finished with it already. It's probably in some skip.'

'All your hard work,' Martha says, her forehead wrinkling as she steps aside to let me in. There are three Masai masks on the wall from when she and Scott went to East Africa, which I always eyeball as I walk in. I expect Martha thinks they look eclectic and cool, but the reality is they are absolutely fucking terrifying – guests always pause slightly, staring at them, like: *Oh, right, Jesus.* Perhaps she will let me make it over, one day. Her flat is such a nice space.

'How's the sleep going?' I say.

'Badly. She doesn't,' Martha says over her shoulder.

I followed the Gina Ford method with Xander, but I know better than to say so – Martha would call the attachment parenting police. It bloody worked, though. He was sleeping through the night within a few months, and has never really stopped, not even when he had chicken pox and spent a furious week trying to sneak away from me so he could scratch. Even now, he sleeps for twelve hours a night, often emerging in the afternoons on Saturdays after more than fifteen hours. Marc and I – though we should be having barbed, *separated* sorts of conversations – still marvel at it. *Still going after 14.5 hours* . . . I will sometimes text. He will send a gif back of a sloth, which always makes me laugh, even though he sends the same one each time.

'I'm starving,' I say, walking into the kitchen and pulling out one of Martha's bright-orange kitchen chairs. I put the beansprouts on the table. 'For stir-fry,' I add.

Martha nods distractedly. She has the sort of tired/happy look of a marathon runner, or a person who's just submitted a PhD. Worthy and happy and worn out. New motherhood. At the time, I was desperate to regain my life, to separate the ties between me and my baby limpet, to get back to wine bars and hobbies, but now I find myself remembering it with nostalgia. Xander had been born with a head of tangled, black hair. Even now, if I see a baby with a head of dark hair my innards twist. God, that second baby. How we wished for it to come, and it never did.

Xander was born at three o'clock in the morning exactly. Marc was there, but nobody else. I was just nineteen. Jesus, I don't recognize her now, the *teenager* who went ahead with that pregnancy. But it felt correct. Meeting Marc, even getting pregnant. From the outside, in the distant past, I would have abhorred teenage Becky getting pregnant by a carpet fitter and dropping out of university. I would have curled my lip in distaste. But, from the inside it was . . . I can't describe it. But it was different. It was Marc's eyes crinkling at the corners as I made drinks without boiling the kettle, presented him with a cold cup of tea. 'Lovely, Samuel,' he said. 'Have you been concentrating?'

What did I love? His nickname for me – Samuel – and how he never, ever called me Rebecca or Becky, like I was reborn when I met him. The way he brushed my hair back from my forehead, repeatedly, when we were watching television, after I said I liked it one time. And – yeah – the innocence of him, too. He led a simple life, he enjoyed plain things. He liked crap films and curries every Friday night and drinking a can of Coke on a Saturday morning. He seemed to enjoy his lowbrow life, and I, subsumed into it, did too. Life, before, had been about adventures across London. Barcelona for a hen do. Marc made it simpler: watching twelve episodes of *Friends* in one day at the weekend. Ordering a Domino's pizza for lunch. Life was smaller, but richer, with him.

Labour had been full of pain, but Marc ensured it was also full of laughter, and I could not wish for anything more for Xander; for his life to have begun with happiness.

'He looks like an ape,' I had said, holding him and looking at that shock of wild, dark hair, soft as candyfloss.

'Like mother, like son,' Marc grinned, and we dissolved into laughter again.

I make tea first. Martha's with no sugar – perfect Martha – mine with three. Martha picks up the steaming mug and sips. She closes her eyes.

'Are you asleep?' I say.

'I'm dreaming of a takeout naan bread . . .' she says, opening her eyes and looking at me.

It is one of our things; we are incapable of attending each other's houses without ordering a takeaway. We vowed, last week, to stop – 'Layla will be full of tikka masala and she's only four weeks old!' – and we said we'd buy vegetables and cook together. 'It might even be good fun,' I had said.

'No,' I say now. 'We said we wouldn't . . . I bought the beansprouts.'

Martha looks at them. 'That is a *lot* of beansprouts.'

There is something mildly condescending in her tone. As though I have even bought beansprouts incorrectly. She would have bought them from a farmers' market, no doubt.

'I know. But sod it. Let's do takeaway. We deserve it,' I say.

We order an Indian and it arrives in under half an hour. I peel away the crimped metal edges of the carton and remove the cardboard lid. The curry steams out. It is more beautiful than the finest art in the world. 'Why do I like crap things?' I say, dipping a finger in. 'Cigarettes and curry. Booze.'

Martha likes running and carrot sticks. She will turn down chocolate biscuits. She willingly drinks sparkling water in bars, even though it tastes like balls – to me, anyway.

'You enjoy the finer things in life,' Martha says. She passes Layla to me and the baby settles into my arms as though they are Martha's.

'Oh – yeah – tobacco and curry.'

'I meant your artistic flair, of course,' she says. 'Your interiors.'

Martha's phone rings, and she disappears off to answer it, so I dish up one-handed, which takes for ever. 'Even getting a takeaway is too much effort, sometimes, isn't it?' I say to Layla.

Martha's flat is big, so I can't overhear her call. I put the plates on the table and hoist Layla up over my shoulder and wander around. Martha, fastidiously organized of mind, does not know how to organize a house. It's full of stuff that's been placed in strange locations: a floor lamp halfway along the hallway, jutting out; two pictures of Layla, framed already but different sizes, right next to each other, no space between them on the wall. I pass the Masai masks as I wander. 'They are going to give you nightmares,' I say to Layla, and show them to her, but her eyes are closed. 'We should replace them with an old driftwood coat hook, shouldn't we? That would go so nicely in this space.'

Layla and I are standing by the full-length living-room window, looking at the nearby still life of the sea, when Martha finishes her phone call.

'That was Ami again,' she says.

Ami is her intern at Stop Gap.

'How often are you taking work calls?' I say, thinking of my own maternity leave, spent tipping bags of Maltesers into my mouth and watching *Homes Under the Hammer* while Xander slept.

She lowers herself on to the sofa, not taking Layla as she usually would. I am glad of it. I am enjoying her warm body against my chest – the baby smell. I had forgotten the baby smell. Xander now smells earthy, of outside air and boyhood. Sometimes, when he's kicking a football against the side of the house, or when he's deep into his computer games, his body moving with the controller, this way and that, I will feel so full of love my chest might burst. When he catches that look, he gives me this lopsided, self-conscious smile. He feels my love, but he is shyly embarrassed by it. It is the way it should be. I hope it stays that way.

But, oh, that baby smell. Marc and I tried so hard for another. At first casually, and then more scientifically, with ovulation sticks and temperature charts. It never happened. I never once had a single symptom of pregnancy. 'It's like our bodies forgot how to make one,' I said one night to Marc. He'd avoided my gaze. Later, I thought I heard him sobbing in the shower, but I wasn't sure.

Martha's phone rings again, silently. She cuts it off. Layla stirs against my chest, her little hand flexing against my finger that she's holding. God, Martha. Don't you realize how lucky you are? That baby smell. Their little fat fists. Their soulful eyes.

'It's constant,' she says. 'She's going back to uni shortly.'

'Then what?'

'I don't know. I can't hire anyone. Well, I don't trust anyone. Not with the big stuff. It's all still being set up . . .'

Stop Gap is Martha's charity, designed to help refugees by providing them with a school in which to play and learn. She saw the refugees on holiday and started setting it up almost immediately after getting home. Her change of career surprised everyone except me. She's always been this way: empathetic, helpful. It made perfect sense, to me, that she would do that.

'You like to be in control,' I say.

We sit in silence for a second. Martha moves into the kitchen and sits at the table. So I do, too, Layla still in my arms.

I look up at Martha. She's rolling an onion bhaji directly into the pot of raita, seemingly lost in thought. She has a husband, a baby, a blossoming charity that's expanded enough to pay her a wage *and* help refugees. I glumly rip off a massive piece of naan bread and mop up some sauce with it. What have I done, compared to her? Had a baby at nineteen. Worked for a load of television twats since. I'm separated, soon to be divorced. A single mum. Probably infertile, or just drinking too much to conceive, if that's even a thing.

It's true that comparison is the surest route to unhappiness, I know, but, God, does that stop us? So is Facebook. So is smoking. So is wine.

'Don't drop tikka masala on her head,' Martha says, watching me bring the naan bread to my mouth as Layla sleeps.

'I'll try not to marinade your baby,' I say, my jealous thoughts forgotten. She is *nice*. She deserves these things. 'Couldn't you do bits and bobs for Stop Gap? To keep your hand in, so you can do it on your own schedule and don't get disturbed all the time?'

'Could I?' she says. Her eyes go wide. I remember it well. Like: *Shit*. There is a world beyond nappies and milk and controlling nap times with the zeal of an army general.

'Of course you could. If you don't trust people. Just do like ten hours a week or something. Remotely. Pay someone to have Layla.'

'I hadn't thought – she's so tiny,' Martha says, looking at Layla, asleep in my arms. 'She's never usually this docile, either.'

'Do you want to?' I say.

'Yes.'

'Then do.' I point with my spoon. 'Scott does. You could get a nanny. Few hours a week?'

'Yeah . . .' She pauses. 'I don't know. It feels wrong.'

'You're hardly wanting to go and do seventy-hour weeks as a trader,' I remark. I spoon some tikka masala into my mouth. 'This is spicier than usual.'

'But I need a nanny who could be – ad hoc. Just when things kick off. At the moment we're trying to hire a proper teacher for the school. That's what that was about.' Martha looks at her phone, then points to the curry. 'It *is* spicier. I kind of like it, though. Listen – I could do ten hours a week, couldn't I?'

'Of course.'

'But they'd have to be . . . whenever I want them. To put out fires, like this. Scott's put the money in, but he doesn't have the time. The gap-year student can't be expected to run it. And . . . I want to. To keep it going. The school is my other baby,' she says with a self-conscious smile. 'It has to be me. Just in the initial stages. Then I can hand it over. But I have to . . . *I* have to find the premises. Hire the people. Don't I?'

'Yes,' I say honestly.

'I need flexible childcare.'

'That's like gold dust,' I say, thinking of Xander's old nursery and its ridiculously ruthless rules. A pound for every minute after 6.00 p.m. you were late picking up.

She looks at me, and I at her, and, I swear to God, we have the idea at the exact same time.

'You could do it,' she says. 'And set-dress much less.'

She says it simply. Neither of us needs to hash out the specifics; we have never needed to. We leap over them. It must be something unique to us, and not our upbringing, because Ethan is never on the same page as we are.

'Be your nanny?'

'Yeah. God – you'd be brill. I can pay you. Really well. If you could—'

'What, be at your beck and call?'

'Basically.'

She doesn't sense the warning in my tone. I want to help. It seems to make sense. But . . . don't take the piss. That's what I meant by that.

We sit in silence for a few seconds in Martha's warm flat. I could sit here, looking after Layla. See more of Martha. Collect Xander from school every day. Not have to worry about bloody set-dressing all the time. I could be around more, stop him playing endless computer game after endless computer game. Get him outside – running, or something.

'Just try it for a bit, maybe?'

'How long?'

'Few months?'

'I could get rid of the worst clients of mine,' I say. 'Keep the rest. The non-bastards.'

She's looking at me so earnestly and suddenly I just think: *This helps her, and it helps me*. It's a no-brainer.

'Let's do it,' I say.

'First-day nerves,' I say, four days later, to a very stressed Martha.

'I'm glad. Means you'll do it right,' she says.

'Whatever,' I say. I know how to look after a baby. Xander is safely at school until three. We have ages. I don't have to set-dress today, and so today is a good day.

Martha is hastily changing a nappy, and Layla is bright red.

'God,' I say, startled at her expression. 'What's she angry about?'

'You need to get her wind out,' she says. 'She's got a bit of reflux. I will be three hours.'

She has expressed some breast milk. She's going to a café nearby, to make calls. To answer emails. She doesn't want to do it in her house, where she can hear Layla cry, she says.

'Oh, like massaging? Xander never really had much wind . . .'

She shows me. The 'tiger in the tree' hold. Laying Layla on her back, cycling her legs. Layla on her front.

'Do you understand that?' she says.

A slice of something cuts through me. Why is she saying it like that? Does she have to be so . . . patronizing? In my head, I imagine telling Marc about that comment, as I often do. In my fantasy land, we are still together, and he says to me, 'Ignore her, Sam. She's a patronizing arse.'

'Yes,' I say to Martha.

'You're lucky. Xander was a total dream,' she says, perhaps sensing my annoyance, as she puts her coat on.

'I know.'

Even when he had mumps, Xander slept. Marc got them, too. God, how we laughed at his huge jowls; we called them his turkey wattles. Marc hadn't been vaccinated, for some reason. He lost loads of weight. It was weeks before the swelling in his neck went down, and months before I stopped calling him moon-face.

When Martha has left, I cycle Layla's legs for her, and she cries and cries. I massage her stomach, hold her in the poses Martha showed me. I feed her. Burp her endlessly. Baby massage. Soothing songs. Little walks. Bounce her.

I start to hear different tones within her screams, by mid-morning. By lunchtime, I feel certifiable, and take her out for a walk where strangers stare at me as we pass, as though I am a lunatic, as though it is me who is screaming.

Martha isn't back by two o'clock, and so Layla comes to the school gates with us, like a very loud alarm I have to carry around with me. Xander is less than impressed, and walks on ahead of us, trying to get away from the noise, I guess. I take him straight to Marc's, who has to shout for me to hear him over the din.

'What do you mean, nannying?' Marc says.

I see it before he can cover it up: irritation. The very specific brand of Marc irritation that only me and Xander can spot. His eyebrows go up, his mouth curls ever so slightly in disdain.

'I'm going to be looking after Layla – for money.'

'Why?'

I shift my weight, moving Layla from one hip to another, and just look at him. 'She needs a nanny. I need money,' I say.

'You don't need money. You've got my money,' he says shortly. 'You don't need them to employ you.'

'I want to stop doing so much set-dressing. I hate it,' I say. Something rises up inside me, as it often does. My mind treats me to a slideshow of my failures and of Martha's per-fection. Baby in her thirties. Strong, stable marriage. A blossoming charity. A flat that overlooks the sea. No unexplained infertility, unlike me. How come some people get it all and some people get nothing? How is that fair?

'Oh, great,' he says. 'Sure, why not just swap jobs without telling me?'

'I don't have to tell you anything any more,' I say coolly to him.

'Alright,' he says, raising his hands, palms towards me, as if in surrender. 'None of my business, is it?'

'No,' I say to him.

He is like this, sometimes. Quick to anger. I used to see it all the time with Xander. He dropped a fork on the floor once and Marc blew up. I had to calm them both down. Xander had cried and Marc was crimson with rage. Over a fork, for God's sake.

I say nothing else, and walk down the drive with just Layla, who is still bright red and crying.

I used to think the desperate mothers asking forums about these babies were exaggerating. *Newborns sleep twenty hours a day!* I would scoff, inwardly.

By the time Martha returns, my whole body is rigid, covered in sweat. I am wrung out. I think about what Marc said: *You don't need them to employ you.* Is it true? Is that how far I have sunk? Am I Martha and Scott's *staff* now?

My next day with Layla is a week later. The nannying arrangement starts to take shape, allowing Martha some control over what's happening with her charity.

But ten days after that, everything changes again.

11

Martha

The prosecution want to call a woman called Sophie. Becky's brow looks heavier. It's an expression I can easily recognize, and I think: *Sophie must mean something to her.* Though I don't know what.

Becky wore a similar expression on that first day of nannying. At the time, I'd thought it was attitude. She'd left every job she'd ever had, I had realized the night before the arrangement began. What had I let myself in for?

I look around the courtroom as Sophie is ushered in. This is what I had let myself in for. This is where it ended.

In death.

In murder charges.

In destruction.

Sophie is young, maybe slightly younger than Becky. Her ankles are slim in skinny jeans and as she takes her place on the stand her hand flutters at her chest. She must be nervous.

Ellen lumbers to her feet.

'Sophie,' she says. 'Can you tell us about the day you saw the defendant?'

'I just saw her. One day.' Her tone is defensive, that of a person who has perhaps said too much, and now she finds herself in a witness box, taking part in a trial for murder.

'And can you tell us a bit more about that?'

She opens her mouth to speak, and then begins.

12

Sophie Cole

Sophie had discovered that she liked to study in dirty pubs. The cheaper the better. She drank gallons of Pepsi – she preferred it draught, from a pump – and ordered chips after she had read fifty pages, the halfway point.

Today's topic was dose calculations. She was studying to be a veterinary nurse. She took her shoes off and sat cross-legged, her knees resting on the underside of the table. It was just the sort of place her father used to take her, this pub in particular. Here, amongst the barmen who called her sweetheart and the bloke who couldn't get off the slot machine, she felt at home.

She checked her phone. Jay was at after-school football until six. She had two hours.

She heard a heavy sort of walk behind her, but didn't turn around. She would only get distracted. That was her deal with herself: she could work in pubs so long as she didn't get talking to anybody.

She heard a baby's cry behind her, and a child's voice, all at once. She reached into her bag for her headphones and began untangling them. She had enough of children at home, thank you very much.

Just as she was untangling the final knot – how *did* they get so entwined? – she heard the woman's voice.

'Alright, what do you want?'

Sophie cocked an ear. That was definitely Becky, from the school. Sophie didn't know her well. She thought she might be divorced. She was always cracking up with Xander, her son. They seemed to get on like friends.

'Coke?' Xander said hopefully.

'No way,' Becky said.

Sophie peeked a look. Yes. It was her. She didn't realize she'd had a baby. It must have been ages since she'd last seen her. She put her headphones in, regardless. Becky was a chatterer. She'd never get anything done if she realized it was her. She'd see if they stayed quiet, and, if they did, she didn't need to put any music on; she could just pretend.

Right. If a spaniel weighs 18kg . . . she diligently copied down the equation that followed the preamble, even though she didn't have a clue what it meant.

Sophie heard Becky's tread again after a few moments, returning from the bar. And then the distinctive splash of liquid on the wooden floor.

'Shit,' Becky said.

Sophie raised her eyebrows and took another look. Wine. God knows, people had judged her, when she still had a young person's railcard and a five-year-old, and yet, she couldn't help but judge back, sometimes. White wine in the afternoon, with two kids. *Huh.*

'Xander, for God's sake,' Becky suddenly said. Sophie knew the tone well herself. She called it the bedtime tone, when she was just waiting for the minutes to slide away so she could justify being on her own. No moans of *Muuum* or sticky hands or random shouts at the television, no legs kicking her on the sofa as Jay, unaccustomed to his new lanky frame, tried to get comfortable, no Robinson's Fruit Shoot spillages on cushions that couldn't be machine washed.

Sophie turned around. Xander was rocking back on his chair, teetering precariously. He wasn't friends with her own son. Jay had once described him as *weird*.

Becky was definitely separated, Sophie remembered now. She had referenced it obliquely, as was her way, saying, 'Oh, I don't need to share the remote control with anybody, now,' at some school social occasion. Sophie had always quite admired her. She seemed to be one of those people who really did *not* care what anybody else thought of her.

Sophie drained the Pepsi from her glass just as the baby started crying, properly crying. *Hmm.* She opened the music app on her phone and scrolled through it, trying to find something ambient and non-distracting. She wouldn't turn around and chat. She wouldn't.

Ed Sheeran, that would do. She found her favourite song. Right before she pressed play, she heard it.

'Xander!'

She turned around. Becky's face was bright red. The baby was in the car seat, crying. Becky was ignoring her, which Sophie thought was odd. She couldn't ignore that sound. Weren't we programmed not to be able to?

As Sophie watched, Becky reached for Xander's hands,

99

her teeth gritted. She pulled on his wrists, forcing him forwards, and his chair back on to the floor. He had to steady himself as he flew towards the table.

'Xander. If you do that again I'm going to smack you,' Becky added.

As if it wasn't already bad enough.

13

Martha

I can't help but look straight across at Becky. Her bottom lip is glistening. She has opened her mouth in shock. The whites of her eyes shine and she looks down, trying, I think, to look dignified.

The constant references to wine are not good. I have often thought – privately – that Becky loves wine a little too much. She will often joke about *wine o'clock* in the late afternoon. Every Friday, without fail, she posts a glass of red on Instagram. But don't a lot of people?

What if the worst moments of my life were paraded in a courtroom? That time I lost my temper in Curry's when Layla was a week old and we needed a new washing machine immediately. The time I huffed at a train conductor when we were delayed for Becky's hen do. The time I leaned on the horn when somebody cut me up on the way to see Ethan after work. How would they look? Anybody could be made to look guilty.

But what about Layla? my mind says. My other mind. Whose side am I on? I am a traitor, caught in no-man's-land between my daughter and my sister. My daughter should trump her, but I know my sister. I look at that still-glistening lip and wonder if I truly do.

'Of course she did it. What do you think happened?'

Scott will say. He isn't as clinical, as dispassionate, as that makes him sound. I try to make myself remember that he is hurting, deep down inside, too. That he blames himself. And perhaps he should. Sometimes he will spend forty minutes in the shower, and emerge with his eyes red. Sometimes, he will say, 'If I had been there . . . if I hadn't stayed longer . . .' and not be able to finish his sentences.

But these witnesses – they were innocent bystanders, and are now forced to recollect, forced to process the events in the light of death, of disaster, of *guilt*. What was it? Situational bias. 'Did the defendant ever seem violent to you?' they will have been asked. Of course they will have stories to tell. Of course they will. Everyone would, when asked that question, knowing what happened to Layla.

Becky had always been hard to read. Sometimes volatile. If you didn't know her well, and know all that she's been through, you could easily assume she was – well . . . a bit unstable.

She had given birth to Xander in the autumn. She should have been starting her second year of university, but instead she was asking for an epidural. I had arrived after he was born. I was twenty-two, and unable to imagine myself in her situation. She had seemed both childlike and grown up to me, then. She told me that Marc had been making her laugh. She'd spent the time in between contractions creased up, laughing, batting him away. As she recounted it to me, I was standing quietly, watching them, thinking: *Maybe this will work out, after all.*

She never went back to interior design school. She couldn't, for a few years, and then she just didn't. She had a string of sort-of related jobs, before set-dressing. Some dressmaking, some space-planning, consultancy work. The television people had been horrible to her but, other than that, she had always seemed happy enough. But maybe the wine said differently.

Harriet is standing up now, and looking pointedly at Sophie. 'So you overheard the defendant threatening to discipline her own nine-year-old.'

'Yes.'

'Did she discipline him? Did she smack him?'

'No. Her hands were gripping his . . .'

'Did she smack him?'

'No.'

'Did she ever seem irritated with Layla?'

'No.'

'Nothing further.'

The judge orders a short break, after Sophie's witness evidence. It's eleven o'clock and so Scott and I decide to walk down to the beach. We need this time, too. This thoughtful downtime. Next week . . . next week, we really will have to move on. Deal with the verdict, whatever it is.

We sit on the sun-warmed pebbles which stick uncomfortably into my dress, but I don't care. His shirt sleeves are rolled up to his elbows. I take a breath, ready to speak.

'Let's not pick it all apart,' he says. 'I can't do it to her.'

'To Layla?'

He looks at me and nods, just once. 'She deserves better than this . . .' he gestures back at the court, 'this circus. About her little life.' His voice cracks.

'I know,' I say quietly. 'I know.' I gulp back the tears which always seem ready to fall, and I look across at Scott.

His blond hair catches the sun. 'Two blond men,' Becky often said of Scott and Marc. 'And yet so different.' Scott is tall and wiry. Marc is shorter, broader, with huge blue eyes and dimples.

I squint, trying to frame the sea in my vision so that I don't get the old or the new pier in the picture, trying to make the sea look just as it did in Kos.

Becky came out to Kos with me, the March after Stop Gap was set up, and I was managing it from afar, while pregnant. 'Would you like to come?' I had said shyly to her, after she had grilled me about it.

'Sounds beyond cool,' she had said, and that was that.

We went straight there after our flight. I opened the door to Stop Gap and found myself holding my breath, like I was about to unveil a new haircut or give a personal speech. Months later, it still smelt of fish. The morning lesson was in full flow, and I forgot about the pain in my limbs, aching and tired from the early start.

'God, it's amazing,' Becky said, looking first up at the grubby ceiling, and then at the expanse of children sitting listening to a story. There was a stilling of the air as I arrived; the two volunteers – gap-year students, whose expenses I just about managed to cover using a tiny EU grant – had stopped and were staring at me. It still felt strange to be that: the boss.

Becky engaged immediately in a way I hadn't seen her do before. She crossed the room to where the teacher was reading a story and sat down next to her. And then she just sat quietly, on one of the children's seats, right at the front of the crowded room. I studied her, my sister, with her elbows on her knees, her hands cupping her face, as she listened to the story, rapt.

And then, towards the end of the story, one of the refugees – Sayid, I thought, though Stop Gap had become so popular I was struggling to keep track – inched closer to her. I saw it happening, felt myself smiling as he did it.

Line by line, he scooted closer to Becky, until by the end of the story he was almost upon her shoes, like a dog might sit at an owner's feet. Unthinkingly – or so I imagined – she reached down and scooped him up, placing him in her lap. And then she didn't turn her attention back to the teacher. She looked straight down at him, at Sayid, smiling at him gently, her gaze encouraging, with just a hint of sadness behind her eyes, in the crease of her brow.

No, I think now, as Scott shifts on the stones and I open my eyes fully and Brighton comes back to life around us. *It can't have been her.* Not that Becky who cradled the refugee child at my shelter; who understood it – and me – completely, reverently. No. It wasn't her.

Then it was an accident. Somehow. A tragic accident. One she either didn't know about, or covered up. But not a murder. No.

14

Martha

The health visitor, Irene Fox, walks into the courtroom, led in by the same usher who brought me in. She has a sleeve tattoo just poking out from underneath a black jacket, and a haircut that looks like a crop being grown out. She seems nervous, her features pinched, her shoulders held stiffly. As she takes the secular oath, she gives a small, sardonic smile, showing pointy teeth.

'When did Layla and her mother first come to see you?' Ellen says. She is thicker-set than Becky's lawyer. Less poised too, but seems affected by the proceedings.

'October time.' Irene looks over at me.

'Do you have the exact date?'

'The eleventh.'

Becky had been nannying for us for just over a week.

'And when was the second appointment?'

'The twentieth.'

The leaves had dusted the car park. Becky was keeping me company. Scott was away, at an overnight developers' conference, so it was just the three of us: Becky, Layla and me. She died at the end of October. Ten days after that, Becky was charged.

'Thank you. And why were they there?'

'Layla was a difficult baby. Lots of wind, the mother thought.' She looks at me again.

How strange this is. To attend a routine appointment, and then to hear it rehashed and repeated back to me, months later. Deconstructed by the court system, and constructed again, into witness statements, testimony, cross-examination. It's so artificial. It was just an appointment. Just us.

'Why?' Ellen says.

'The baby – Layla – cried a lot, especially after food. Writhing, going red and angry. Looking uncomfortable.' She pushes her hair back from her forehead. It's getting in her eyes. 'Raising her legs up.'

'And did she have reflux?'

'Yes. I diagnosed that. I asked the GP to prescribe Gaviscon Infant. And then, when they came back on the twentieth, I asked him to prescribe ranitidine, which is stronger.'

Becky pushed for the second meeting. By that time, I was on the phone for three hours a day, trying to sort out the staffing and the equipment and taking new premises. There was so very much to do, and nobody could do any of it but me. They seemed so vital, those calls that seem so stupid now. Was Becky concerned for Layla or was she . . . at the end of her tether? 'Martha, you need to sort this out,' she had said fiercely to me one night. Was that motivational, or had it been a threat?

'Did the Gaviscon seem to work?'

'Not really, no. The mother said that she was still symptomatic. Still crying a lot. Not being sick very much, though, so I thought it might be silent reflux.'

'Silent reflux?' Ellen balances her fingertips on the desk and leans her weight against them. The tips blanch white.

'Reflux without so many outwardly obvious symptoms. The babies are uncomfortable, but it's less clear why. They don't always vomit. Sometimes they swallow back the stomach acid. It causes discomfort and wind.'

I sink my head forward on to my hands. Scott shifts in the gallery next to me, placing an arm across the back of the bench and curling it around my shoulders. Mum tuts, behind us, a soft, sympathetic clucking noise.

Becky is looking at me, as she always seems to be, when I raise my eyes again.

'How much – in your experience – do babies have to cry, before people seek professional help?'

'Your Honour, if I may . . .' Harriet says. She stands and looks attentively at the judge, her mouth set. 'This witness is a witness of fact. She's not an expert.'

'I entirely agree,' the judge says, simply and quietly.

'I'll rephrase,' Ellen says. 'Do you know how much Layla was crying?'

'No,' Irene says. 'I don't. But Martha seemed to suggest it was more than other babies – more than was normal. Her symptoms were on a par with classic silent reflux.'

'And how was she when you got the GP to prescribe the ranitidine? In the second appointment?'

'The same. She needed walking around a lot. She needed jiggling after meals. She was crying for much of the second appointment.'

'So would it be a reasonable assumption that a typical refluxy baby, with these symptom patterns, prescribed what you prescribed . . . would have been crying pretty much all the time?'

'Not all the time. But a lot. For many hours per day.'

'Crying for many hours per day,' Ellen nods. She pauses, letting it sink in for the jury, then turns to look at them meaningfully. The pause stretches out in the courtroom. Still, she doesn't speak. I can almost see the awkward, loaded silence, stretched thin, its surface like gossamer.

Here was a baby nobody could cope with, the silence says. Here was a woman lacking the resilience needed to cope with a baby in as much pain as mine. *Did it hurt Layla, when it happened?* I wonder. *Did she know her heart was stopping, her brain dying?* My eyes are damp and I blink.

'And in what percentage of cases would you say the ranitidine works?'

'Thirty – forty? Sadly, reflux often seems to have to run its course. Sometimes the medicine works, but more often reflux has to go away on its own.'

I can't help but look across at Becky. She has stopped looking at me, and is instead focusing her gaze up at the judge, or perhaps at the crest behind him. She looks impassive, but I can see the areas of tension she's holding in her body. Her jaw is quivering just slightly. She always used to feel the cold so much more than me – and I now remember what her jaw used to do. Our walks home from school, from Brighton to Hove, along the coast. We'd talk about what our adult lives would look like; where we would travel, what we would do for a living. How it would feel to own an entire house, ours to decorate exactly the way we wanted. Her jaw would always be chattering like that. When she would arrive at pubs with Marc, to meet Scott and me, in the winter, her jaw would be working like that against the cold.

It's not cold in the courtroom. She is condemned. That is how she looks.

'And did it work? For Layla? Was she in the thirty to forty per cent?'

'I don't know,' Irene says. 'I never saw Layla again.'

Ellen sits down, triumphant, and I can barely look at her. The point-scoring of it. The games. The wordplay. The strutting theatre. Peacocks. It is despicable. Disgust rises up through me, unexpectedly, and I swallow, trying to dampen it down.

Harriet stands up and looks at the health visitor.

'How many babies do you see with reflux, Ms Fox?' she says icily.

'How many babies . . .?'

'Say, per year.'

'Well – four times a day, maybe, it gets mentioned. Forty-six weeks per year, for me . . .'

Harriet looks at her notes. 'So we're talking, what, up to a thousand a year?'

'Maybe – I really have no idea.'

'I wonder how many health visitors there are in the UK,' Harriet says.

Ellen turns her head and looks sharply at Harriet. Her mouth parts. Her brows draw together.

'Just wondering,' Harriet says. 'Seems like quite a lot of refluxy babies.' She brings her attention back to Irene. 'So reflux is – I would say – all round pretty common.'

'Common-ish. Yes. Maybe fifty per cent of babies have an episode of it.'

'Fifty per cent!' Harriet says, like she's been handed a rare diamond.

Irene doesn't care, I see. It's not her baby. It's not her sister. She is cool, up there on the stand, and has no opinion about my sister's likely guilt or innocence. She hasn't taken a side. She will leave the courtroom, after this. Head home and watch television, no demons in her living room, sitting over her shoulder in case she relaxes.

'Right. So fifty per cent of babies are refluxy.'

'Yes, at times.'

'What would you say the outcome is – with these babies?'

'The reflux passes,' she says immediately.

'They are not killed. Thank you,' she says.

'If I may . . .' Ellen says, rising to her feet.

The judge doesn't even say anything. He merely looks at Harriet, exasperated.

'Nothing further,' she says. 'Withdrawn.'

We break for lunch. It's all so civilized, like we are playing cricket or at a training course, not like we are watching a trial play out in front of us.

The door creaks behind Ethan and me as we make our way across the hall and out into the sunshine. Mum, Dad and Scott are just in front of us. Mum's body language is hunched. Perhaps she, too, is thinking of Layla, in pain in her final weeks.

Ethan looks at me over his menu in the café we end up in. He doesn't say anything for a second, but I can tell he wants to. 'Now it's started,' he says tentatively. 'I just feel so sure she's innocent.'

I shrug, not wanting to discuss it. I have nothing – and everything – to say on the subject, but I'm exhausted. 'Who knows,' I say.

'But if she is . . .' he continues.

'Hmm?'

'Imagine if she's totally innocent.'

'Yes.'

'Then she's wrongly accused. And hardly anybody believes her.'

I gulp. I can't imagine. 'You do,' I say instead. It is easier to be prickly, to be spiteful, than it is to be nice, for the first time in my life.

How did we get here?

I gaze down at the menu, not pondering what to eat, not really here at all. Instead, I am back in July last year.

I was seven and a half months pregnant when it happened. When I did it. The most significant event leading up to Layla's death. It was late one night. I couldn't sleep, was too uncomfortable, and was idling on the internet.

I had three internet tabs open; two for grants of a couple of thousand pounds, and one for much more: the National Lottery's charity page. I wanted to show Scott that I had used his money well. That it had been worthwhile. That we were helping people – together.

I would just fill in the charity details, I thought.

On the next page I had to fill in the financial information. It was dark in the spare room, just the glow of the monitor, and the cursor was blinking, the only movement in the still summer night. I knew the sea was rolling outside, but I couldn't see it, couldn't hear it through the triple glazing. I reached to open the window, my bump pushing against the desk as I did so. I reached and stroked it, instinctively; the first time I had done so.

Ambivalence, we kindly called it. The broodiness didn't hit in the way I thought it might. But one morning, the day before my thirtieth birthday, I was baking, and carried a sugar bag on my hip from the pantry to the kitchen. That was the first time I felt it. A solid presence in my arms. How nice it might be to look after a baby, a child. The rest of the leaps came easily. 'Why not?' we said. And then, the sex: so easy to have unprotected sex. So unconnected with the decision-making, it seemed to us. The pregnancy test. And here we were, and I was stroking my bump for the first time, like: *Hello to you.*

It was partly the bump grazing against the desk that made me fill in the rest of the form. A real and tangible touching. That touch. My baby. It brought to mind the large brown eyes of the children in Kos who queued up from sunrise to come to Stop Gap for the day; to get a meal, to talk to someone, but mostly just to play. At home, they never played; they had adult concerns. Finding food. Being quiet in the refugee camp. At Stop Gap, they could play – and be as loud as they liked. That was what they were queuing for, I thought.

I rubbed my taut bump and reread the information, then clicked: Next. A personal statement. And then all of the children were my bumps, too. Bana, whose hair had lightened in the sun. Moonif, with the scar across his forehead that he wouldn't talk about. Amena, with the dirty koala toy. The queuing. Their disappointment.

I looked at the blinking cursor, as regular as the heartbeat inside me, and began to write.

15

Becky

The reflux appointment has been all I have been able to think about, once I found out about it, as if it were a wrapped, pristine packet of cigarettes in my handbag waiting to be opened.

Even Marc, just now, texted me saying: *It's the day!* Mind you, he's nice like that.

I read the message a few times, thinking: *How come you're like this now?*

I remember, a few weeks before we split up, I walked in the door, having been away on a hen do for the weekend. Xander was already in bed – sleeping, of course – and Marc was alone in the living room, a can of Carling on the arm of the sofa. 'Alright?' I said.

He didn't reply, merely nodded. I took my shoes off, waiting for him to say something, but he didn't. Not a single question about my weekend, nor an offer of a drink for myself. Nothing. He didn't even turn his head to look at me. Kept watching *Match of the Day*, his gaze fixed.

He had wanted to have sex with me the previous day, right before I left, but I'd said no. I needed to pack, get going. It had been ages, he'd said, but I ignored him. He'd been off ever since, not saying goodbye to me, and not saying hello, either. His temper was one thing, but his sulking was worse. Something had changed with him. Was it the pressure – the tedium – of parenthood, or was it something more? I never knew, and things unravelled soon after.

Now, almost a year post-separation, he sends texts like that. If he had been . . . if he was this nice *then*, what would have happened? My heart answers before my brain can stop it, and I close my eyes with the pain of it.

I reply to him, now: *Thank you – hope it goes well.*

Me too, he responds immediately. But then he adds: *This has gone beyond a joke now.*

The arrangement. I know he means the arrangement. I wrinkle my nose in distaste and put my phone away. Before Marc withdrew completely, he developed this curious, macho attitude to life that reared its head at times when Xander was little. He would say things like 'They need sorting out,' and 'He's got it coming to him.' Sometimes he would snatch noisy toys from Xander, and slam doors, and bang saucepans around in the kitchen as he cooked. I could never reason with him when he was like that. It worried Xander, I know it did. But they never lasted long, his moods. He always snapped out of them. And he'd snap out of this, too; this disapproval of the nannying arrangement. Or so I hoped.

The health visitor will sort Layla out, and then we will be alright. She won't cry so much, won't be angry and tearful when Martha gets home.

It is late in the afternoon when we go for the appointment.

It is almost getting dark, and I perch in the window of a lit-up café nearby. I can't go in. It feels like too much hangs on it. My hands feel clammy with nerves. Because . . . if they can't sort it. Then what?

I sip my overpriced flat white and glumly watch the people walk by outside. A man with a poodle, both cowering a little against the wind. Perhaps it won't always be this way. Soon, one day soon, I won't be looking after my sister's baby who cries all the time. I could get a loan. Go back to design school. Finally finish. Become more like Martha: achieve something, instead of languishing in mediocrity. I don't want a big, flashy life. Somehow, being with Marc taught me about smaller pleasures – watching *The X Factor* with a Chinese takeaway, a drive-through McDonald's on a Sunday night – and I have no desire to become a high flyer, a traveller, a big shot. I just want life to be a little better. A little easier. To make money doing something I enjoy.

Marc's right about the arrangement, even if he expresses it poorly. Something needs to change. I know it. Martha has taken advantage of me, and why shouldn't she? I am a shadow of her, a pale imitation.

The door opens, letting in a blast of smoked autumn air, and I am immediately transported somewhere nostalgic, though I'm not sure where.

Martha and Layla emerge in the doorway, behind a woman in a polka-dot mackintosh. Layla is strapped to her mother's chest, and is crying. My jaw sets.

'How'd you go?' I say.

'Oh, rubbish,' Martha says. 'Last time we got Gaviscon. Now we have ranitidine.'

'I still can't believe they prescribed Gaviscon,' I say.

What next? A prescription for Hall's Soothers? Homeopathy? Probably.

'What does ranitidine do?' I say.

'It stops the production of stomach acid. Same as Gaviscon, but more powerful. To be honest,' Martha says, digging in the changing bag for the prescription, 'it sounds like it's just one of those things.' She shows it to me. Ranitidine. Three times a day.

'One of those things?'

'She'll just – grow out of it. I already think it's a bit better. Don't you?'

The shock must show on my face because Martha steps back, covering Layla's head with her hand.

'God. Maybe,' I say, covering it up. Though I mean: *Are you deluded?*

We leave the café and Martha's hair blows across her face in the cold air. We have the same hair, so much of it, brownish red. We don't know where we got it from. Our parents both have thin hair, wispy, and here we are with massive manes that required special hairbrushes ordered from a catalogue by Mum. Dad used to clear all the hair that clogged up the drains when we were growing up. He never said a word about it until I saw him doing it one day and he admitted he did it every Monday. That was his way: stoicism. Ethan has inherited it.

'How long until the drugs work?' I say.

Layla's whimpers become louder as we walk across the car park, and Martha reaches around for her hand.

I can't get in the car with the crying. I can't bear it. But how can I tell Martha that? *Actually, this arrangement isn't good for me. I can't stand it any longer.* I can't, can I?

'Feckless, unreliable Becky,' Martha will say to Scott, and then they will roll their eyes about me. Their *staff*, gone rogue.

No. I can't have that happen. I will make it work: I am too proud.

'Up to a year.'

'Wow.'

'I know. But you're so great with it. And think of next year, and how easy it'll be,' she says with a wide smile. And then, as if she is trying to make things seem better, she says, 'It'll either work or it'll pass.'

It is a very *Martha* thing to say. The logic of it. We sat up late, one night, on the day of her thirtieth birthday, post-takeaway, and she said to me, 'I think I want a baby more than I don't want a baby.'

'Right,' I had said, with all the annoying, knowing smugness of a parent. 'It's not that simple,' I added. Though, really, I suppose I was jealous of her. Her decisiveness, and her control. She would never have an accident and spoil her career as I had.

'We're going to start trying tomorrow.'

'*Tomorrow?*'

'It can take years, and you only get two IVF cycles on the NHS if you are under thirty-nine.'

'IVF?' I said. 'What?'

'In case we can't conceive.'

I shook my head. She sometimes made no sense in this way, was five steps ahead of herself, having imagined nine disasters along the way.

'Look,' I had wanted to say. 'Look at the women who get pregnant immediately, the women who have all of their babies in their forties, the women who look like they might *miss out* but who it works out for, seemingly at the last minute.' But anyway, this is what I love most about her. My lens is wide-angle. Hers is narrow, but clearer. I like the hyper-logic of it. She makes perfect sense, just not in the real world.

'Everything is a phase,' she says now.

I blink. The crying. Layla's face, even now, is streaked with tears. This job of mine, this nannying a constantly crying child. It is going to go on and on. A year. The tears, mine and hers. I could get another job but . . . it is working, for Martha at least.

'This too shall pass,' I say faintly, remembering seeing it on Mumsnet one day but never having needed to apply it to my own child. Xander was a sleepy newborn, a docile toddler who played alone. It is only now, as he approaches his tenth birthday, that I foresee any problems; I can suddenly see him as a sullen teenager, withdrawn. But not quite yet.

'Yep,' she says, seeming happy.

Layla is her baby. I am thinking: *It is different for me.*

Her phone rings. I can hardly make it out at first over the crying.

'Oh, hang on,' she says, lifting Layla out of her sling and placing her in my arms. She walks over to the car, leaving me in the middle of the pavement. Just like that. She doesn't even check if that's okay with me.

Offload the baby on to the nanny, why don't you? I think spitefully. As Layla cries, I get my phone out and text Marc back. *Fucking right*, I type, my head full of the reflux prognosis – 'one of those things' – and the way Martha presumes our arrangement will continue for ever.

I stand rigidly with Layla. *It's normal*, I am telling myself. She just left the baby with me while she went to get her phone. But it's another imposition. One in a whole line of them.

When she gets back, I don't ask her who it was. That is, until I see her face. She's white.

'What's up?' I say.

'We got the grant,' she says quietly. It is her tone that makes me look up properly. Her phone is still lit up by her side.

'The Lottery grant?'

'Yes.'

'How much?' I say.

She whispers her answer. 'One point two million pounds.'

'Fucking hell.'

'Yes. We can do so much with it all,' she says.

'You can.'

'We could – we could even buy somewhere. In Kos. Somewhere – permanent.'

'Jesus,' I say.

She has this serious expression on her face, the one she only ever gets when she's thinking hard. 'Ami thinks I need to go. Next week. To look at places. She says there are a few great ones on the market at the moment, but they're getting snapped up. And Scott's going to be away again.'

'Yeah,' I say. 'Where is Scott?'

'This developers' conference ... I can't take Layla, Beck.'

'I know,' I said, thinking of the flight, the premises, the

hundreds of children. She can't take a baby into that chaos.

She is going to ask me.

She turns to me. Layla is held close to my chest, but is looking up at Martha in adoration. Mother and baby. 'I need to go next week.'

'I know.'

'It's chaos there. I can't be viewing properties with an eight-week-old. She hasn't even had all her vaccinations . . .'

I wait for it. Braced.

'Could you have Layla for a night? Scott is away for one night, but he can have her for the other. I'll only be away two nights.'

'Of course,' I say, my voice husky.

'And then, after the trip . . . I could set up loads of things. A place where kids could learn how to use computers and learn English and . . .'

'Who are you going to get to do all that?' I say sharply.

'I could. With this money,' she says, like it's obvious. Like she doesn't even *have* a baby to look after.

'I thought you were just arranging the premises and then handing over to someone?'

'But everything's changed, Beck,' she says, her eyes bright. 'This is really working, isn't it?' she adds, gesturing to me and Layla and demonstrating – as usual – a total and complete misunderstanding of reality. How she runs a charity is beyond me.

'What?'

'The nannying. Look – we could . . . couldn't we make this long-term? You could stop all of your freelancing. I could pay you *handsomely*,' she says. She's absolutely pumped.

'Oh – I don't know,' I deflect, a fixed smile in place. *Like fuck we will make it long-term*, I am thinking.

'We can get out of the fish market . . .' She pauses, then adds, 'We teach them every day in the old fish market and it stinks, Beck. They even queue up to come – to spend their days in a horrible old market. If we had somewhere new, I could teach them seriously, with proper equipment, about geography, and science . . .'

I can't argue with her altruism. It comes from a good place, I tell myself with gritted teeth. She takes Layla off me and she stops crying. For a moment, the night is blissfully silent.

In the quiet, I tell myself that I'll do the night. The one night. I can handle it. I take a few breaths. Of course I can. But I can't continue after that.

'Let's get – let's get you to Kos for the premises and then see. Okay?' I say.

I'll tell her when she gets back. I'll tell her that it can't go on.

16

Martha

I don't eat lunch. Everybody else orders fry-ups, and they arrive, steaming and greasy in front of them. I wonder what Becky eats for lunch with her legal team. She always had funny taste in food; would eat beans and processed pork sausages on toast, drink Cherry Coke. She'd eat Angel Delight when hung-over. The sound of the whisk would signal it for me when we were teenagers. I hope she's eating rubbish somewhere now, that she's happy.

I can still remember the words Ami used as she told me about the premises in Kos. She wasn't passing on the information just so that I, as CEO, would know, so that I would be kept in the loop. No. She was *expectant*. 'You'll come, won't you?' she said. I recognized the tone, too: used by employees who give their all to work, who have nothing else to balance it with. 'Of course you'll come,' she was saying. There was no question. She wasn't asking one.

And how could I not go? I needed to sign the documents. It was my charity. There were hundreds of refugees who were relying on me. In that moment – on that phone call, with Becky already nannying – it seemed so obvious, so logical.

It was only when I went to say goodbye to Layla that I saw the things I had missed in making that cold, dispassionate choice: that I loved Layla more than I had ever loved anybody. That my chest ached when I was away from her. That time away from her felt suspended, unreal, and only recommenced when I held her again. And that I suspected she felt the same about me.

I couldn't go, I remember thinking, as I brought her close to me for the final time. I just wouldn't go. But the details of cancelling – the people I would let down, the flight I had booked, the premises viewing I had lined up – seemed insurmountable. And so I went. As I prepared to settle Layla in the Moses basket, she shifted her head closer to my chest and wrapped her little warm hand around mine, nuzzling into me. She didn't want to be put down. I gave her one last breastfeed, even though I was late. She sucked until her eyelids were heavy, milk drunk. I tried to unlatch her, but she wouldn't let me. Every time I did, she sucked again. Eventually, I unlatched her with my finger, breaking her seal, and she wailed.

I left with both of us crying.

My tea is delivered on an old-fashioned wooden tray that says *potatoes* on it. The teapot is transparent and has a miniature milk bottle with it. Dad taps the lid once, awkwardly, and looks at me. It's just a silly gesture.

Chin up, he is saying. Or maybe, *I'm thinking of you*. He doesn't know how to say these things.

I stare across at him and a memory forms in my mind. He'd taken us to the park. It must have been when he was looking after me and Becky. His year as a stay-at-home parent. I'd climbed to the top of the steps of a slide. He'd been holding Becky's hand; she was walking carefully across the bark chips towards us. He raised a hand to me and waved.

'Remember when you looked after Becky and me for a year?' I say to Dad.

He blinks, looks at Mum, then back at me. He doesn't like to take sides, to have difficult conversations. If he could, he would have simply watched Sky Sports all day, every day this summer and never mentioned the trial.

'Yes,' he says. 'It was tough and brilliant.' He winces.

Nobody knows what to say to me. To admit the positives of parenting, or to complain, is insensitive. Nobody can win.

I smile reassuringly at him.

Scott reaches for my hand and grasps it, under the table. 'I wish I'd done more. More,' he says to my father, his voice cracking slightly, fractures showing in his stoic demeanour. 'Like you.'

It surprises me. I should feel warm towards him, but instead I want to push him away. *How could you have left her?* I want to say. But then: I did too.

'How do you think it's going?' I ask Ethan quietly, later. I feel Mum tense next to me.

Ethan rests his elbow on the table and gestures with his fork, finishing his mouthful. And then he puts another slice of sausage in and chews that, too. 'How do *you* think?' he says back to me, when he has finished.

Will *nobody* here just say what they're actually thinking?

I think of the reflux appointment in full, now, without the distraction of the cross-examination playing out in front of me. Layla wasn't crying as badly as she often was. Isn't that always the way? And so I was over the top, with Irene – 'She's normally much worse than this!' – but Layla wasn't exactly happy, either, looking back. She was giving a low murmur, a kind of cat's growl, when Irene examined her, her feet kicking in her footed pyjamas. Images walk onto the stage in my mind, unbidden. Layla's tiny feet, soft after a bath; they would fit into the palm of my hand like lucky rabbit's feet. Those feet, those sounds: all gone. I swallow.

Ethan pours my tea for me. It's fresh, and a tea leaf makes its way into my cup, floating for a second on the top, glossy black, before being doused away by the milk he adds second.

'Badly,' I answer, eventually.

Mum takes a bite out of a toastie. Beyond her, the sea is moving steadily. The movement of it makes me feel drunk.

'It's unfair they're talking so much about Layla's crying,' she says. 'It's irrelevant.'

'God, Mum – it's obvious why,' Ethan says.

I wonder when he became so snappy. He didn't use to be like this. He broke his leg when he was fifteen, and I spent the whole summer inside with him, watching *Friends* DVDs. We are word perfect on the early seasons, can recite them at length. One recent Christmas, we moved the sofa to fit the tree in and both shouted 'Pivot!' at the same moment.

He picks up the spoon and stirs my tea for me, even though I don't take sugar, as if I were an infant who needed caring for.

'It's to make it look like Becky lost control. Because of the crying,' I say to Mum, who looks baffled. As I say it, her expression closes down.

As I stare at the sea, a memory comes back to me. Becky and I as teenagers, sneaking off one Saturday to the Brighton naturist beach. Becky was so excited, the day we decided to go, telling Mum and Dad we were going to the Lanes. Finally, we arrived, our feet sore in flip-flops in the heat. There were naked people for miles. I felt my cheeks heat up.

'I can't believe it's *pebbled*,' was all Becky said as we reached the sign and stopped, gawping.

'Why?' I said.

She arched an eyebrow and shot me a sidelong look.

'All the beaches are pebbled around here,' I reminded her.

'Martha.'

'What?'

'*Pebbles*. Hardly comfortable on a bare arse-cheek or two,' she said. 'Or, indeed, a bollock.'

'*Becky*,' I said, but her humour was infectious; always was.

'Jesus, look at them.'

'There's . . . so many of them,' I said faintly.

'I have never seen quite so many dicks in my whole life,' she said. With that, she took off her top and skirt and ran into the sea. Just like that, right in her underwear, just a teenager herself. She never thought. She was so impulsive. I'd been both in awe and frightened of her. She didn't care. She just didn't care. It was that self-destructive streak again. Only *the moment* seemed to matter to her. Not afterwards, when her clothes clung to her wet skin, when she was shivering on the way home. Everybody had seen her body: her teenaged body.

Later, when we got back, we didn't tell anybody where we'd been, not even Ethan, who was sort of our ally. Becky had wet hair, but nobody seemed to notice.

I blink, now, looking at Ethan, who's gazing intently at me.

I know he's going to ask it before he does. I can see it in the way he moves the wooden tray.

'Do you think they're going to vote guilty?' he says. The words fire into me like bullets. How could he ask so casually?

'I don't know,' I say tightly. 'Ask them.'

It's what I tell myself every day. Trust the justice system, and we will know for sure next week, after it has performed its excavation, its deep, focused mining of that night in October last year.

'I think the prosecution case is strong,' he says. His tone is resigned. 'I'm worried it looks convincing.'

'I don't want to talk about this . . .'

'Let's not,' Mum says.

'She is *adamant*,' Ethan says. After he has said it, he stares at me again. He's got Becky's jawline. It looks clenched, sometimes, even when it isn't. He has said it before. I thought he would be cynical, but he isn't. He is almost as staunch as Marc about her innocence. 'I've never seen her so adamant,' he says now, again.

'The evidence is quite clear,' Scott suddenly says tightly.

'Oh, is it? Let's just do away with trials then,' Ethan says. 'Lock her up and throw away the key.'

'That's not what . . .'

Mum is staring down at the table. Her shoulders are tensed. They start to shake. It is almost imperceptible, but I see it. She is suppressing tears.

'This is why I don't want to discuss it,' I say. 'This always happens.' And it has: over and over and over again last winter, we picked it apart and it always blew up.

Ethan protesting her innocence.

Scott arguing for her guilt.

And me, Mum and Dad, not knowing, just not knowing, our shoulders shaking.

'This always happens,' I add.

'Forget it,' Ethan says bitterly.

We cannot possibly make up our minds. Becky swears she didn't do it, but all of the evidence points to her. We are in limbo. My parents live with her. They still – presumably – eat meals together and take walks and talk about the weather. Their judgement is suspended, too; has been for almost a year now.

'I don't know,' I say, my voice rising several octaves. '*I don't know.*'

Ethan is silent for a few seconds. Behind him is an entire wall of clocks. They tick out of sync with each other.

'Nobody knows,' I say. 'Clearly. How many professionals are involved in finding out?'

'Loads,' Ethan says quietly, his mouth drawn tight. He pushes his plate of unfinished food away.

I suddenly feel deflated, guilty. He struggled to get this week off. Emails answered, calls returned quietly in side rooms. He doesn't need to be here with me, watching a trial, eating awkward lunches, but he is.

'*She* knows,' I say. 'But that's it.' I shrug.

'I feel like I know,' he says. 'I know Becky.'

Mum darts a look at me, and I see her eyes are wet. How must this be for her? Her two daughters: at war. Unwillingly.

'*You* know Becky,' Ethan says.

Mum flags a waitress down and mimes for the bill.

'I didn't know either of them,' I say, the punchline open to me like a swinging door.

But the words I say aren't true. I thought I might not know Layla, when I sat looking at her for the first time in the hospital, feeling unable to understand how I was now somebody's mum, that my daughter was there in front of me. But I did. I knew what her cries meant and when her tiny hands were about to tighten around my fingers. It was as if somebody blurred the edges, just slightly, so that she and I continued to overlap.

And I knew Becky. I knew before she told me that she was separating from Marc. I knew from the way she held her shoulders when she was desperate to interject with an anecdote of her own, at parties, and I knew when it would be to tell the story of the time I was so nervous about my SATs results that I wet myself.

But did I know my sister and my daughter now? Did I know them *together*? No. I was too busy being busy; being absent.

'I really don't know,' I say, my eyes feeling watery. 'Do you?'

'I know when she's lying, and I don't think she is,' he says.

I tilt my head, looking at him. He never understood Becky like I did, at least, I didn't think so. He was sometimes dismissive of her, in adulthood, referring to her *whims* and, occasionally, unfairly, her status as a single parent. His life was so orderly. The big legal job. His wife. Children in their near future, I thought. But he didn't engage, would avoid even the most banal questions – 'How are you?' I would ask, and he'd wave a hand and say, 'Same old.' He could have no idea whether Becky had done it, because he didn't know what Becky was about. Not like I did.

I can picture her innocence completely. Becky, frantically calling 999. Becky who was hugely unlucky — wasn't she always so unlucky? — all the evidence pointing to the aunt in the post-mortem results. Becky facing trial alone, without the full support of her cold sister, Martha, who merely watched from the public gallery, undecided.

But I can see her guilt, too. That temper. That *attitude* she sometimes seemed to have. The self-destruct button. Consequences be damned.

But what if there's something else? Something beyond the *unknown asphyxiation accident* the defence alleges? What if it was an accident that she's covered up, in that hasty, messy way of hers? What if she's got in too deep?

There was an entire evening on the night of October 26th. An entire evening during which anything could have happened. What if somebody else was there that evening? What if it had been them?

17

Martha

My eyes don't adjust readily to the dark of the courtroom foyer – it is that blueish darkness that follows sunshine – and I can hardly see as I am scanned and frisked and my handbag is opened for the fourth time in two days.

And then, as I take a blinded step forwards, there is Becky. So real and so tall and so near to me that I can smell her perfume.

I can feel Ethan next to me. Becky is in front of us. And here we are. The three of us. Two sisters and a brother, just as we have been for decades before this. Becky has Ethan's green eyes. Becky and I have the same nose. We all have the same faces that look serious at rest.

I brush past her, not acknowledging her.

I can't.

In the courtroom, the jury files back in, and Ellen stands up for the prosecution.

'An agreed statement will now be read out,' she says slightly pompously.

An agreed statement? I look sideways at Scott. He shrugs. Just beyond him, I see Ethan's brow has lowered. He is scribbling on a blue legal pad which he passes to me. *Has Becky got a conviction??* he has written.

I almost scoff, silently, here in the public gallery.

No, I write back.

Ellen stands up and begins to read.

'It is agreed that on the twenty-eighth day of April 2015 the defendant Rebecca Blackwater was convicted at Brighton Magistrates' Court of using threatening, abusive or insulting words or behaviour, contrary to section 4A of the Public Order Act 1986 and fined the sum of three hundred and fifty pounds.'

The judge clears his throat and begins to speak.

'The defendant's previous conviction is something that you may take into account and weigh in the balance. But you must not convict her on the evidence of that alone or mainly on that evidence. If you give it any weight, how much weight you give to it is a matter for you. The Crown says that it supports their case because it demonstrates that the defendant has a propensity to lose control and commit acts of violence. The defence, on the other hand, submits that you should not give it any weight because it is a crime unrelated to the offence of which the defendant is accused. You can take it into account only if you consider it to be fair to do so.'

I am staring hard at Ethan. He looks over at me and shrugs.

What does it mean? I write on the back of a receipt to him.

Ethan writes back to me. He passes the note to Scott, who holds it out for me between his index and third fingers.

It's road rage, he has written.

He gestures for the note back, a flick of his fingers. It returns with more writing on it.

It's damaging because it raises the question: what might Becky be capable of?

The parties say no more about the road rage. It is introduced, and left hanging, for the jury to decide upon. A secret from Becky's past, unearthed, and shown to us, and then put away again.

Road rage. I had no idea. When did she . . . what possessed her to . . . had she attended a hearing, and told none of us? How could she? I try to remember April 2015, but I can't. I can't find the day. It must have just been a normal day, for me.

Road rage. Shouting at somebody in the street. My body chills with the shock of it. Jesus, what else was she capable of?

Most of the time, with Becky, I can relate. Sure, she is impulsive. Sometimes she is temperamental, dramatic. But then sometimes, other times, she does things like this. Running into the sea with no regard for who was looking. Riding her bicycle into a car. Raging at another driver so seriously that she got convicted. Who is she?

No, I tell myself. She's Becky. This is just the justice system, shining a light on the worst parts of her personality. I never doubted her before all of this. I never thought she was capable of anything truly bad. I was never frightened of her. Never.

'The prosecution calls Jasbinder Kaur to the stand,' Ellen says. 'Jasbinder is the defendant's neighbour, and overheard a phone call on the night in question.'

A woman with long, shiny hair is let in by the usher and sits down at the stand. Her large eyes dart around the courtroom, from the crest behind the judge to the jury to Becky in the dock.

I stare at her. Yes. That's who it is. It's Becky's neighbour, at the back. She's a particular sort of young woman – fastidious about order and bin night – but that's all I know of her.

'And what happened on the night of the twenty-sixth of October?'

'I overheard a phone call.'

'Made by whom?'

'The defendant.'

Goosebumps appears on my arms. *The night of.*

Until now, the witnesses have all been peripheral, like planets orbiting the sun; relevant but far removed from the event. These next witnesses: they were all there on that night.

The neighbours.

The paramedic.

The doctors who couldn't help her in time.

The police.

The case is closing, rushing towards its devastating conclusion, and I can't stand it.

18

Jasbinder Kaur

7.30 p.m., Thursday 26 October

Eventually, the weeds got the better of her, as they always did. She couldn't resist cleaning and tidying, these days. Since the miscarriage, anyway. The mess of it.

Kev said it was getting worse, the cleaning, but she thought the house looked brilliant. Sometimes, she would sprint up the stairs, trying not to look at the carpet in case she saw crumbs, and not bother to brush her teeth in case she spotted the beginnings of black mould again in the bathroom.

The security light clicked on, as she knelt down on the ground, legs tucked underneath her. The night was silent. That's what she liked about Hove. Six houses overlooked her garden, but there wasn't a sound from any of them. All she could hear was the spraying of the weed killer and the sloshing of the liquid. Spray, slosh. It was just like vacuuming or ironing: strangely satisfying. She squirted again, thinking of the weeds withering overnight.

A patio door slid back, in the garden in front of her.

'Yeah, she just won't stop,' a voice said.

Becky, she thought it was. It was coming from the right

direction. She carefully set the spray bottle on the ground, then sat back slightly, listening. It was nice to forget the cleaning for a moment. She closed her eyes. It was okay if she didn't do it. She didn't *have* to do it. If only that was true. How sweet life would be if it were.

'*No*,' Becky's voice said, surprisingly loud in the clear night. 'She's not hungry. Definitely not.'

Jasbinder reached a hand out and twirled the stem of a dandelion between her fingers. It was rough, like fine Velcro, sticking against the broken skin on her hands. She had always liked Becky. She was very *real*. Jasbinder often went to confide in people – to tell them about the miscarriage, to tell them about the cleaning – but always stopped herself. But Becky knew. She had told Jasbinder about her inability to conceive. They'd talked about how hard it was, together.

'Inside,' Becky said. 'I'm in the garden. Having a break.'

Jasbinder strained to hear. Yes, she could hear a baby's cry, coming from inside. Who was that? Becky didn't have a baby. She must be babysitting. Jasbinder felt her innards twist. The snug, warm weight of a baby. The tiny fat hands, gripping her thumb. Maybe she could go and visit. Pop over. Just to – to hold it, to smell it.

'No. God, no need for that,' Becky said.

Jasbinder could hear Becky's feet on the pavement as she paced. Was somebody offering to come over? Jasbinder thought that would be best: babies were hard work on your own.

She held a tall weed in one hand as she squirted it with the other. As she looked at it, she thought perhaps it was actually quite beautiful: thick, ragged leaves, rough like goose-fleshed skin. Little purple flowers in the centre. It suddenly pained to her do it, but she squirted it anyway: weed, be gone.

'Don't,' Becky said. 'But will you be there? I don't know. Just be on the end of a phone.' There was a long pause. 'No. I know. Don't be silly. Of course I won't.'

Becky hung up shortly after that, and Jasbinder heard the patio door slide slowly shut behind her.

19

Martha

No need for that. That's what Jasbinder said Becky had said. No need for what? To come over? I sit back in the public gallery, my thoughts racing. What if he had come over? What if she had lied?

'It's not very easy to piece together half a conversation, is it?' Harriet, Becky's lawyer, says, as she rises to her feet. Her eyes are narrowed, looking carefully at Jasbinder. 'I am surprised you can recollect it at all.' Here she is: the defence lawyer, on the full defensive. She is small and slight compared to the hulking Ellen, but her voice rings out loud and true in the courtroom. 'How clearly do you remember it?'

'Very.'

'How do you recall so clearly what was said, when you only heard half of it?'

'I could hear it very clearly. And then the next day I learnt that the baby had died, which made me reflect on it.'

'Thank you,' Harriet says, holding up a hand. 'But what I am wondering is . . . did this conversation sound out of the ordinary *at the time*? And not in retrospect?'

Jasbinder hesitates. 'No. Not really,' she says eventually. 'No.'

'Were you worried that night, at all, for Layla's welfare? Given what you'd overheard?'

'No. Not at all.'

'So it was a pretty normal, non-alarming conversation?'

'Yes.'

'Thank you. Nothing further,' Harriet says.

Becky's eyes are narrowed, in the dock. After this, if she's . . . if she's free. Will she move back in? Nod hello to these neighbours? Surely not. How could she? What is the way forward, from all of this?

'The prosecution calls Devorah Friedmann to the stand.'

I watch as a wiry, tiny woman with dark hair wound into a bun strides quickly over to the witness stand.

'Mrs Friedmann,' Ellen says.

'Yes.'

'What do you remember about the twenty-sixth of October?'

20

Devorah Friedmann

Devorah opened Candy Crush on her phone. She was on level 980.

Her grandson, Ezra, was at her feet, playing with an old Lottery ticket.

The bell above the door rang, and Devorah raised her head. Ezra looked up, too. He looked just like her husband, David.

A tall woman walked in. Devorah ignored her, but got up off her old stool and turned Candy Crush off. The tinny background music cut out, leaving the shop in silence.

'Sorry,' the woman in front of her said after a few minutes. 'Just these.'

Devorah glanced down at them. Two bottles of Calpol Infant Sugar Free.

'Six pounds, please,' she said. She was glad the baby years were behind her. Lordy. She could drop Ezra back at her daughter's, go home and actually *relax*.

'Thanks,' Devorah said as the woman handed over the

exact money. At least she didn't have to bother with change.

'Baby won't sleep,' the woman said with a rueful smile. She picked up both bottles in one hand and left.

21

Martha

'Two bottles?' Ellen says, repeating what she has just been told. Her upper-class rasp rings out in the courtroom. I close my eyes against it.

'Yes, two,' Devorah says.

'And she said the baby couldn't sleep.'

'Wouldn't, I think,' Devorah says, looking thoughtful.

'And tell me – was the defendant alone?'

'Yes.'

'Members of the jury, please note. The defendant was in sole charge of baby Layla at this moment.'

The jury nod, saying nothing. *She left Layla alone.* It thrums through me.

'What time was it?'

'Seven forty-five.'

'Nothing further,' Ellen says. She pats the front of her robes and sits down heavily on the chair.

'Devorah, if I may,' Harriet says.

'Yes.'

Devorah looks nervous; small and slight in the witness stand. Her slender arms are drawn across her.

'Were the bottles of Calpol on any sort of offer?'

'Two for six pounds.'

'Nothing further.'

I can't believe she left my baby alone.

My throat feels tight with it.

I start to count the faces in the room to distract myself. There are only women in this case. Me. My sister. My daughter. Two female barristers. The almost all-female jury. The witnesses. All women, so far. Mothers, daughters, friends. This tiny world seems to revolve around us. It discards the men. They are not expected to look after their children, and they are not blamed when they don't.

The barristers want to discuss something and the jury dutifully file out. The public gallery is permitted to stay, but we don't. The legal arguments are lost on me. Scott suggests a coffee, and I follow him.

We all come out of different doors – Becky, her lawyers, and the public gallery – but we all end up in the same place, like water being drained from a colander and into a sink. I stop, momentarily, not knowing where to go. Becky is just a few feet to the right of me. I can tell in the same way I can tell her mood from her stance – tense, today – and where she's about to go – to the toilets. Our bodies have been so close to each other for so many years that they know each other, like two tennis players whose limbs can predict their opponent's actions. She serves; I return it effortlessly.

Except I don't see the backhand coming: Mum crosses over to her and follows her in. 'How is it?' I hear her say before the dark wood door swings shut behind them.

She left Layla *alone*.

What if she has done it? What am I doing here? Panic

rises up through me. I'm here, ostensibly supporting her, and she might have done the worst thing in the world to me.

I try to calm myself down, snap out of it, but these days I know it'll pass. In a few hours I will be back to feeling irrationally supportive of her. It is the way of it.

I sit on a bench, ignoring Dad and Ethan and Scott hovering nearby.

Ethan goes outside for a cigarette and I sit on a hard metal bench and watch him through the tinted glass windows. It's warmer, today, the sky a heavy white above us, like being trapped inside a dome. He has started smoking roll-ups, again, after five years off them, held between his index finger and thumb, and the gesture doesn't suit him. It's like seeing someone from work in their pyjamas, or a celebrity on the Tube. Becky always said Ethan hated everything about smoking except how it looked, but I don't think that. There is pleasure in the way he closes his eyes when he inhales. *Good for him*, I think: life is too short anyway.

Scott comes up behind me and catches my hand. His glasses mirror the fluorescent courtroom lights above us.

'Think they will let us go?' he says.

'Early finish,' I try to smile.

He sits down next to me and I run my fingers down his arm. I read somewhere that every single skin cell renews itself after seven years, and so the arm I am touching is not the same one I was touching seven years ago. It feels just the same, to me.

'Do you think it will be better, when we know?' I say.

'Maybe,' he says, but a faint frown crosses his features.

'I think so,' I say.

The frown deepens. 'Marth.'

'Hm?'

'I think you need to prepare yourself, for the verdict . . .'

He has often tried to protect me in this way. Straight talking. I have always liked it. I never wanted to be babied. He seems to read my mind, as he has always been able to, because he pulls me close to him, just like he does in bed, at night. Our sides are touching each other, right down the length of our bodies.

'Why?' I say softly.

'Because I think it's going to be guilty.' He rests his head against mine gently. 'I'm sorry.'

'No,' I say faintly. 'She died of . . . she died of lack of oxygen. It doesn't mean somebody did it. It doesn't even mean it's suspicious. It could have been an accident. The police thought it was, for ages, remember? And the doctors.'

'Marth . . .'

'She could have rolled over or leaned against a blanket and wasn't able to . . . to pick up her head. Or it could have been a co-sleeping accident. We haven't had the medical evidence yet. We don't know for sure it was . . . it was definitely suspicious.'

'But Becky would admit that, wouldn't she? If she said she'd co-slept with Layla, or she'd found Layla tangled up or something, then she wouldn't have been tried.'

'I don't know,' I say. I close my eyes and pray for it to have been an accident. I've lost my daughter. I don't want to lose my sister, too. 'They might say it's—'

'What?' His tone is soft. He is not being harsh. Or, at least, he does not mean to be.

'They might say that they don't know,' I say desperately.

'Science is science. That's what they'll say. Somebody did it.'

The words thrum through me.

Somebody did it. Just as I had thought earlier on. What if *somebody* had been there that night? And not Becky?

Something fires up in my mind. *Becky left Layla alone.* What if something had happened while Becky was at Londis at 7.45 p.m.? The times check out. Layla died between eight and nine thirty. It could have been somebody else.

'Somebody killed her,' Scott says softly, unaware of my mind racing. 'We know that. Even if the verdict is not guilty, we still know that. Babies don't die from asphyxiation for no reason, Marth.'

I can't handle that. Not guilty, but no explanation either. *No.* I will trust in the system. Somehow, somehow, we are going to find out what happened.

'I was away. From her. I was away,' I say, the saliva clogging my throat like a viscous syrup.

'So was I.' His voice is anguished, too. 'It was me who should have been there. Not you.'

'We both should have been there,' I say tightly.

'But you only went because you knew it was only one night – that I'd be back for the second night. And I wasn't. I just didn't come back to her.'

'It's different for you,' I say, wondering if I truly believe that. If I am simply caught up with the narrative surrounding the case. I draw a deep breath. No. I'm not. 'I was her *mother*,' I say to him. And that is what I believe. My role in our family was senior to his. However unfair that is. However sexist.

'That's bullshit,' he says. 'It was both of us. It was *me*.'

And now I see his anger for what it is. He wants to feel

like he is fighting back. Ethan is smoking. Mum is with Becky, in private, mothering her. And Scott is getting angry.

And here we are: the culpable parents. The parents who were not there. We're not in the dock, but we should be.

Marc hasn't been allowed in the public gallery, because he will be a defence witness, later in the week, and he has Xander, so I am surprised to see him walk into the foyer. The day outside, through the windows, has a faintly autumnal feel, as though the light outside has been heavily filtered through a grey curtain.

Becky emerges from her meeting room, flanked, as ever, by her legal team: she is expecting Marc. She crosses the foyer to him, reaches for his arm, her fingertips just touching it. It's impossible to read the expression on her face. He nods at her, smiling shyly, and follows her across the foyer to the room.

The things that must go on behind those doors. I watch them, still walking closely together like a couple, arms almost brushing, and I cannot help but remember the reason for their separation. What she did to Marc. It is not evidence; it is not admissible, but it is the truth. I put it out of my mind. I can't think about that now. Besides, I am sure the court will come to it. They ransack your personal life, your history, your mistakes, when you are accused of a crime. They will come to it.

'He did these courses on the internet,' she told me, two Christmases ago, twenty-five days after they had broken up. 'FutureLearn, they were called, and they were the end of us.'

I'd been contemplating getting pregnant for some time.

Sort of. In my own way, taking literal years to reach a decision: the Martha way of life. Some decisions were merely made for me, in the end.

Marc had moved out on the first of December. Becky had joked she was having a bottle of wine for every day of Advent, but her voice sounded strangled as she said it.

'Why?' I said. We were in Mum and Dad's living room. Christmas-stocking bunting was strung across the fireplace and *Elf* was playing in the background. My socked feet were flung over the arm of the sofa, mulled wine in my hand. Would I give up the wine for nine months, and the peace for ever? I wasn't sure. I rested my hand on my stomach and tried to imagine it full and pregnant, little realizing that the beginnings of my baby were already curled up inside me.

Becky shrugged. 'I think by the time you've done twenty FutureLearn courses your marriage might be over.'

She was sitting cross-legged on the floor, in front of the television, with her back to it. She often sat in that spot, like a cat; she said the pipes crossed and there was a warm patch. She was always so cold. She was picking at the skin around her fingernails.

'Forensic profiling. Beginners' Mandarin. Hedge funds. You know?'

'Right. That's . . . not like him,' I had said. Marc had always seemed to me to like simple things. He would always eat the same packet of cheese and onion crisps during half-time in the football. Every single Saturday, match day, he would check in, on Facebook, writing: *Fingers crossed!*

'No. He got kind of obsessed,' Becky said.

'I see.'

'By the time – I don't know. By the time I emerged from the early years of motherhood it was too late.' She shrugged.

It seemed a strange gesture, twenty-five days after her marriage had ended, but she was like this. Prickly, sometimes.

'It's hard. Having a baby, I guess. Wasn't Marc . . . wasn't he good, though?'

Becky gaze locked on to mine. 'They can only do so much,' she said. 'It's the women who suffer. It's always the women.'

'Is it?' I said.

'Of course it is. We try to reach equality, but we never fucking will. Breastfeeding. Labour. It's all us.'

'You were a kid yourself, anyway,' I said, trying to talk her down. 'Besides all of that.'

'Yep. We limped on for seven years. Almost eight. But think about that. It wasn't that we were too young or whatever. We didn't stop having sex – we were always so good at sex.' She gave a little laugh, a sort of puff of air out of the side of her mouth; a half-smile. 'It was just the good old-fashioned daily slog of parenting that did it. Isn't that fucked up?' She stopped picking at her fingernails and raised her head to look at me.

'Not really,' I said. 'You're pretty textbook.'

'Cheers to that,' Becky said. Even there, on the floor at Mum's, a single mother in a Christmas jumper, she looked cool. She looked directly at me. 'So I slept with someone else,' she said. 'That was the real nail in the coffin. After the FutureLearn, obviously.'

Becky. A dishonest cheat. I never thought she would be unfaithful. Could she surprise me in other ways, too? How dark did her personality go?

'I . . . oh,' I said. 'God . . . when?'

'Five weeks ago. I told him – Marc. I couldn't live with myself.'

'Where was it?' I said.

'Where?' she said, looking at me with a sudden look of distaste. 'At his.'

I blinked, imagining affairs to be seedy things, taking place in alleyways and across office desks.

'So you went to his.'

She waved her hand again, then went back to chewing her nails. 'It wasn't what it sounds like,' she said. 'Not like that.'

'How was it, then?'

'If you must know, we were shit at getting pregnant and even shitter at being married,' she snapped.

She didn't say any more than that. I wish she had. But she had all these barriers up all the time. Humour was one. Barbed comments were another. Underneath that – occasionally glimpsed – was soft, yielding Becky. But she was hard to find.

I sigh now as I think back to their marriage. How she and Marc used to be. Their obvious sex life. 'I'm going to bed, and you're coming with me,' Becky had said, tugging on Marc's hand, only two summers back. Their desire to spend all their time together; Becky following him to his carpet-fitting appointments, sitting on kitchen counters and in the next room, just talking to him. So different from me and Scott.

The most Scott has ever done is bring me fruit and vegetables from his patch of land. A bunch of fresh broccoli. A punnet of strawberries, grown by him. He means well. It's just . . . practical. That's all. Love, for Scott, is cooking a meal, changing a light bulb, buying me a book I've expressed an interest in. He makes my life run seamlessly, and I loved that once. So capable and calm. He made me ham sandwiches every morning after his paternity leave, cutting them into bite-sized pieces so I could eat them one-handed. He didn't leave a flamboyant, loving note, as Marc might. But there was love there. There was love for me. I try to remind myself of it now.

He is at his grandfather's land so much, lately. Too much. Three hours one night recently, until long after dark. He's bringing home no produce. I don't know what he's doing.

I snap back to reality, and return to the memory of Becky in our parents' living room. My mind was reeling from the shock of her confession.

'Who was it, anyway?' I asked.

She would answer me on this. Becky dealt in facts just fine. It was feelings she didn't like.

'Bloke from television. Absolute wanker, as you can imagine,' she said.

'After work?'

'Early Christmas party, yeah. November party. Went back to his.' So she was on self-destruct.

'Oh, Becky,' I said.

She just shrugged again, her eyes misty.

But, since then, she and Marc have never instructed solicitors to divorce them, and they have never quite moved into hostility, either. He sits too close to her at the family barbecues he still attends, laughs too loudly at her sardonic jokes.

Now, in the court foyer, Marc holds the door to the meeting room for Becky, and she throws him a look.

It's a look I've seen them exchange before; one they've never stopped sharing. A kind of mutual understanding. Their eyes scrunch up at the corners. Each of them, perhaps, is in sharp focus to the other, the backgrounds blurred around them.

I wonder how Marc's coping with Xander.

I wonder how Becky's coping without Xander.

I want to keep looking at them, as they gaze at each other, walking into the meeting room together, oblivious to me, but they close the door behind them.

It's another neighbour's turn next. Theresa, my sister's neighbour since for ever, is about to take the stand. I have known her – in a sort of once-removed way – for years. She's probably more similar to me than to Becky. She has a serious, quiet way of talking. She goes for a run twice a day, extremely early in the morning and late at night. So late that, even in the summer, while Becky and I have been scoffing takeaways, I have seen the street lights catching her reflective running gear. Illuminated and then in darkness. Illuminated and then in darkness.

She and her husband have no children, but they have three dogs. A huge one, a medium-sized one and a little one. Becky and I called them the Three Bears.

I've only ever observed her from a distance. From afar, she is statuesque, looks like an athlete, pounding the streets. Up close, she looks different. Doesn't everybody? Don't we? And now, here she is, a witness.

She has been observing us, too. And she is about to tell us what she has seen.

22

Theresa Williams

9.10 p.m., Thursday 26 October

Ian was away, in Bratislava, at some stag do. No, go, *go*, she had said, smiling broadly. Let him see the strippers. Let him drink himself unconscious. If you tried to control them, they played away. Hadn't she learnt that lesson once?

She faced the fridge, the chilled air bringing goosebumps out across her arms and legs – she was in a vest top and pants, the heating turned up as high as could be – and scooped a dollop of Marmite with her breadstick. It was disgustingly rich, the Marmite tarry in her mouth. She almost felt self-conscious, as if, even though she was alone, people might be able to look in on this private moment of hers.

She vowed to make this her last breadstick, putting the Marmite back in the cupboard. She drank a glass of water poured from the jug she kept in the fridge.

She checked her phone, standing in the living room, her bare feet on the old tiles she had restored last summer.

Ian hadn't texted her. She checked WhatsApp and scrolled to his name. *Last seen: 21.05.* Five minutes ago. He could have texted. Perhaps he was . . . no. She wouldn't go there again. This wasn't then. This was now. That's what the counsellor said they had to say to themselves. He was sorry, after all. If they wanted to move on, they had to actually *move on*. Ian had seemed especially keen on that approach, in the counselling. Somehow, it had become her fault.

No. She was just in a bad mood tonight. Too much time alone, too many carbs. She would sleep it off.

She went to lock up. She didn't like locking up when Ian was away. Their old Victorian house seemed to loom larger, somehow. She would never admit it, but she always expected to see a face, peering in through the dark glass, as she reached to turn the key.

She took a peek. No face. She was alone.

As she turned the keys in the door, she heard it. A strangled shout. 'Shut up! Just shut up!' she thought she heard.

Really? she asked herself. Surely not.

Her stomach clenched anyway; the anxiety of being alone. It was Becky, she thought. It seemed to come from the left. Becky was by far her loudest neighbour – since she had complained about the reggae-playing neighbours, anyway. Becky played rap music at weird times; she seemed to work from home. Theresa heard occasional hoots of laughter when her ex-husband, Marc, came over. That was so weird.

They were so friendly, still. She didn't understand it. Sometimes, she thought her fantasy man might be based on Marc. That openness, the way he looked at Becky, the way they laughed ... Theresa hadn't complained yet, about the noise they made, though she might soon.

Maybe he was over there now. She cocked an ear. Maybe they were arguing.

Even if Becky was shouting at something else, would she shout like *that* if she was totally alone? Theresa thought not. Those sorts of outbursts were for one thing only: sympathy. She listened again.

Was that . . . she could hear something. A faint murmur. She stayed completely still. No. She must have imagined it.

She stepped away from the door, but the keys were still swinging, and she held them so they were silenced.

The noise came again. 'Oh honestly, if you don't shut the fuck up, I'll—'

That was definitely Becky. But that was where it ended. The shouting. The threat hung in the air. Who was it aimed at?

She didn't hear anything else after that. Only the sound of wind in the trees, a hooting wood pigeon outside, her own breathing.

She didn't think about that uttered shout for days afterwards. Until the police came. And then she remembered it and – oh God. The significance of it. It made goosebumps appear all over her arms and legs, just like when she had been standing in front of her fridge. When that little baby had still been alive, and she could have still stopped it, if she had known.

23

Martha

I am making a scene in the public gallery, but I can't help it. I knew it would be hard to hear Theresa's testimony, but I didn't anticipate this. This huge bolus in the back of my throat, this heaving feeling. My baby daughter's last moments. Being shouted at. And the phrasing, the swearing: it is undoubtedly *Becky*, whatever happened afterwards. My hands shake as I reach to wipe the tears away.

'So that was the night of baby Layla's death, but you had another encounter with the defendant and baby, did you not?' Ellen says. 'The previous day?'

'Yes, I did. I don't know the exact time.'

'And what happened then?'

'Becky was just getting out of the car, on her drive. Layla was in the car seat. Becky explained their arrangement to me. Layla was crying.'

'How much?'

'A lot. Enough for me to ask if she had been fed.'

My cheeks heat up. *Had she been fed?* I can't even contemplate that. Of course Becky had fed her. My fingernails dig into my palms. She would have. She just would have. Please let her have been feeding Layla properly.

'And what did the defendant say?'

'Oh, she just huffed. She was a bit defensive, you know.'

'But you were concerned enough to ask if the baby had been fed.'

'Yes.'

'And then on this night, when you heard shouts . . .'

'Yes.'

'The defendant sounded . . . frustrated?'

'Yes.'

'Did you consider going over?'

'Well, I didn't know. I . . . didn't think. And, anyway, you can't, can you?'

Ellen shrugs, looking regretful. She adjusts her robes. 'I don't know, Ms Williams. But that'll be all from me.' She sits down

Harriet rises. 'Do you have other neighbours, Theresa?' Her angle is clear, and she is homing in on it like a bird of prey.

'Yes.'

'On the other side?'

'Yes. It's a row of terraces.'

'How many in the row?'

Theresa looks up, thinking. 'Six?'

'So your house is flanked on either side. And then . . .' Harriet pulls out a photograph of the rows of houses.

Our lives have become merely legal evidence. My sister's house, *exhibited*. Her neighbours, *witnesses*.

'. . . turn to page four of your binder, please, jury. Your house,' she says to Theresa, 'has three on one side, two on the other.'

'Yes.'

'So are you telling me that, standing *inside*, and equidistant from each of your neighbours' living rooms, you are one hundred per cent sure that the voice you heard was the defendant's? Despite these *five* other houses?'

'Yes.'

'Even though there is both a house on your left and your right. At equal distance?'

'Yes.'

'One hundred per cent.'

'Well, I can't be one hundred per cent because I didn't see her, but—'

'Yes,' Harriet says, cutting her off. 'So, it might easily have been other neighbours. Somebody outside. It's a city. People must walk by all the time – do they?'

Theresa says nothing, looking confused. 'Do people walk by all the time?' Harriet says again.

'Often, yes. They do.'

'Is it fair to say that you know the defendant better than your other neighbours?'

'Oh, yes,' Theresa says. 'A lot better. I would know her—'

Theresa walks right into the trap.

Harriet opens her mouth to speak. 'And so you're more likely, aren't you, to assume that the voice you're hearing is that of the person you know best? When really it could have been anybody . . . a stranger. Another neighbour. A neighbour's friend?'

'Maybe,' Theresa says, battered on the witness stand.

How clever they are, I find myself thinking, *these lawyers*. How they can take something that is virtually certain, and turn it inside out, so it becomes unformed and unsure of itself. Turning a truth into a mess; into lies and false-hoods and incorrect memories. A beam of pure white light, refracted into a complicated rainbow.

159

I am certain Theresa did hear Becky, painful as it is for me to admit it. They are her speech patterns, peppered with her swear words. She sounds just like that when she is . . . when she is angry.

'Did the anonymous shout sound – how did it sound to you?'

'Angry.'

'In its words or its tone?'

Theresa looks up at the lights, which makes me look, too; strip lights, garish ones. She takes a while before answering. 'Both,' she says.

'So then,' Harriet says, 'I'm afraid I have to ask . . . you knew the defendant had a babysitting arrangement with the mother of Layla?'

'Yes.'

'And you were struck by the menace in her voice – if, indeed, it was even her – which was, conceivably, directed at the baby.'

'Yes.'

'And yet, what did you do? You did nothing.'

'No,' Theresa says softly.

'So I'm inclined to wonder, Ms Williams, whether you really were as worried as you say. Perhaps, really, you thought this was quite usual. A woman, frustrated at bedtime by her child. We have all been there, have we not? Perhaps, now, with hindsight, you remember it differently. Incorrectly.'

I study Theresa. She isn't looking at Harriet. Instead, she is looking down at her hands, which rest on the wood of the witness stand.

'Maybe,' Theresa says. 'Yes.'

I look down at my hands, folded neatly in my lap. Half-moon-shaped dents are at the centre of my palms. Shouting at bedtime. I have been there. I certainly have. I can't bring myself to look up at Becky, or across at Scott. They have both seen the worst of me. I know Becky will be looking at me, wondering if I have done as she did. Of course I've felt angry. Of course I've shouted.

What I once said to Scott keeps returning to my mind. It was two and a half weeks after Layla was born.

Labour had been . . . God. Like something else entirely. Almost medieval. I remember every moment of it. There is actually a place where you can go where pain is *unbelievable*. And everybody is casual about it, and will leave you in that state for hours, will tell you to pull yourself together and push, after thirty hours of it. There are laws about hurting people's feelings in the workplace, but there are no laws about this, this brute force, forceps, a cold hand, reaching unexpectedly and urgently right up inside me.

After nineteen hours of contractions, I was one centimetre dilated. I went in, but they sent me away again. At home, I could only sit in one position: on the floor, with my left leg cocked on the bed. After labour I had hip pain for almost as long as the bleeding lasted.

The contractions came and then they went but they would surely come again, and perhaps they would never end, I thought, as I stared at the wall. The problem was I had been ambivalent. So on the fence that I could have teetered either way. My only evidence for going forth and procreating had been that most people seemed to rather enjoy it – in a kind of grim *in the trenches* way, admittedly – and that most people had more than one child. Never mind that I lacked the urge and the hormones and, seemingly, the inner grit. Never mind all that.

After thirty hours, she was born, by forceps, and at that moment, with the metal inside me, I no longer cared. *Cut me open*, I thought. *Kill me.*

They handed her to me, but I don't remember it. After an hour, a nurse took me to the toilet to wee and brush my teeth. She combed my hair for me. While I was in there, they got a cleaner to come in and mop the floor. They mopped the blood away, the water turning burgundy in the bucket that I saw as I emerged from the toilet.

Ten o'clock at night came, and Scott had to leave. ('Visiting hours are over,' a bewildered-looking nurse said to me.) And there I was, alone in the hospital bed, with my daughter – my daughter! – to my right. And the decision – that tiny decision, it seemed to me – to ditch the pill and to tip ever so slowly on to the other side of the fence and drift slowly downwards loomed so large it almost seemed to sit inside the room with me.

It got easier, of course. The disorientation faded. Once I got home and I'd had a bath and a cup of coffee, it was alright. But what helped bring me back from the medieval world, as I called it, was seeing Becky, who said, 'I didn't want to have to tell you about the labour bit – but Jesus!' Classic Becky. 'You're doing alright, though, here?' she said, as though she knew. *Here.* The new world I inhabited. It was different. I was for ever changed. And I was glad she was there with me. Here.

And then the love came. Like my milk, it took a few days, but it arrived, as though somebody had taken my soul and replaced it with something much bigger, much more inclusive.

Scott had taken two weeks off work, and we spent them sequestered away together. Days blended into nights. He made sure he was awake every minute that I was. I protested, but I loved the company. Somebody to hand Layla to while I made toast for the two of us. Somebody who *got it*, whose bones ached, too, with tiredness. After a week or so, we were both – remarkably – in bed, Layla asleep in her Moses basket across the room, and he pulled me towards him. It had been like returning home after a long stint away. Here we were: on the other side of it.

Scott went back to work, though, and by then the love for Layla was no longer new. The novelty of changing nappies had worn off, too. I was in the en suite, sitting on the floor. I don't know why I was in there. I was in a rare petulant mood where I wanted to demonstrate how unhappy I was, and how shocked I was, and how I didn't realize it could be this way. I chose to do so by sitting on the bathroom floor, five minutes before Scott was due home.

He arrived, shirt sleeves rolled up, and there I was with Layla. Screaming Layla.

The floor of the en suite was dusty and I think it was making Layla snuffle and sneeze. She had been crying for over two hours.

'She's been like this all day,' I said.

Scott made a funny kind of gesture. A sort of *what can you do?* Meant well, of course, but I didn't take it that way.

'I wish we'd never had her,' I said spitefully.

Scott didn't react. He stopped looking at me, looking

instead down at the sink. He wiped away a smidgen of yet more dirt, then inspected it on the end of his finger. He was trying to distract himself. 'Give her to me,' he said.

'I don't wish we hadn't had a baby,' I said.

'Right?' he said.

'I wish we hadn't had *her*,' I said. 'Layla.' It came from a nasty, hollow place inside of me. It was a statement meant to hurt him. To worry him. So that he would help me more. After that blissful paternity leave, his career had returned to how it had always been – as if he'd merely gone to Italy for two weeks, not changed his life for ever – while mine floundered, calls from assistants unanswered for days as I ran on the treadmill of feeding, changing, settling Layla to sleep. Over and over. When one finished, the next began.

He took a step back. His eyebrows drew together in surprise. 'What?' he said, though I'm sure he didn't want me to say it again.

'I can't think of a worse baby to have,' I said. I stood up and handed her to him. Even as I did so, my arms missed the weight of her: the paradox of motherhood.

He never mentioned it again, and neither did I. But sometimes, in the dark days that followed her death and Becky's arrest, I wonder what he really thought, then, and what he thinks now, too. Motherhood was such a tangled knot, and I had only just begun unpicking it. Most people had years to unspool it, to inspect it. To come to terms with life changing for the worst, and the better, all at once. To understand that life was much harder, but strangely more fulfilling, because I had split my life in two – into mine and Layla's.

But we didn't have time.

'Thank you, Ms Williams,' Harriet says. She sits down.

A strand of my hair drifts down and lands on my arm.

Ellen stands up to re-examine.

'In your opinion,' she says, darting a glance at the defence lawyer she was laughing with just hours previously, 'how did the shouting sound?'

'Like somebody very angry. At the end of her tether.'

'Frightening?'

'Yes, certainly,' Theresa says. 'Especially for a child.'

'Witness can't possibly know—' Harriet starts to say.

'I can't control her answers,' Ellen says to Harriet. 'Nothing further,' she adds.

As she sits down, I catch a tiny smile on her face. It's a good day at the office, for her.

24

Becky

I am in Sainsbury's and had forgotten how difficult every-thing can be with a baby. Xander never cried quite like this. The health visitor called his sleep abnormal, but Marc and I didn't care.

'Our baby sleeps too much!' Marc said to me one night while we were lying together on our cheap IKEA bed, Xander asleep in the Moses basket just a few feet away.

We spent hours in that room, in those early days. We used to eat dinner in bed. We weren't tired, and Xander would have tolerated sleeping downstairs with us and being carried up when we went to bed. We just enjoyed being lazy in there, together, watching television on the old TV set and eating.

'Can you imagine what a doctor would think about that for a complaint? *Please help us; we're fully rested!*'

'Besides, he's pretty fat,' I said, sitting up slightly on the bed and leaning over to look at Xander. The rings of fat around his wrists and ankles. It was warm in the bed-room, and he was naked save for a nappy.

The memories are bittersweet, these days. 'Don't worry,'

a friend once said to me when I mentioned Marc's name one too many times on a night out. 'Everyone has an ex they're still in love with.'

I had blinked, and denied it. And yet, later that night, in bed, I thought: *Of course. Of course I am. But it's too late for us, anyway, now.*

Is it?

The quiet question rises up inside me. But it is. I am incapable. I am incapable of telling Martha how hard the nannying is, and I am incapable of telling Marc how sorry I am about what happened between us. What a fuck-up I am. Martha knows how to apologize. And Martha can cope with Layla. What's the point of me? God, I want a glass of wine as big as my head, now. I'll buy a fucking bottle.

Layla has cried in the ready meal aisle of Sainsbury's, and through all of the fruit and veg. As I reach to grab a bottle of milk in the dairy aisle, Marc texts me, just a photograph of a beautifully laid carpet.

Lovely! I reply, gritting my teeth while Layla cries as I adjust her in order to respond.

You okay? he replies immediately. It's true it's unlike me to send such a short, dismissive reply.

In baby hell, I send back. *Lovely carpet though, really*, I add.

I love how a carpet can transform a room. I know I would've been an excellent designer; I could always select the exact right colour. There's a huge difference between oatmeal and fawn, trust me.

When I started set-dressing, and back when Marc was still my husband, I would gather up my materials and go with him on his carpet-fitting days. I would sit in the room next door to the one he was fitting in, spread out my cardboard and sequins and Sellotape, and we'd chat, and he would swear at the carpet stretcher, and his bad knee. We'd play games – listing celebrities beginning with every letter of the alphabet, or playing I Spy – and he'd make me proud of him with how fastidious he was, how neat. I loved to watch the transformation take place, from bare floor to fluffy carpet. I loved the smell of it. Marc later told me it was caused by something called 4-phenylcyclohexene, which rather took the romance out of it. 'No, it smells of *newness and hope,*' I replied, and he threw his head back with laughter.

You need to tell her no, next time, Marc types back now as I stand in the supermarket. *Takes the piss.*

Doesn't it just, I reply, but say nothing further.

What else is there to say? The last thing I want is Marc getting protective, intervening, trying to *fix it*, as is his way.

I buy only the necessities, now, alone: milk, a reduced baguette, some hummus. I have four bottles left of Martha's milk, so Layla will be okay. I need to get home and tidy: I cringe as I think of the house waiting for me. I have always had a tendency to let things get sinful before I tidy, enjoying the dramatic transformation even a bit of housework brings about. I'm looking forward to removing the soiled dishes piled high on the kitchen window sill just as soon as Layla gives me a moment.

My phone rings in the car and I answer it on hands free. Marc's deep voice booms through the in-car system. 'I can already hear her,' he says.

'Don't, Marc,' I say.

'Don't what?'

'Don't . . . it's fine. Just don't.'

'They're taking advantage of you,' he says.

'They're not. They're really not. I volunteered. It's only tonight. One night.'

'But it's all the time, Sam,' hc says.

I shrug in the car as I wait at a set of traffic lights, even though he can't see me. 'Yeah,' I say. 'I know. I know it is.'

'Why is she crying so much, anyway?' he says. 'What's wrong with her?'

'She's a baby,' I say. We hang up soon after that. God, I don't need him to tell me they're taking advantage of me. It makes it worse, not better.

We are hot when we get home, and Layla is bright red and screaming as I open the car door. It won't open fully, and closes back on to my hip, and I clench my jaw. 'Please be quiet,' I say, taking a moment to lean against the side and try to breathe. 'Please, please just be quiet.'

As I scoop Layla up, I see her. My neighbour, Theresa. She's in yoga wear. A vest top and a long-line cardigan. Leggings. Ugg boots. No doubt about it: she has been eating avocados and meditating. Straight out of a fucking romcom.

She lifts her arm in a wave. The smile dies as she sees Layla's bright-red screaming face.

Theresa once complained about one of the other neighbours, Sheila, who liked to cook and listen to reggae every Saturday afternoon. I liked to hear the reggae drifting through the walls, and smell the spices and the jerk chicken. Sometimes Sheila brought leftovers round on paper plates covered in foil, and I liked that, too – like party food. She had stopped bringing Theresa leftovers, she told me, after the complaint. And she had turned her music down, too, so on Saturdays I had to strain to hear it.

'My sister's baby,' I say, swinging Layla's car seat. It's weightier than I remember with Xander. How did I carry this stuff around all the time? I must have had absolute guns for biceps, like Michelle Obama, or something.

'Oh, is she struggling? Your sister?' Theresa says.

'No, no. Not really,' I say. 'Her job is . . . I'm stepping in. Sorry for any crying,' I say with a grimace. 'She's not very settled. At times.'

'Why are you . . . that's so generous,' she says.

'Yeah, well. She couldn't find a nanny who she could just call up. You know?'

She lifts her chin and looks at me squarely. She has moaned, in the past, about me, too. About Xander and his footballs. She doesn't much like children, is my guess, and she doesn't want there to be a baby next door. She is one of those people who sees kids, somehow, not as volatile little humans with fat hands and short legs and tempers, but as another species entirely. 'Give him a bloody break,' I have wanted to say, over and over, when she texts me: *Another ball in our garden*. Always full stops at the end of her sentences.

Layla has been crying for the entire conversation.

'You see?' I say with a laugh as we turn to go in, holding tightly on to the car seat, even though it is making my arm tremble. *Oh well*, I think bitterly. *Martha's life may be perfect, but her baby sure isn't*.

'She's very noisy,' Theresa says. 'Has she been fed?'

'Yes,' I say, testily. Does everybody — *every single person* — insist on treating me like a piece of shit? Like a child? A rubbish *employee* who needs micromanaging? I clench my jaw in rage.

As I turn to leave, I see Theresa's eyes taking in the plates in the kitchen window, piled so high it looks as if they may fall at any moment.

25

Martha

Scott puts the television on, low, when we get in. We both behave in this way. Taking up as little space as possible. We hardly make any noise. It is as if we have spent most of our happiness. The dregs are being meted out, and they have to last a lifetime. That's grief, I guess.

I drum my fingers against my leg as I try to think about it. I consult the lists I made the previous night, holding the pages close so that Scott can't see. Timelines, but nothing more. What am I doing? I rise and go into the bedroom. Scott says nothing.

I spread the timelines out on the bed and look at them.

Layla died between eight and nine thirty. Becky was out at quarter to eight. Somebody could have been in the house. With or without Becky.

No. That's mad. Ludicrous.

I start a To Do list, instead.

Visit the house.

Research wrongfully convicted mothers.

My handwriting is shaky, unpractised. It looks more like Becky's spidery scrawl than my own.

I stand by the window and hold the list in my hand. Scott appears in the bedroom. He asks me a question with his eyebrows.

'Nothing,' I say. 'I'm not doing anything.'

'What is it?'

'Just . . . solutions.'

'Solutions?'

He takes his trousers off and changes into shorts. Our flat is always too hot during the summer. The veins are standing out on his hands.

'Just explanations. Other than . . .'

His face drops. 'Other than Becky?'

'Well. Yes.'

'I thought you were leaving it to the jury,' he says. He runs a hand through his blond hair.

I am standing, framed in the floor-to-ceiling window, staring at him. 'No. Why should I?'

His hand drifts slowly down to his side. 'You know what I think.'

'I don't know how anybody knows what to think.'

'Who could it have been, other than Becky?'

'I don't know. Anybody. There was a whole evening where we don't know what happened, Scott.'

'But everything points to her.'

'No, it doesn't. It's just slander. Road rage and leaving Layla alone and forgetting Xander – none of it is evidence about how Layla died. About what actually *happened*.'

'But it is,' he says softly. 'That's why it's being brought up.'

'But . . . there is other evidence.'

'Is there?'

'Yes. Like *who she is*. What I know about her . . .'

'People act out of character all the time,' Scott says.

'This is killing, Scott.'

'I know,' he says, spreading his hands wide. 'But.'

'What? What's the but? I'm just trying to see if there's anything else that someone might've—'

'Nobody's missed anything. Sweetheart.' He moves towards me, slowly. He reaches a hand out. 'I just want you to be happy again,' he says. He waits for a moment, looking at me, then sits down heavily on the bed.

I can hardly believe he is the same person whose arm would feel weighty and secure across my shoulders as we walked along the river together at university.

'Martha. You're hurting yourself. Going over and over it like this. It's like picking a scab,' he says gently. His eyes are damp.

Our gazes have finally locked, after what feels like months. Suddenly, I am anchored. I was adrift, and now, here I am, not yet at shore, but anchored by him, my husband. Safe.

'What was the but?' I say, still frozen in the window.

Scott is looking at the floor.

'Say she gets off . . .' he says.

I grit my teeth at the phrasing.

'Would you leave another baby with her?' When he looks back up at me, his eyes are watchful.

'No,' I say quietly. 'Not at the moment. But maybe something will happen?' It sounds hopeless, even as I say it. 'Maybe someone else was seen.'

I think of the near-endless procession of witnesses to come.

Experts and doctors.

And Marc . . .

'We're not going to know anything. They will either decide that she did it or she didn't. There's nothing you don't know. The trial won't help. You've got to stop thinking it will provide the answers. The answers are . . . the answers are in moving on. Keeping on,' he says.

He has said it to me before: during bad jobs and the recession, when we were in negative equity. During a horrible holiday, once, staying in a hotel that had slugs. 'Keep on keeping on.' I had always loved that. His calm optimism. On the last night of that holiday, with the slugs leaving trails around the bed late one night, I said, 'Keep on keeping on,' and felt actually, properly happy, a bubble of pleasure in my chest, there with my husband in a slug-infested nightmare. It was as though he had taught me to enjoy life *despite* itself, and not merely to wait for the good times. I felt dizzyingly liberated. *I can choose to be happy, no matter what*, I found myself thinking. 'Exactly,' he smiled at me. 'Keep on keeping on.'

I shake my head now. There seems to me to be an endless amount of information I wasn't aware of. Hardly any of it is material, but almost all of it is new. The previous conviction. Maybe the defence have bombshells, too. Maybe there is a medical reason; a pre-existing condition. Something congenital that caused my baby to suffocate. Is there such a thing? Oh, please say so: that she died naturally, not knowing it even herself. In my mind I can see her eyes closing peacefully; those translucent eyelids.

But . . . maybe Becky went somewhere before or after Londis? Maybe Becky left Layla with *somebody* when she went to Londis?

On my pad I write down everybody's name. As many as I can think of. All of us: Mum, Dad, Becky, Scott, Marc, Xander, Marc's parents, Becky's neighbour Theresa. I strike through the names of those who have strong alibis at the time of death.

There they are. A list of suspects. I hold the pad close to me. I'll never show it to anybody – of course I won't – but it feels both good and horrible to see them written down. Like I am doing something.

Next to each name left, I make a note of where they say they were between 8.00 p.m. and 9.30 p.m. on the night Layla died.

My pencil stills across one name: Marc's. Where was he? Alone. Fitting a carpet for work, so he said. Could anybody vouch for that?

Wednesday

26

Martha

'Ms Blackwater, is it true you were in another country the night it happened?'

It's the same reporter again, the one with the curly hair. She's wearing a wrap-around top. I can see the top of her ribcage above it, two small sweat patches underneath her armpits.

I look at her, again, and she looks back, expectant.

I push past her and into the courtroom.

The next witness, Alison, is one of the few people in Becky's life who I didn't really know. She is the mother of a school friend of Xander's. She was at Becky's house at 11.50 p.m. on the night in question. A few hours after Layla's death.

I tried to ask her about it – what she saw – at the school gates, where I lurked for a few days until I saw her, back in the winter. But she told me she couldn't discuss it. I went again the next day, but that time, she looked frightened of me and my pale, haggard form. I didn't go back again.

It's like a fragmented nightmare, a kaleidoscope. One piece of evidence to my left, one to my right. Another behind me, another in front. Perspectives of paramedics, nurses, neighbours, friends. I look at them all, these different angles from which to view the same crime, but I can't piece them together myself and decide whether or not my sister is guilty of killing my child.

Alison enters the witness box at ten o'clock. Outside the windowless courtroom, the sun blazes relentlessly. It's the kind of weather that would once have had me wanting to take a sabbatical and do insane things. Get a tabloid newspaper and a smoothie – one of those ridiculously huge ones from Costa or similar – and head to the beach, buying a disposable barbecue on the way.

She is wearing flared jeans and a kimono. I almost smile to look at her. I know exactly what Becky would think of her, and I dart a look across at the dock. 'Fucking hippie,' Becky would say. 'A kimono.'

Alison tells the prosecution barrister that her son Forrest goes to school with Xander, and that she has one other child.

'Tell me about the night of October the twenty-sixth,' Ellen says. 'You saw the defendant between three and four hours after, as we allege, she had smothered Layla to death.'

27

Alison Jones

Alison poured herself a measure of cucumber fizzy water in her kitchen. She had organized her day around this evening. She'd written one thesis chapter – she'd had to turn off the internet to do it – and here she was, halfway through her reward. She was watching reruns of *Sex and the City* in the snug. Jones, her husband – she'd always called him by his surname; everybody did – was out, and the boys had a friend over. It was totally joyous, these hours alone on the cracked old leather chesterfield.

She took the drink back into the snug. Upstairs was utterly quiet, and she immersed herself in Carrie and Big's world.

It felt like only moments had passed but, when she checked her watch, it had been three hours.

She walked across the landing and stood outside Forrest's room. She could hear something from within. Creepy music, but complete silence otherwise.

She opened the door a crack and recognized the film immediately. Oh shit. It was *The Shining*. She would recognize it anywhere. For fuck's sake. Jones loved horror films. They must have found his recording.

'What's this?' she said. The words were out before she looked at Xander, and her heart seemed to expand in her chest. Oh, no. Poor, anxious Xander, who earlier had asked her innocently if there would ever be another world war. And now this. Her unmanageable children had indoctrinated him into watching hardcore horror. She would be the talk of the school gates.

His long, lanky legs – he was huge for a nine-year-old – were drawn up to his chest and he was so frightened, so bloody frightened, that his shoulders were jerking. His eyes were fixed on a point on the wall to the left of the television. He couldn't even look.

'Okay, that's enough horror,' she said brightly. 'Off,' she commanded.

'It's not even that scary. It's so crap it's funny,' Forrest said.

Ralph didn't look bothered, either. She guessed it was too much to expect her two children to think of Xander, and his nervous disposition. No. Not nervous, exactly. Worried. Wanting to please people, to not be in trouble, so much so that he would go along with watching a terrifying movie.

'You alright, Xander?' she said to him.

'Not really,' he said, meeting her eyes across the room. And then he unfolded his limbs and came to her.

Oh shit. This was real. He was upset. He would tell Becky – and Becky could be *fierce*.

'Oh no – it's not real. It's not real at all,' she said. 'I always imagine the cameramen and the sets, when I'm frightened.' She looked at where they were on the Sky player. It was paused just ten minutes from the end: the damage was done.

'I want to go home, Alison,' he said. He often spoke in this formal way. She doubted her children knew the Christian names of any of their friends' parents.

He wiped his cheek with one of his adult-sized hands and looked at her, standing in his pyjamas in the middle of the room. Forrest snorted derisively and she gave him a look.

'Oh, no, Xander. It's not real. Let's watch something nice to get rid of the memories,' she said.

'*Beauty and the Beast*?' Forrest said snidely.

'I want to go home.'

'Okay,' she said, realizing there was no use trying to salvage the night. 'You'll all have to come in the car.'

She texted Becky and then bundled everybody into the car. She didn't make them put their proper clothes on. Becky hadn't read the text by the time she was turning the key in the ignition. It was unusual for her. She was usually an immediate replyer, one of those people who responded seemingly before you had even sent your message, and always with questions.

Forrest and Ralph were quiet in the back of the cold car. Xander was in the passenger seat, mostly because he was almost as tall as she was, but also because he was still shivering with fear. *The Shining*. What were they thinking?

It was less than a five-minute drive to Becky's, and she still hadn't read the text by the time Alison pulled up outside the house. She called Becky's mobile, but it rang out and went to her chirpy voicemail, so Alison sat in the car for a few minutes longer.

She looked at the house. All of the lights were off,

except one. The front room was in darkness. The kitchen, too, the taps just catching the reflection of the street lights. Only one upstairs window was illuminated. A bedroom. Surely it was alright to knock? Anyway, what was worse: risk annoying Becky by disturbing her at a late hour, or risk traumatizing her child by making him stay the night with her tiny psychopaths?

She got out of the car, pulling her coat around herself, and rang the doorbell.

There was no answer. Ten seconds went by, then twenty. She glanced back at the children in the car. Forrest and Ralph were watching something on an iPad. Xander was staring straight ahead. Alison wondered if perhaps she should just try the door, and send Xander in by himself.

No. She'd wait. Her breath clouded the air in front of her and she stamped her feet, trying to keep warm. The early-winter cold seeped through her thin trousers and she drew her coat tighter around herself.

Ah, finally. Light pooled in the hall, and there was Becky, showcased in the frosted glass. She was tall, but tonight her frame seemed unusually hunched, her shoulders rounded as she undid the locks. She was usually so confident, so self-possessed: a quality Alison greatly admired.

'So sorry, Becky,' Alison said to her now. 'Did you see my text . . .?'

Becky's face was grey. She swallowed. 'No,' she said, sounding spaced out. Her eyes looked strange. Not teary, exactly, but older. More lined, somehow. Like she hadn't slept for a few nights. Like she had the flu.

'Xander . . . um, well, Forrest and Ralph, they watched . . .'

'Sorry?' Becky said.

Her hair was bundled on top of her head. She had no make-up on, and Alison was struck by the circles underneath her eyes. One of her hands was shaking, and the other was wrapped around her waist. Was she ill? Perhaps, Alison thought, looking closely at her, she was drunk.

'Sorry – what?' Becky said again.

'No, no, I'm sorry,' Alison said, 'disturbing you like this.' God, she really was grey. Alison had never seen a complexion that colour. Little dots of sweat sat on Becky's upper lip, which she dashed off when she saw Alison looking. Her finger came away wet, and she wiped it on her jogging bottoms.

'They watched a mental film. I'm so sorry, I should have noticed, and stopped them. Xander is . . . well, he's very frightened. He wanted to come home.'

'Right, okay,' Becky said. She nodded distractedly and then – for the first time in the entire exchange – looked beyond Alison to her son in the car.

She didn't ask what film. She didn't say anything further. She merely made a defeated kind of gesture, motioning to Xander, who went dutifully inside. He disappeared into the house, into the rooms beyond the kitchen. To bed, alone.

'It was *The Shining*. I'm sorry,' Alison said.

'Sure,' Becky said. 'Whatever.'

Whatever? 'I didn't get the impression he'd watched anything like that before.'

'I don't really know, to be honest,' Becky said, not looking at her.

'Anyway, I'm really sorry for any anxiety he—'

Becky waved off her apologies with her hand, then went to close the door on her.

The rest of the house was silent, she noticed.

Completely and utterly quiet.

28

Martha

'Thank you, for that,' Ellen says. She looks pretty pleased with herself. 'So, just to clarify: you definitely could not hear baby Layla crying when you dropped Xander back?'

'No. Absolutely not.'

'How sure are you?'

'One hundred per cent,' Alison says.

She is firm and clear, just as Becky would be in the witness box. Becky was always good at choosing friends that are just like her. Fat lot of good it's done her, though, that selectiveness. They've shopped her. Every last one of them.

'Good.' Ellen sits down.

Harriet rises. 'How distressed would you say the defendant appeared, on a scale of one to ten?'

'Um,' Alison says. She pushes her hair back.

'Slightly distressed? Very?'

'Only slightly. She was just . . . weird.'

'Right. So not, perhaps, as distressed as somebody might be had they committed murder just hours before?'

'The witness cannot possibly answer that,' Ellen says. She doesn't stand, doesn't even look up.

'Okay. Not *very* distressed, then? Not in shock?'

'Well, no.'

'And remind us why you were there. With Xander.'

'He was frightened.'

'He was frightened and who did he want to see? Who did he ask to see?'

'His mum,' Alison says quietly, a slight catch in her voice.

'His mother,' Harriet says, turning to the jury, her voice loud, almost too loud, for her small frame. 'And how did he seem when he went into the house?'

'He just . . . he just walked past her and went in.'

'Entirely at home, then.'

'He seemed at home, yes.'

'Did he – who knows his mother best – seem at all troubled by her behaviour?'

'No.'

'Nothing further.'

They don't mention the lack of crying. Whether or not Becky did it, by that point Layla was dead. And she ought to have known it. What spin could the defence put on that? None.

I stare at Alison as she leaves.

Could Marc have been there? Is that why Becky took so long to answer the door? Was she hiding him?

'Now,' the judge says. 'The prosecution is going to play the 999 call made at 7.59 a.m. the next day.'

A clerk moves towards the back of the court. Her robes sweep across the carpet as she brushes past us. She is messing with a computer at the back.

And then Becky's voice starts to play:

Ambulance. My niece is . . . she's not breathing. Oh God, she's not breathing. Help, please help. How can she not be breathing? I don't . . . I can't . . . I didn't . . .

There is a beat of silence, and then a soothing operator asks for Becky's address, the address I could rattle off without any thought at all. I always liked the way her postcode tripped off the tongue: BN3 3AA.

Operator: Okay, Becky, how old is the child?

Becky: Eight weeks. Layla.

Operator: Okay. We're going to perform CPR. Five rescue breaths, into Layla's mouth. Okay? Make a seal with your mouth around hers. Blow steadily until her chest rises. Has anything happened to the baby that you know of?

Becky: [silence]

Operator: Becky?

Becky: Her skin is totally white. She's not moving. I . . . she's not moving at all.

Operator: Have you done five breaths?

Becky: Yes.

Operator: And now the chest compressions. Two fingers, okay? Just two fingers, not hands. Thirty compressions. Depress the chest by one-third of its own depth. Do you know what that means?

Becky: Oh God, I've been using my hands. Oh, two fingers. Okay.

Operator: The ambulance is on its way. How long has she been this way?

Becky: Her skin is totally white.

Operator: Two fingers on the chest and thirty compressions, okay? Push down by one-third of the depth of her chest.

Becky: One-third. Okay.

Operator: Twice per second. To the rhythm of 'Stayin' Alive'. Do you know that song, Becky?

Becky: Yes.

Operator: Now, Becky, is the front door unlocked?

Becky: Yes. I've sent my son down. I didn't want him to see . . . Xander, unlock the door, yes?

Operator: Okay, Becky, I can see the ambulance is less than two minutes away. Keep going with the compressions. Can you see any signs of life?

Becky: Signs of . . . life? No. None.

Operator: Ambulance is one minute away, Becky.

Becky: She's not breathing at all. Her limbs are . . . I think her limbs are stiff. Oh God . . .

Operator: Keep compressing, Becky. 'Stayin' Alive', yes?

Becky: Yes. Oh God, oh God, come on, Layla . . .

Operator: The crew have arrived now, Becky, so I'm going to hand you over . . .

I dart a glance at the jury as the tape stops and the courtroom falls silent. I can't look at anybody else. Not Becky. Not Scott.

The tape exists in the few minutes right after Layla was found, and right before she was declared deceased in A&E. Right in the middle, where things might have turned out otherwise, though I know they never could have. It is harder to think about what Becky might have done differently in those minutes than it is to think about what she did the night before. I don't know why.

'Thank you,' the judge says to the clerk.

Ellen stands up. 'The prosecution calls Natalie Osbourne, the attending paramedic.'

A large woman, in a short black skirt, white top and black long-line cardigan is brought in by the usher. Her hair is dark and glossy, curling to her collarbones, and just the ends hint at auburn.

She is sworn in, and confirms she's a paramedic, and has been for six years. As she confirms it, a flush overtakes my body. It works its way up my torso and down my arms.

This woman in front of me who is self-consciously adjusting her cardigan held my baby in her dying moments.

29

Natalie Osbourne

They were approaching the house, there within six minutes of the call. It was the very start of her day, and, already, something grim awaited. An unconscious baby, the operator told her. Her skin was white. Not breathing, no pulse. CPR being performed. It didn't sound good.

Natalie had a head cold. It had kept her up for most of the night. In the end, at four o'clock, Adam had made her up a bowl of Vicks, just like her mother used to do for her.

But she wasn't fuzzy-headed any longer. She was completely and utterly alert. An unresponsive baby. Adrenaline pulsed through her body.

The house was tall and slim. They abandoned the ambulance on the drive and opened the door. Immediately, Natalie could hear the commotion upstairs.

'Oh God, oh God, come on, Layla,' a woman was shouting.

Natalie ran up the stairs. The nursery was the first door on the right. Her eyes were on the baby, and the woman who she presumed to be the mother. Her colleague saw the other child, the nine-year-old, tear-stained and standing on the landing, peering in horror at his mother, and took him downstairs.

They didn't call the deaths of babies. That was Natalie's immediate thought when she saw the body. And, later, she wished she hadn't had it, that she hadn't been so pessimistic. Would she have done anything differently, she thought, later? No. She wouldn't. She knew she wouldn't, and yet . . . she couldn't help but relive it again, just to see.

That baby. She stood on the landing and stared at it, for just a second. You learnt to spot it. You learnt to spot the signs. Not blue as she would have presumed, when she first started out in the job. Not blue, no: white. Floppy.

The room was almost empty: a makeshift nursery, it looked like. A Moses basket. A chest of drawers. A faded carpet, worn in patches in the middle of the room and good as new at the edges.

Natalie was measuring doses and felt a lurch of sympathy and wished she could tell the mother, then. To save her the hope of the resuscitation, of the ambulance journey, of the cold, sterile resus room in A&E, the doctor's sombre expression and, finally, the baby being wheeled away to the morgue. They could do it now; a black body bag might be kinder, in a way. But she couldn't: the list of deaths she could call was minuscule. Dead on arrival: it was the doctor's job.

It was rhythmic. Natalie moved in. The air bag. The adrenaline. It came naturally to her. But the whole time, she was thinking: *This is futile. Absolutely futile.*

Natalie glanced at the mother. She was ashen, a tissue clutched in her fist, brought up to her face. She was shivering violently, pulling a cardigan around herself as she turned and closed the bedroom window. The sound of it closing seemed to reverberate around the bedroom.

The finality of it.

30

Martha

'No questions,' Harriet says demurely, standing briefly before settling back into her seat.

Ellen rises. 'The prosecution calls Amanda Thompson,' she says. 'The treating doctor in A&E.'

I am determined to stay for the entire examination, which will be led by the prosecution. I am pinned to my seat as though forced to watch a beheading, although I will never be able to unknow what she tells the courtroom.

I turn my eyes away from Ellen and watch as Amanda Thompson collects herself, ready to give her initial evidence. I look down at my hands. Everybody's eyes are on me.

Scott's kind gaze.

Becky's.

The jury's.

I hear Amanda clear her throat. She must know the pain she is going to cause me. She's a doctor.

And then, I can't resist any longer, and I look up at Becky. When she sees me looking, she takes a step closer to the dock and holds a palm up. The guard removes it. It leaves a misted, sweaty mark against the glass, which fades after a few seconds.

31

Amanda Thompson

8.20 a.m., Friday 27 October

Amanda hung up the red telephone: the ambulance was on its way into A&E, carrying an unresponsive eight-week-old baby.

She reached for the alcohol gel dispenser and squirted a generous amount into the palm of her hand. It was cold.

People were right to revere medics, she thought. Amanda's colleagues said they were tired of being treated like demigods, of being asked questions of life and death at New Year's Eve parties, but the reality was they did know stuff. Amanda knew, for example, that a call at eight in the morning about an unresponsive baby was almost always a bad outcome. She knew exactly what had happened. The parents had woken up, and had found that the baby was dead. It was as simple as that: Amanda would bet her career on it. Not that she was too fond of that asset – particularly at the moment.

She found the senior house officer eating toast in the kitchen. He was seriously young, a bespectacled child prodigy, she assumed. 'Is there a paeds nurse on?' she said to him.

He started, butter dripping down his chin. 'Fiona's off,' he said. 'Costa del somewhere.'

'Damn. Thanks. Red phone's gone – get ready. Happy Friday . . .' she said grimly. It was usual, in a hospital, this black humour, gallows humour. But there was nothing funny about this.

Eight weeks. The baby would be about five kilograms. Amanda worked out the drug doses and lined them up. Adrenaline, glucose, fluid volume, sodium bicarb, calcium gluconate. She hoped the baby wasn't very fat or very thin, or she would have to recalculate, and there wasn't time for that. Or perhaps, she thought, perhaps there was no rush at all. Perhaps it was all over. Her hands stilled over the drugs as she thought it, and she shook her head. *Concentrate.*

The team arrived quickly. They had been well trained by her. They formed around her, becoming a functioning unit, like a swarm of honey bees, caring only about the good of the group.

'You take the airway,' she said to the anaesthetist. He immediately walked around to the head of the bed in the resus room, a curtained-off area in A&E where people came to live or die. Afterwards, after the resuscitation, it would be littered, like a war zone of plastic packaging, blood, bodily fluids. Nobody knew about the indignity of it, except the medics. The medics knew. People were deposited in here by paramedics, splayed naked, catheterized, bruised by paddles on their bare chests. They coughed and vomited and wet themselves, and afterwards, it was swept away, mopped up, like it had never happened.

'Paeds reg – sorry, I don't know your name – please do circulation. Nurse, take times and scribe. Please.'

'Okay,' the staff nurse said.

Shame she didn't have paeds experience. Amanda could do with the help.

'We have a baby, eight weeks. Found unresponsive this morning,' Amanda said to the team.

'Shit,' the paeds registrar said.

Quite right, she thought.

The second staff nurse arrived, and Amanda told her to get the Hartmann's fluid bags ready: pump them full, get them warm. The first rule of A&E medicine. Especially with children. Everybody thought medicine was the job of brain-iacs, but it wasn't, not really. It was largely as rudimentary as plumbing. Luckily, it was usually more interesting. Though, like most truly interesting things, it broke your fucking heart.

'I'll lead the resus,' Amanda said. She checked the watch in the top pocket of her scrubs. They'd be here any second now.

They had asked her what drew her to A&E in her regis-trar interview, and the truth was that Amanda was better in a crisis than anywhere else. Without a deadline almost upon her, she did nothing. She had two switches: work-aholic and complete dosser. She never occupied the middle ground. She needed blood and gore and red telephones. She used to occasionally crave a car crash to occupy her night shift. Now, she didn't recognize that crass woman in her registrar interview. But what would she say, today? 'They die,' she would say simply. 'Don't give me the job. I can't handle death.' Why had she thought she could han-dle it? She didn't remember even thinking about it at medical school, but wasn't death at the very centre of her occupation? Death, not life, as she had previously thought.

The ambulance arrived outside and the paramedic, Natalie, rushed in to hand over to her. Amanda didn't look at the baby, not yet. She looked at Natalie's brown eyes, ringed with thick kohl, and she listened intently. This was the second rule of A&E: bleed your handover dry. They always knew more than you.

The nurses moved Layla on to the resus trolley while Amanda listened.

'This is Layla,' Natalie said. 'She is eight weeks and two days old. Normally fit and well. Found unresponsive in her Moses basket. No signs of life. CPR commenced eight minutes ago with no ROSC. Adrenaline given.'

Her anaesthetist bagged and intubated immediately, as instructed, but Amanda stood there, watching, deciding what to do. That was the third rule of A&E: always think, even just for a second, before acting. That valuable second's thinking time had saved lives, before. 'Wait,' she had said a few weeks ago, looking at the way a middle-aged woman who had fallen off a horse held herself. 'Scan again,' Amanda had said. And there it was, on the second X-ray. A slight misalignment of the spine which would have left her paralysed if they had relied on the first X-ray and discharged her with analgesics.

She turned her gaze to baby Layla. And there it was. The evidence that she had been right to pause, momentarily. She took a deep breath. Right: at least now she knew.

'Adrenaline,' the paediatric registrar said.

She reached an arm out to him, and one out to the anaesthetist, too, both of her arms stretched wide like a bird's wings. 'Stop,' she said.

The anaesthetist looked up at her, both of his hands

around the endotracheal tube. His hands stilled around it. It was impossibly small. Only 3.5mm; the third-smallest size.

'No more,' she said softly, and the registrar stopped fussing with the joules setting for the paddles. 'She has rigor.'

Rigor. The paramedics couldn't call death – that was Amanda's job – but there it was, right in front of her. Layla's arms were frozen, held rigid by her sides, as though she was steeling herself against the cold; tiny frozen fists against her fat thighs.

The nurse was still determinedly working on her, stripping her yellow Babygro off – it had bear patterns on the feet – ready for more CPR, but Amanda just repeated herself, calmly but firmly: it took different staff different amounts of time to accept it. It always had.

Layla's skin was already mottled and blemished. The blood had slowed, stopped, and was settling in the dips and undulations of her body like snow in valleys and at the bottom of hills. Her lips had turned a darker, deeper shade of red. Burgundy.

Amanda blinked slowly. 'Please stop, now,' she said to the nurse. 'It's inappropriate.'

That was the word that did it. *Inappropriate*. It meant something to medics. It carried weight: it meant *cruel* and *futile* and *not in the child's best interests*. They had all attended lectures on the meaning of these phrases. Nurses, doctors, paramedics. Separate lectures, the same meanings. Ethics.

Amanda couldn't help but reach out a hand to touch Layla, though. Not to assess her. Not for any science. Just to comfort her in her final moments. Even though Amanda knew that those moments had taken place long before she got there.

Layla's skin was waxy, and room temperature, like a doll's. Amanda always found it so very strange to reach out and touch a body and it not be warm. Like a bubble bath that was cold upon entering. It was always a shock.

Amanda said a small prayer for Layla. Another thing she never would have done, back then, when she was an ambitious registrar.

'Eight thirty-two,' she said. 'Pupils fixed and dilated.'

Another death.

Called.

She took the baby's rectal temperature. The police would want it to time the death. If it was suspicious. They used a nomogram, which Amanda vaguely recalled learning about in some extra training session given on an evening a couple of years ago. Some calibration between the ambient temperature of the room where the death occurred, the rectal temperature in the body upon discovery, and the weight of the body. With that, they were able to estimate the time of death to within minutes.

Layla was taken to the morgue by a porter, her skin now the exact shade of the grey linoleum floor passing quickly underneath her. Just hours previously, she had slept in a Moses basket. Amanda blinked, and thought perhaps she wouldn't be a doctor for much longer. She shook her head, trying to clear her thoughts. She should go home; get some sleep.

She left the resus room and had a moment to herself, just for twenty seconds. Deep breaths in and out. Feelings weren't feelings. They were tangled mixtures of hormones:

cortisol, adrenaline, rushing through her system, telling her lies. She knew this, and still they felt real.

It was time to tell the parents.

She didn't immediately spot the mum. She usually did straight away – it was obvious. Maybe she was tired, at the end of a night shift, her body wrecked and tense. But no, she thought afterwards. Really, it was because the woman – Becky, she later learnt – was acting strangely.

It had been something about her stance. Too upright, and expectant, like somebody waiting to make a complaint, not to hear the fate of their child.

'Yes?' Becky said, when Amanda ventured forwards, which Amanda thought was stranger still.

'Are you the mother?'

'On a plane. I'm the aunt,' Becky said.

She would have to do this twice. For just a moment, Amanda felt like she could never do it again.

'I'm very sorry . . .' Amanda said.

And that was all it took. The rest of it was normal. The immediate bending over double that everybody did upon being told of a death. The hollowing of the cheeks, as though the wind had been knocked out of them. Eyes downcast, darting, thinking: *Can this be?*

And so it followed the usual patterns. Becky's tears. The hysterical call to Martha, the mother, as her aeroplane taxied along the runway. Becky had to repeat herself three times to get the message across to her sister.

But Amanda had not forgotten those initial reactions. And then, when the scans were done, the post-mortem complete, and the arrest had taken place, she had thought: *Yes.*

32

Martha

I dart a glance at Becky. She is looking straight at me, tears running down her face. I wonder how many tears she has shed, since it happened. Does Marc comfort her? Does he *believe* her?

Marc. My mind keeps coming back to him. I have seen him only twice since the night of.

The first time was at the hospital, once I got there. I hardly remember it. I remember only tiny pinpricks of that day.

I remember staring blindly out of the window for the entire flight home after getting the call. I had never before experienced utter and outright denial. Never. But all I could think of as I watched the ground become smaller underneath us was that I would get to the hospital and then I would sort it. I was the mother, after all.

And then. And then.

I remember the constant feel of my hand against my mouth, my breath hot against it. *Was I still breathing?* I was thinking, after two minutes, and four minutes, and six. Surely life had not gone on while my new baby lay dead in the morgue two corridors down from A&E, wheeled there in her cot – her final cot – just like that? It was two hours ahead in Kos, I couldn't help but think, and perhaps, somehow, I could bend time so we went further back than two hours.

Three.

Four.

Twelve, I later learnt.

I remember a pair of eyes belonging to a doctor. She is on mute, the rest of her faded out. I think her hands are placating me, somehow, out of focus, but all I can see are those eyes. Those round eyes, a funny greenish grey.

I remember the curtain hooks above the bay where it happened. One of them was half-formed, a C instead of an O, and it swung more than all of the others when everybody brushed past. And there was a lot of brushing past. So many people. At times it felt like hundreds. The admin of death.

The death certificate followed much later. Oh, with that damning cause of death, that *damning* cause, Becky. Asphyxiation.

I remember Layla's mouth. It had darkened – the blood pooling in her lips – so it looked gothic, like a blackened rosebud.

And yes, I remember Marc. He was skittish, nervous, shocked, but weren't we all? When I arrived, he was holding Becky's hands in his. Then they turned to me, together, and he told me he was sorry for my loss. It was oddly formal. Did he know something then?

The second time I saw him was one week after. One week post. He rang our doorbell at the most civilized time he could find: Saturday, at three o'clock in the afternoon. He was cordial like that, considered. I saw him through the spyhole in our front door, and stopped still, in case he saw me. His brow was wrinkled and he was bobbing on his toes, as he often did, flexing his feet, so his blond head kept dipping in and out of view.

'Marc,' I said when it became apparent he wasn't going to leave.

I couldn't open the door, but I stopped looking through the spyhole; it reminded me of the tunnel vision I experienced at the hospital when I saw the doctor. He didn't answer me, and in the end I got my phone out to text him, my soon-to-be-ex-brother-in-law – why wasn't there a simpler way to say *the man my sister used to love*? I saw the last message that was on there. He had asked for the dimensions of a chest of drawers we wanted to give away. I'd sent across that it was about eight of my handspans, and he had sent a row of hand emojis back, saying: *Never mind, I'll measure it myself soon*. We never did sort that.

I really cannot discuss it, I texted him, standing there in my too warm hallway.

In typical Marc fashion, he simply said: *Okay xx*.

But now I look back on that and feel differently. It was too dismissive. Too easy. I'd let him off the hook. And that was that.

What if I contact him now? What if I speak to him, soon, and ask him if he's telling the truth about that night?

My insides feel hollowed out, my arms shaky and numb. I never knew the things the treating A&E doctor had seen. I knew the basics. But I didn't know the rest. The details of my baby's skin – when I saw her she had been preserved, somehow. Washed with her own toiletries, brought from her changing bag – that's the policy – and dressed back in a white Babygro that I always thought was her favourite.

She smelt of Layla. The golden hair was just the same. The skin was cool, and waxen, but not that different.

My breasts felt full as I held her.

'Right,' Ellen the prosecutor continues. 'What were you thinking had happened to Layla, at the moment she presented in A&E?'

'At that stage, it could have been absolutely anything. My thought processes were: infection, trauma, metabolic disorders, seizures, cardiac events. Sudden infant death syndrome, though that is a diagnosis of exclusion.' Amanda's words are perfunctory, clipped, but her voice is low, her tone mournful.

'And so, could you exclude any of those conditions at the time?'

'We use a process called the surgical sieve. We think: was this acquired or congenital? And then we look at what happened – the heart stopped – and we work backwards, to work out why. But the answer is: we can't confidently exclude them. There was no rash suggesting infection, but I ordered bloods and cultures to look for infections anyway. There were no outward signs of trauma – bruising, deformation. I understand a CT scan of the body was done as part of the post-mortem. There was no family history of seizures or cardiac events. And even if there was no family history, that's not to say it's excluded. So at that time, it could have been anything.'

'Anything. I see. And how long do you think Layla had been dead, when she presented at A&E?'

'She had rigor. It doesn't set in uniformly in babies so it's hard to say, but . . . hours.'

'If Layla had suffered some trauma, is there a way you could know when it happened?'

'No. I understand the pathologist will be using the Henssge nomogram to assist you with the time of death.'

'Yes. Which will be explained later, jury,' Ellen says. 'But for now we must rely on the factual evidence, such as the testimony of other witnesses.'

Harriet folds her arms, watching but saying nothing.

'So if Layla was killed at some point between eight and nine thirty in the evening, would that fit with what you saw in A&E? If she were, say, smothered and died immediately, at 9.20 p.m.?'

'Yes, that would fit perfectly with a baby who presented as Layla did in A&E.'

'Thank you, Amanda,' Ellen says, shutting her folder triumphantly and sitting down.

Harriet stands up.

'The defendant called 999 early in the morning, didn't she?'

'Yes. At eight, I believe.'

'As soon as she found the baby.'

'I don't know about that,' Amanda says.

'I'll withdraw that,' Harriet says, before anybody can object. 'And you yourself didn't note anything that led you to suspect violent action, when the baby came into A&E?'

'No. I refer to the coroner, as I always do – as everyone has to do – when a baby has died.'

'So you saw no evidence of fractures . . . no bruising. No red marks, across the mouth or nose?'

'No.'

'So there was nothing, really, to arouse your suspicions?'

'No,' Amanda says, making a futile sort of gesture, her

hand lifting in the air and coming back down again immediately. 'I wasn't suspicious.'

'And as you're actually a witness as to facts, and not
providing expert evidence, I shall leave it there,' Harriet
says, glancing at Ellen.

I look back over to the dock.

Becky's features have relaxed slightly. Her jaw has
stopped quivering. Her shoulders have fallen. I see her
take a deep breath.

But, oh, Becky: the worst is still to come.

'The prosecution calls Detective Sergeant Johnson,' Ellen
says.

It is just before lunch, and the lawyers look tired. The
jury don't. They look alert, keen to be finally getting into
the details of the case. Not the neighbours or the social
workers, curiously distant from the night in question
itself. Here they are, mid-season in the box set of our lives,
pleased to be getting some answers at last.

I see Becky's body language shift, and mine probably
does, too. This woman, Keysha Johnson, was the beginning of it. It began – and it ended – in A&E, of course,
but the legal proceedings truly started with Keysha, and
with the interviews, and then the charge.

I blink, looking at Keysha as she crosses the court. She
is regal-looking, wearing a charcoal-grey suit with a tur-
quoise silk blouse. She holds herself upright, like an actor
in a play. Her hair is braided in perfectly straight lines.
They could've been done with a ruler. Between the plaits,
I can see her scalp.

She doesn't look at the jury, or the judge, and certainly

not at Becky, either. She takes her jacket off and lays it on the wooden shelf behind her, utterly at home.

'Detective Sergeant Keysha Johnson,' Ellen says.

'Yes.'

'You are the DS in charge of child protection at Sussex Police.'

'That's correct,' Keysha says, tilting her chin slightly upwards.

'You were the first police officer on the scene after Layla was brought to A&E and declared deceased, and then you went on to investigate the defendant, overseen by Superintendent Christopher Jones, whose evidence is agreed and won't be presented here today.'

'That's again correct,' Keysha says. She sounds almost bored.

'I'll leave you to talk me through it, then,' Ellen says. 'From the beginning, please.'

33

Detective Sergeant Keysha Johnson

Morning, Friday 27 October

When the call came from A&E this morning, she had
answered it in a bored tone. Drunks, domestic violence,
more drunks. Thursday was the new Friday, and so Friday
mornings were now as bad as Saturdays. But no. A dead
eight-week-old. And the sister was looking after her, and
not the mother. In suspicious deaths of children, it was
always the parents, in Keysha's experience. These calls
always involved the parents. The investigations always
involved the parents. They would deny it, but that's how it
always came out in the end.

The atmosphere in A&E was strange. They should be
used to death, she thought, but they didn't seem to be.
The consultant was red-eyed, leaning on her elbows over
the reception desk, having an in-depth conversation
with the triage nurse. Keysha was pointed in the direction
of the aunt.

There she was. Rebecca: *Call me Becky*. A strange thing
to say to a police sergeant, but she would let her off for
now. Keysha was watching, though. She appraised her
body language. Arms folded across her chest. Defensive.
Yes, Keysha was watching.

Becky was tall and imposing, with bright, clear eyes, and had on a cardigan and jeans. No make-up. Middle class, Keysha observed dispassionately. It probably hadn't been violent, then. A few years ago, she would've winced at such a sweeping generalization, but not now. It was simply the truth.

'Becky, I know this is a very difficult time,' Keysha said. 'But I am going to need you to take me to the house where it happened.'

'The house,' Becky repeated.

It was funny. The woman was looking straight at Keysha, but there was nothing going on behind her eyes. Shock, Keysha supposed, though that didn't exonerate anybody. Lord knows, criminals, too, are shocked by the results of their own depraved actions.

'Martha will be here soon . . .' Becky said, checking her phone. It was ablaze with messages.

Keysha frowned. She would have that phone off her, soon enough, once she got the warrant, and she would search it properly.

'. . . she's on a plane.'

The mother, Keysha guessed, though nobody thought to tell her. 'Okay,' she said. 'But nevertheless, because an infant has died, there is a procedure to follow, and I am going to need you to come with me now.'

They travelled in Keysha's car, in silence. Keysha's phone in the glovebox vibrated once and she did her best to ignore it. It was less than five minutes to Becky's house. 'Here on the left,' were the only words that Becky spoke for the entire trip.

The Scenes of Crime Officer met them there. She was

standing outside, handbag held in front of her. She was a prim old woman, married forty years, and she photographed crime scenes every day of her working life. Keysha found her fascinating. Did she go home and tell her husband of the things she had seen that day?

Becky went inside with her, while Keysha waited in the car. It didn't take them long. Keysha was dying to know the state of the scene, but she didn't ask. She couldn't go in. That was the Scenes of Crime Officer's job. Hers was to sit here and wait. To think.

Next, she took Becky to the station. The first interview was exploratory. At least, that's what they said. Becky didn't want to come – she wanted to wait for Martha – but Keysha promised they'd have her back by the time her sister was home; that it would take less than an hour. The husband and son were waiting back at the hospital for her. The house was sealed off: a crime scene.

'What happened?' Keysha said in the interview. She didn't bother trying to look friendly, these days. She was forty, and she couldn't be bothered any more.

'I was in with her. All evening. She cried all evening. I was texting Marc about it.'

'Who's Marc?'

'My ex-husband.'

'What did you do with your evening? You and Layla?'

'Tried to stop her crying.' She darted a quick look at Keysha. 'Watched TV.'

'Oh, what did you watch?' Keysha said conversationally.

'A film. A TV programme. About house-hunting.'

'So a TV programme.' Keysha tilted her head to the side.

'Yes. All evening.'

'Did you do anything else of note?'

'Talked to Marc, on the phone, as well as texting. Nothing else. At all.'

'When did you put the baby to bed?'

'Elevenish.'

'Right. What were you doing with her until then?'

'Trying to stop her crying.'

'Okay. How?'

'Feeds. A bath. Walking . . .'

'I see.'

'And then my – our – son was brought home. He'd been at a sleepover and he hadn't been . . . he had been scared. He's an anxious type.'

'And when was that?'

'Around midnight.'

'And then . . .'

'I did one last check, later. Two . . . three? I had some wine. She was still grumbling. She hadn't stopped, really. I fell asleep on the sofa. Woke up and checked her. And the next thing I remember is in the morning. I woke with a start, you know? When you're used to being woken by the baby.'

'Why were you used to being woken by the baby?'

'I am – I *was* – Layla's nanny. Unofficially. For a while. I'd had her the previous night as well . . . Martha's husband was supposed to come home after the first night, but he stayed an extra night at a developers' conference . . .'

Keysha blinked. 'I see.'

'And then I . . .'

Keysha waited. The silence seemed to fill the tiny

interviewing room. Becky's eyes started to water, but Keysha remained impassive: she could wait all day long.

'I guess I sort of knew, then.' Becky winced. 'I mean, I didn't. But I was worried. When she hadn't cried. So I got to the spare room and she was . . . Jesus. She was dead. I called 999. Did CPR on her . . . her little . . .'

'So the last time you checked Layla was – when?'

'That time I told you about, in the early hours.'

'And how was Layla then?'

Becky's eyes moved to the side, avoiding contact. Keysha clocked it immediately.

'She was fine. Normal.'

'And you would've expected to be woken between the small hours and eight, by her?'

'God, yes, absolutely.'

'But you weren't.'

'No. And I was so tired and, I guess, quite drunk that I slept until eight.'

'What do you remember about Layla at the one or two o'clock check?'

Becky's head sank to her chest. 'I don't know.'

'You don't know?'

'I poked my head around the door. It was dark. She was quiet. I don't know. I just . . . I just didn't want to wake her. That screaming had been . . .'

'What?'

'Intense. So I just opened the door a crack. All seemed well. I thanked my lucky stars she was quiet.' Becky gulped.

'How much wine had you drunk?'

'A bottle.'

'Okay. So quite drunk, then.'

'Yes.'

'Is your memory of those small hours clear?'

'No.'

'No co-sleeping?'

'No. None.'

Becky was taken back to the hospital, and, while it was fresh in her mind, Keysha took a note of their conversation. It always started with a timeline. Then she sat back in her chair, and looked at the papers through narrowed eyes.

Cot death, she hoped, despite herself.

There was nothing found at the scene. The officer showed the photographs to Keysha. A Moses basket, which was seized and tested but showed nothing suspicious. A changing table with a mattress on the top. A blanket. A cuddly toy on the floor. No signs of violence. No blood. Nothing unusual or out of place.

A week later, the call came. The post-mortem: the cause of death had been given as asphyxiation. Blood and blanket fibres in Layla's lungs. Smothering, as far as Keysha was concerned.

Well, shit, she thought. She genuinely hadn't expected that.

Was she losing touch with her instincts? She thought back to Becky in the interview. She'd been shifty, that much was true, but Keysha didn't think she was a murderer. Well, not until now, anyway.

She looked again at the photographs of the Moses basket. Accidental asphyxiation was surely unlikely. Eight-week-olds couldn't roll.

Had the baby actually been in Becky's bed? A bottle of

wine. Accidental smothering: that would do it. But she'd denied co-sleeping. If she'd said they'd co-slept, she wouldn't have been charged.

Interesting. In her denial, she had incriminated herself.

Becky got a lawyer immediately. She no-commented like a pro, and asked for the Duty Solicitor. Keysha telephoned him: an affable, sporty young solicitor from Hove, called Pete. She had always liked him. After fractious initial interviews, sometimes, late at night, they would smoke outside together. Disgusting habit, she knew.

'Becky, if you were co-sleeping . . . charges wouldn't be pressed,' Keysha said in their next interview. 'Rolling-over smothering is very common.'

Becky's cheeks turned pink. 'I wasn't co-sleeping.'

'Tell me exactly how you found her.'

'On her back . . . white. Unresponsive.'

'How did the room look?'

'Just . . . normal.'

'No signs of anything? A discarded blanket? A sign she had rolled over, maybe?'

'No.'

'Was the door closed or open?'

'Closed.'

'Okay, and how was it when you entered the room? What do you remember?'

'It was dim. Um . . .'

'Did you alter anything in the room, anything at all?'

'No.'

'Did you move the blankets? Move the Moses basket?'

'I pulled the blankets off Layla to try and revive her.'

Pete became obstructive after that, rendering any questioning pointless, so Keysha decided to look at the papers properly, then recall Becky.

She took her time over the evidence, just the way she liked to. The phone. The Fitbit. The internet search history. She looked at them in turn. They were strange; they sat on the knife edge between normal and suspicious. Hadn't she had her fair share of desperate evenings when Lebron was little, after all? The texts she, herself, had sent . . .

She took them in turn.

The text messages to Marc at seven o'clock:

Becky: *Jesus, I'm worried about Layla. And me!*

Marc: *It always feels worse at the time. I still had a list from when Xander was small. Here it is. Feed. Change. Burp. Fart. Tired. Dirty nappy. Cold. Hot. Lonely. Teething. Pain. Overstimulated. Understimulated. Ill. No Reason. xx*

Marc: *Internet says if crying for no reason: sucking, swaddling, music, white noise, fresh air, bath, motion, massage. Take a break. You didn't ask for this, Samuel, when you took it on. I know that. xx*

A phone call to him at 7.31, lasting three minutes.

She turned to the Fitbit. Keysha's tech assistant had downloaded it all for her.

She clicked on the folder: data from 26 and 27 October. And there it was, a map of Becky's movements, right on the screen in front of her.

Keysha traced her finger across the map on the screen. She checked, then checked again: always double-check everything, her old boss used to say to her.

She sat back in the chair and folded her arms, looking up at the ceiling rose. How interesting this Becky was shaping up to be.

On the screen, there were two blue lines. One moving away from her house, one moving back four minutes later. She had been four hundred yards down the road at 7.45 p.m., after the texts to Marc and the phone call. Keysha brought up Google Maps and typed in the address, then zoomed out, her eyes scanning. Ah, there it was. A Londis. The Calpol, purchased immediately. It wasn't indicative of anything. It *wasn't*. And yet, somehow, in that sensory part of her gut that came to life in investigatory moments like this, it just *was*.

But, more than that, Keysha's gut cried out: Becky had said she hadn't left the house.

Becky had lied.

Becky had, Keysha suspected, left the baby alone.

Later that evening, she went to Londis to get their CCTV.

'I went to Londis for the Calpol, yes,' Becky said in the third interview.

Pete crossed and uncrossed his legs next to her. He shot Keysha a look.

And, finally, Keysha found the Google search. Two words, googled at 9.12 p.m.

Calpol + Overdose.

Those two condemning words.

Keysha brought up the medical evidence of the post-mortem on her screen. Blanket fibres in the lungs. Minor signs of a struggle. A bruise on the back of the ear lobe: an unusual location, almost always indicative of abuse.

But more than that: the time of death. Between eight and nine thirty. *Absolutely* no later, the pathologist said. It would be impossible. Becky hadn't even put the baby to bed by then. That was a strange thing for her to have said. Keysha suspected she'd been drunker than she said and had no idea of the timings, because Layla was found dead in the bedroom.

And then: the delay. Potentially twelve hours between death and calling the ambulance. Delay in seeking medical attention: the biggest red flag there could be.

It was always the way. They tried to fix it, to cover it up, concoct a story.

Becky had looked in on Layla in the small hours, by her own admission. Keysha gritted her teeth and shook her head. It was fabricated. To make her look attentive. But, of course she hadn't looked in. A few hours earlier, at between eight and nine thirty, Layla had died, and Becky had been the only person in the house.

And so, when perpetrators realized they couldn't cover it up, they faked it. A frantic 999 call, made hours after the event.

The texts.

The solo trip to Londis. The lie.

There would be more evidence, but that was enough.

Becky was charged with murder forty-eight hours later.

34

Martha

Calpol.

Overdose.

Two incriminating words. Or are they?

The more I think about it, the less sure I am. What would *I* google, if I were unsure of dosages? Maybe that, yes. There was no Calpol found in Layla's body. That is not how she died. For the prosecution, this is about intent: evidence that my sister couldn't cope. That she was looking for solutions.

I glance sideways at Scott, sitting here next to me but not speaking, not allowed to speak. I shift my body closer to his, feel the warmth coming off him. His jaw is quivering. He's trying not to cry. We link hands together in the public gallery.

They show the jury the Scenes of Crime Officer's photographs. I can't see them, and I don't want to, though I can imagine them. The Moses basket in the corner, on the floor. The blanket. The changing mat on top of Becky's old white chest of drawers that she's had since university. Flappy, the yellowing old cuddly toy, found on the floor.

The defence lawyer, Harriet, stands up. She doesn't say anything for a few moments. She looks down, shuffling her papers, but doesn't speak. Eventually, she looks up, and straight at Keysha.

'Detective Sergeant Thompson,' Harriet says, 'how many days passed between each of your interviews with the defendant?'

'Between the first and the second: seven. Between the second and the third: one.'

'I suppose, then, that Becky could easily have deleted those texts, and cleared her Fitbit?'

'Yes.'

'She could easily have already deleted a phone call.'

'Yes.'

'A text.'

'Yes.'

'A Google search, even.'

'Yes.'

'And she didn't.'

'Evidently not.'

'When you asked the defendant whether she had been to Londis, what did she say?'

'She admitted it.'

'*Admitted?* Or just answered honestly?'

'Well, she previously led me to believe she hadn't been anywhere—'

'In her first interview she gave you an extremely brief account of her evening, which did not revolve around going to get Calpol.'

'She omitted it entirely,' Keysha says smoothly.

'But as soon as she was asked, she told you?'

'Yes.'

'Now, if you don't mind, I'd like to take you to the Google search. It was exactly this: Calpol *plus* overdose.'

'Yes.'

'Detective Sergeant, if I wanted to know the limits of how much Calpol to give a baby, what might I google? I might google Calpol plus dosage limits. I might google Calpol instruction leaflet. But I might also google Calpol plus overdose.'

Keysha says nothing, merely stands and stares at the barrister. Then she folds her arms, very slowly.

'Witness is not a Google search engine expert,' Ellen says.

'Nothing further,' Harriet says.

Ellen stands up. Re-examination. The last-chance saloon to rescue the witness from things admitted in cross-examination.

'Detective, what might a criminal google if they were searching for ways to give a baby too much Calpol – a lethal dose?'

'Witness is not an expert,' Harriet says, leaping to her feet. Her cheeks are flushed. 'You just said that yourself,' she says to Ellen, looking childlike, hurt, almost.

'Please refrain from asking the witness to comment on what *criminals* might google,' the judge remarks benignly.

Keysha has said nothing, but the damage is done.

35

Martha

'Let's go for a walk or something,' Scott says to me in the foyer at lunchtime. His body language is off: his gaze downward, a hand to his throat. 'I can't deal with any more of this shit.'

Ethan is standing in the foyer, looking at us. No doubt he has views on the damning evidence, but I don't want to hear them.

'Okay,' I say to Scott, last night's conversation forgotten, subsumed into the swamp.

So what if we disagree about what happened to our daughter? It won't change anything, after all.

We stand on the steps together in the blazing heat.

'It's too hard to listen to,' he says. 'Like watching a car crash.' He runs a hand through his hair.

I think about what he said about Layla deserving better. He won't unpick the events of *the night of* out of respect for her. Somewhere, something quiet and soft and optimistic swells in my chest. He is a good person. A better person than me, maybe.

'There isn't even an accusation of a Calpol overdose,' I say quietly, unable to stop myself from going over it.

'I know. It doesn't make any sense. They're trying to establish evidence of a motive, I guess. That she was looking for ways to . . .'

I tune him out.

A couple of years ago, Becky and I met up one Sunday for a walk. It was early spring, and Marc had moved out a few months before. The weather was just beginning to warm up, and Becky was wearing a striped T-shirt. She brought a hand to her face to gather her hair – it was windy – and I saw her knuckles were grazed.

'Been fighting?' I said with a small laugh.

'Only with walls,' she said.

'Walls?'

'Marc and I had a row. He wanted to switch our weekends around because of a *curry with the lads* when he wouldn't switch with me so I could come to London with you.'

'You punched a wall?'

'I felt like an idiot, afterwards,' she said ruefully. 'I *did* wait until he'd gone before I did it.'

'Jesus,' I said.

I'd laughed it off with her at the time but, now, I think: *Would I have ever done that?*

No. I wouldn't.

Was it normal? I didn't know. That edge of hers, that temper.

I open my mouth to talk to Scott. But then he turns to me, and his blond hair catches the sun, and here we are, together, on the steps, and all I can think is: *He looks so much like Layla.* Strawberry blonde. The slightly turned-down mouth. The wide-set eyes.

The look of sadness that crossed both of their features, sometimes.

*

Scott heads back inside but I stay out on the steps, telling him I want five more minutes. I walk back to the seafront, my phone in my hand. I think about Marc's lack of alibi, about Theresa's testimony in which she wondered if Becky was alone, about Becky leaving Layla as she walked to Londis, and suddenly I know what I'm going to do.

My fingers find Marc's contact details on my phone and then I'm calling him before I can stop it. I shouldn't be. It is probably a crime. We are witnesses on opposing sides of a murder trial.

'You have no alibi,' I say when he answers.

'Martha?' he says.

'You have no alibi,' I say.

'For that night?' he says.

'Of course, for that night.'

'God, Martha,' he says. 'I was at home.'

'Did you go and help Becky? Were you there? Did you go over there when she was out?' I say, the words rushing out. 'Are you letting her take the rap?'

'*No*,' he says.

'Theresa said Becky didn't sound like she was alone.'

'Well, she was alone,' Marc says. 'Nobody came over. I won't listen to these questions, Martha. I've been asked too many times.' His voice is tight.

'By who?' I say.

And then, to my surprise, he hangs straight up, without answering me. Without explaining at all.

It is only later that I consider the very specific language he used. *Came* over. Nobody *came* over.

A word he would only use if he had been there himself.

36

Becky

Early evening, Wednesday 25 October

'Can I play, though?' Xander says.

'Yes, yes,' I say impatiently. I am looking after Layla until Friday, and it's only Wednesday evening. Martha left for Kos this afternoon. Scott was supposed to be coming back tomorrow but has decided to stay *two nights* at a *really useful* developers' conference. Thanks, Scott. No, no – you booze away, don't mind me. I wouldn't mind, really, except he didn't *ask*. He merely told me. As though I was the help. His text pinged in as I was unloading the shopping from Sainsbury's.

I drafted text after text in response:

Well, yes, actually, I do rather mind, and I think your crying daughter does, too, one said.

Or maybe: *Sure, my overtime rates are £500/hour.*

In the end, I sent them all to Marc, wordlessly. He rang me immediately, his voice deliciously low and amused. He didn't know what I was talking about. I tried to ignore the way that voice made me feel, tried not to look at the goosebumps that appeared on my arms.

'You gone mad, Samuel?' he said.

'I was going mad at you so I don't go mad at Scott,' I said. There was a pause.

'Ah,' he said, after a few seconds, no doubt replaying the text messages in his mind and working it all out. 'I see. Jesus, Sam. They're playing you.'

'He's a twat,' I said.

'Yes. What's he doing? They can't *both* be away? For another night? She's only eight weeks old.'

'Maybe he's sleeping around,' I said. I didn't mean to say it. It just slipped out; mindless speculation with no basis.

Marc paused. It was awkward.

God, why did I say that, after what I did to him?

'I doubt Scott gets around much,' Marc said.

I was grateful for his gentle humour. That humour carried me through years of ovulation kits, of pregnancy tests, bought needlessly and used before my period was even due. Once, Marc used one, too, just to cheer me up. 'There,' he'd said. 'We're both not pregnant.'

'No,' I said into the phone then, with a small smile. 'I doubt Scott does.'

'I was thinking I might say something to them,' he said to me. 'About this arrangement. If you'd like me to — if you feel you can't?'

'No, Marc,' I said. 'No, don't do that.'

'Her crying is annoying *me*, and I'm not even experiencing it,' he said. 'Maybe she's unwell.'

'She's not unwell. She's just . . .'

'I could come over. I can get babies to stop crying.'

'No, you could get *Xander* to stop crying, but I'm learning he was a pretty easy baby.'

'I bet I could,' Marc said.

I remembered him holding Layla one evening at Martha's. 'She's seriously loud,' he'd said to me, over the crying. 'Why won't she *stop*?'

I hmm-ed, instead of saying anything, and said goodnight.

Layla is crying in her bouncy chair. I jiggle it with my foot while I unpack Xander's lunch box, removing a blackening banana skin, but it does nothing to stop the crying.

'How long have I got?' Xander says, hanging around the door frame of the kitchen.

'One hour,' I say to him.

'You cut my hour short on Monday, by five minutes,' he says. 'Remember?'

'Did I?' I say vaguely. Layla's tears escalate, so I reach to get her out of the bouncer. I cast about for her blanket to swaddle her; something which occasionally soothes her.

'Yes! Because we were late for swimming? And then when we got back it was too late, because we had to have the oven chips?'

'Right, right,' I say. Children are so strange. The detail of it! Oven chips.

'One hour five minutes,' he says, looking at me.

He always used to be so eager to help me, to please. This exacting, relentless questioning is new. Perhaps he will grow up to be one of those combative journalists on TV. I shudder.

'Fine,' I say, disposing of a crust from his lunch box into the bin and holding Layla close to me. 'You should eat it all, you know. Crusts, too.'

Layla is still crying, her face turning purple. 'Stop shouting,' I say. 'There's nothing to be angry about.'

As Xander goes to leave the kitchen, he turns to me. 'I wish she wasn't crying,' he says.

'Me too. It's loud,' I snap.

'No. I just mean, I wish she wasn't sad.'

My eyes fill with tears. Like, here he is. My boy. My boy that I've known and loved for nine years. I stretch my arm out to him, and he comes over, briefly, and leans his body against mine in an imitation of a cuddle.

Layla continues to scream, one navy-blue eye making fleeting contact with mine until she looks away again. She looks just like Martha.

'One hour, five minutes,' I say, as Xander leaves the kitchen.

I set Layla down on the kitchen floor, even though it is tiled and cold. The bouncy chair doesn't work. Holding her doesn't work. She can lie there, swaddled, just for a moment. I'm ashamed that I feel angry. I feel angry with her.

I boil the kettle to cover her screams.

37

Martha

It's time for the medical experts. The people who weren't there at the time, but have *views* on what happened on that night, because my baby's body is merely evidence to them. A specimen, a slab of muscles and bones and blood.

There are two experts, one for the prosecution and one for the defence, paid hundreds of pounds each. Their words are expensive. I look across at Becky in the dock. She knows what happened, either through her own actions or because she knows what she didn't do. I contemplate her. After a few seconds, she must sense me looking, because she looks straight back. Our eyes meet. Neither of us smiles. Neither of us looks away, either. We just look at each other, holding each other's gaze, for a few seconds.

Scott clears his throat next to me – a soft, familiar *uh ah* – and he moves his hand to my knee. I stop looking at Becky and look down at his hand instead. I place mine on it and wonder whose Layla's would have grown to look more like. Scott's hands are small and square, with neat, rounded fingernails. Mine are long. 'Piano player's hands,' Mum always used to say, even though I was rubbish at music.

Scott and I met at a dinner party, which is far too grand

a term for what it really was. He was heartbroken, recently abandoned by an ex, and spent much of the evening talking about her. 'There was just no warning, you know?' he kept saying to me. Somehow, the friendly counselling I offered became something more and I remember thinking, one night, at age twenty-three: *God, you will do.*

I didn't think like that when he proposed. *He makes me happy*, I thought, picturing his freckled nose, the calm way he embarked upon tasks. He believed in equality, did half the housework, if not more. He never shouted at me, always asked me pleasantly how my day was. Yes. We were happy. We turned our mobile phones off every Wednesday evening – 'hump day' we called it – and cooked together. I'd fry the meat while he chopped the onions. The dishes got more elaborate – two courses, three – and the conversations deeper, less formal, as we lost self-conciousness, absorbed in the cooking. Every Thursday morning, I felt as though I had taken a holiday.

But then, two weeks after the wedding, the day we got back from our Sardinian honeymoon, I woke in the night and remembered that thought I'd once had: *You'll do.* I stared across at Scott in horror. His form was exactly the same. The same sleeping position. How could I have thought such a thing? I suppressed it, pushing it downwards like compacting soil.

It's funny how a single thought can come to define something – a marriage, a baby – but it has. *You'll do.* And now, even though years have passed, and what it was then isn't what it is now, I still repeat that phrase to myself, often, in the shower, or late at night when he's away. *You'll do.*

Did I mean it? Were we doomed from the start, or did

I once love him fully, completely? I don't have a clue. In the haze of what's happened since, and the grief, I find I don't know. But we were three, and now we are two: he is everything I have.

'The prosecution calls Julia Todd,' Ellen says.

Scott shifts on the seat – he's tall, with long legs, and the public gallery is cramped – and we watch the consultant paediatric and perinatal pathologist make her way to the witness box. The courtroom is hushed.

The pathologist.

The post-mortem.

The autopsy.

I grit my teeth and stay sitting. I have to be here. I have to find out the truth.

For Layla.

38

Julia Todd

Afternoon, Thursday 2 November

People were always surprised by what Julia did. She had stopped telling people, at parties and events. 'Housewife,' she sometimes said, letting Jim talk about his work in the library instead.

She spent her mornings writing up reports and her afternoons dissecting young babies. That was the truth of it. But how do you tell somebody that at a wine tasting event? It shocked people. It was, she thought, because she was fat and old and wore glasses. How dare she enjoy gardening, Merlot, reading the *Telegraph*, and the clean slice of a knife down the centre of a corpse?

She approached the metal table where that afternoon's baby was laid out for her.

She checked the record sheet. Layla. Layla's skin was a pale grey, translucent. Entirely normal, though Julia spent so much time with dead people that living people sometimes seemed unusually flushed and warm to her. The flutter of a pulse, the steady rising of a chest: how unusual, how *animal*, she sometimes thought.

She checked the ID and hospital number, then removed

the white Babygro. She put it on the other long, spare metal bench. The babies always seemed so small on the bench, like putting them in a huge bed, but Julia rather thought the notion of tiny beds in a morgue would be much more depressing, somehow.

Julia could see immediately that Layla was typical, but she checked anyway, for low-set ears, hernias. Abnormalities. She measured limbs. She worked quickly, but accurately, getting into the rhythm of her afternoon, like going swimming or riding a horse.

It was an odd case, she had learnt when reading the notes that morning. The baby brought to A&E by ambulance, found by her aunt, moonlighting as her nanny. Off the record, the consultant, Amanda, had told Julia she had a *bad gut feeling* about her. Amanda was always having bad gut feelings, though – one of life's overthinkers – so Julia didn't pay too much attention to that. She started checking over the body for injuries, hoping to find none. She supposed she was hoping for sudden infant death syndrome: a death for no reason at all. Tough on the parents, but the best outcome of a bad bunch, like trying to pick the best way to get food poisoning.

She deliberately hadn't checked the scans. She liked to look at the body, first, the primary source, and then the secondary sources, to see if she agreed with them. There was no substitute for a body.

She took a couple of steps back and looked at her. Not just in case she had missed something global in her careful, detailed inspection, but also because she wanted one last look at her as a baby, as a person, before she irrevocably changed her.

She turned her over. But what was that, on the back of her ear lobe? A blueish tinge. She looked at it from this way and that, then noted it. It could be a birthmark. Or it could be an injury. It was unusual to find a bruise on non-bony soft tissue. And it was very suspicious: babies couldn't bruise their own ear lobes.

Her hands stilled. There it was, halfway through the autopsy. Evidence of suffocation. Blood in the lungs. Fibres. *Shit*, Julia thought. *Shit.*

No matter how many times Julia saw such things, the hairs on the back of her neck stood to attention each and every time.

Right then, she thought grimly. *Now. We are looking at suffocation.*

She checked the scans. She couldn't wait. She leafed through them quickly. Nothing on the tox screen. Blood cultures normal.

She turned to the eyes. And there they were, as she expected. Retinal haemorrhages. Little, dotted red sunspots on the retina. Blood where there shouldn't be. She checked the mouth, too. Bruised gums.

It was one of the most obvious cases Julia had ever seen. And she was of the opinion that this could only mean one thing: Layla had died from being smothered, whether accidentally or deliberately, she couldn't tell. But she had died because she couldn't breathe.

Something had obstructed her airways.

Something or someone.

39

Martha

I can feel that my eyes have filmed over, the courtroom blurred, but I am not crying, not really. Julia's detached way of talking has helped to delude me. It is not Layla she's talking about. No. It is someone – *something* – else. We've had the funeral. It's gone. I'm glad I didn't know then what had happened to her in that post-mortem.

I try again – I've tried so often – to recall whether or not Layla had a birthmark behind her ear. I've looked at hundreds of photographs of her, but none capture the correct angle. I've gone over and over my memories of her, but I can't recall. I just can't. I am the world's worst mother.

'Thank you, Julia,' Ellen says. 'It is agreed between the parties that the experts who examined the pathologist's slides – the ophthalmologist as to her eye injuries, for example – will not be questioned. Their evidence is not in dispute.' Ellen says it more to the judge than anybody else. 'I wasn't sure, Your Honour, when to address that agreement with the jury.'

'That's fine, Ms Hendry.' He turns to the jury. 'Does everybody understand this? The evidence you are hearing has been agreed by other experts. We have deemed only Ms Todd's evidence to be relevant, because the other findings have confirmed her views, and we wished to avoid a parade of experts in the court, confusing matters.'

The jury nods at him, one uniform mass of heads.

'Okay then,' he says, turning back to Ellen. 'Please resume.'

'Alright, Julia. Almost done,' Ellen says. 'Let's just be clear about these findings.'

'Let's,' Julia says, pleasantly, as if they were discussing what they would eat for dinner that evening. 'I found evidence of asphyxia in Layla's post-mortem.'

'What evidence?'

'Each piece?'

'Yes,' Ellen says slowly, slightly exasperatedly, I think.

'She had blood in her lungs, together with fibres. She had little haemorrhages around her nose, mouth and eyes, which indicate struggling to breathe, or a physical struggle. She had bruised gums.'

'And the significance of this is . . .'

'They all point to asphyxia. And the bruising can indicate smothering.'

'Why?'

'Because pressure is applied.'

'Thank you,' Ellen says, clicking her pen and looking down at her notes. She lets the pause yawn. She lets the jury digest it.

'Let's talk about the bruised ear lobe.'

'Yes. Layla had a blueish mark on her ear lobe, at the back.'

'What can this be an indicator of?'

'Non-accidental injury. It's unusual for areas of soft tissue to bruise in this way. Layla wasn't mobile, so I would expect her carers to be aware of what had caused it.'

'What could a bruise there be caused by?'

'Not many things. Trauma. Inflicted by someone or something.'

'Thank you.'

Becky and I went through a phase, when we were sixteen and thirteen or so, of leaving notes for each other at home, on one of the pillars on our landing. They never said much of anything. They were more diary-like, about our days and our thoughts on school. I try to find something damning in the memory now. I am always doing this, these days. Re-examining the past in the light of our current situation. Were her notes angry? Were they sociopathic? Once, we were passing on the landing, me heading into the bathroom, she coming out with a towel over her hair, steam curling around her shoulders. I could see the water evaporating off her hot skin, like water in a hot frying pan. 'I owe you a note!' she said in that way of hers. There was nothing malicious about it. Nothing angry, nothing suspicious. She signed them with hearts next to her name.

I look across at her now.

'Now one more question. This is very important, Julia. The attending A&E doctor took baby Layla's temperature. You have seen that temperature, and you have also seen a report from the Scenes of Crime Officer who has not given oral evidence. That report shows the ambient room temperature, which is an agreed fact between the prosecution and defence.'

'Yes.'

'And so, in your report, tell us how you have arrived at the time of death in the case of Layla.'

'When you know the weight of the deceased, the ambient temperature of the environment they died in, and you have a temperature reading taken at some point after death, there is an algorithm called the Henssge nomogram which enables you to tell at what time the baby died.'

'And what time of death did your calculation give?'

'Between eight and nine thirty,' Julia says, pushing her glasses up her nose. 'It's impossible for it to be after nine forty.'

'Why?'

'Because of the differential between the ambient temperature of the bedroom and Layla's temperature on arrival at A&E. It places the time of death between eight and nine thirty, but it would be impossible to be later.'

'How sure are you?'

'One hundred per cent. There is no way Layla was alive after nine thirty, nine forty.'

'And at between eight and nine thirty only Becky was in charge of Layla,' Ellen says to the jury. 'Becky *alone*.'

'Okay,' Julia says.

'And ten past nine was right after the neighbour heard the defendant shout at the baby,' Ellen says.

'That's hearsay,' Harriet objects.

'Thank you. Nothing further.' Ellen smiles at Julia and ignores Harriet: they're old pals.

Harriet stands up. She seems about to speak, then stops, running a finger down a sheet of paper in a binder and taking a breath.

'Ms Todd,' she says. 'I only have a few questions.' Her voice is strong, loud, in the courtroom, but she wipes her brow.

I wonder what Becky's said to her.

'The bruise. What else could this be?'

'A congenital mark called a Mongolian blue spot. It's a birthmark.'

'Is there any way to tell whether it's a bruise or this blue spot?'

'Not now Layla is deceased,' Julia says, bowing her head. 'A bruise would fade if she were living. A birthmark wouldn't.'

'And without photos of the back of Layla's ear, or recollection from the parents – who say they don't know, can't remember, understandably – it's impossible to say. And it's impossible for you to say, isn't it?'

'Yes.'

'You say the toxicology screen was normal?'

'Yes.'

'There was no evidence of Calpol's active ingredient, paracetamol, in Layla's bloodstream?'

'No, none.'

'And so certainly not an overdose?'

'No.'

'And finally, if Layla had somehow rolled over and became stuck in the Moses basket . . . if she hadn't been able to turn her head . . . would her injuries look like this? The bleeding around the eyes, nose and mouth? The bruised gums?'

'Yes. Maybe. It's very hard to distinguish between accidental and homicidal smothering. But these do indicate . . . pressure applied.'

'Nothing more from me, then,' Harriet says, but she remains standing, allowing Julia's words to linger in the courtroom.

Impossible to tell. It could be a horrible, tragic accident that we will never understand.

It is over. The pathologist is led out by the usher.

I look straight at Becky. I'm not watching her, as I have been for the rest of this case, instead just exchanging a glance with her, as is natural to me, to us.

She is turning her head to look at me at the same time and our eyes meet. And there it is. That understanding. She widens her eyes and—

No. I cannot do this. I cannot connect with her. Not until I know. I think of my notes that I hide from Scott, back at the flat. Reams and reams, copied out from the internet, about wrongly accused women: women whose babies died for no reason, whose babies had accidents. Women released from prison years later, exonerated but unbearably damaged. But that's not her. Not yet. I can't exchange glances with her like this, and certainly not in open court. But I can still feel her gaze on me and I can't help but dart a glance up again. God. She looks awful.

What's her barrister going to do about it? What's their explanation for this damning evidence that's been given? There was blood where it shouldn't have been in my baby's body. Somebody made that happen to my baby's tiny eyes, nose and mouth that I grew inside myself, every single cell.

The bruised gums.

The fibres in her lungs.

The overheard shouting.

Like finding the knife, the body, and Becky's DNA on the fucking handle. How could it be an accident? How could it not be Becky?

And yet, against all the odds, something seems to rear up in my gut and speak: *It wasn't Becky.*

There was somebody else there that night. I think back to what Marc said: *came over.*

She wasn't alone. He was there.

I need to see him.

40

Becky

One. Two. Three. Four. Five.

I promise myself I will go back in again when I get to fifty. I'm sitting in my car. Well, hiding in my car, really.

I don't understand why it is like this. Xander was such a fantastic baby. The *judgement* I felt towards other women, women whose babies were non-sleepers, whose babies wouldn't accept dummies, bottles, who wouldn't be weaned. Xander was easy; he did all of that. And, even then, it was too hard for me and Marc. We drifted apart. But then I cheated, severing us entirely from each other.

We ended in separation, like so many couples before us. I remember his clear blue eyes meeting mine as we said our wedding vows. I would've put money on us. We used to laugh so much. That was the healthiest way through life, we agreed.

But then he changed. Not fully. But a little bit. Some of the time. He developed an edge which I'd never seen before. 'Get to your bedroom and out of my sight,' he once said to Xander, after he'd discovered Xander had lied about having spent his pocket money on fidget spinners. It hadn't been fair, and I'd told him as much, and he'd thumped the arm of the sofa, not looking at me, his jaw set. I'd opened a bottle of wine that night. That beautiful tannin lining my mouth, staining my lips. And, later, that lovely numbing effect.

Layla is upstairs, crying, and I am in the car, breathing. It's 4.00 p.m. and Xander is with his dad after school. I have tried everything with her. I googled it.

Wind.

Food.

Cold.

Hot.

Tired.

The internet no longer offers up answers. The search results are all purple, not blue, already clicked on. I haven't asked Martha. Not while she's in Kos. I could kill bloody Scott for leaving her with me for a second night, though I sent him a breezy text back.

Why am I like this? I wish I was one of those people who could say, coolly, 'No, that doesn't work for me.' No explanation. No second-guessing. No self-flagellation. But I'm not. I'm just not.

My phone beeps. It's Marc.

Samuel, his text begins. *How you getting on?*

I smile at that. He has called me Samuel for years. Martha and Scott find it bizarre, always exchange glances when Marc uses that special name that has its roots in the time when we used to love each other.

It originated when we were watching *University Challenge.* We liked to smirk at the nerdy team members. 'Their mothers didn't love them,' Marc would say. We would hoot with laughter at their geeky sweaters and milk-bottle glasses.

Anyway, at the precise moment Paxman asked, 'Which Beckett served as a member of parliament for Whitby from 1906?' Marc said, 'Drink?' and I said, 'Samuel.'

How we laughed. 'Sorry, drink, Samuel?' Marc said, and we chuckled some more. The answer wasn't even Samuel Beckett; it was Gervase Beckett – Samuel Beckett was a *ridiculous* guess. He was an Irish writer who lived in Paris, not a Whitby MP! That just made us laugh even more.

I don't think Marc has ever called me anything else since. Not even when it all unravelled, when we forgot to kiss each other properly – dry kisses, perfunctory kisses before work – and forgot to be Marc and Becky, not Xander's parents. I was still Samuel, then, to him. Even the day he left, he said, ''Bye, Samuel,' in this sad, mournful way that I've never forgotten.

Alright, I reply to him now, but nothing more.

There's no time. Besides, he's just checking in with me, I think. I hover on his name, wanting to call him. To say, 'I love it when you call me Samuel.' To say, 'I miss you, thanks for checking up on me.' But I can't. No matter how nice he is now, he won't want to hear it. The romance is over. Those laughs, that life, snuffed out. By me. Because of me. I'm lucky we can even remain friends. That he remains nice *at all* after what I did.

I glance up at the darkened bedroom window where I know Layla is still crying, still bright red, still writhing around.

I have to go back in, soon. I didn't ask for this, didn't

know what it would involve, but here we are. There's no point being furious about it, I tell myself. But nevertheless, fury burns through my veins.

I'm angry at myself. But I'm also angry with her.

With Layla. For crying.

It's irrational, but it's true.

Forty-eight, forty-nine, fifty.

41

Martha

There is a paediatric neurosurgeon up next. She is wearing a blazer which is the exact colour Layla's cheeks used to be: the pale blush of an apricot.

'Please state your name for the court,' Ellen says.

'Helena Armstrong.'

'And what is your job?'

'I'm a consultant paediatric neurosurgeon.'

'And how many years' experience do you have?'

'Twenty,' Helena says.

She folds her arms and tilts her head to the side. She doesn't look forty-five to fifty. She barely looks thirty-five.

'Seven as a consultant.' She reaches and takes a sip from the plastic cup of water on the edge of the witness box.

Her hands are steady. She is utterly used to this, I can tell.

Ellen is staring down at her papers. This is her moment, after all. This medical evidence is what the case turns on. This is her proof.

'Let's take it injury by injury,' Ellen says to her witness.

I feel my mouth filling with saliva.

'Okay,' Helena says.

A paediatric neurosurgeon. I can hardly imagine what her life is like.

'The pathologist told us that Layla had haemorrhages around her nose and mouth. Blood in her lungs, together with fibres. And bruised gums.'

'Yes, she did have those, according to the scans and reports I have seen.'

'And why is that so unusual, Ms Armstrong?'

'If there is blood around the nose and mouth, it indicates that the baby was struggling for breath, or perhaps even struggling hard against somebody who was inflicting harm. When strained, veins and arteries burst. The same happens in the lungs, with forced attempts to breathe before death. The bruised gums indicate force.'

'Force?'

'Yes. The bruised gums are indicative of Layla perhaps having had something applied quite tightly across her nose and mouth.'

'I see. So, in your expert opinion, Layla died from asphyxiation. But do you have a view as to whether this was accidental or deliberate?'

'It looks deliberate to me. The bruising is suspicious. The haemorrhages could be down to the body struggling for breath, or down to violence being inflicted on Layla. It's impossible to tell.' She indicates the folder again. 'I have replicated the scans.'

'Please turn to pages thirteen and fourteen, jury,' Ellen says.

'Here are Layla's MRI scans, performed after she died,' Helena says. 'You can see the blood in her lungs very clearly: the white spots on the scans. Likewise the white lines on the retinas, which indicate retinal haemorrhages.'

'Thank you,' Ellen says. 'How sure are you that these

injuries are attributed to deliberate and not accidental smothering?'

'With the bruised gums, as sure as I can be.'

I swallow the saliva.

What was I doing in Kos, the moment it happened?

At 8.30 p.m., 9.00 p.m., 9.30 p.m. The experts are all sure. It was between 8.00 p.m. and 9.30 p.m.

Asleep, perhaps. Perhaps I was removing my make-up in methodical swipes. A mother, becoming an ex-mother, in one unknowing motion.

'So it is not possible that, for example, the baby rolled and became trapped somehow in the Moses basket?'

'Layla was only eight weeks old. She hadn't rolled over yet. So I would be surprised by that.'

'Thank you.'

'And now to the bruising on her ear lobe.'

'Yes.'

'Why is that unusual?'

'It's very difficult to bruise a baby's ear lobe. It is not bony, and so it is not likely to be bumped. It therefore raises red flags to medics.'

'Why?'

'It's consistent with signs of abuse. Deliberate trauma. Pinching.'

Pinching.

'Thank you. And finally. The pathologist has timed the death as occurring at around eight or nine at night. Is that consistent with what you have read?'

'I have no reason to dispute that. Yes.'

'And would Layla have died instantly, following the suffocation?'

'Yes.'

'Nothing further,' Ellen says.

Harriet stands up, looking contemplative. Her eyes are narrowed and she upends her pen and taps the end of it on the desk until it clicks off, and then on again. The noise seems to echo in the courtroom.

'Would retinal haemorrhages be present in an accidental smothering?'

'Yes, probably. But not always.'

'Would bleeding in the lungs?'

'Yes.'

'Bleeding in the skin surrounding the mouth and lips?'

'Yes, sometimes.'

'Bruised gums?'

'Not always.'

'Sometimes?'

'Yes.'

'Thank you. Is it not, also, possible that some of these injuries – the retinal haemorrhages, for example – are *incidental* findings, left over from, say, if not accidental smothering, then a traumatic birth?'

'Possible, but unlikely.'

'So with that possibility, we cannot be certain that this baby was smothered at all, either accidentally or on purpose. There are plenty of explanations.'

Helena huffs. 'I can't answer that.'

'I think you have to,' Harriet says, raising her eyebrows to the judge.

He makes a motion with his hand. 'Ms Armstrong, an answer to this is both helpful and necessary,' he says.

She pauses, then says slowly, 'I would like to think I am as certain as I can be.'

'Nothing further.'

Ellen stands back up. 'If you had to say, in terms of likelihood, whether these injuries were more consistent with accidental or homicidal smothering, which would you say?'

'Homicidal.'

'Thank you.'

'We'll take a break there,' the judge says.

I thought he might intend this for Becky's benefit, even though she's been sitting there impassively, her chest rising and falling, but he's looking across at me and Scott.

'We only have one more witness,' Ellen says. 'Then the prosecution can close.'

The judge looks across at us, over his glasses, and raises his eyebrows. He reaches a hand up to scratch underneath his wig. It must be itchy in the heat.

I look at Scott. His eyes are wide, panicked, even though he has always suspected Layla's death was not accidental. He looks at me, raising his eyebrows, wondering if we can go on. I lift a hand, which is supposed to mean *go ahead*, but the judge remains looking at me, forcing me to speak.

'Please, go on,' I say, my voice sounding loud and confident.

I must look calm on the outside, but I'm not. Marc's name has been running through my mind repeatedly as I sit in the public gallery.

I know what I'm going to do. I have decided. I am going to speak to Ellen about him. I'm going to tell her that he has no alibi. Perhaps I can speak to her after this next witness. Tell her about Marc. Maybe there'll be an opportunity.

'The prosecution calls Jane Ghale.'

After a few moments, a small, bent-over woman arrives in the court, brought in by the usher.

'Please state your name for the record,' Ellen says.

'Jane Ghale.'

She is sworn in and confirms she is a radiologist and has been for ten years.

'Have you reviewed the MRI scans of Layla Blackwater?'

'I have.'

'Please talk us through them. Jury, please turn to pages thirteen and fourteen again for the scans.'

Jane reaches forward and holds two slides up, showing my baby's chest. 'The white area indicates bleeding.'

It looks like a cloud over Layla's lungs.

'Is there any doubt about what that represents?'

'No. It represents blood.'

'Thank you, nothing further,' Ellen says.

'Nothing from me,' Harriet says.

Ellen rises again, tugging at her robes which keep slipping down over her shoulders. 'The prosecution rests,' she says.

And just like that, the onslaught of the State is over. There is no more. It didn't end with a revelation or a bang. Just a radiologist confirming in a small voice what we all already knew.

I look up at the ceiling behind the dock where Becky sits and think about it all.

The trip to Londis, leaving my baby alone in that house.

The Google search.

The neighbours overhearing the shouting, right before the exact time of death.

Alison, Forrest and Ralph's mother, seeing Becky grey and shaking, the house eerily silent behind her, when we all knew that Layla cried so much, all the time.

And the medics, of course. Convinced that it couldn't have been an accident, not feasibly.

Layla could *only* have died during that evening. That evening when Becky was alone with her.

It is a compelling case.

I glance at the jury. They're shuffling in their seats, at the halfway point, as they wait for direction from the judge. Would I convict, if I were seated there, and not here? If the victim wasn't my baby, and if the defendant wasn't my sister? It is only halfway through the case – the prosecution is at its strongest, like the winter solstice, night at its longest – but I cannot ignore the voice inside me that says: *Of course I would.* It's like Scott said: there is no other explanation. The only way she is innocent is if we shrug our shoulders and pin our hopes on spontaneous, unexplained bleeding, on coincidence, conjecture.

Becky's defence is that she has no defence at all. She doesn't know, can't explain. That isn't a defence. They have no explanation, only the holes in the prosecution's explanation. And as for the rest, the non-medical evidence, they'll say: *But she's a good person.* What defence is this? It is nothing. There is no defence case. It is only: *Not that.* A finger pointed at the prosecution. It was an accident, but not one Becky caused: she admitted that in her police interview. If it wasn't a tragic, co-sleeping accident, then what was it?

Murder.

Scott is right. He is always right; the most reasonable person in my life. My sounding board, my voice of reason.

I look across at my sister in the dock, her head bowed as the lawyers shuffle their papers, as the judge takes stock, as the players prepare to metaphorically switch sides. I look at her and agree with Scott. Here was a smothered baby. And here was the person looking after her. She must know. She must know what happened. She must know more than me, anyway.

'I think we should leave it there for today,' the judge says. He looks at the digital clock on the table down below him, its giant numbers glowing red. 'We've made very good time thanks to the meticulous preparation, prompt witnesses and the jury's flawless attendance. We'll be looking to conclude early next week. We can commence the defence case in the morning. Everybody fresh.' He directs a kindly smile my way.

I linger and see the security guard releasing Becky from the dock. He hands her over to an usher. She waits obediently at the door, clearly schooled in what to do, and only moves when the usher motions her out. She's bailed. Not in custody. She's not dangerous, surely. But then I think of Xander, moved into Marc's house, her contact with him supervised by our own parents, and I wonder. Social Services must think she is dangerous. The State does, too. Is it only me who doesn't?

I look at her slim wrists, at her ribcage visible at the top of her thin, open-necked shirt. If she is convicted, what will I think then? Will she transform, in the dock, as she is sentenced? Into my sister, the murderer? I can't imagine it. I just can't. Perhaps I will always believe her.

'Shall we go?' Scott murmurs to me.

I'm watching the barristers. Ellen leaves first. My eyes track her across the courtroom and out the door. Through the little glass window in the wood, I see her disappear into a meeting room opposite the courtroom.

'Yeah,' I say.

The room is clearing out around us. The jury is looking pleased with their early finish, off to enjoy the sun and put loads of washing on and collect their children from school, probably. Becky's team has closed around her and escorts her out. She's got a tan line around her neck that I spot as she reaches to pull open the door. She must have been outside a lot. *It's only sun*, I tell myself. You can sit in the sun but still be miserable.

It's just the two of us, now, in here together, looking at it all. The dock. The royal coat of arms. The places where the jury sit.

All of it.

Layla's life.

Her little fat fists that gripped my hand during night feeds, her dark, soulful eyes that looked into mine as she suckled, her golden hair that smelt so good, like cooking biscuits and lavender and summer days. Those are all gone. Instead, we have juries and witnesses and experts' reports about haemorrhages.

The detritus of a life.

I tell Scott to go home without me. He looks surprised, for a second, then obliges. He doesn't question it any more. He doesn't try to maintain a sense of togetherness. Neither of us does.

I wait in the foyer, listening for the sweep of Ellen's robes.

She arrives out of the meeting room after ten minutes and I hover nearby, looking vague, as though I might be waiting for somebody, or looking for the vending machines.

She catches my eye, briefly, and I think I see something sympathetic behind her professional, neutral expression.

'Ellen, I . . .' I say softly to her.

She stops fussing with her briefcase and looks at me.

'I was thinking – listen. About . . . about Becky's husband.'

'Marc,' Ellen says.

'Yes.'

'Look, I'm just wondering . . . has anyone ever looked into his alibi, for that night? Really looked?' I swallow, not saying I've asked him, not admitting that. Trying to forget it, but not able to, either. Those words he used. *Came over.*

'Marc's alibi?' she says. The expression on her face is suspicious, irritated. She looks as though she is about to tell me to stop, to let her do her job. That I am inappropriate. But, at the last moment, she seems to take in my skinny form, my thinning hair, and she looks at me kindly, instead. 'I'll look into that,' she says to me. 'Tonight.'

'Thank you,' I whisper. 'Thank you.'

42

Martha

When I walk through the door of the flat, Scott doesn't look at me.

He sits on one of the armchairs covered in fabric from India and I sit on the sofa and wonder why the flat feels so cold as summer starts to wane. We watch the sea in the distance, still lit up by the sun. Even though it's just there, it's four storeys down, and behind a glass wall. It may as well just be a big flat-screen television tuned permanently to the seascape. People are swimming in it, some paddling at the edge, some in wetsuits, their strokes confident and strong.

'I'm going out,' Scott says.

Most evenings from late spring to early autumn, he would go to his patch of land and harvest it. This time of year we would be looking forward to blackberries and apricots. Boxes of them, every evening. They were always fresh and sweet. Scott would fold his lips in on each other as he brought them in, otherwise his proud smile would show. He's been going more, lately, but not bringing any fruit back with him. He's maintaining the status quo, I guess. Going through the motions.

'Please don't do any research. It's not good for you.'

'Sorry?' I say sharply.

'No more research. It's time to . . . we need to . . . we need to accept it.'

'Why do you care if I research it or not?'

'I just don't think it's good for you . . .' He pauses, and looks at me sympathetically, as if I were a mad person. 'Listen, anyway. At the land, I've been working on—'

'Can you not? Can you just not? I don't even really like fruit, actually.' The words are out of my mouth before I can stop them, and I see Scott's face fall. 'I've been pretending to,' I add spitefully.

It's the truth, but it's not the time to tell it. It's not about the fruit. I know that. It's about what he said. *We need to accept it.* But how can we? How can we ever?

'Okay,' he says. His tone is so measured, always controlled. 'Whatever.' It's not dismissive. It's weary. Sad, even.

'Sorry,' I say. He must think me a diva. Who rejects presents from their spouse, after years and years of receiving them silently, complicitly? 'I just . . . I didn't want to tell you.'

He walks past me, pulling his shoes out of the hall cupboard. 'Don't worry,' he says wearily. 'I'm going anyway.' He reaches towards me, just slightly. But when I don't take his hand, he lets it drop to his side. He lingers for just a second, looking at me. 'Love you,' he says softly, so quietly I have to strain to hear it.

'Same,' I say back.

I'm blinded, momentarily, by a memory of wandering the streets of Verona with him, queueing up to see the Juliet balcony with dripping ice creams clenched in our hands. He laughingly licked the wafer cone of mine, and

I swatted him away. We were happy. We *were*. Perhaps it is just grief, my mind marinating in negativity, affecting everything, colouring it black.

'I mean it,' I say to him.

He gives me a quick, warm smile, and then the door closes softly behind him, leaving the flat in silence.

He texted me the day after the dinner party at which we first met. *It was nice chatting*, he said. *It really helped*. And so it went. It wasn't so much the beginning of a relationship as a general moulding together. I had just started teaching, in my NQ year. He had been a teacher, too, for two years, but had just left to do a Masters in programming. We used to work together, in my kitchen and his, late into the night. I liked the way he worked. The calm, quiet tidiness. The single desk lamp. Muzak that he found on streaming sites. We were study buddies, best friends, and then more. There was no moment. It was inevitable, like the quiet, calm movement of the tide up the beach.

Staring now as I walk into our bedroom and run my fingers over his rows of neatly hung shirts, I wonder: *Shouldn't it be ... something more?* The kind of something that Becky and Marc had. The thoughts rise up but, methodically, I push them back down again. They will not come in here. They are not welcome.

He hasn't brought a single piece of fruit back from his land recently. I pause at the window, watching his car headlights as he drives away into the twilight. Is he really going there? Who knows? I can't ask him. It would be barbed and loaded. But he's been there more and more. Perhaps he's just sitting, on his land, not tending the vegetables, not doing anything. Just sitting, letting them die.

I go and get my notepad and look at it.

Marc. He would do anything for Becky. Give her an alibi. Cover up a murder. He would help her, in her hour of need. Maybe he hated our arrangement. Maybe he got frustrated with Layla himself, and her constant crying. He was temperamental, too. Quick to anger. Maybe he resented Layla. They had wanted another child. Maybe it's that: plain old jealousy. Maybe all of it, put together, tipped him over the edge.

I go for a drive. My muscle memory takes me naturally to Becky's. How many times have I driven here? Hundreds, it must be, over the years. Thousands. The car idles as I stop outside Becky's. The night is warm and I wind down the window to let in the air. It's clear here, not salty like the gritty sea air near my flat, but fresh and soft against my shoulders.

I rest my head against the seat and survey the house. It sits empty, now, virtually since *the night of*, the black windows ghoulish-looking in the darkening evening. Becky and Xander left, like evacuees, to separate locations. He to Marc. She, home, to Mum and Dad. I stare at the garden gate, the three steps up to Becky's front door, then my gaze trails upwards to the bedroom window.

That's where it happened. Up in that room, the furthest on the left.

I get out of my car, pulling my jacket around me.

I stand on the pavement and look at the window. What happened in there? Only Becky and Layla know for certain.

Layla.

She was small when born: just six pounds, dead on, as if

maybe she intended to be an exacting person – my favourite kind. Her arms would for ever be disappearing up the sleeves of her Babygros. It frustrated me. I was trying to mould her to a fixed world, like, *This is how we do things, we wear our sleeves down to our wrists.* But she had other ideas. Once, when her hand had disappeared up again, she reached out and grasped my finger through the fabric, and looked at me. It felt warm and deliberate, that clutch of hers.

I try to remember those moments, standing here, now, outside the spot where she died. I try to forget the moments when I was bored, or frustrated. There were so many of them. That time, on a coach, when she vomited up all of the milk it had taken me three hours to express. The times when she just wanted to be held. The love I felt for her hid behind it all – like a stunning view from a house, appreciated at first, and then ignored. The main emotions I felt had been frustration, boredom and guilt. My nipples hurt, until I stopped breastfeeding, and then they dribbled milk in my bra, leaving impressions like pale inkblots. The love somehow did not come to the forefront like it should have. Perhaps I needed time. I don't know.

How could Scott have left her? Anger rises up through me, but I try to suppress it. How could *I* have left her?

Whatever happened with Becky, it wouldn't have happened if I had been there. I would never have slept until 8.00 a.m. like Becky did. If I had loved my baby more – if the love had been more prominent, like a spice in a dish that overwhelms everything else – I wouldn't have been able to leave her, would I? I would not have gone to Kos.

I would not have begrudged the impact she had on my life. I would not have been frustrated by her tears and her dirty nappies and the insatiable hunger of those early days, those cluster feeds. If I had been a better mother. If I had loved her better.

'You have to be here,' my reliable gap-year student, Ami, said to me on the phone one day in mid-October. 'A property's come up.' She was still getting the emails, even though she was ex-acting CEO of Stop Gap and now at Warwick University studying history. 'I called up about it.'

'What?' I said.

'There's a premises,' she said. 'It's just come up. There's a viewing this weekend. You can buy it with the grant. It has – Jesus. It has, like, forty rooms.'

'How much is it?'

She gave me a number. We could afford it.

I was standing in the bedroom, a hand dangling into Layla's Moses basket. Only, instead of seeing her navy-blue eyes, I saw the other children's. Slim cheeks, with little hollows. Big brown eyes.

'What is it?'

'An old hotel. The government owns it. They'll sell it to us. They were keen, on the phone. I pretended to be you.'

'Where is it?'

'Right next to the fish market. You'd hardly have to move. But you should see it. Martha, you should see it.'

A few moments later, she sent me a photograph. It wasn't the venue that did it; it was her dedication. Nineteen, a fresher at university, and there she was overseeing commercial property purchases for me. Stepping in as CEO. Let alone the rest.

'Can I just do it remotely?' I said.

'Well, no, it's fine. I could go. In my reading week. It's just . . .'

'God, no. Don't do that.'

Could I go, and see it, secure it, buy it? Get someone in to fit it out?

'You need to be there to sign. You have to physically sign the deeds.'

Shit. The signatures. Of course.

I stared out of the window, not looking at Layla. I could go for two nights. Just two. Sign for the premises. Make sure everything was okay. Get it sorted, then hire someone once I was back home. Somebody who could oversee it properly, once the premises were sorted.

'There's already interest in it. Because it's at such a discount.'

It would be fine. It was five hours away. She had been good for Becky last week. Quiet, apparently. My breasts ached, but that was my problem, not hers. I'd set it up, secure it, and be back before she knew I had gone. It would be fine. It was the right thing to do. She was fine, and they . . . those children weren't.

Layla's eyes met mine and a slow smile spread across her features. Her first ever smile. My baby. She'd be safe and warm, here, with Becky. And I would go to help them. The other children. They needed me. They had nobody for them. That's what I thought then. Looking back, now, I don't recognize that Martha, that decision I made. Layla needed me more than anybody could. Because I was her mother.

But if it had never happened, if she had lived, I know I would never be thinking these thoughts. I would have been helping the children in Kos, and would have returned to my own family. It would have been lauded, that I set up a charity *and* raised my child.

Hindsight.

'Let me ask Becky,' I said.

I flew out to see the premises. I signed the document early, my signature a familiar scrawl. The date was stamped next to it: 27/10.

It is the day she was found dead. The day she was declared dead in A&E, even though she died on the twenty-sixth. Her death certificate, and that dated signature, all bound up together.

Evidence of their own. That I cared about other children more than my own.

My focus shifts back to Becky's house again. To the window of the room in which it happened.

Somebody knows the truth, I find myself thinking. Becky or Marc or Becky's neighbour . . .

I picture each scenario.

Marc, letting himself into her house, snuffing out my baby's life so callously, just like that.

Becky, accidentally killing my child, and asking for help.

The images before me, the theories in my mind, are all wrong. Or are they? Maybe almost all of them are absurd . . . but maybe *one* of them is correct. I just need to find the right one.

The barrister will sort it, I tell myself.

But I know I'm going to confront Marc again. I have

to. And then, if not Marc ... Becky. Even though it is illegal. Even though it isn't right.

I have to do it.

For Layla.

The bed is already warm from Scott's body by the time I get into it, much, much later.

43

Judge Christopher Matthews, QC

Christopher takes a wander down to the beach. It will be Thursday tomorrow. The trial will end early next week. *It will be a long jury deliberation*, he thinks. All that medical evidence.

He hates long deliberations. He can't settle to reading anything new, waiting for a jury to return a verdict. Other judges begin new cases, but not him. He waits like a caged lion pacing its cell. The jury often send questions, or notes asking for a majority direction, and every time one comes through he hopes it will be the verdict and he will be able to move on, and start his next case.

Sometimes, they take days and days; over a week, once.

He can't imagine how Becky, the defendant, feels.

The prosecution has been sure of itself, moving through the waters of the case like a cruise ship, determined in its direction. The defence has been trying to stop it, to manoeuvre it, but it has been as ineffectual as a person tugging on a rope, trying to get a 200,000-tonne ship to change course. He feels sorry for Ms Smith, the defence barrister. She is good, but she doesn't have anything to work with. Maybe there'll be a last-minute miracle, like in the movies.

He doubts it.

He decided, last night in bed when he couldn't sleep, that she had probably done it. They almost always have, after all. She should just say she rolled over on to the baby in her sleep. She'd get off.

Why doesn't she? Indeed.

He pauses for thought. This is strange. He is sure she's smart. Maybe she did it in some other way. Or maybe it really *was* someone else, somehow.

But she doesn't look guilty. She just doesn't.

He sits on his favourite wide, flat rock and watches the sea turn itself over. As always, his mind roams to Sadie, and the events just before she left him. She now lives in a tiny flat, in Hove, quite near to the defendant, actually. She didn't take the dog with her. She never even comes to see him.

He and Sadie divorced eighteen months ago. Irreconcilable differences. The usual. He was distant. He didn't care about her job, only his.

He picks a pebble up and throws it into the surf. Then he brings his mobile phone out – an old, second-hand thing – and scrolls down to her number. Something about this case has got under his skin. He thinks it is the sisters. The way they look at each other all the time across the courtroom. The fact that the mother, Martha, is there at all, watching proceedings, clearly hoping for a not guilty verdict.

The love, he guesses. That's what it is.

They all loved each other, until they were splintered apart.

Thursday

Defence

44

Martha

'Martha—' the reporter says.

I turn and see her familiar face. Her curly hair is clipped back. She has a larger microphone, I think, and she thrusts it towards me more confidently, as though I might be about to speak, today, when I haven't all week.

'Have you ever asked your sister whether she did it?'

It's time for the defence.

'The defence calls Marc Burrows,' Harriet says.

There is no defence speech. No pacing barrister like on the television, posing thoughtfully like a catwalk model. Instead, there's a shuffling of papers, a clearing of the judge's throat, and then Marc enters the witness box. Just like that. We've gone from prosecution to defence, the wind has changed direction, the interval is over. And here we are. Marc. Finally, his evidence will be examined, scrutinized.

We might find an answer.

And, if we don't, then afterwards ... I am going to find him.

We saw him out in the foyer, waiting for his turn in the witness box. We didn't greet him. We know not to *interfere* with witnesses, despite my earlier call to Marc, despite my plans, but there's no Crown Prosecution Service leaflet on what happens when every single witness is somebody you know.

Neighbours.

Acquaintances.

Friends of friends.

Relatives.

When the key defence witness is your ex-brother-in-law. When the defendant over there – already in the dock as we enter the court – is your sister.

'I do solemnly and sincerely and truly declare and affirm that the evidence I shall give shall be the truth, the whole truth and nothing but the truth,' Marc says.

I close my eyes against his words. I had forgotten his easy manner, his simple, straightforward gaze.

He dips his head a little, then raises it, and looks directly at Becky.

Ex-lovers: one in the witness box, one in the dock.

'Mr Burrows,' Harriet says, 'could you explain how you know the defendant?'

'I am her ex-partner.'

'When you're ready, please tell us in your own words what you remember about the night of the 26th of October.'

Goosebumps appear on my arms.

This is it.

45

Marc Burrows

It was ingenious. The television power cable was long enough to stretch out into the hallway, and he had balanced the screen on the bottom step of the stairs, facing him. He had reluctantly agreed to lay this carpet out of hours, but he hadn't checked the fixtures. His stomach dropped when he saw the schedule on Sky Sports – plenty of action in the European leagues – and he considered cancelling. But what a decision showing up had turned out to be. It took ninety minutes to fit a carpet. He had a perfect view of the football. And he was being paid to bloody watch it.

His phone beeped at seven o'clock just as the underlay was down and Real Sociedad had scored. He paused, hands on his hips, standing in the centre of the room, to watch the replay. Decent finish, but where was the marking?

He turned away from the television and got out his phone. Becky.

Jesus, I'm worried about Layla. And me!

This baby situation. It was madness. Utter madness. Martha was taking advantage of Becky, and Layla was a nightmare. Total nightmare baby. He couldn't understand why Becky put up with it.

He had spoken to her yesterday about it, and he thought he'd heard something a bit desperate in her voice. She wasn't usually like that. She was resilient. She'd stuck it out for years with those wankers at the television studio. She was caustic, often, even dangerously full of rage at times, but never desperate, not recently. The last time he'd seen her this way was when they were trying for a second baby. What began as a preference slowly morphed into something essential, one he had been unable to make happen. They were ruled by a twenty-eight-day cycle of hope and despair. Perhaps if he held her closer, after, his skin on hers, he had once thought . . . perhaps if he imagined sperm meeting egg . . . perhaps, then, it would happen for them. But it never had.

They weren't just robbed of a chance to conceive. They were robbed of the full potential of a *life*. How they wanted to make silly faces at a new baby. To teach a second child to walk, and talk, and run. To develop new inside jokes about a second person. But nothing would materialize, no matter how hard they tried. There was nothing. They were creating nothing, month after month.

And then she had slept with somebody else. The oldest trick in the book, though he couldn't say he blamed her, not really.

She had confessed immediately. Came home, walked in the door one cold November day, and said, 'I slept with somebody else last night.'

Her dispassionate tone shocked him almost as much as her words. He wondered, at first, if it was a result of the drinking. That had been steadily increasing, hardly any days without a glass of red, the clink of the recycling getting louder and louder each week.

But it wasn't. He watched her lower her handbag. It made a thudding sound as it hit the floor. 'Who?' he found himself saying, though he didn't care who it was.

'Carl from work. And no, I wasn't drunk.'

'I thought you were staying with Jenny.'

She met his eyes, then, and her gaze wasn't pleading, or contrite, or anything, really. There was a challenge, in it. *Let's address it*, the face said.

He thought of all the times recently when he'd avoided talking about their relationship. Their recent meal out at a steakhouse, without Xander, where Marc played on his phone for the entire meal. Rolling away from her in bed one morning because *Super Sunday* was on and he couldn't be bothered to go down and press pause, come back and have sex. The courses he did on the internet, late at night, instead of joining her in bed. Something had settled between them, widening the more they ignored it, until it became too big to cross. They had become lazy about their own relationship, and that idleness had killed it. It had been amazing how easy it had been to fall out of love. It took hardly any effort at all.

'I see,' he had said quietly.

'Should I go?' she had asked.

'Do what you want,' he'd replied.

Those four words sealed it. There was to be no reconciliation, no recovery, no *intimacy*, physical or otherwise. He moved out on the first of December. She'd already had half a bottle of wine by the time he'd packed his things. He saw Xander the next day, and the one after that – Becky had always been reasonable about shared residency – but it wasn't the same. Of course it wasn't. They were broken: a broken home. She'd left him no choice.

He typed a text, now, standing in the living room.

It always feels worse at the time. I still have a list from when Xander was small. Here it is. Feed. Change. Burp. Fart. Tired. Dirty nappy. Cold. Hot. Lonely. Teething. Pain. Overstimulated. Understimulated. Ill. No Reason. xx

It was half-time, so he googled it, then texted again.

Internet says if crying for no reason: sucking, swaddling, music, white noise, fresh air, bath, motion, massage. Take a break. You didn't ask for this, Samuel, when you took it on. I know that. xx

She didn't reply to him, so he got the carpet out of his van. He wished he'd brought a beer, now. Could've made an evening out of it. Still. It was alright, he had the second half to look forward to. Perhaps he could pop out and get a beer later.

The second half had just started, and right as he was stretching the carpet – the *worst* fucking part – his phone rang, with the ringtone he'd set just for Becky. The lilt of it still made something open up in his chest.

'Alright?' he said. 'Still crying?'

'Yeah, she just won't stop,' Becky said.

Marc put the carpet stretcher down, reached over, and switched the television off. The football players disappeared.

'It will get better. And you can give her back,' he said. 'Soon.'

She didn't respond to that. If she were here, she would be looking at him, head tilted, eyes to him. *Yeah, right*, her expression would be saying.

'Have you fed her – loads? She's definitely not hungry?' he said.

'*No*,' Becky said. 'She's not hungry. Definitely not.'

'Where is she?'

'Inside. I'm in the garden. Having a break.'

'Don't worry about it,' he said. 'Babies can handle being upset. She won't remember.'

'I'm not,' she said. 'Honest. I'm not. It's just – *ugh*.'

'Yeah,' he said. 'I can come over? I'm doing a fitting but I'm almost finished.'

'No. God, no need for that. Don't,' she said hurriedly. 'But will you be there? I don't know. Just be on the end of a phone.'

Should he go? He thought about it. He could pack his stuff up. Surprise her. Go to help.

'You know I will, Samuel,' Marc said. God, it hurt him, remembering those nights, when Xander was just a baby and they would have to stifle their laughter into the pillows in the bedroom. Becky always lay on the top of the duvet, on her belly.

'Look how much the mattress dips on your side compared to mine,' she had said to him on one such night.

'Thanks,' he'd said. 'I'm huge.'

'It's like being on a waterbed,' she'd laughed.

He could still conjure up the entire image of her. Her curved back. Her smiling eyes. They always had the heating up too high – their bills were astronomical – but it was worth it for those hours they spent on top of the duvet.

'I've had a big dinner,' he'd said, and she had laughed even more.

How had they gone from that to this?

'Don't make this your problem,' he said. 'It's a job. If it's not working for you, then you leave. Not your circus, not your monkeys. Leave, if you want to.'

There was a long pause before she replied. 'No. I know. Don't be silly. Of course I won't.'

He sighed. She wouldn't leave. He wished she would. He had never liked Scott, in particular. He liked him even less now. Cheeky fuckers. He would sort them out.

Marc looked at a slight wrinkle in the carpet, from where he had had to stop stretching it suddenly. It would need to be redone, but it didn't seem to matter any more.

'You'll be alright,' he said. He hoped he was right.

His phone rang again at just gone eight the next morning. He had showered, when he got in, little curls of new carpet coming off his arms and hands in the shower. And then he had drunk too much, thinking of Becky and that special tone of voice she had used with him in the past, her curved back on their old shared IKEA bed.

His head was thumping as he answered the phone.

She was screaming.

He sat up in bed, his body lurching forwards, elbows on his knees. 'Becky? What's . . . what's?' The room swam dangerously, as a result of his hangover or shock, he didn't know.

'Layla's . . . I'm pretty sure she's dead, Marc.'

A horrified chill moved through him. 'Dead?' he said faintly. 'Dead?'

'She died in the night.'

'Where are you?'

'There's paramedics everywhere. They're here . . . they're working on her. Oh, Marc. Please come. Please come.'

46

Martha

I think of what Marc said to me on the phone. *Nobody came over.* Followed by the beep, beep, beep: call failed. His tone was not even angry; it was incredulous.

'And did you feel concerned when Becky called you that night?' Harriet says. She looks agitated.

Ellen shifts in her seat, and the judge interjects. 'Sorry to stop you,' he says, putting a hand out like he is placating a wild animal or a child in the throes of a tantrum, 'but can you please ask that in a way which is non-leading?'

'How did you feel that night when Becky called you?' Harriet says.

Marc shrugs. 'I just felt bad for her. The baby was crying a lot.' He looks over at Becky in the dock. He has the same solemn expression he wore at their wedding. 'I wanted to help her. But I wasn't . . . concerned. Not exactly.'

'Well, you put the words in his mouth,' Ellen mutters under her breath.

Harriet looks at her sharply.

'I mean I was worried,' Marc adds. 'But only because Becky was worried. I wasn't worried *for* her. I was worried *with* her.'

Harriet pushes her short, dark hair behind her ear, under her wig. 'How did you feel about the content of the text messages?'

'I just felt sad because she was worried about Layla.'

I can almost see the thoughts flitting across Marc's mind. He can't say that he was worried for her. He can't say that she was having a hard time. He can't say that Layla was difficult, that Becky had been blessed by the minimal demands of her own sleepy son, was inexperienced, out of her depth. All he can offer up are these platitudes. He wasn't concerned, *not exactly*, he says.

But then he raises his hand to his forehead, and I see him wipe sweat from his brow. He is nervous. He's giving evidence. Maybe it's just normal nerves. But something about his body language is off.

'I know her well,' he continues. 'I was worried that she was in a difficult situation. But I never – if I *ever* thought something might happen, I would have gone over there.' He swallows. I watch his Adam's apple bob up and down. 'And I didn't.'

I look across at Ellen. She is watching him closely.

'Thank you,' Harriet says. 'And how did you feel the next morning?'

'Complete shock, when she called me.'

'And finally: had you previously been irritated when Xander had walked into traffic?'

'Yes. I had.'

'And so you can understand why he had reason to lie in A&E.'

'Yes. I can.'

'Thank you.'

Ellen stands up. Her first cross-examination. 'Marc,' she says.

'Yes.'

'You separated from the defendant. About how long ago?'

I look at Marc, then at Harriet. She's watching the proceedings, sitting back in her chair, her left arm slung across its back.

'Eighteen months or so,' he says.

'And why was that?'

Marc spreads his arms wide, expansively. 'Why does anyone?' he says. 'There are loads of reasons.'

I am struck, suddenly, by how unlikely it would be for Scott to have this broad view of us. If we ever broke up. He would say, nodding seriously, 'It all unravelled because I failed to stack the dishwasher one Tuesday.'

But Marc has always understood that. And Becky, too. They would never become bogged down by details and miss the broad view. 'I've got a lovely wife and a great kid and the sun is shining,' Marc once said happily at a party before cracking open a can of beer. The big picture. At least, that was how I had always viewed him. Before.

I close my eyes. Am I mad, suspecting my brother-in-law? People don't know when they're going insane, do they? Perhaps I am. Perhaps I have been sent mad with grief.

'You can't ask that,' Harriet says, getting to her feet and looking at Ellen. 'What relevance is the defendant's marital breakdown?'

'Given you have called her ex-husband to give evidence, I'd say it's very relevant.'

'I will allow it,' the judge says.

'Our child, I guess,' Marc says carefully. 'Well, no. Not him. Parenthood. No. Just . . . life. That led to our problems.' His eyes look wide and frightened.

Who can possibly say what has led to the breakdown of their marriage, under oath?

'Your child?'

'We had Xander, unplanned, when we were very young, and it was . . . it's a lot of pressure, and change, for a relationship. We couldn't have a second. We tried for . . . for ages. We grew apart. And then she was unfaithful.' He says this in a low voice, quieter still.

He doesn't look at Becky, but I do. She has a palm on the glass again, like a monkey at the zoo, waiting sadly for escape.

'I see,' Ellen says. 'So she has form for deceit. But you are on good terms with the defendant now?'

'Yes. We still see quite a lot of each other.' He ignores the dig. *Form for deceit.*

He has sidestepped it in that adult way of his, but the jury has taken it in, that unchallenged comment landing like a fact in their laps.

'How much?'

'We text most days. It used to be about Xander but it's more than that, now. Jokes. We sometimes chat. On Friday nights. We get the same takeaway. We choose it, from afar, and eat it on the phone. I don't know.' Marc shakes his head. He's babbling.

I want to warn him, my brother-in-law. 'Stop giving them this stuff for free,' I want to say, but then I remember the words he used – *nobody came over* – and how shifty he looked when asked about that night on the stand, and . . . I want them to catch him out.

'Why do you do that when you're separated?'

'Text?'

'Yes.'

'It's just . . . you know.' He shrugs again. 'We like each other, still. We mean a lot to each other.'

Becky is staring at Marc, her eyes round. I have seen that look before. She had it on her wedding night. She had it when she brought Marc home to meet all of us at Christmas.

Despite myself, my eyes fill with tears. To be separated, on the verge of divorce, and to have all your personal history gone through, ransacked, in the witness box. Your poor, blurred boundaries. The weird things you do that you are glad nobody knows about; here they are, looming large in a courtroom for all to see. Projected on the wall just over there. The jury will remember it for ever, Marc and Becky's private business.

'So you wanted to help her, when she asked. It was natural to you.'

'Yes. Of course. We don't fight or anything like that. We just help each other.'

'She said she was worried about Layla *and herself.*' Ellen reads from the sheet of paper in front of her, even though the words are surely burnt on the brain of everybody in this courtroom. She is building up to it. I can tell. She's going to ask about his alibi.

'But she didn't mean . . . it was just a figure of speech. It was her way. She was . . . she's, like, quite comedic. She's very funny. So she was just making a joke, you know? Like, I'm worried about this bloody crying baby and I'm worried about myself, too. In case I . . . but she didn't mean in case I *do* anything.'

281

Ellen is watching him like he is prey, letting him fill the silence with his prattle. 'So what did she mean, then? If not *in case I do anything*?'

'She just meant it as a joke.'

'Sorry, Mr Burrows. What's the joke here? Am I missing it?' Ellen's face relaxes into a friendly smile.

Harriet crosses and uncrosses her legs, then leans forward, looking at Marc.

I wince. It is like watching somebody get fired. Like watching a public humiliation. And isn't it?

'Well, she was talking about what she might do but it was a joke.'

'What she might do. As in, harm Layla? That's the joke?'

'Yes. But it was just a joke.'

'A joke, right.' Ellen looks meaningfully at the jury, as though joking in such matters was so abhorrent. But it was *before*: that text. That silly text. Wouldn't all of the contents of our iPhones look pretty damning, if read out selectively at a murder trial? I had said this to Scott, a while back, and he had given me a strange look that said: *Um, no, mine wouldn't.* And I suppose his wouldn't. He's straight-up like that. A pragmatist. A simple soul, like Marc but also totally different.

Ellen pauses, picks a pen up, and clicks it twice. In the silent courtroom, it sounds like the cocking of a gun. *Click, click. Click, click.* She appraises Marc seriously. This is it. She is going to ask about his alibi.

Eventually, she speaks. 'Are you really saying under oath that you weren't worried about her?'

'I wasn't worried she would do something.'

'That's not what I asked. You were the last person to

speak to her, Mr Burrows, before she killed baby Layla. Now answer my question: were you worried about her?'

'Yes, I was worried about her.'

'Because she seemed disturbed during the call?'

'Not disturbed, exactly, no. Just upset.'

'*Upset.* I see. What do you think she was upset about?'

'Because she couldn't settle Layla.'

'Ah, I see. She was upset with Layla.'

'No, *for* her.'

'So,' Ellen says, 'why do you think Becky was contacting you that night?'

'Why?'

'Yes. You specifically.'

'I don't know.'

Ellen pauses again. 'You see,' she says. Here it comes. 'I would say that, given your closeness, and everything you have told us, Becky would turn to you, out of desperation, if she thought she might be about to do something she would regret. If she was feeling desperate, and frightened, and fearful that she might lose her rag. Do you agree?'

'No, I . . .'

'No? Who else would she turn to?'

'If she was—'

'Yes. If she was desperate and frightened and angry. Perhaps she couldn't say as much. Perhaps she couldn't admit seriously that she was worried about *herself*. And what she might do. But is there anybody other than you who she might turn to, if she were feeling such things?'

Marc's eyes flit towards me, in the public gallery, and then he looks away again. 'No,' he says. 'Not in those circumstances. It would be me.'

'Yes. She turns to you in her darkest hour of need. Sends a cry for help. Nothing further.'

She didn't ask. She didn't ask if he was there that night. If he has an alibi. I am deflated, and furious, all at once. It's not about him, I suppose. He is not on trial: Becky is. She's the prime suspect, so why would they look to somebody else? I shouldn't have asked the prosecution. I should have asked the defence lawyer. Harriet would have been more likely to help me than Ellen. Ellen wants to secure a prosecution.

Marc looks across the courtroom. Not at me, but at Becky. Their eyes seem to meet, and something seems to pass between them.

I keep staring, watching them. Nobody else seems to be looking. He is conveying a message to her. A slight shake of his head. She nods at him. She looks grateful. He looks . . . what? He looks like he's done her a favour, that's what.

He has lied for her. I am certain of it.

Any remaining belief in his honesty evaporates, right there in the court. They're in it together. He's testified for her because he once loved her. But look! They're communicating.

They're still looking at each other. I can't take it any more. I'm going to ask him. I'm going to ask him in person what the fuck went on that night.

47

Becky

'Layla, there really is absolutely nothing to be crying about,' I have said about a hundred times. She should be in bed. Xander is out, at a sleepover, no doubt not sleeping. The only one of us who truly wants to be in bed is me.

We have both had less than two hours' sleep. I don't know how she is still crying. We still have one more night together, before Martha and Scott are back.

She is fed – boy, is she fed, three ounces! – and she isn't wet, and she doesn't seem to have any wind and her legs aren't tucked up in the frog-like newborn way. But she is crying. Crying and crying and crying. The sounds have taken on tones within themselves, like a vast orchestra or – more apt – a heavy metal band. I grit my teeth against the noise. How many hours until Martha is home? Sixteen? I look down at Layla. It will be okay. I'll take it one hour at a time. No baby ever came to any harm through crying, I tell myself.

I do another bottle. I google how much is the maximum amount of Calpol she can have, and decide I'll save that like a trump card. Besides, I know babies. She's not in pain. Not physically, anyway.

You'd think you would get used to the noise, but let me tell you, you don't. Martha and Scott would know the science of it, no doubt. We're not supposed to get used to it, or something. But Martha and Scott aren't here. Nope. It's just Layla and bloody useless Becky.

I am aware of something hot and volatile inside me. The sort of dart of anger you get when you're stuck in traffic and are very late, or like last year when the bathroom ceiling caved in, just like that, on a bloody Tuesday night, or when your period arrives for the thirty-sixth time in a row, like the 07.49 to London: often delayed, tantalizingly so, but nevertheless always there in the end. We stopped trying, after four years, and split up soon after that. Xander, conceived so easily one night, was not to have a sibling, no matter how hard we tried.

I open a bottle of red. Ah, that satisfying pop as the cork slides out. I'll have two glasses. *No more.* Just to take the edge off. As I sip, I think about what Xander said earlier, after school: 'She seems very upset.' He was resting his weight on his elbows, on the breakfast bar. He kept lifting himself up on it, like a pull-up.

'Stop doing that,' I said. 'You'll fall over.'

'What's she got to be sad about?' He raised himself up again, the muscles in his arms tensing.

It was such a simple question that I felt my heart expand in my chest, relieved that I could still feel that warm, hot centre within me. That deep well of love for my son. I reached across and ruffled his hair. Such a simplistic thing to say: *What's she got to be sad about?* Such a nine-year-old thing to say. But then, maybe it's not to do with his age. Maybe he got it from Marc. It's actually totally the sort of thing Marc says. 'Why be sad when you can eat a bag of Doritos?' he once said to me, and I really think he meant it. Why indeed? I feel a lurch of pain, remembering that. God, I loved him. I loved him so much. Nothing else compares. I can picture the evenings spent just doing nothing. Mundane things. Television. Ironing. But I always felt so lucky, just so lucky next to him.

How could I ever have it again? I can't, that's the truth. But, actually, isn't the Marc I know now – the Marc I text constantly now – the exact same Marc I once loved so much?

I can't answer that.

What might've saved us? More *date nights*? Were the clichés really correct? We'd been arrogant; so confident in our relationship that we didn't even notice it failing. The truth is, they all take work.

It could still work. No, it couldn't. I slept with somebody else. Another fuck-up in a long list of them. Martha would never cheat. Scott would never cheat. Marc would never cheat. It is just me, always only me, who succumbs to temptation. Who smokes and drinks and sleeps around.

This is just the nostalgia talking. I am looking after Layla, and the texts with Marc are getting more and more frequent, and it reminds me of those early days with Xander when we had been so happy. That is all.

'She's not sad,' I said to Xander. *She's angry*, I realized. She was angry with the world. I didn't share this with Xander. Instead, I said, 'She's only just come into the world and it's cold and she's hungry. She's shocked.' *As am I*, I wanted to add.

'She wants her mum,' Xander said, with curious insight for a nine-year-old.

I nodded and gulped a bit. She wanted Martha. Angular, calm Martha. Layla would, of course, know her over blobby, impatient me. We were so different, Martha and I. Layla couldn't be fooled by me, the lesser Blackwater sister.

Now, it's just Layla and me in the living room. Xander is away overnight; the first time he's not with Marc or me in his entire life. He seemed glad to be going to a quiet, calm house without any crying babies. I try to pretend he's with Marc. It's easier that way. Marc was the only other person as watchful as me, when Xander was a toddler. 'He's got a Lego block in his hand,' Marc would say. 'Mind he doesn't eat it.' The anxiety of parenthood had been divided equally between us. There was no helpless man act, no inability to stack a dishwasher or remember a birthday card while seemingly having not lost the ability to go to work or remember what time the boxing was on. There was none of that bullshit, thankfully. Of course, there was another kind, as there always is.

I stare at the wall, now, and not at Layla, and try to count to ten in my mind again. That doesn't work, so I watch the second hand of a clock on the wall as it completes a full circuit. Sixteen hours. Perhaps I could ask Marc to come over. Share the load. But no. That's not fair, is it? It wouldn't even be fair if we were together. This is our mess. Mine and Martha's.

Layla's face is bright purple, her gums like angry red watermelon slices in her mouth, and I wearily make up another bottle. I consider texting Martha, but I don't. What's the point? It would only upset her. And she wouldn't be able to come home any sooner. Scott should be here, but who am I to tell him that? I cringe as I imagine writing the text. *Come and look after your child!* I would say. And Martha and Scott would roll their eyes at silly, dramatic Becky: the hired help, the nanny, unable to cope with looking after a baby. 'This is what we pay you for,' Martha would admonish, and I would feel small and sad and shit at being unable to do yet another job.

Instead, I get out my phone and text Marc. It's weird, I know, but I am sort of beyond caring. Marc and I always had a wonderfully weird relationship, and we will forever. We were weird when together, and weird when apart, so why not sit comfortably in the wasteland between parents, friends and ex-lovers?

Jesus, I'm worried about Layla. And me! I write to him.

The crying is so loud I think I might actually go mad. I look at her little red face and shift her from being up against my shoulder to the 'tiger in the tree' hold. Her limbs are bunched up, angrily, but her left arm swings down like a monkey's. I pat her back, which feels tense. It doesn't feel like wind, but what do I know? It feels taut with stress. Like she is carrying the weight of the world.

For fuck's sake. For fuck's sake. Just shut up. Anger seems to suffuse me, like I have been dipped in lava. Just shut *up*. I down my first glass of wine, and wait for the numbing effect to kick in.

I stand again and stare out of my living-room windows and out into the night. Jesus, I'd take a difficult boss over this, any day. Layla is more difficult than the very worst of the television people. I try to bring a smile to my face at the irony of it. But that's the thing: you can only laugh at your situation if you are not frightened of it. I am frightened, here tonight, with a baby who won't stop screaming, trapped in an arrangement I didn't intend to turn out this way, and so nothing is funny. Nothing is nice. Nothing is comforting, except wine. I imagine I feel similarly to Layla.

My phone pings, the special tone I have assigned to Marc. He has sent a lovely text full of advice.

I consider the list while looking at Layla and find a song at random to play on my phone. Green Day blares out, and she cries harder. I leave it on for a few seconds longer, but it seems to anger her further, so I turn it off. I go back to the text and, over the next half an hour, I work my way down the list. She refuses the next bottle. I give her a bath, which she cries through, and put her into a new nappy and yellow sleep suit with bears on the feet. I grasp her little hands. They feel just the right temperature, but I turn the heating up regardless. I add a layer and then I remove two. It is like the worst exam of my life, like some vast logic puzzle I have to do while my ears are being tortured. I pour a third glass of wine – *fuck it* – and take her upstairs and over to the feature wall in the bedroom and show her the black and white polka dots. And – ah. At last. Silence. My ears ring in the unexpected quiet, as if they have simply started to scream, too. Layla stares at the polka dots in awe.

I was six months pregnant with Xander and couldn't stand on the stepladder to paint the ceiling because I was so unbalanced with my bump.

Marc found it hilarious. 'Hang the wallpaper with me, instead,' he said.

We left the ceiling half done. We were like that.

'Are you bothered about a half-painted ceiling?' he said to me.

'But,' I said, 'it should be *finished*. When we sell—'

'Do *you* care?' he had said.

The arguments that I had stacked up – my parents' arguments, Martha's voice in my head – fell away.

'Not at all,' I said.

He brought the dining table up. My job was to spread the paste on to the back of the wallpaper. Marc set a bucket beside me and brought me a chair.

The paste looked like cheap porridge, thick and gluey. I dipped the brush into it and pulled it out. The paste dripped off it.

'None of that ready-glued wallpaper shit,' Marc said. He showed me how to paste it on to the back of a sheet while he hung one on the wall.

'It's quite methodical,' I said, breathing it in. The paste smelt comforting, somehow. Starchy, almost straw-like. I was standing in a slice of sunlight, the light warm on the tops of my feet, and Marc was humming gently under his breath, and I thought: *How is it possible to be this happy, at nineteen and unemployed and pregnant?* It couldn't be true, and yet it was. It so clearly was.

'You've dropped loads on the floor,' Marc said with a laugh, reaching down to blot the drips with a wad of blue tissue.

I liked that laugh. That laugh that said: 'I will never shout at you. Life simply isn't that serious.'

I was scrolling through my phone while Marc hummed under his breath. He'd tagged us on Facebook – he loved Facebook – as *hanging out*. Only I knew we were hanging wallpaper, and I liked that: our secret, inner language. Our own code. It only got richer over time, like a slowly marinating stew.

We were obsessed with renovating our house – the little house, we called it, for some reason – in time for Xander's arrival. We did six rooms in two months, becoming like a one-dimensional couple who work together and talk only of *the business*. We had become obsessed with the idea of the mantelpiece. We would fantasize about when the house was done. We would have things *on the mantelpiece*. Curated pieces: dishes from Nepal, pretentious trinkets, the sort of thing Martha started buying after she met Scott. Whenever we saw anything – a stupid wooden box in HomeSense, or the ugliest handmade ornament for sale on Facebook – we would say, 'For the mantelpiece?'

Later, when we did the living room, I was too large to even hang wallpaper, so I just sat in a corner of the room while Marc did it, instead. I read quiz questions to him off the internet. 'What's number one in the UK charts right now?' I would say, and accuse him of being old when he didn't know. 'Coldplay . . .?' he would say, and I'd hoot with laughter. 'It's Drake,' I'd say, rolling my eyes, and Marc would say, 'Who?'

I sat with my back to the radiator in the bathroom while he tiled, one cold Sunday. Xander was kicking away inside me while I drank a can of Coke and watched Marc grouting. He was meticulous with it, like an artist, I always thought. He knew so much stuff. That was one of the things I loved most about him. He knew where the electricity cables ran behind the walls, where the hot and cold water pipes went. He was like a magician who could see behind the scenes. And he'd learnt it all himself, too. His father was rubbish, had never taught him to be handy. He'd gone on all these courses to learn how to do all of it. Basic mechanics for cars. Carpet fitting. And now he did everything. He had about nine jobs. He listened to football podcasts all day at work and finished sometimes at three o'clock. I loved that about him, too. He made me somehow see that life didn't have to be experienced in a *big* way, and that happiness was small, really. I still have that attitude now. I can have as much fun in the bakery aisle of Sainsbury's as in a club in Ibiza. It's all about attitude.

'Do you think our baby will have kids?' I said to him as he moved the trowel back and forth, his eyes flitting over the tiles. Afterwards, I knew, they would all be identical, perfectly uniform. I would always have a lovely house, thanks to him. Design school or no design school.

'Who knows?' he said, stopping to look at me.

'I'd love to know whether or not I'm going to be a granny,' I said.

'I just think,' he stood, his hands on his hips, and looked at me, 'I just think I'm going to have a rather nice life either way. No matter what.'

That optimism. I closed my eyes, relishing it, like the sun on my face on a hot day. Was it possible to fall in love with a mindset? If so, I had.

He put an arm around me. We hugged for so long that a bit of grout, thicker than all of the rest, dried and set before we could remove it. He kissed the top of my head. He didn't care.

Layla starts crying again after a minute of the wallpaper — one minute's blissful silence — and I sigh heavily. I take her into the bathroom and find the piece of grout. I put my fingers around it and try to pull it away, but it's stuck fast, like a barnacle. Good, I think, anchoring myself to it.

I put her down in her Moses basket, but the crying only gets worse. Little tears are dripping out of the corners of her eyes and gathering in her ears like caught rainwater. Her gummy mouth is moving, angry, frightened. I understand it, suddenly, somehow: she wants her mother. Of course she does. It's obvious.

I leave her there and sink down the wall to sit on the floor. It's not fair. Men go to work but women can't, because of this. These tears and this unhappiness. I am the closest Layla has to a mother and yet I am nothing — not a patch on Martha. I don't smell like her, I don't dress like her — stylish but classic, like a royal — and I don't sound like her, either. She needs Martha's warmth, her calmness — she's so serene — and her quiet organization, her firm, angular grasp. None of my stupid jokes and fumbling disorganization. She needs Martha. Not me. Not Marc. Not even Scott. It isn't fair, none of it.

And so instead of trying to stop Layla, I simply join in. After a bit, I pick her up, and together we rock and sob on the spare-room floor, my feet lying underneath the bed, toes just touching the underside of the mattress.

Jesus, the garden is cold. It's seven thirty. I didn't think. I just stumbled out here, desperate to get away from the crying, the relentless, sheer bloody-minded determination not to sleep. God, it's horrendous.

I dial Marc's number without thinking.

'Alright?' he says. 'Still crying?'

'Yeah, she just won't stop,' I say. My voice is full of tears; I can hear them. There have been too many tears in this house recently. Mine, Layla's. Even Xander was strangely mournful the other morning, tired of the all-day crying, as we all were. I hope he's alright with it. That it isn't affecting him. That he knows I love him.

'It will get better. And you can give her back soon.'

But it will never end, I think, looking up at the sky and blowing a bloom of air out. There will be more work, not less. Martha has always worked too much. Too many good bloody causes. And I will never get to design school. God, what was I thinking? I wanted to escape the set-dressing, but I didn't think beyond that. And now what? I wish I could quit. Go to design school. Or even just get a normal job again. But Martha will never find another nanny willing to be so flexible, will she? And then all those children in Kos . . . they will suffer, too.

'Have you fed her – loads? She's definitely not hungry?' he says.

'*No*. She's not hungry. Definitely not.'

I think of Layla writhing around as I offered a bottle. I'd defrosted it correctly, and then she'd refused it, and I had thrown it angrily in the bin. Fuck's sake. My own anger scares me, and I try to breathe through it, to let the thoughts go. Don't attach meaning to them.

Have more wine. That'll help.

'Where is she?'

'Inside. I'm in the garden. Having a break.'

She is upstairs, in the makeshift nursery, in the Moses basket. Her legs will be kicking up, clenched to her body. Her face will be red. Little arms and legs making cycling motions as the anger fills her body, too.

Something rises up inside me. Something dark and furious. How could Scott leave me like this? How could Martha? This isn't supposed to be my job. This isn't my child. It's not fucking fair.

'Don't worry about it,' he says.

'I'm not. Honest. I'm not. It's just – *ugh*.' I try to play it down. I don't want him to worry.

He wants to come over. To help. But I can't let him do that. He can't help me. I raise my eyes heavenwards and try not to think about it.

He gives some pat advice, about it not becoming my problem, but it is: it is.

I stand in the garden for a few more minutes, scrolling through the texts again. I'll get her some Calpol. To calm her down. To numb any pain she's in. And maybe then I will calm down, too.

A strange plan is forming in my mind, unwittingly, as though it is not my own; mental weeds growing, obscuring my home-grown plants. I could leave. Go to Londis. Buy the Calpol. That could be my breather. And then I wouldn't have to put her in the pushchair, bring everything with me: the changing bag, the endless bottles.

It's almost the same as standing in the garden and having a smoke and a cry. I'll be less than five minutes. I put her on the kitchen floor yesterday, and she survived that. It's not cutting corners: it's survival.

I set her down in the Moses basket. Her crying doesn't get any louder, and so, satisfied, I leave her, closing the door behind me softly. I lock it, too, to keep her safe.

48

Martha

Frannie is next. A curious woman who lives opposite Becky. I know her to say hello to, but then, I know almost everybody Becky knows, and vice versa. This is how our relationship was. Her oldest friend became my friend, and came on my hen do. We forgot how we knew the people in our lives, only that they were tangled up in the web of me and Becky.

Frannie's very fair, and very serious. Becky says she is *too earnest*. I have only met her a handful of times, and know that she used to live with her sister – they were often to be seen reading in their garden – and had a dog together called Patrick who they took to a dog nursery every morning at eight o'clock. Becky called it Malory Towers for Dogs, and would only ever refer to it as this. But then the sister left. 'Got married, had a baby,' Becky said bitterly.

Frannie enters the courtroom, brought to the witness box by an usher. She's wearing a pair of huge glasses. Her hair is dip-dyed, near blonde at the ends and dark at the roots. 'Very Brighton,' Becky would say.

She's wearing a paisley dress with bell-bottom sleeves that drape absurdly over the wood of the witness box.

'Are you Francesca Lewis?'

'Yes, I am.'

'Will you tell us a bit about what you saw on the night of the twenty-sixth of October?'

49

Francesca Lewis

7.20 p.m., Thursday 26 October

Frannie was trying to French-plait her hair. It wasn't so bad, living alone. It felt fat and full. Plus, she felt sometimes like she was a more interesting person when she lived alone. She was a cross-stitcher, a woman who liked to take a walk around the streets right before bed, a lipstick-lover.

She propped the phone up on the window sill, paused on the first video. She liked to do her hair there. She could stand the phone up against the glass and use the pane as a mirror. This is how she did the hair tutorials, even though she was thirty-four and alone and should probably be depressed.

She was just reaching up to loop a complicated bit of hair that didn't seem to belong anywhere into the main plait when her eye was caught by a woman at the window opposite. Ah. Wasn't that nice? Her neighbour, Becky. Cradling her sister's baby. Becky was looking after her a lot at the moment.

They were always exchanging things: the car seat Becky had given to Martha, the pair of shoes Becky had borrowed for a night out. 'See you Thursday,' Martha would say, 'and bring the chutney.' Things like that. Family stuff. She missed that. Her sister, Olive, now lived in Cornwall with her new husband. It had all happened very quickly.

Frannie looked across again at the image in the window. It gave a new meaning to the word *tender*. One hand around the baby's head, protectively. The other around its bottom. Comforting. Her body bent towards the baby. The room softly lit, amber, behind them.

She couldn't help but wonder as she stared at the mother and baby framed in the window, like a Madonna and child.

Despite herself, Frannie couldn't help watching them for a long moment. Aunt and niece.

50

Martha

'Thank you,' Harriet says. 'So how would you describe the defendant's body language towards the baby?'

'Warm and protective. A hand around the baby's head.'

'Nothing further.'

'How far away were you from the window?' Ellen says, as she gets to her feet, as though she can't possibly wait.

She shouldn't be going in for the kill already. I fiddle with a loose thread on my jeans. Let us have this moment, the moment where this nice woman saw Becky with Layla. Let us remember it. Less than an hour or so before Layla died, she was held, a hand cupped tenderly around her head. Perhaps Layla thought it was me, momentarily. Perhaps Layla leaned in, ever so slightly, the longer, golden hairs along the nape of her neck just tickling Becky's hands. She was safe, and Becky was calm and protective, her body soft, her voice low.

'Erm . . . God,' Frannie says, tucking a long strand of hair behind her ear. 'I have no idea.'

'Your house backs on to theirs, right?'

'Yes.'

'The nursery that Layla was in has two windows – front and back. It's a long room. Let's look at the Scenes of Crime Officer's photographs.' She flicks through the bundle and directs the jury to look at them, too. 'Here is the bedroom,' she says.

I close my eyes. No, not the Scenes of Crime Officer's exhibits. Not during this defence witness's evidence that Becky was doing nothing wrong during Layla's final hours.

She holds up a photograph. It was taken in the morning and the light is wintry, milky. The Moses basket lies, discarded, on the floor. Flappy scrunched up next to that. The first photograph shows the front window, the second one the back. I had always liked that room. Last night, looking up from the street, I could see right through it. Front to back, like it was a tunnel.

'So the back of your house backs on to the back of Becky's. Right?'

'Yes.'

'So there are two gardens between you.'

'Yes.'

Ellen puts the photographs down. 'Twenty metres, thirty, would you say?'

'Yes. Probably.'

'It's thirty-two.'

'Okay, thirty-two,' Frannie says.

I wonder why they play these games.

'How clearly can you really tell someone's emotions, their stance, their real body language, from thirty-two metres, and through two windows? Thirty-two metres would be . . . it would be out of this room, and into the corridor beyond. Notwithstanding the fact that it was night-time, and, by your own evidence, the room was dimly lit.'

'Is there a question in this monologue?' Harriet says, not standing up, merely turning her head towards Ellen like a polite patron to a waitress, eyebrows raised.

'How clearly could you see?'

'Well, I thought I—'

'Can you clearly see the faces of the public gallery here?'

'Just about, yes.'

'Well, they are only fifteen metres away, Frannie.'

'I could see her.'

'Did you like looking?'

'I . . . what?'

'Did you like looking at them?'

Frannie blushes. 'Yes, it was . . . I was . . . it was a hard time, and I liked looking.'

'A "hard time"?'

'Well, I was living alone for the first time, and I liked . . . I liked looking at that image, of Becky holding a baby.'

'And so you saw what you wanted to see.'

'No, I—'

'Nothing further.'

When we get home, Scott sits down in the big love seat, right next to a framed black-and-white photograph of Layla on the wall.

When I told Becky about my first date with Scott, she raised a hand to me and said, 'Let me guess – he's a *nice guy*?'

'Yes,' I had said. 'But isn't Marc?'

She smiled, then, dimples showing either side of her cheeks. 'He's not a Nice Guy,' she said.

I hadn't known what she meant. She seemed to know more about life and its rules than I did, and that night, when I saw Scott's number flash up on my phone, I thought: *Are you a Nice Guy?*

I supposed he was. But what was wrong with that? As I answered, a cold fear arrived in my stomach: was I *settling*? I ignored it. If I didn't pay it any attention, it would go away.

I pull the laptop on to my knees, now, and begin to google.

Babies who died for no reason.

Babies who look like they were smothered but were not.

Accidental smothering false conviction eight-week-old.

There are some relevant hits. I read them, voraciously, making meticulous notes on my pad. I think of Frannie's evidence, of Becky cradling Layla in the window, backlit. Becky is innocent. I let the words turn around in my mind. Could she be? Her damning Google search, the overheard shouting. Could they all be nothing? Bits of stray evidence caught up in the search, like ocean debris? *Okay*, I think to myself. *Maybe.*

Could Marc have let himself into Becky's house during that five-minute Londis window? Is it even possible something could have happened then? The prosecution said the death wouldn't have been after nine thirty but could have been as early as eight. Becky was at Londis at seven forty-five. It's possible something could have happened when Becky was at Londis . . . something accidental. Something they then covered up. What was that bruise? Maybe it was that?

Maybe Marc came over and something happened. Together, they staged an accident. Positioned Layla in the cot. Waited it out. Called the ambulance in the morning.

They'd thought they could fool everyone into thinking it was cot death; that the medical tests wouldn't reveal the truth.

Or maybe Marc had done it – I recall that shouty, fatherly temper of his – and Becky was covering for him. They figured she would be more likely to get away with it than him. A man. The sister would never be convicted, they'd reasoned.

That could be it.

But why wouldn't they have a party line? Why didn't they concoct something? A fall? Co-sleeping? She could've said co-sleeping, and got off.

It doesn't make any sense.

I read and read the internet, and my notes stretch to four pages, before Scott looks up.

'What are you doing?' he says.

'Research.'

'Researching what?'

'Accidental smothering of young babies,' I say. 'And I've been thinking about whether somebody else could've been there that night, too.'

Scott doesn't say anything, which is almost worse than a diatribe. He merely exhales, nostrils flaring, and shakes his head. He reaches for the remote control and turns the television on.

The local news blares out into the room. They're covering our case, and he changes the channel.

51

Judge Christopher Matthews, QC

'I can't believe the ex-husband said all that stuff,' Christopher says to Rumpole in the garden. 'Bloody idiot.'

The dog is sniffing the hydrangeas Sadie planted one Tuesday afternoon when he was working. They are turning brown around the edges of their petals.

'Can you imagine?'

Christopher has seen plenty of ill-advised witness performances. Ex-lovers, barbed answers to questions not asked. Lies told, of course. Contempt of court, and the rest of it. But he's never seen anything quite like this. An ex-husband, sure his wife is innocent, despite all the evidence to the contrary. And looking at her from the witness box with that look on his face. Maybe they *were* in on it together.

Nevertheless, he thinks the barrister was nasty, going for their relationship history. He almost said something, but decided not to after a moment's thought. *Let them go for it*, he thought. Whatever.

He stands, now, in his garden, worrying away at Marc's evidence, but can't find what bothered him most about it. He goes inside, leaving Rumpole in the flower bed, and sits at the breakfast bar, not knowing what to do with himself.

It comes to him, five episodes of *Game of Thrones*, four beers and six hours later: Marc respects Becky. He looked at her with respect in the courtroom. And so when she told him she was innocent, he believed her.

When was the last time Christopher looked at Sadie that way? He remembers, once, referring wryly to her nursing career as *wiping bottoms* in an unusually vicious, alcohol-fuelled moment at a dinner party when he chose to prioritize the cheap laugh over the offence it would cause. She never mentioned it, but he saw her shoulders tense. He should have apologized. Why didn't he?

What did she think of him at the end? Does she miss Rumpole? She's never said, and he has never enquired. Does she still love him? Not according to their divorce petition, no.

He sets his can of beer down on the arm of the sofa and pulls his laptop over. He will email her, he thinks.

As he types, a peculiar sensation comes over him. It is something to do with the stillness of his house. The only sound is Rumpole, turning around in the corner of the living room.

Layla.

That's who Christopher is thinking of. The baby who died: by accident or from something sinister, he isn't yet sure. But there is something weird about it. That is where the goosebumps come from.

Something isn't quite right.

Something isn't quite fitting together, somehow.

Friday

52

Martha

I go to Becky's house in the early morning. This time, I let myself in.

I wonder dimly if Scott knows of my absences: my late-night wanderings, my early-morning outings. He probably notices, as I notice his. Maybe he thinks *I* am seeing somebody else. That I don't love him.

I shifted closer to him in bed last night, my skin against his, but he didn't wake. He would have had no idea it had happened.

I'm standing in the hallway, my spare key in my hand, and it's the overpowering smell that does it. The smell of their home. I never used to be able to smell it, I was there so often. I close my eyes as I think of it. Takeaways with Marc and Becky while Xander played on the floor, back when they were happy. White wine in Becky's garden. Taking Layla over there for the first time, when she was just three days old and it still hurt to sit down. Xander cradling her clumsily while we watched anxiously. It was all ahead of us, then, or so we thought.

It was one such night, maybe just over a year ago, when she was still raw from her split with Marc, when she asked me about Scott. A couple of glasses of wine down on a Saturday night, she said, 'Do you honestly really love him?'

'What?' I almost laughed. 'Scott?'

'Well, ignore me, if you want,' she had said, sloshing wine everywhere as she gestured. 'I married for love, and look where I am.'

'But what do you mean?' I said. I shouldn't have asked. I knew what she meant.

On my hen do, in the quiet underground of a spa, I had asked her how she knew Marc was the one. She had wiggled her toes against the hot wall of the sauna, and said, 'If you have to ask, he's not.'

'I just don't think you're that into each other,' she said simply, pouring more wine for herself.

'Don't be ridiculous,' I said.

But now, I remember the ruthlessness of it. Ruthless. That is one word I might use to describe her.

There will be evidence upstairs. I know it. Poked around in – by the Scenes of Crime Officer, the police, and maybe the medics. But there'll be other evidence, too. A life, stopped. A glass of water, half empty, on Becky's bedside table, perhaps, or a half-full laundry basket.

I can't take any more steps into her hallway. It's enough, for now, to smell Becky's house smell. I leave after just a few minutes more.

As I'm walking down her drive, my hand on the cool metal of her garden gate, I feel it. It's conviction. That's what it is. The complete, assured conviction that *somebody* did this to Layla.

And that it wasn't Becky.

A murder happened here. My body knows it. And it tells me it was Marc.

I get in my car and drive in the direction of his house.

Marc answers his door with a confused expression on his face. It's six o'clock in the morning.

He's wearing a grey T-shirt and jogging bottoms. He looks up the stairs behind him, then shuts the door, standing barefoot on the welcome mat outside in the heat. I guess Xander is there, and he doesn't want him to hear.

'God,' he says. 'Martha, if this is about—'

'Was it you?' I say, unable to stop the words tumbling out of my mouth.

He says nothing.

'Was it you?' I ask again.

He pauses for a second, raking his hand through his hair. 'This again,' he says. His voice breaks. 'You really think I did it.'

'Did you go over to see Becky? What about when she went to Londis?'

He raises his head to look at me. 'I can't imagine you're going to believe me,' he says. 'But it wasn't me. I didn't do it. I wasn't there.'

'You tried to help her, didn't you? After? You covered it up . . . you said nobody *came over*. You didn't say *went over*.'

He blinks, and that sentence – *evidence* I was so sure about – seems to evaporate into nothing.

'I didn't go there,' he says. 'I wish I could tell you how I felt the moment I got that call, Martha.' He meets my eyes. 'The call in the morning about Layla. It was the

worst moment of my entire life. And Becky, she . . . I don't
know what you think, but, Martha, her heart is broken.'

'Because she is accused?' I say.

'No. Because she lost her niece. Her niece that she
loved and cared for so much. She feels guilty. Not because
she *is* guilty, but because she *feels* it. Layla was in her care
and . . .'

He doesn't break my gaze. His eyes dampen, but still he
keeps looking at me.

'You never doubted her?' I say. 'You never once thought
she'd done it?'

'No,' he says. 'Not once, not ever.'

'How can you be so sure?' I say. I'm genuinely curious.
How could he possibly know?

'Because . . . because I know her. Inside out,' he says.
'And I know grief, too. It's obvious. She doesn't eat.'

I don't say anything. I just carry on looking at him, feeling utterly lost, on my brother-in-law's doorstep.

'Look, Martha, if you come again, I'm going to need to
inform somebody,' he says gently.

I turn and walk away without another word.

He is convincing. His tearful gaze is convincing. His
threat, imparted gently, reluctantly. It is the Marc I know
well. My brother-in-law. No wonder the barrister didn't
ask him. Of course he wasn't there.

I'm an embarrassment. A desperate woman.

I walk to the beach and try to forget I saw Marc. Try to
forget the look he gave me.

The trial will close on Tuesday and then the jury will
commence its deliberation. At the start of this week, I

couldn't imagine today. But here we are. The days are the same length, the same rhythm, meted out by God, even though their weight, on us, is heavier than mercury. Scott is right. I've got to stop trying to solve it and move on somehow.

The sea sparkles in front of me.

I flew to Kos on the Wednesday afternoon. A few hours. Hardly anything, I thought. Like driving to Oxford. Hardly any distance.

I would sign the documents on Thursday. Get a lawyer instructed to purchase the property. Return Friday morning. A fleeting visit to ensure all was safe; to see the children and hold their warm hands for a few moments. To ensure they had a premises. And then I would hire somebody: properly. Spend the rest of my maternity leave with Layla. And with Becky. Maybe we could do the admin between us, jointly.

I was already on the return plane, waiting on the runway, when I got the call. The door hadn't shut yet, people were still milling about, putting their hand luggage above me – a man's zip from his hooded jumper swung perilously close to my face – and so I answered my phone, ringing in the depths of my handbag.

It was Becky. The last call I ever took from her. It's still in my call records, frozen in time.

It took me more than two iterations to understand it. It wasn't true. It couldn't be true. The man was still trying to get his bag into the overhead locker. His zip was still swinging. Towards me and then away from me, towards me and then away from me.

We started taxiing. I woodenly turned my phone off.

Logical Martha overrode the other. Just get home. Get home and sort it out.

But I never came home again. Not really.

Scott is in a shirt and boxers in our bedroom when I return at eight in the morning. I don't like the vertiginous sensation of being up in a flat that overlooks the sea: the expanse of it. I don't tell him where I've been. What I've asked Marc.

'You don't need to wear a shirt,' I say, suddenly irritated at the pretence of it all. At the Masai masks hanging on our wall that we brought home from some exotic holiday or other. Status symbols. That's what they are. And where did status get us? I want to pull them off the wall, but I resist. I rage at the sea views we purchased, like they were a tonic to cure all modern ills. At the shirt he insists on wearing to the trial for the murder of our daughter.

'I know. But it's . . . you know. It's court,' he says.

He likes to follow the rules. They are the scaffolding of his life. Taking a bottle of wine when invited to somebody's house for dinner. Sending birthday cards, thank-you cards, sympathy cards. He's good at all of that: etiquette. I've always found it charming, like he has fully bought into the world he lives in, not questioning his choices, like I am.

I could tell him, I think strangely. I could say it, right here, and unravel my marriage: I married you because I thought I should. I never liked the fruit and vegetables you brought back for me. I don't want any more children with you. I don't know you.

'Never mind,' I say, instead.

I try to think of the good times, the good memories, but they are only *things*. The excellent champagne we had at our wedding. The venue with its sandstone walls that I snuck off to run my hand over. The bike with a basket he bought me for my thirtieth birthday. The £17.99 pregnancy test I took – digital – which told me I was between one and two weeks pregnant. The damned raspberries and strawberries he brings back. They are all so material. What is the substance beneath it? I look out to sea, but it's shifting, the bed of the sea churning itself up and spreading itself out over the beach. What is underneath that – the core of the earth? I want to press myself against it, to feel its heartbeat, to feel its stability underneath my chest and hands as I lie there.

'We've got to go,' Scott says. 'We'll be late. I know it's . . . I know you'd rather be anywhere else,' he says tentatively.

See? I tell my mind. *See?* He is always thinking of me. My stoic, gentle, thoughtful Scott. Why can't I reach him?

He looks at me, in the mirror, his eyes on mine as he flattens his shirt collar down. There's a question in those eyes, I am sure of it. I want to ask him what it is, to put it out there, but I don't. I rack my brains for a nice memory, trying to find one amongst all the *things*, like a hoarder with a room full of useless stuff. Eventually, I find it, while still gazing at him.

We were lazing by the river, in Cambridge. It was in the early part of summer, or late spring maybe, when days like that still felt like such a treat. Winter had gone! We had a picnic blanket out but Scott was lying with his feet in the grass.

'I keep getting ants on my legs,' he said.

'Move your feet then,' I said.

'I can't. I like to—' He stopped.

'What?'

'I really like to dig my toes into the mud. Look.'

He waved a foot upwards, swinging it towards me. His toenails were encrusted with mud. A lone ant made its way across the arch of his foot.

'That's gross,' I said.

'I know. I must stop. But I like the feel of it. The squashy feel. I'll wash later.'

'You'll get threadworms,' I said.

'Maybe so.'

Yes: that, I think now. I cling to it. We are all the other has. And we were happier. We never laughed, exactly – not like Marc and Becky – but perhaps there's something here, underneath the earth.

That solid mud. That earth between our toes. I am sure we can find it again, somewhere.

53

Becky

As soon as I walk up the drive, I hear the screaming. I almost go out again, but it's been too long. She must be terrified, I think guiltily. The double-edged sword of motherhood. I had forgotten. Every uncomfortable emotion comes with an unpleasant side order of it: guilt. Feelings were one-dimensional, when life was lived just for me. But when Xander was born, and now, while looking after Layla, feelings are experienced twice: the initial emotion, and then the guilt. The bitter aftertaste.

The crying gets louder and my jaw locks into place. The glint of empathy I felt has disappeared behind a smokescreen, and all I feel is steeliness. There is something hard in the centre of my gut, unyielding. It's taken root, and I can't stop it growing.

What is it?

It is anger. I am angry.

When I reach the front door, something is different. The key won't turn left.

The door is already unlocked. I open it, my heart pounding.

There is Marc, right on my sofa, holding Layla, staring up at me, an unreadable expression on his face.

54

Martha

The curly-haired journalist says nothing today. A new tactic. I appraise her silently as we ascend the steps to the courtroom. She looks back at me, impassive. I wonder if I can see a hint of something in her eyes. An apology, maybe. Perhaps she has a mortgage, is a single parent. We all have our jobs to do. The microphone drops to her side and she makes a funny kind of gesture, her hands just twitching by her sides, the palms turning to me, slightly.

Surrender. It is surrender.

The defence proceeds in a more shambolic way than the prosecution, it is less carefully meted out. A medical expert was due today, but she got her days muddled up. And so the defence skips to a social worker, who is available, having answered her phone at 9.45 a.m. and saying she would be in as soon as possible.

Between nine and half past ten, we do nothing. The jury are sent back to their holding room, but we aren't. Instead, Scott and I watch the barristers milling around, offering each other water, talking about colleagues in common. Becky, too, is taken away again – who knows where? – and for fifteen minutes Mum, Dad and Ethan leave the courtroom. I guess they are with her, though they won't tell me; they never do.

I visit the tea machine and stand in the foyer, delaying

the moment before I go back into the stuffy courtroom, then decide to use the toilet to put it off for a few minutes more. I've not been to the toilet here yet, going only in cafés at lunchtime. I must be dehydrated, not looking after myself in the wake of it all. Perhaps my cheeks are sunken, dark circles beneath my eyes. I wouldn't know. I am buried in the cemetery just over there, with Layla.

The dark wood door swings shut behind me and I enter a cubicle. There are tufts of wet tissue paper lining the edges of it. One of them sticks to my black shoe. I hear someone else come in. I listen carefully, but it is not Becky's walk, her stomping. It must be somebody else.

I emerge, and it is Becky's lawyer. She's only come in to wash her hands, fix her hair, it would seem. Our eyes meet in the mirror for a moment. A few days ago, I would've spoken to her about Marc, but not now: he is telling the truth.

We both look away.

She looks back as she leaves, just once. Our eyes meet. She looks sorry. She looks sorry for me.

The social worker is finally called to the stand, though we are almost stopping for lunch. She smiles at Harriet, a quick smile, eyes crinkling, but in a way that is too practised, as though she has perfected it in the mirror. She has attractively pointy canines. She doesn't look much more than twenty-five.

'Can you please confirm your name?'

'Lynne,' she says, and I'm surprised by such a sixties name. 'Lynne Oliver.'

'Isn't it right that you are the social worker who investigated the incident involving Xander and the defendant in Accident and Emergency?'

'Yes.'

'Can you tell us what happened after the incident with Bryony Riles, the safeguarding nurse in A&E? When Xander and his mother gave a conflicting account as to the cause of his shoulder injury?'

I look across at the judge. He has pulled a handkerchief from his robes, somewhere, and I can just see the edge of it, pale blue, peeking over the top of his bench before he wipes his glasses with it.

'I received a report from A&E. Xander's explanation of his injury was that his mother had pulled his arm in their kitchen. His mother's account was that she pulled him out of traffic. It's reasonably common but, nevertheless, I wanted to speak to Xander.'

'And so you arranged for a home visit, with him, on his own?'

'Yes, I did.'

'And what was the date of that home visit?'

'The twenty-first of September.'

'And what happened?'

'The defendant let us in, and then went into another room while we spoke.'

Harriet fumbles with the papers. 'Yes. And what did you discuss?'

'We discussed the events that led to Xander's admission to A&E,' Lynne says. 'He told me that his father had become frustrated with him walking into traffic and—'

'Hearsay,' Ellen says. 'That's Xander's account. We want yours and yours alone.'

'Alright,' Harriet says, through gritted teeth.

'Did you have any concerns following your talk with Xander?'

'No.'

'And during your visit at the defendant's home, did you assess their home life more generally?'

'Yes. The defendant lives – *lived* – alone with her son. She and her ex-husband are on good terms.'

'Go on.'

'Becky's home was completely normal. Clean. Bright. Plenty of food in the cupboards. Xander's artwork on the fridge.'

'And Xander?'

'Perfectly well adjusted,' she says.

I think of Xander with his quiet, people-pleasing personality. I think of the surprisingly good poem he wrote for me a year ago, and the computer games he loves to play.

I think of Marc's expression outside his house and feel deflated all over again. What was I thinking? I had *no* reason to suspect him. What was it based on? His lack of alibi, and flashes of temper here and there? That doesn't mean he's capable of *murder*.

God, I have been a fool.

'And what was the house like? Did you see the bedrooms?'

'Perfectly unremarkable. The house is over three floors, and Xander's room is up in the eaves. Xander had his things everywhere but it wasn't untidy. There were no signs of substance abuse or violence. Xander's behaviour towards his mother was completely normal.'

'And how did the defendant herself seem?'

'Normal. Funny, actually,' Lynne says.

I like that she noticed it. You cannot help but notice how funny Becky is; it is her defining characteristic.

'Very jolly. A bit nervous, which I would expect, and hope for. It was important to her, what I thought of her during that visit. Which is a good, and normal, sign.'

'Yes. Did you notice anything else?'

'No. Nothing at all. It was a completely normal set-up. A normal family home.'

'Thank you,' Harriet says, giving Lynne a warm, broad smile.

Ellen stands up immediately. 'Lynne.'

'Yes.'

'Why were you instructed to review the defendant's family life?'

'Because there was suspicion about whether she had been violent to her child.'

'How long elapsed between Xander's version of events in A&E, and you seeing him alone, without his mother, to discuss what he had said?'

'Nine days.'

'During which time he was living alone with . . .'

'His mother.'

'Who could easily have asked him to lie for her.'

'No.'

'*No?* How do you know?'

'I . . . I don't.'

'Thank you. Nothing further.'

We are dismissed early. The judge has to hear another case, or something, and so we leave just after lunch. The summer heat continues relentlessly, and Scott takes my hand outside the courtroom. 'Home?' he says gently, but it irritates me.

'Okay,' I say.

We stand on the steps for a moment in the sun. Becky's already left, and Mum and Dad, too, with the air of people leaving a wake. It's almost over. The verdict is almost upon us. No matter how hard I try – and I do try – I just cannot imagine that verdict happening, nor the things it will bring with it.

A new image springs to mind. Becky in prison, her cheeks gaunt and chiselled, her humour stamped out by prison's relentless, unvarying ways.

And then, when she's released . . . How will we continue? There is no way out for us. Something has to happen.

Something will happen, I tell myself. I'm just not sure what.

'She got a lawyer right away,' Scott says to me. He is squinting up at the sun.

'Huh?'

'She didn't answer questions with an open mind, like somebody who's innocent. She got a lawyer before she would speak to anybody.' He runs a hand over his chin.

'Yeah. But Becky is – you know. Pretty savvy. She's . . . you know how she is. Streetwise. A cynic.'

'Streetwise about what?' asks Scott. 'Because I sure as hell don't know.'

'I don't know, either,' I say. 'Sorry. I don't know what I'm saying.'

I suddenly feel flat. There's no solution. It *wasn't* Marc. Oh God, so it was Becky. Of course it was.

'I wouldn't know how to get a lawyer so fast, anyway,' Scott concludes.

Ethan appears behind us. 'Don't worry about that,' he says quietly. 'They all get lawyers right away. I'm telling you, she didn't do it.'

'Hmm,' Scott says.

Privately, today, in this moment, I agree with Scott.

I'll go there, one night, I decide. Before the trial ends. Stay at Becky's house. Not to investigate it, but to accept it. To accept what has happened to me.

To all of us.

55

Martha

I go for a walk alone, and microwave a pizza when I get back to the flat. It cost 89p from Sainsbury's Local. It is one of those cheap children's ones. Plastic cheese and tomato. No sun-dried tomatoes here; no fresh baby spinach, no buffalo mozzarella like we would usually have. Just an 89p pizza, obliterated in the microwave, tipped whole on to a small plate and cut with scissors.

Scott is in bed when I walk into the bedroom, carrying my dinner on its plate. His chest is tanned. I hardly recognize it.

I set the pizza down on the end of the bed. It'll stain the Egyptian cotton sheets, but I don't care.

'What're you eating?' he says as I sit down and look at him.

'Nothing,' I say. 'Pizza.'

'I had a cold quiche.'

'Nice.'

He ignores me and goes back to his iPad. He is reading the *Telegraph* on it, something which Becky always found hilarious. 'Just educating myself,' she would mimic him, when Scott perused articles even on Christmas Day. I wince as I think of her. I think of her often in this way, in this normal, benign, friendly way. *Oh, Becky would love this spotty mug*, I will think in a shop, and then remember, suddenly, and stop.

I take a deep breath. Perhaps it is time to follow my husband's advice. No sleuthing. No investigating. Just a quiet acceptance of the tragedy that has befallen us.

'Scott?' I say.

His head snaps up. 'Yep?'

'Do you think she did it? Really and truly?'

He puts his iPad down. 'Yes,' he says.

'Because of the evidence?'

'Yes.' He stares at me.

His eyes look navy blue in the dim bedroom light. The posh carpet curls around my toes – it's so deep – and it smells artificial in here, of the Glade plug-in our cleaner changes every other Thursday.

'Marth,' he says softly. He removes the iPad and puts it on the bedside table.

'Mmm,' I say. I cross my legs in front of me, balancing the plate. The stringy cheese feels molten in my mouth. I proffer him a triangular piece and he takes it. 'Surprisingly nice for 89p,' I say.

'Martha.' He looks at me now, and his shoulders slump. 'I'm sorry. I just . . . I think the easiest explanation is the correct one.'

My back is turned away from what is in the corner of the room, but I can feel its beam, like a lighthouse sweeping back and forth over the sea: the Moses basket. It's still there. Still has her hair and skin in it, no doubt; her smell. The police returned it to us, after they were finished with it. She breathed her dreamy, milky breath into that basket, with us, for eight weeks of her life, before it was snuffed out.

I can see Scott's eyes keep darting to it.

'Do you really think that?' I say.

'I do,' he says.

We say nothing more for a few minutes. It's time. It's time to accept it. And it's time – however painful that is – to move on from it.

I meet his eyes and he blinks, and I see the Scott I met, all those years ago, at the dinner party. The man who then became my husband.

We *were* happy. I feel it with a sudden certainty in my gut. He is the man who knows me best in the entire world. I can say anything to him.

He reaches over and takes another piece of pizza.

'Watch it,' I say, 'it's mine.' The banter, the casual inter-action, feels nostalgic to me. It's been so long since we have done it. I had forgotten we ever did.

'Got a taste for it,' he says with a quick grin.

I remove my tights and stretch my legs up the bed to him, enjoying the feeling of the cool sheets on my bare skin. He rests a warm hand on one of my feet.

'Anyway. We weren't there,' he says. 'We're to blame. Really. We should be to blame. *I* should.'

'I know.' I hold his gaze again. 'We weren't there enough. We were . . . we were inept. In that way.'

'Yes. We were. So really . . . I don't know. It was more than one person. It was us, too.'

'Yes,' I say. 'I think that's the part I find hardest. We're not on trial.'

Scott holds his hands out, half a tiny pizza slice still held in one. A string of cheese and tomato smears across the bed and he wipes it up with his finger, which only makes it worse.

'Leave it,' I say. 'I hate these fucking sheets.'

Scott splutters, a real, genuine, surprised laugh. 'Do you?'

'Yeah. I hate this whole flat.'

'Why?'

'It's like . . .' I look around the room. At the white dressing table dotted with my make-up and brushes. At the huge grey vase in the corner, serving no purpose: it's too massive to ever contain flowers. 'It's all fake. Isn't it?'

'Is it?'

'What's the word for when you're doing things because other people are?'

'Keeping up with the Joneses?'

'No, more than that. I don't know . . . I just feel like my whole life . . . I don't know.'

'What do you mean?' His expression is becoming more alarmed, and he sets his uneaten pizza down on the plate.

I give a half-smile. 'Pretension. I got a job because I had a good degree. We got a flat overlooking the sea because – well, because why not? Everyone likes that, right?'

'I don't love this flat. I thought you did.'

'It feels like a show home,' I say.

I always loved show homes. I loved the matching cushions and ornaments and fake photographs. I loved the little artificial lemons in the bowls. But you can't live like that.

'I want mess and stupid bedspreads. Seventies bedspreads.'

'What else did you do just because everyone else did?' he says.

'Got a mortgage.'

'Yeah.'

'Had a baby,' I whisper.

His head drops at that. 'I see.'

'I thought it would be . . . it was just the next thing, wasn't it? Spend twenty thousand pounds on a wedding. Kit out a nice flat. Have a baby. I never knew it would be so . . .'

'So what?'

'So complicated. So hard. I didn't know any of it. I wasn't ready. Stop Gap was too important to me. It was the only thing besides you that was *real*. I wasn't ready to give that up. And neither were you, with your job.'

'No.' He eats the final part of the pizza. A few crumbs cascade down on to the duvet. 'We weren't.'

He is looking at me, saying nothing. We both know it's illogical.

'I loved her so much,' he says, his voice thick with tears.

He opens his arms and I scoot up the bed towards him.

'It was enough. That you loved her,' I say softly. 'It's just . . . complicated. If we'd been trying for years, or something, and we'd loved every moment of having Layla, do you think it would have been different?'

Scott doesn't answer. How can he? Of course it's true – if we had been there, Layla wouldn't have died, so say some of the experts – but the reasoning is flawed. She didn't die because we didn't love her enough. She died because somebody stopped her breathing. Because Becky stopped her breathing.

Scott heaves a huge sigh. I bob up and down on his chest like a tiny boat out at sea.

'It's pointless. Talking like this. It has happened,' I say.

'Yeah. But I miss her,' he whispers.

Neither of us speaks for a while.

'It was my fault,' he says.

'What?' I say.

'It was my fault, not yours. I shouldn't have left her. If I hadn't got carried away, socializing, wanting another night of freedom, it wouldn't have happened.'

'No. It was both of us.'

'You've been blamed for it. For everything.'

'I know,' I say softly.

'But it was *me*. I'm the one who changed my plans. You were always going to be away two nights.'

I look up at him. His face is wobbling, trembling with the effort not to cry.

'Why did you?' I say. I have never asked. Instead, I have avoided him, shifted away from him in bed, my body rigid with anger. He left her.

He sighs, his chest moving up and down. 'I don't know,' he says. 'I don't know. It was hard for me too.' He holds a hand up. 'It was harder for you, I know. A million times harder. I suppose that's what made it hard for me. I didn't know what to do about it. And the guilt. Of seeing you struggle. Of seeing Layla struggle. And I had to earn the money, but I was also being selfish, Marth. I could've taken more leave. I could've gone part-time. We could have shared it. I see it now. It's so clear. But I didn't then. I wish,' he says, his voice rising, 'I *wish* I'd taken her off you. Thrown that bloody expressing machine out of the window. Formula-fed her, so I could help. But it's a bloody hornets' nest. I nearly said it to you so many times, but I didn't know how . . . I thought you'd think you'd failed her. All I wanted was to make it easier for you, for her, for everyone. But instead, I avoided it, because it made me uncomfortable. Because I was a selfish bastard who wanted another night away. And now, she's gone and . . . I never thought she'd be gone,' he says, tears coursing down his cheeks. 'I never thought this would happen. Because of me,' he says. 'Because of that one stupid, *stupid* text.'

I hold him closer to me. I can feel his heart beating underneath my ear. Strong and steady.

'Thank you for saying that.' I don't argue with him, and I don't try to convince him otherwise. He's learnt his lesson. We all have.

'That day in the en suite, when I said . . .' I begin, tentatively.

'Yes,' he says.

I don't want to get the memory out and examine it, but I have to.

'I didn't wish we had never had her.'

'You were just so broken,' he says. 'It was so hard. I wish I had helped you.'

'It was just the shock of it,' I say. 'New motherhood.'

He pulls me closer to him. 'I know,' he whispers in my ear. 'I know.'

We lie there for five minutes, then ten, crying, my head on his chest. Something about it feels cathartic. We're cried so many times over the past nine months, but this time, we're together. We're in it together.

'Becky said something to me, you know, after she was arrested. She said it wouldn't have happened if I had been there,' Scott says after a while.

I blink, listening to his breathing, thinking. 'I'm sorry,' I say eventually.

'I think she was just furious. I didn't know. I didn't know how hard it had been for her, when I texted about staying another night. And she sent this really nice reply saying not to worry.'

'She didn't say. She didn't say to anybody how hard she had been finding it.'

'Yeah. Anyway,' he says, heaving a sigh.

We lie in silence for a while.

'Any more regrets?' he says lightly. 'While we're confessing?'

I almost say it, then. That I married him because I thought I was supposed to. A developer-in-training. A nice bloke. Uptight, sometimes, but kind to me. A man with whom I didn't have a huge amount in common, except a commitment. But to what? To the cause, I guess. To normality. To nice flats and mortgages and babies and pressed napkins on the tables at our wedding. To Italy in the summer and skiing in the winter. To the establishment. To life. To living life the way *one should*.

I think of his toes in the mud at the river, that day in Cambridge. I see his fingertips, now, stained orange with cheap tomato sauce, and notice how I feel, deep down in my stomach, right underneath my heart, about him. How I can remove my tights in front of him, eat a cheap pizza and get it everywhere. I think of the things he has just said to me: his guilt, his regrets. How differently he would do it all again, if he could. How he *wanted* to do things differently, but just didn't know how. There is love for me, there, buried deep underneath his layers.

Still waters run deep.

I think of the way he has held my hand through every

334

day of the trial. His calm coaching of me the morning I was due to give evidence. His warm presence every lunch-time. His sympathetic smiles. The way he shields me from the reporters. The way he tells me it was his fault, not mine. The father *and* the mother. Not just the mother.

We may never be like Marc and Becky, but they're not together. And maybe, just maybe, they're not perfect. I had always so admired their relationship, their hundreds of in-jokes, but it must have been flawed, cracked, too. Because it failed. When it came to it – a child, jobs, *life* – their marriage cracked. Its foundation wasn't strong enough.

Maybe there is hope for us. Perhaps we can sell up, here. Quit our jobs. Go part-time. Go and get muddy at the weekends.

'Regrets?' I say softly. 'No. Nothing further.'

Later, after, my husband goes to the wardrobe. He's naked, and I look at his form in the dim light of the bedroom.

'Can we get a rambling old house?' he says.

'Yes,' I say. 'No ambient lighting. No fucking Glade plug-ins.'

'Zero,' he says. 'I want to tell you something.' He looks at me, his expression serious. 'About where I've been going in the evenings.'

He sits down at the end of the bed. He looks braced, as though I might not like what he's about to say.

My mind starts racing. Affairs, divorce, loneliness. 'Okay,' I say.

Oh, please don't leave me, I am thinking. Not after we have reconciled. I can see it so clearly now. We don't have to be like Marc and Becky. Not silly. Perhaps there is another way.

Here is a man in front of me to whom I can say, 'I sort of regret having a baby,' and he hasn't judged me. There are so many kinds of relationships, and Marc and Becky's is just one of them. Ours could be another. Not jokes, but other stuff: vulnerability, maybe. Intimacy.

'Can I show you something? At the land?'

'Now?' I say.

He spreads his hands wide in front of me. 'Why not? Didn't you notice the fruits have stopped? Since?'

I look at him, intrigued, then smile what feels like my first smile since it happened. 'You've been there loads . . . I have wondered.'

'This is why.'

We get dressed and get in his car and drive there. It's less than five minutes, and I can't believe I haven't been in almost a year. The night is cool and calm around us, and Scott turns the heaters up so high the hot air makes my face feel tight and shiny.

His patch of land is down a hill, left at a gate.

I notice as soon as we descend the hill that it's not how it was.

'Where are the plants?' I say.

He shrugs shyly.

We walk further down and open the gate.

And now I can see them properly. And I can hear the sea, rather than just see it, like an illusion. And I can taste the salt on the breeze.

There they are. Maybe forty of them. Tiny trees. Calf-height, just like Layla would have been by now.

'You got rid of all the plants.'

'I don't care about the fucking plants,' he says softly. 'What use is growing fruit that only I eat?'

We stare out at the trees together. They won't yield fruit. They won't save money. Their ferns waft slightly in the breeze. They're pointless. They're pointless, and I love them.

'They'll grow as she would have,' Scott says.

I look more closely at them. Every trunk has an L carved into it. They're all for her. And for me.

'I love them,' I say to him. And I do.

Monday

56

Martha

The reporter isn't there today. I look around for her, on the steps, but she has disappeared.

Scott and I spent the weekend not talking about the trial. We slept too much, ate too much, but we were together.

By tomorrow, it will be over. Or, at least, the evidence will be, and it will be for the jury to decide. But today, it's the defence's expert. This is it: the woman who can give us an alternative truth, if there is one.

She is called Jada, and she is younger than I thought an expert might be, maybe only in her early thirties.

She confirms her name and her job title, which is a jumble of words to me by this point. Her eyes keep flitting to me. Perhaps she thinks I wish for Becky to be found guilty. And do I? No. I don't. Quite the opposite. Despite myself. Because of myself, and because of her, and who she is. My little sister.

'Ms Browne,' Harriet says. 'It's important that we get this right.'

Jada pushes oversized glasses up her nose. 'Yes. For the sake of the deceased child.'

Layla was just beginning to recognize people, right before she died, but it was only me who could spot it: the tracking of her eyes, the interested eyebrow raises. She had fantastically expressive eyebrows, her back arching as she tried to hold her head up, to turn and look at everybody.

'Yes, I couldn't agree more,' Jada says. 'Sometimes, accidents happen, and we'll never know what occurred.'

'So can you talk us through the evidence, piece by piece?' Harriet says.

Jada nods. 'Nine hundred babies died in 2014 from accidental suffocation and strangulation in bed.'

'Yes.'

'A *very* small percentage of suffocations are homicidal.'

'I see,' Harriet says. 'So if we were to consider the hypothesis that Layla was accidentally smothered, how could that have happened?'

'If, at any point, you perform an autopsy on a baby, the baby's body will show a snapshot of what its body has been through in those past few weeks or months, at the moment you cut into it. Whenever doctors perform a test looking for one thing, they often find other, benign, things that then require investigation. Ever had a scan of your appendix and then they found a liver cyst, and so on? Well, that can happen with babies. The honest answer is that if you take a snapshot of a baby at any one time, you won't always know what was wrong, and what had a material effect. The scans are just snapshots. They are not as diagnostic as you might think.'

'So the scans are merely showing the body as it was as the time of death. But perhaps not everything observed in the scans caused the death? In babies, in particular?'

'Yes, exactly,' Jada says. 'If you were admitted to hospital right now, pronounced dead on arrival, and we performed an autopsy, what might we find? An old bruise to your hip from that table? A blood clot on the brain that might've ruptured one day soon, or years from now, or never? A blocked artery? The beginnings of cancer, somewhere? The thing with babies is that their bodies are so . . . well, so *new* that it is just impossible sometimes to tell what caused what. We are still learning, every week, every month, about them, and what's there right after they leave the womb. What we cannot – what we mustn't – do is assume that every sign found on the scans indicates force or a struggle. We must also accept that, ultimately, we weren't there. And so we may never know.'

'And sometimes,' Harriet says, with a look at the jury, 'the tendency can be towards *knowing*, and so we convict, where it would be wrong to do so. Do you have an alternative hypothesis, based on your examination of Layla's case?'

'Let's take the evidence step by step. The bruise behind the ear could easily be a Mongolian blue spot: a congenital birthmark. Now that Layla has died, we cannot test whether it had always been there or if it was a new bruise. But we shouldn't assume.'

'Yes', Harriet said. My eyes pool with tears. How can I not know whether a mark had always been on my own daughter? I have been through my hundreds of photographs of her, over and over, hoping to find one with the answer. But I never do.

'The bleeding in the lungs and the blood spots around the mouth, nose and on the retinas could all be caused by accidental smothering.'

'Yes. And how might Layla have been accidentally smothered?'

'She might have rolled over. Eight weeks is early, but not unheard of. The defendant could have remembered incorrectly, and could have placed her face down, misre-membered. Perhaps.'

'And the haemorrhages?'

'Could have been caused by accidental smothering but could also have been there from birth.'

'How?'

'During a prolonged and difficult labour – or one where the baby's head does not easily fit through the birth canal, or the baby is large – the blood vessels in the eyes can rupture.'

'So those symptoms may have been there since birth?'

'Yes.'

'And would they look like the retinal haemorrhages we have seen on Layla's scans?'

'Yes.'

Harriet pauses. She looks down at her papers, then up at Jada, then at the jury.

'Please can the members of the jury turn to page eight-een of their folders,' Harriet says. 'The pathologist's photographs of Layla's retinas, taken with a magnifying camera through the pupil.'

Jada reaches for a folder, too, and holds up a photo-graph. It looks like a sun, or a ball of lava. 'Full retinal haemorrhages would have blood across this entire orange area,' she says. The eyes have thin, red cobwebs over them, interspersed, in the centre, with fat, sprawling drops. 'Layla's are only in the centre, here,' she says, point-ing to one of the blobs.

'What would you conclude might cause retinal haem-orrhages like this?'

'Many things. Birth trauma. Accidental smothering.

Crying violently. CPR, for example. CPR performed by the frightened defendant. Shaking, to wake the baby up.'

'Thank you. Lots of explanations. None as far-fetched as abuse.'

'No.'

'And, finally: do you agree with the pathologist's time of death as between eight and nine thirty – nine forty at the absolute latest?'

'Yes. I agree there could be no way Layla would have been alive after nine forty.'

'Thank you, Ms Browne,' Harriet says. 'That will be all from me.'

That's it? That's it?

I sit very still, hoping for more.

Where is the counter-evidence? The moment of *truth*?

Ellen looks completely cool as she stands up. She stands silently for a moment or two, one arm across her body, left hand cupping her right elbow, right hand up to her face. Her head is tilted thoughtfully.

'Right,' Ellen says, sounding exasperated. 'At no point has the defendant, the victim's mother, or anyone who had care of Layla said that she was accidentally smothered. Becky had sole care of Layla at the agreed time of death – between eight and nine thirty that evening. She would have known, and indeed would have admitted, that it was accidental, if it was. If it was accidental, the baby would have been discovered having rolled over, or caught in her blankets. The defendant's own account is that Layla wasn't even in bed at that time.'

Harriet stands, but Ellen gets there first. 'I will withdraw that commentary,' she says. Then, looking at the witness, 'So your evidence that Layla's injuries might have come from an accident are irrelevant, because that isn't the evidence we have.'

'That we know of.'

'You say these injuries would present themselves in a case of accidental smothering. Would they all? Even the bruised gums?'

'It's possible.'

'All the time? Every single time?'

'Not every single time, no.'

I find myself looking across at Becky, wondering what she thinks about all of this. If she did it, if she didn't . . . because if she didn't do it, all of this – this conjecture – it's pointless, isn't it? An expert saying one thing, the next saying another . . . she might be sitting there, knowing that she didn't do it. How strange that would be.

'Retinal haemorrhages – how often do they last *eight weeks* from birth?'

'It is possible that they do.'

'Is it likely?'

'It's possible.'

'Is it rare?'

'It is quite rare for them to last eight weeks.'

'Right.' Ellen sighs, as though she is dealing with an idiot, a criminal. 'So your *hypothesis* is that Layla did not die because of homicidal smothering. She died of accidental smothering, or of something benign and *undetectable*, and the findings of haemorrhages were incidental to this? Or maybe that she rolled over prodigiously early, for the first time, that night – and nobody saw? And she was found on her back, by the defendant's own testimony?'

'Yes.'

'Is that likely?'

'It is possible.'

'You say CPR or shaking to wake a baby can cause retinal haemorrhages.'

'Yes.'

'So your position is that the injuries might have been caused after Layla's death, after she was found dead in her cot?'

'Yes, they could have been.'

'Are the other injuries consistent with taking place after death?'

Jada looks at her feet. 'Well . . .'

'Because the body behaves differently before and after death, does it not? The blood stops flowing, for example?'

'It does.'

'So the quality of the injuries – do they look to you like they occurred before or after death, in terms of inflammatory reactions?'

'Before. But it is possible that—'

'Right. Thank you.' Ellen leaves a meaningful pause. 'Nothing further.' She heaves a sigh. She sounds exhausted, baffled, confused. Just confused by this expert, and all of her unlikely, ludicrous evidence.

And she's not the only one.

So that is that. I sneak a look across the public gallery, at Scott. He was right. There is no defence. There are no facts. They have bent each beam of truth, refracted it naturally away from Becky, but it is a construct. The truth of it is that one beam – abuse, a spotlight explaining every single injury – fits. This defence – that one symptom was caused by one unlikely event, another by another – seems unnatural. Precarious. Like it could tumble down at any moment.

The conviction I felt in Becky's front garden has disappeared. This isn't a murder investigation, and I am no sleuth. It's just a slow unravelling of a tragedy, a tragedy my sister caused. It must be.

The truth is, there is no truth. We will never know.

Conviction or acquittal. I am never going to know.

That is the truth of it.

57

Becky

'You left her?' he says. He's holding her close to him. Her mouth is right by his ear. The noise must be unreal.

'Only for five minutes,' I say. I wave the bottles at him, both held in my right hand. 'Calpol.'

'Oh,' Marc says.

Credit to him, he doesn't labour the point. I shouldn't have left her, obviously. But he knows, more than most, the stress of it.

'You sounded like you could do with a hand anyway . . . and I wanted to talk to you,' he says.

'Okay,' I say dully.

'What's going on, Sam?' He rises, going to stand by the mirror over the mantelpiece. 'Who's that?' he says to Layla, pointing to her reflection.

'Nothing,' I say sullenly. I'm not sure he hears me over the crying. 'It's just . . .' I say, looking at my husband in the mirror.

His smell lingers in the living room. Not aftershave, not deodorant, not washing powder. New carpets, that's what he's always smelt of. And I have always loved it.

'This arrangement,' he says. 'It can't be long-term, can it?'

'I don't know,' I say, over her screams.

Marc sits down again with Layla. 'It's mad,' he says.

'It's mad how incompetent I am,' I say. To my surprise, my voice cracks, expanding around a lump in my throat. 'Mad,' I say.

Marc doesn't say anything. He just looks at me. Blue eyes open wide, so trustworthy. I could tell him anything.

'Look at their life,' I say.

I gesture and Marc passes Layla to me. She quietens, still crying, but more of a low, discontented grizzle. I lay her down in my lap and her fists close around my fingers. Her little warm hands.

'Martha and Scott's?'

'Yes. Look at it. They're running a charity. He earns a shitload with his computer stuff. It's perfect, isn't it? Their perfect flat, their perfect, charitable endeavours, their perfectly planned baby.'

'Is it?' Marc says. He rubs a hand thoughtfully over his chin.

This is what I've always loved about him. He considers my opinions. He doesn't dismiss them, as Martha and Scott do. *Bloody Becky*, they think, exchanging a wry glance. But Marc never does. Never would.

'And then look at me!' I say, sounding hysterical, even to myself. 'Failed at design school. Failed at set-dressing. Failed at marriage,' I say, catching his eye.

'I failed at that, too,' he says softly, sadly. 'Not to mention the baby making.'

I take a deep breath. And suddenly, here I am. After years of avoidance, of *pride*, of defiance, here I am, ready.

And I know it's not just the wine talking. It is me. 'I'm sorry, Marc,' I say. 'I should never have given up on us. I should never have slept with somebody else. It was . . . *God*, it was beyond stupid.'

'It was,' he says. 'It was.'

'I regret it every day. I regret *this* nannying every day,' I say, looking at Layla, 'and I regret that.'

'Well, at least you've admitted it,' he says, a small smile on his face.

'How do you mean?'

'Oh, Sams. I think sometimes you're so prickly, worrying about what people think of you, that you never truly say how you feel. You think they'll judge you.'

'But they do.'

'So what?' he says, looking at me. 'So what.'

'Thank you,' I say to him. But I'm not done yet. The weeks of pent-up thoughts are racing out, across the living room, to my ex-husband. 'And now this. I'm a failed nanny, too. I was never a good mother,' I say thickly, my voice sounding coated. 'It's just that Xander was easy.'

'No,' Marc says, standing up and coming to sit next to me on the chair. He sits on the arm, his hand dangling casually behind my back. I can feel the warmth of it. My entire mind is focused on it. 'No way. Remember when Xander had winter vomiting? And then teething right after?'

'Vaguely,' I say. I think it was the only time I'd ever been seriously sleep deprived. 'In the spring,' I say. I only remember that because I ate an entire Easter cake, in bed, at 4.00 a.m.

'He was sick for three nights straight,' Marc says. 'No sleep. I had a big job on and you just did it all, Sammy. Cleaning up the sick. Changing the beds. Comforting him. And then the teething. I got home one night and your eyes were just black with how tired you were. But there you were, rubbing Bonjela on to his gums even though it was late.'

I remember that night. He sent me off for a bath. I fell asleep and woke in the tepid water. He dried me off, in the bedroom, and I fell asleep in the towel.

'You just did it all,' he says again. 'You can do anything you put your mind to.'

'You remember all that?'

'I miss it,' he says. 'I've missed it so much. I have Xander half the time, since we split. But I miss it. The other parent.' His eyes meet mine. 'You.'

'I wouldn't miss me,' I say.

I have never once considered how hard it must have been for him. I slept with somebody else and, out of respect for himself, he had to move out. But I'd never once thought I had consigned him to co-parenting, to McDonald's trips alone with his son, to lonely evenings and solo school runs. How selfish I am.

'Sam, listen. You got pregnant at nineteen and you coped with it. You gave up your career for Xander. You found a job that let you work around him. You never resented it, even though you weren't doing what you wanted. And as for us . . .'

'Well, yes,' I say. I look up at him, and his arm shifts, finally connecting with my shoulders. I lean into it. I can't help but do anything else. 'What about us?'

'You ditched your arse of a husband. As you rightly should.'

'I slept with somebody else. Somebody I didn't love. What an idiot,' I say forlornly.

'With good reason,' Marc says with a sigh.

His other hand reaches down to rub Layla's stomach. She's still grumbling, but also watching us, her navy eyes catching the lamplight.

'Not really,' I say. 'You were a bit . . . we were withdrawn and lazy. That's all. The usual.'

'It wasn't usual,' he says. 'It wasn't laziness.'

'No?'

He sighs, then says nothing, looking across the living room in silence.

'What?' I say.

'Do you remember my mumps?' he says.

'Yes,' I say.

How we had laughed at his moon-face. Martha had said it was cruel, and we had just laughed even more.

'When Xander was two.'

'Yes, I remember.'

'Well, that's why,' Marc says simply.

I'm still looking up at him. His expression is unreadable.

'When we started trying again . . . when it took ages, I saw the doctor. I didn't want to, but Dad said I should. So I did. And that's . . . I'm the reason. The mumps. I couldn't give you a baby because . . . I can't,' he says. 'That's why.'

I look down at Layla, then up at him again. His eyes are wet. I don't think I have ever seen him cry.

'Oh,' I whisper.

'So,' he says, dragging the back of his hand underneath his eyes, 'I withdrew. I just couldn't handle it. I developed this dickhead persona. Shouting at Xander, at you. Acting macho because—'

'Marc,' I say.

'I know. I know I should've told you. You could've left. Had a baby with someone else. Or at least stopped hoping your period wouldn't come.'

I swallow hard, remembering those months – those *years* – of bathroom tears. Of checking my boobs so often that I convinced myself they were sore, a phantom pregnancy symptom created by checking for one. Of pregnancy tests done anyway, in hope, and searching for lines that weren't there.

But then I think of Marc. Ill with mumps. Rendered infertile. Being told by a doctor and acting normally that night – whenever it was – around us. Not feeling like he could complete his family, because of something that had happened to him. Mumps. So quotidian. So unfair.

'Marc,' I say again.

'I'm so sorry, Sam. I should've said. Instead, I went the other way. Those stupid FutureLearn courses. I felt like if I filled my head with other stuff, with distractions, then maybe it wouldn't matter. God, what a twat. It's no wonder you slept with somebody else. I don't blame you.'

'God,' I say, trying to take it all in. Trying to work out whether it's a betrayal or a welcome confession. I scout around, searching, but I find no resentment. I find only one thing: sympathy. And regret. 'You poor thing,' I say. I reach up for his hand and hold it.

He starts to cry properly, fully. 'I'm so sorry I didn't tell you.'

'I'm sorry, too ... I'm sorry we didn't find a way through.'

'Yeah,' he says. 'I wasn't surprised, though. When you slept with someone else. I know how many nights you wanted to . . . and I just rolled away from you. I just couldn't. I felt faulty.'

'You're not faulty,' I say, leaning against his body. 'You're never faulty, to me.'

'That's why I was so nasty, anyway. *Being a man*, I suppose.'

'You weren't nasty. You were just a bit – hey. You had a lot going on.'

'I was trying to assert my masculinity. With tellings-off. With temper.'

I breathe in his new-carpet smell and say nothing as he shakes beside me. I rhythmically stroke the rough skin on the back of his hand, letting him cry. 'That's why you were nice, when we split up,' I say. 'That's why you've always been so nice to me.'

'It was like a pressure cooker. And then when I moved out, I felt like . . . I felt like me again. I wasn't going to make any babies, and nobody was expecting me to. And we just reverted, didn't we? I didn't imagine it, did I?'

'No,' I say. 'We did. We did just go back to the way it was. The way we were.'

'And now . . .' he says.

He shifts his weight, and I move over, and suddenly we're both sitting, squeezed in too tight, in the armchair together.

'Not sure this is big enough for my arse and yours,' Marc says.

I can't help but let out a laugh. That humour of his. So base. I have always loved it.

'And now what?' I say.

Layla starts crying again and I try my best not to feel irritated. Marc looks at me.

'She's loud, isn't she?' he says. 'No wonder you've been going bonkers.'

'She's so loud,' I say.

'You need to quit this job,' he says carefully.

'I know. I do know that. I can't do it any more. I feel so – God. I feel so *mad*. I forgot Xander the other day. I left him at the school gates again, because Martha was late, and I didn't have a phone.'

'Oh, Sam. We can't let that happen. Their needs can't trump our little family's. And you're not mad.'

'I am. I feel angry at her,' I say. 'I feel angry at Layla.'

'I see,' he says. 'I see.'

He's nodding, thinking. Wondering what to do, I suppose.

'Well, Samuel,' he says. 'Enough of that. We hardly stopped being together, anyway, did we?'

Layla shifts on my lap. Her eyelids are drooping, but she startles awake each time sleep approaches.

I realize I'm holding my breath. 'No,' I say. 'We didn't.'

I look at the clock on the mantelpiece. Close to eight o'clock on the twenty-sixth of October. The day we worked it all out. The day love won out.

'So how about we . . .' he says, looking at me carefully.

I say nothing, just look back at him, the widest smile in the world on my face. Ever so slowly, he leans down, and kisses me deeply, his tongue tantalizing, his lips soft.

Home. I am home amongst the new carpets.

Home.

58

Martha

The defence has two witnesses remaining: a midwife and Xander. Becky is not giving evidence – exercising her right to silence – which is a fact I try not to dwell on.

Ethan tells me it's what most defendants charged with murder do. That she will have been advised to do it. That, because she has no explanation, the best way forward is to not state her case. That if she takes the stand, the jury may judge her. But still.

The midwife is called. She is a no-nonsense West Country woman called Bridget Evans.

'Just a few questions,' Harriet says, looking tired and pale after the expert witness evidence.

'Okay,' Bridget says. She has a dark, low ponytail which spreads down her back, but the roots are a bright white, like a badger's. Her face has an earthy, ruddy quality. No make-up. A sort of plump smile; her cheeks fill out as she smiles at Harriet.

'Tell me about Layla's birth.'

'It was – gosh, I do remember it so well,' she says. 'It was a bit of a bugger, to be honest. Martha—' she indicates me, perhaps unprofessionally, and I nod, embarrassed. 'Well, let me tell you. I saw Martha when she was hardly dilated at all. She kept coming back, she was in so much pain! I felt for her. She has one of those brittle bodies, skinny, that feels pain easily. That's my theory, anyway. I sent her away, then she came back, I examined her, sent her away again, and so on. On the morning of Layla's birth, she came back, told me she'd been sitting with her leg cocked on the bed all night. I admitted her at that – not because I thought she was in established labour, but because I felt sorry for her. I wanted her to believe that it was happening, you know; that it was time. The body follows the mind, sometimes, in that way. Anyway. Things did move after that. She spent some time in the pool, which she didn't want to get out of, to be honest. Then it really ramped up, and she was moaning, but Layla got stuck in the birth canal. We just couldn't get her out for love or for money. The ventouse followed, then the forceps.'

'I see. Sounds traumatic.'

'It was.'

'And so, in your opinion, it was a traumatic birth?'

'Yes.'

'The birthing canal was too small for the baby?'

'She needed assistance, yes.'

'And so her injuries could stem from that traumatic birth – old injuries that hadn't quite healed?'

'Yes.'

'Your witness,' Harriet says to Ellen.

'Are you an expert as to Layla's specific type of injuries?' Ellen says.

'No.'

'Do you know how those injuries result – whether from physical suffocation or from birth?'

'No.'

'No more questions,' Ellen says, throwing Harriet a look of disbelief.

59

Becky

I've shouted at Layla. I'm so pissed I'm shouting at her even though I'm on my own. I've googled all sorts of things to try and help her.

I'll just go to bed. I'll just go to bed and maybe all of this will go away. Since Marc left – he said he could stay, but I didn't want to subject him to the crying. I want to be with him properly, alone – all I've done is drink.

I bring my arm up to look at my watch, but I misjudge, and my wrist hits me in my face. I can't see the time anyway. Everything is blurred. The room moves with my gaze, like when I had bad flu one Christmas. I shake my head, which makes it worse.

Bed, anyway. And then tomorrow Martha will be home and I will have one hell of a hangover for sure. But just bed, bed, bed, now, and I can forget everything.

I sit on the sofa. Not moving.

The noise of it.

60

Martha

I'm alone in the bathroom in the court, until Becky comes in.

In some ways, I knew it would happen; perhaps she intended it, waited patiently outside with her legal team until I came inside. Or perhaps just because it was bound to occur, with us existing in such close quarters all week.

Bathrooms. A no-man's-land between camps. They trust us, for some reason, to enter this room and not speak to each other, even though they keep an eye on us every-where else. But then, I suppose, Becky is bailed. Neither of us is a prisoner. We are free to wash our hands on our own time.

She joins me at the sink. She doesn't pretend to use the toilet. She is here for me and only me.

Her eyes meet mine in the mirror. That green gaze I had almost forgotten. Direct. Her dark eye make-up. I know Becky: that's war paint. Armour.

I look at our faces, side by side in the mirrors. How simi-lar we look. The same bone structure. I was always slight where she was broad, but now we are almost the same. Both diminished. She is gaunt, underneath her cheek-bones, her décolletage herringboned where her shirt lies open at the neck. I have become stooped. She still has the

Blackwater mane of hair. Mine has visibly thinned at my temples and lies flat and lifeless against my collarbone.

She's still looking directly at me, while my eyes rove all over the place.

'Becky,' I say.

'Yeah,' she says simply. Like: *It's me.*

And it occurs to me now that I haven't heard her voice for nine months. Every single action in that courtroom – the witnesses' oaths, the sweep of the barristers' robes, the jurors listening so intently – is about her, and yet she has no voice in any of it. None at all.

She gets a tube of hand lotion out of her bag and rubs it into her fingers. She was always good at stuff like this. She liked self-care. Would often send me photographs of her feet in candlelit baths, her eyes green behind a mud face mask. *I can't tell you how much I need a bath-time wine and face mask,* she would sometimes text. Or, occasionally, a message would come through at seven o'clock in the morning: *Manicure day today,* it would say. A running commentary from her, to me, about her life. It was a privilege. We were so lucky.

I watch her massage the lotion over and under her palms, her hands twisting, the fingers interlacing.

I can't stop looking at them. Clearly, she is here to say something to me. *She knows,* I can't help thinking, as my eyes dart to meet hers again. And those hands . . . those hands know. Those eyes know and that brain knows and her mouth knows. But is she lying to me, my sister standing here in the bathroom, using a sage and sea salt hand cream like she has no cares in the world.

'Come tonight. To the old spot by the bat house,' she says to me. 'Nine o'clock.'

'Okay,' I say. 'Okay.'

She says nothing further. She replaces the hand cream in her handbag, hoists it over her shoulder in that way that she always did – the movement used to look assured, dramatic, almost like an actress, but she is too frail to pull it off now – and she leaves the bathroom, the dark wood door banging softly behind her.

We are dismissed again. The defence is stop-start. Xander needs a morning slot to give his evidence by video, and tomorrow is the final day of evidence. The judge just lets everybody go, like children the day before half term when nobody can really be bothered any more.

Except this isn't a primary school; it is a courtroom. The defence needs the momentum I, for some reason, urgently feel.

We go home and look at Rightmove; at places where we would like to live. Places different to this sterile flat. Rambling old houses. Doer-uppers. Squat bungalows.

'We could go anywhere,' Scott tells me, which I like.

'Kos,' I say with a tentative smile.

He shrugs and says, 'Maybe.' Then he adds, 'Anywhere with you, really.'

He holds me to him, the lengths of our bodies pressed together, and I feel truly safe.

For the first time in months. Years.

At ten to nine, I excuse myself.

'A walk,' I tell him.

I am here. Back at the stretch of grass by the water which overlooks the sea, where normal grass blends with tough marram grass. The bat house stands on a raised part which banks upwards, gently, and underneath the bat house there's a flatter patch of ground, almost thatched-looking, where we used to sit.

I can still see the childhood things we used to imagine here. The lamp post we pretended was a giant friend of ours. The old electricity box with the *Danger of Death* sign peeling off it. We ignored the sea. We were far more inter-ested in other things.

She is not there before me but arrives two minutes later. She was always late.

She sits next to me, slightly too close – she was always so tactile – and says nothing. Together, we look out to the sea, sitting on the flattened grass. It's still warm from the sun, even though it's late. The breeze is soft against our arms, feeling rounded. It's body temperature, as though we were sitting in a tepid bath of air.

She looks at me, now, her eyes meeting mine. Our eyes are completely different. Mine are round and close together, brown, hers spaced far apart, and a clear green that catches the moonlight. Above us, a bat squeaks, and she winces.

'Can't believe we used to come here and let the bats flap around us,' she says.

'I always thought it was kind of cool,' I say.

'You would,' she says, with a little laugh; a sad little exhale. 'You geek.'

'There could be a retrial, if they knew about this,' I say.

She shrugs. 'You've given your evidence.'

'But still.'

'Yes, I know,' she says. She tugs at a clump of grass. She flashes me a quick smile. 'Don't tell Ethan.'

I put off the inevitable question I must ask her tonight, and instead say, 'What's with the road rage?'

'Oh, God,' Becky says, putting her forehead in her hands. 'They made that sound so much worse than it was.'

'What was it?'

'It was just – this guy cut me up going into a car park. I got out and had a word with him.'

'What, and he called the police?'

'They were there anyway. Passing. He flagged them down. He was a tosser. BMW wanker.'

'I see.' I would have laughed at that, a year ago.

We lapse into silence.

'You're tanned,' I say.

'I've been sitting in the garden, smoking, for three months straight. It's all I do,' she says. 'Mum and Dad hate the smell. They say their roses smell of Marlboro Lights.'

'Oh,' I say. 'I see.'

So I was right. She's not been sunbathing. She's been worrying. Haven't we all?

We don't say anything for a while.

'I want to say something, before we talk about it,' Becky says suddenly.

'Okay,' I say in a small voice. I never could argue with her, not really.

'Did you know?'

'Know what?'

'How jealous I was of you.'

'What? No,' I say quickly. 'No.' I look across at her in surprise. Her nose is turning red in the cool summer air. 'Of me?'

'God, Martha, you're so obtuse,' Becky says, rubbing at her forehead. 'I was so bloody jealous of you. Every day. Every day of my life.'

'When? Why? I was jealous of *you*, Beck. All your jokes with Marc. You were like . . . I don't know. You seemed so together.'

'Wow,' she says softly.

'Why were you jealous of me?'

She looks at me. Her green eyes are bright in the night. 'You really don't know?'

'I have no idea,' I say.

But slowly, slowly, something clicks into place. Becky's barbed comments. Her cageyness. Her sarcastic attitude. 'Martha will have a sensible orange juice,' she would mock, sometimes, in restaurants. 'Well, Martha and Scott read the *Telegraph* every weekend,' she once said to Ethan, as though it explained something. Of course. Of course she was jealous. The oldest, most timeless reason for comments like that.

'After Stop Gap was probably when it got really bad. But, if I'm honest . . . since for ever.'

'But . . . why?'

'You just *had it all*, as they say. Husband. Baby. The ability to make a baby, which I'd somehow lost. Beautiful flat. Job – charity work, too. You seemed to – I don't know, Marth – you seemed to pass through life so smoothly. It was so organized. You were always so organized,' she adds, with just the ghost of a smile.

I look at her, not quite believing her. 'I didn't,' I say in a small voice. 'I definitely didn't.'

'I started drinking, you know. Not too much, but

definitely too often. Wine o'clock here and there. Then Wine Wednesdays to get through the midweek dip. Wine Thursdays, because Thursday is the new Friday. Every night of the weekend. Then no days off wine, all week. In the end.'

'I thought you drank a little too much,' I say quietly, wondering what's to come. A confession?

'Yeah, I did. I've stopped now. Totally. It's the only way.'

'I see. But why were you drinking?'

'The jealousy. Everything. I just felt like a fuck-up. I missed Marc, in the evenings. What started as a treat became a weird kind of companion. And then – well, I was hooked. But the jealousy . . . I saw you all the time, you know? And I just felt so inferior. That's it. And then I went home – alone, with no baby, no husband, just a shit job – and I sank red wine.'

'Oh, Becky.'

'I know.'

'Is that why you asked me about Scott? You seemed to think, sometimes, that he wasn't good for me. Was that jealousy?'

'No,' she says. 'No. I was just concerned for you, then. I thought maybe he wasn't right for you. I was wrong. It's nothing to do with me. Concern grew into jealousy, I guess, when I saw that he *was* right for you. That he made you happy. Like I said, you had it all.'

I can't help but be touched by her misguided concern. She was looking out for me. As sisters do.

'But, Beck,' I say, 'I was just doing everything I thought I should do. I didn't want any of that material stuff. I didn't want any of it.'

'No?' she says, sounding bitter, an eyebrow raised.

'No. I want to live in a rambling old house. I don't want to be a slave to a job. I don't want to do *the done thing*. No matter how much everyone else expects it of me.'

'But you did.'

'I don't want to. Not any more.'

'Right,' Becky says softly.

I hope she realizes. I hope she realizes that I didn't have it all. And even if I did before, that I don't any more. I have lost it all.

We watch the sea in silence. Not talking, but being together, is companionable. It shouldn't be, but it is.

'Okay, so,' Becky says in a sort of breathless way. 'Marc . . . he came over that night.'

The twilight air seems to still around us. *Marc came over.* I was right. I was right. I wasn't mad.

They have lied.

They have lied to the court.

'What?' I say.

'He came over to help.'

'What? When?'

'He was there when I got back from Londis. He stayed for a bit. We talked. We . . . well, you don't need to know that.'

'Know what?'

'We reconciled,' she says with a shrug. She looks down at the grass.

'You're back together?' I ask, even though I want to ask her why they lied, and what happened to my baby. I ask because, despite myself, I still care. I still care about their marriage. And about her.

'Yes,' she says, finally glancing up to look at me. 'We are.'

'He believes you,' I say.

'Of course he does.'

'Did he always?'

'Completely. Unfalteringly. Yes.'

'Oh.'

'We said he wasn't there because . . . God, it escalated so fast, the suspicion, and we didn't want both of us to be investigated. He needed to lie, for Xander. Otherwise we'd *both* be tried. And where would Xander——?' She stops herself just in time.

Where would he go, indeed? At least she still has him. At least she still sees him.

'You could have told me,' I say. 'I've been – bloody hell, Beck. I've been going mad theorizing. I even spoke to him.'

'I know,' she says.

'You owed it to me to tell me.'

'I couldn't tell you because . . . because I love him.'

I stare at her. Loyalty. Hers is with Marc. Who is mine with? Scott? Layla? The refugee children? Suddenly everything seems unbearably complicated.

'But another thing,' she says, sitting forward slightly.

Where is this leading? I am finding myself thinking. I haven't uncovered any truths. There has been no confession. The truth has become more confusing the longer we have spoken. I don't know who's guilty or who's innocent any more.

'And I need to say this,' she says. 'Marc coming over that night made me realize something.'

'Okay.' My shoulders tense up.

'I found the nannying really fucking hard,' she says. She holds a hand up as I begin to protest. 'No, listen, please, Marth. I found it really difficult, and I was very angry a lot of the time.'

'Why?' I say. Fear breaks out across my body. Goose-bumps spread across my skin. She was *angry*.

'At first I thought it was because . . . Layla was . . .' She is choosing her words carefully. 'She was quite demand-ing. Far more than Xander. And I was . . . I was so shocked you would leave your baby. I wanted another baby so badly and I would . . . I'd never have left my baby, I kept thinking.'

'Yes,' I swallow. None of it is easy to hear.

'And I was frustrated by how hard I found it. And then I was frustrated because I could never tell you how hard I found the nannying. I felt like such a fuck-up. I thought it was the solution. The bloody set-dressing job had made me forget Xander God knows how many times . . . I needed an out. I thought nannying was it. But it was even harder, and I couldn't say it to you. I'm so inept, I couldn't even say it to you.' Her eyes go glassy

I look away. Oh, please don't let this be leading where I think it is.

'Looking after children is always hard,' I say neutrally. 'I would have understood.'

'I know, but I had this complex about Xander having been an easy baby. I thought you'd think I was hopeless if I said . . . if I said I couldn't do it any more.'

'But I could barely do it,' I say. 'Why are you telling me this?' I look sideways at her. She looks beautiful, here in the dusk. 'What did you do?'

'I put aside so much for it. For our arrangement. I forgot Xander again, and the school went wild – as you've heard.'

'Yes,' I say quietly.

'I gave it all up for you. I had her whenever you wanted me to. Even though I couldn't have my own.' Her voice is thick and strangled. '*We* couldn't have *our* own.'

'I know,' I say. I want to go on, to defend myself, but she stops me again.

'I want to tell you what I found so hard, first. I realized something. I realized what was actually difficult about it. For me.'

'Okay.'

'I found it so hard not because of the imposition on my time, but because of how I felt *for* Layla.' She is speaking quickly now, her words ringing out in the night.

She is earnest. She is so rarely earnest. I meet her eyes and listen.

'What?'

'She just wanted you, Martha. She just wanted you.'

'I know,' I say, my voice thick. 'I know. And I wasn't there.'

'I was a poor substitute. That's what I found so hard. I've thought about it a lot, lately. I felt so fucking sorry for her. And I'm sorry to say that, Martha. I know you won't want to hear it. But there it is. That's why I was angry: I was angry with you. She needed her mum.'

'I know, Beck. I know she needed me. Not her dad, either, really. But me. You can't say anything I haven't thought.'

'Well, yes.'

Tears film my eyes. Becky found it difficult because she was sympathetic to Layla. I blink. I hadn't expected that. She had lied to protect Marc, and she had hidden her true feelings about nannying to protect me. She was proud, yes, but she was also compassionate. My sister. I had forgotten.

Please let her be good. Please say she didn't do it.

Becky closes her eyes and blinks. 'God, I miss her,' she says. 'My little niece.' Her voice breaks. 'I know I shouldn't be saying that, sitting here, with *you*. But I do.'

'I miss her, too,' I say.

We're talking around in circles, ignoring the elephant in the room, and after a moment I can't stand it any more.

'Did you do it, Becky? With him – or by yourself?' I say after several minutes.

The courtroom fades from my mind, here, in the summer air with my sister. I turn my gaze to her and it is as if she is taking the stand, and this is her evidence.

She opens her mouth to speak.

'I don't know,' she says. 'I don't fucking know.'

My entire body heats up, then cools, like I've been plunged into hot and then cold water. She doesn't know. She doesn't know.

Guilty, guilty, guilty.

'You don't *know*?' I say, barely able to speak. My vision narrows again, just like it did in A&E when the doctors told me. I can't see properly. I shake my head.

'I thought I knew, once. I thought I knew myself, once.'

'What do you mean?'

'Marc left around nine. We just talked – over the crying – but then I poured another glass of wine and . . .'

'Why should I believe you, when you've said he wasn't there this entire time? He lied in the witness box,' I say.

But then I think of the expression on his face outside

his house that morning. Of course. He believes her both because he was there, and because – that night, for them – it was love. Reconciliation. That's their story, anyway.

'I know,' Becky says, her voice flat. 'You don't have to believe me. Nobody does. I can see why.'

I look at her features. Her eyes are blurred with tears. I don't know if I believe her. Why should I? I can still see so clearly a scenario where Marc and Becky covered it up. Perhaps my instincts about him were correct, all this time.

'What happened after he left?' I say, swallowing my doubts.

'If you'd have asked me early on – right afterwards, before I got charged, or even after I was bailed and the press slept on Mum and Dad's lawn to try and get an exclusive – I would've said I was innocent.'

My mind seems to spring to life. *I knew it.* I knew I was right when I was leaving her house. Somebody murdered my baby.

'But . . .' Becky says. 'I was drinking. I drank so bloody much. A bottle of wine.'

Despite the warm, clammy air, my body chills. This is it. She's going to say it. All of my hopes, the benefit of the doubt, all my optimism will be dashed, just like that.

She's still looking directly at me. That full hair. That face; my sister's face. What expressions haven't I seen on it? Hardly any. I have seen that upper lip curve in a sneer of disdain, the mischief when she cracks a naughty joke, the stress that appeared around her eyes while in that bloody job that led us to this. But now her emotions are stripped away. Her expression is blank as she looks at me.

'Lately, I've been starting to think . . .'

'What?'

'I don't even know what happened myself. How could I? I was so drunk.'

'Yes.'

'I spoke to my lawyer. I said maybe, with the wine and everything, maybe I was a little . . . that maybe I held her too close,' she whispers.

'Too close, too close,' I say, my hands clasping together like fighting snakes. 'Too close.'

'It must have been me. Everyone says it.'

'Close how?'

She shakes her head. 'We were in the bedroom. I was on my way to bed. Pissed. I was frustrated with her. I held her to me. I must have obstructed her airway – it must have been me.'

'But *did* you? *Was* it you?'

'I was angry.'

'I was angry at Layla a lot, too. What did you do, Beck?'

'I don't remember. I don't know. My lawyer has told me not to say. She says I didn't hold her too close. That it couldn't have been me. That I have made it up, subsequently, to explain it.'

The language she's using isn't quite right, isn't quite normal, to my ears. It's not like she is remembering something, but rather, *mis*remembering.

'She cried afterwards, anyway, I thought. I could've sworn she was crying around eleven, off and on, but I can't remember any more. And fucking *Alison* says Layla wasn't crying at midnight. And the experts say she was dead by then. So what do I know? I was trashed. Trolleyed.'

'When did you hold her too close, Becky? I'd rather know, before tomorrow. Before the end.'

'I must have held her too close.'

'Are you going to tell the court that?'

She brings her lips close together, clamps them so they blanch, then shakes her head. 'No.'

'Why not?'

'I'm not telling the court anything. My lawyer said not to. I wanted to, Marth,' she says, looking at me, her eyes damp. 'I wanted to get up there and tell everybody the truth. The messy truth.'

'But what *is* the truth?'

'Six months ago I would've wanted to take the stand and tell everybody it wasn't me,' she says.

'But now . . .'

'The truth now is that I don't know. I've always said it wasn't me, but recently I've started to think it must have been. I was drunk, and holding her close. That's what must have happened.'

'But why?' I say.

The marram grass shifts around us in the breeze.

'Because it must have. Imagine this,' she says, and I see some of her old flair return. 'Imagine this.'

'What?'

'You're driving along, at the speed limit, you'd say, or thereabouts. Thirty.'

'Right.'

'You hit a child and they die.'

I swallow. 'Yeah.'

'And ten experts say your car's skid marks, they indicate you were doing fifty.'

'Right.'

'The injuries say fifty, too. The state of the vehicle. Fifty. Right?'

'Yes.'

'And then you think: *Well, I can't actually remember looking at the speedometer.* It was just a belief you had. That you were doing thirty. It's not *based* on anything. It's formless. And, in the face of all this evidence, it disappears. It just disappears. Replaced by doubt. And doubt can be huge.'

'I see.'

'So I would've said six months ago that this never happened but, Marth, there's been a campaign against me. Constant witness statements on retinal haemorrhages and bleeding lungs and my overheard shouts. And do you know what? I think: *Just hand me over.* I obviously didn't know what I was doing. I'm not of sound mind, I can't remember! So just deliver me up to the justice system. Okay, I was doing fifty. Because I don't fucking know.'

'But if you had to say which one was the truth – which is it, Beck? Thirty or fifty? If you had to bet your life on it. Experts aside. What's *your* evidence?'

'Thirty,' she whispers. 'I never speed.'

We don't speak for a few minutes. What's to say?

We shift closer to one another. We watch the iron-grey sea together.

'I just wanted to know if you did it,' I say to her.

A fine mist is rising from the sea and spreading inland. I don't remember this from our childhood.

'It's not that simple,' she says.

It's another fiction. Because what could be more simple than this question?

'What time did you hold her too close?' I say.

'Around nine thirty?' she says hesitantly.

The latest time of death.

The fingers of my left hand twitch and curl in, involuntarily. It goes against my gut instinct, and believing in Becky's innocent intentions, to feel this twitch of anger, but I feel it anyway. It was her. It was probably her.

The world turns dark, a mess of smothered babies and blood and gore and fear and . . .

Oh, the fear Layla must've felt.

61

Martha

I leave Becky there, eventually, but I go back to her house. I know now that there is nothing here, no concrete evidence, just insubstantial memories, like the sea mists I have left swirling around Becky.

It's time to put it behind us. To say goodbye.

The house stands empty. Tall and slim and dark. I text Scott, telling him where I am, and he calls me immediately.

'Why?' he says when I answer.

'I don't know,' I say. 'I just . . . it's almost over and I just, I guess I wanted to be here. Where she was last. Maybe Becky will move back in again, after . . .'

Scott sighs softly down the line, but doesn't correct me, doesn't feel the need to say: *Of course she won't; she'll be in prison.*

'I just wanted to be here,' I say.

Not to figure it out, not now. Just to be here. To accept it. The messy truth. And to bid farewell.

'I see,' he says. He pauses. 'Do you want me to come over?'

'No,' I say quietly. 'No. It's fine.'

'Are you going to stay there?'

'I think so,' I say.

I can't explain it to myself, so I don't try to explain it to him. I just feel as though I might figure it out if I stay here. A full night.

'Do you mind?'

'No. Do what you need to,' he says simply, and we hang up.

The door is soundless as I slide my key in the lock and open it. The house sits silently, like a sleeping animal, and I close the front door behind me for the first time.

I'll just explore a bit. Wait it out. Sleep here, the night before we find out what truly happened.

The living room is a time capsule of what happened that night. Xander wasn't taken from Becky until the post-mortem results came in, but once the spare bedroom was declared a crime scene, and Layla dead, they left. That morning. They never came home again.

I pick my way across the living room. Becky's mess surrounds me. She was always so chaotic.

The walls are a slate grey, with accents of white: a white fluffy throw, a white rug. White candles in bell jars. Becky is a natural. She should have stuck out design school, somehow. Or gone back, maybe. But she'd been subsumed by motherhood, and then defined by her own failure, too bitter to change it.

A collage of black-and-white photographs adorns the wall behind the sofa. Layla is one of them. Framed and hung during her short eight-week life. It is the same photograph I had framed.

My body remembers the way upstairs, even though it has been almost a year. A left turn, halfway up the stairs, that I make instinctively. A fine layer of dust has settled on the bannister and I wipe a finger through it.

Becky's room is at the front of the house, and I walk in and stare at her bed. That, too, is a freeze-frame. Her duvet pulled back, half of the bed bare, as she must have rushed frantically from the room. A hair dryer is discarded, plugged in, switched off, lying on the floor next to her pine wardrobe. A wine glass is by her bed.

I shake my head, leave the room, and head up the second flight of stairs to Xander's room. I can't go into the spare room, the nursery. Not yet. I'll start slowly.

Xander's room has a raised step, where the door frame protrudes upwards, and I almost trip on it. I've hardly ever been in here – only a handful of times. When was I last here? I can barely remember: our family's shared past is a speck on the horizon, these days.

Xander used to walk alongside me, sometimes, when we were all out together. He seemed to like to chat to me, though he pretended he didn't. What would we talk about? School. Sport. Television. How much he wanted a dog. It was a lifelong dream of his; I admired his dedication to it. Marc had said when he was ten he could get one if he walked a lead every day for a year, to prove his commitment. 'A lead?' I had said, in disbelief. 'How bizarre.'

'He has to come home from school to get the lead. He can't just walk around at lunchtime at school and count that,' Marc had said.

There was a beauty to it. Xander was going to log the walks on Becky's Fitbit. There'll be no chance now.

His bedroom is entirely blue. Navy walls, royal-blue double bed. The only thing not blue is his enormous Xbox One set-up. Gaming paraphernalia lies everywhere.

I sit on the bed. It still smells of him. A musty glass of

water sits by the side of the bed. I wonder if he's sipped it since, in the afterworld.

Xander and I played *Tomb Raider* just two years ago, on Boxing Day. I came up to say hi to him, but ended up staying for hours in his room. I couldn't move along a snowy pathway in the game. I kept falling off, flailing with an ice pick. How we both laughed at me. In the end, he took the controller from me, and ran easily along the ledge, then passed it back. We ate an entire box of Roses during that cold Boxing Day.

Curious, I boot up his Xbox. What was he last doing? God, he loved his games. Why hasn't he got them with him at Marc's?

Xander2000. That's what he called himself, and that's what it says in green at the top right of the screen.

He'd been playing a game called *Call of Duty: Infinite Warfare.*

Xander2000: Last saved: 27/10.

Weren't we all?

Last seen then. Last saved then. Before.

The nursery is darker than I remember. The curtains are motionless at the window. I reach to touch the glass. It's cool against my fingertips. The Moses basket is gone, examined by the police, and then given back to us, and so the room is almost empty, only a makeshift changing table there, a foam mattress lying atop a chest of drawers. Becky's things are piled into a corner, away from where Layla would have slept. An empty picture frame. Trivial Pursuit and a sack of Xander's old clothes that I was going to go through for Layla.

I sink down, on to the floor by the changing table, and allow myself a fantasy. I hardly ever indulge.

Layla is here. She will be one soon – in two weeks.

I'm stressing over a cake. Becky is sardonic – 'She won't even remember it' – but helps me ice it, anyway, the butter-cream forming peaks that mimic Layla's spiked-up blonde baby hair. I hold her out, cast in the dim light of a single candle, and try to encourage her to blow it out, which she doesn't.

Xander pushes his fringe back from his hair and reaches for her, his cousin, and he holds her as Becky and I sit and watch.

I close my eyes, thinking . . .

When I open them, the room is just the same. Bare. It holds no clues. Nothing in the house does, of course not. What did I expect? That I would find something the police missed? Solve the case myself, right before the last day of the trial, when it's solved already?

It was Becky. She got drunk, and held my baby too close. That's all. That's it. A tragedy.

No. There's no evidence left, of course. I don't know what I expected to find. There is nothing here. No evidence.

Just a space, where my baby once lay.

A hole.

62

Judge Christopher Matthews, QC

Sadie doesn't want to know.

It has taken him until now to stop reliving the email, the bubble of hope that sat in his chest as he opened it, which popped violently as he read her curt response, poisonous pessimism spreading throughout his body.

Thanks for the apology, though. I do actually – strangely – appreciate it, she wrote.

Strangely. Strangely. Because she no longer cares, he guesses, is the context.

He is a lawyer, after all. He can do linguistic semantics.

They may have a verdict tomorrow. He will distract himself with that. It seems like a slam dunk for the prosecution, to be honest. Nevertheless, the decision will be monumental. The jury must always consider it seriously, no matter how strong the prosecution's case.

'Anyway,' he says to Rumpole. 'She doesn't want me back, old lad. But at least I realize. How I've been.'

Rumpole regards him seriously, then goes back to sleep.

Christopher pads upstairs, later. He doesn't sleep well the day before the case closes for deliberations. That feeling of goosebumps settles over him again, just as he is about to fall asleep, and keeps him up for several hours.

Tuesday

63

Martha

I wake in Becky's house on the last day of the trial and I know, somehow, that this will resolve itself today.

Not the verdict. Not the suffering. But something. As if one layer is being resolved, slowly, like a preliminary fine coat of paint upon a wall, barely transforming the surface at first.

Perhaps it is just that the trial will be over, and we will all move on.

I lay in Becky's bed, looking idly across the corridor at the nursery for most of the night, saying goodbye to Layla. I've hardly slept. Instead, I've relived my most favourite memories of her. The one where she was placed on my chest, skin to skin. Part me and part her, bound for ever. The first time she made eye contact and it was as though Cupid had struck me, there and then, right in the heart. Her first smile, a small upturning of her mouth that spread and spread until – my God – there it was. A true, genuine smile, baby to mum, for what felt like the first time. I had put all this effort in – food, winding, nappy changing – and here was something back. It should have felt like almost nothing in return, a token gesture, but actually it felt like the whole world, delivered to me by Layla, in that smile.

The guilt crept in alongside the memories, but I tried my

best to nudge it away. Yes, when I first held her I was pre-occupied with the pain in my groin. When she smiled at me I was sleep deprived, wishing she would nap for longer. But those things didn't matter. Perhaps she never knew.

I brush my hair using Becky's brush, which I quickly fill with my own hair, and then borrow her blusher, like I've done a thousand times before, just to make myself look alive again. When I am ready, I linger at the door to the nursery, my hand on the wooden frame, and say goodbye to her.

Goodbye, and that I am sorry.

I arrive at the court and Scott holds my hand tightly but releases it when we see Xander arriving in the foyer. My natural instinct is to go to him, my nephew. To ask how school is going, how often he sees his mum.

They like to interview children early on in the morning, the website guidance says. I have not been permitted to see him, either. He, a witness for the defence, and me, for the prosecution.

He's grown taller now he is ten. His legs have grown before his body, like a grasshopper's. His hair is longer, falling in front of his eyes. I am struck that, suddenly, this child in front of me, this little boy I held, bewildered, on Becky's behalf, ten years ago, is almost a teenager and soon will be an adult. Adolescence. It sort of suits him; he has always had an insouciant air, as if he has been waiting for it, was ready for it.

He's ushered upstairs, away from us, but as he is, the worker assigned to look after him glances over her shoulder and looks at me, just once.

The morning's proceedings take a while to get going.

The judge is fussing over something, back in his chambers, and the barristers talking quietly. It is the final day of the trial, and the end is in sight.

Ellen passes Harriet a note, which she reads, and smiles, two long and ageing dimples appearing each side of her mouth. I almost reach across to intervene, to stop these playmates who are supposed to be behaving seriously, but I don't.

And then. And then. The judge arrives, and an usher is directed to turn on a monitor. It springs to life, and the courtroom hushes, as if a curtain had gone up on a stage at a matinee.

And there he is. At the centre of it. The final defence witness. My nephew, sitting on a tiny chair, a child's chair, in a tiny pale-blue room. He looks just like Xander, but also not. The same massive blue eyes, from Marc, the same thick hair, from Becky, but the way he is sitting is slouched. Legs spread wider than before. He runs a hand through his hair, and the effect is complete. His hands are no longer fat and childlike; they have been replaced by a kind of adult leanness.

'The barristers will ask you questions, now,' a male voice, off-camera – offstage – says to him.

'Thanks,' Xander says.

I'm surprised to find his voice is deeper, too. I think of Xander in all of his guises. Newborn Xander with that whorl of dark hair that Becky carefully washed with Johnson's shampoo. Toddler Xander, carefully collecting leaves from the garden and handing them to me. Xander in reception at primary school, wanting only to kick a ball against the wall of the house for hours at a time. Xander of late: a computer gamer, a boy who wanted a dog. And now here looms another: teenage Xander. All of the other Xanders, the various incarnations of my nephew, are gone for ever, consigned to family history and photo albums.

'Hi, Xander,' Harriet says, standing up slowly. She looks at the wall-mounted television. As she reaches to sip her water I see that her hand is shaking, the surface of her drink trembling as though in an earthquake.

What are they going to ask him? Layla died at eight or nine. He arrived just before twelve. He didn't see anything. All he will be able to do is verify that Becky wasn't abusive, which we all know. And yet I can feel the tension in my shoulders, my clenched jaw. I look across at Becky watching her son on the monitor, and wonder what she's thinking, her face impassive.

'Hi,' he says back, simply.

He was always polite to a fault. Becky hadn't drummed it into him – she didn't care about that stuff – but he always, *always* asked about my day, right from when he was five, in that curiously adult way of his. Perhaps it came from Marc, I don't know.

I look across at Becky. She has closed her eyes.

'Can you tell us a little bit about your mum?' Harriet says gently to him.

'Yep,' he says, then a childlike pause as he realizes he's supposed to be doing so. 'She's . . . I see her every weekend at Granny and Grandad's for four hours.'

'And how is she? What sort of mother is she?'

'A good one. She is kind,' he says softly, running a hand through his hair.

'And did your mum . . . has your mum ever been violent towards you, Xander?'

'No, never.' He looks confused.

I wonder what he knows about what's going on, how he finds living with his father, seeing his mother with my mum and dad watching. There is a stab of sympathy right in my heart. For him, of course, but also for her.

'Does she ever shout?'

'Yeah, sometimes.'

'What does she shout about?'

'When I play on the Xbox when she's said I can't,' he says, with perfect comedic timing.

But nobody laughs. If anything, the hush gets more pronounced, the silence crowding into the courtroom with us. Somewhere, an air-conditioning unit creaks. A member of the jury shifts in their seat. Otherwise, there is only silence.

'Anything else?'

'Lots of things,' Xander says, the ghost of a baffled ten-year-old's smile crossing his features. 'She doesn't like it when I don't tell her if I'm going out to play with Barnaby. And if I don't tell her where I am.'

'Okay, I see,' Harriet says gently. She looks tired this morning, her eyes squinty.

I would be tired, too. I *am* tired, too. But today, it will be over.

'Tell me about the incident with your shoulder.'

'I walked into the road and Mum yanked me back. Because there was a car.'

'I see. And then, when you went to A&E and the nurse was strapping your arm, what did you tell her?'

'I said it was something else, but it was a lie. Dad was there and he gets angry about traffic, and other things, too. He says I need to pay more attention.'

'And so it was definitely a lie and not something else?'

'She pulled me too hard out of the way of a car,' he says, with a strange adult finality. 'I'm sorry I lied.'

'And when the social worker interviewed you, did you tell her the truth?'

'Yes.'

'And Mum didn't tell you what to say?'

'No. And my mum hasn't told me what to say now, either.'

'And what about when Mum forgot to pick you up from school?'

Genuine puzzlement crosses Xander's features. 'She just forgot.'

'How did you feel?'

'I didn't feel anything. I was annoyed she was a bit late, I guess.'

'Right. So, last October, on the night Layla died. You came home on that night at just before midnight?'

'Think so, yeah. We watched *The Shining*. I didn't like it. So I came back.' He shrugs. Simple as that.

'And how was your Mum when you came home?'

'Fine. She was fine. She was normal.'

'What did you two do?'

'I went straight to bed, and straight to sleep. Within ten minutes.'

I almost smile. His fantastic sleep skills: alive and well.

'Did you look in on Layla?'

'No. The door was closed.'

'Thank you,' Harriet says.

Ellen stands up. I can see a cream blouse underneath her robes. It looks softer than her usual attire.

I am staring at Xander as something seems to swirl and dip around me, like I am at the waltzers again with Becky on the Pier.

'So you remember nothing of the night Layla died?'

'No. I woke up when the sirens came.'

I close my eyes. The sirens. But something . . . something is nagging me. It feels vital that I reach it before the lawyers do; before *he* does.

'So you went to sleep immediately? Did you notice anything unusual when you came in? How did your mum seem?'

'I went straight to sleep.'

'Do you remember the time?'

'I didn't notice anything.'

I frown. Something is off in his tone. It is not defensive, exactly, but it is strange. It is the same tone he uses when asked if he has done his homework. When he hasn't.

I stare at my nephew on the television screen and wonder what I am thinking.

'You didn't hear anything at all? Do you know what your mum was doing?'

'No.'

'You didn't hear anything at all?'

'No.'

Xander2000: Last saved: 27/10.

But how could that be?

The day my baby died.

The day my baby was found dead.

He said he went to bed, after he got home just before midnight on the twenty-sixth.

'Just to confirm: you were asleep the entire night? Sorry to labour the point, Xander, but you are the only witness as to what your mum was doing in the hours surrounding Layla's death. Can you tell us whether Layla was awake? Did you hear her crying?'

'Well, maybe I stayed up a bit,' Xander says. The needling of the questioning has got to him.

'Well, for how long?' Ellen says.

'A few hours,' he says evasively.

'A few *hours*? And so did you hear anything?'

'No, I said I didn't.' He folds his arms and stares directly at the camera.

Xander2000: Last saved: 27/10.

'Were you awake all night?'

The judge addresses Ellen, stopping the monitor, and Xander's face freezes on the screen. 'Where is this line of questioning going, Miss Hendry?'

I look across at Becky. Her face is still expressionless, but there is something screwed around her eyes. She is steadfastly not looking at me. Looking instead at the monitor. Looking terrified.

'I think it's important to establish if Xander heard anything at all. He's admitted he was awake.'

'He has said he was awake, and that he didn't hear anything, already,' the judge says.

'Fine, Your Honour,' Ellen says, looking exasperated.

The video screen flickers back to life.

'Xander. You heard nothing that night, then—'

'Miss Hendry . . .' the judge says.

Ellen continues anyway. 'You are under oath, Xander . . .'

'Less bullying, please,' the judge says crisply. 'I am warning you now.'

'Yes,' Xander whispers.

'So . . .'

The judge observes them, not speaking. His eyes are watchful. One more bad question and he'll halt it.

'Xander. What did you hear?'

'Nothing.'

'Under oath, nothing at all?'

'Yes, okay, yes,' Xander says suddenly, tears making his voice sound watery and thin. 'Yes. I did hear something,' Xander says.

Becky's head drops to her chest.

'Xander, what did you hear?'

Becky's face is ablaze. Her cheeks, her neck, her forehead. All red.

My own head pounds as I look at her. Oh God. What does he know?

'Xander, it's okay. It's fine,' Ellen says gently, her voice as soft as a whisper.

But it's not safe, it's not fine, I want to tell him. She is softening him up, and soon, she will sting him, like a poisonous insect.

'Okay,' Xander says, his voice shuddery.

She backtracks. 'So, you were awake from when until when?'

'I was awake a lot. I don't know. I couldn't sleep,' he says. 'She was quiet when I got in,' he whispers. 'Then she started crying again.'

Ellen looks flabbergasted. 'Really? When did she begin crying again?'

'Later.'

'What were you doing?'

'I was . . . I was . . .' the words seem to die as they

tumble out of his mouth, each getting weaker until they make no sound at all.

Becky's hands are on the plate glass of the dock again. She's staring at him. Her face is no longer red: it's white.

'I couldn't sleep. Because of the crying.'

'At what time did she start crying?'

'When I got into bed.'

Layla is supposed to have died between eight and half past nine. The entire case centres around that medical, scientific fact. The time of death. This doesn't make any sense.

The courtroom is completely silent.

'And then, she kept crying. For hours. So I went down to . . . to see her. To help her.'

'To help her?'

'I wanted to stop the crying and sleep. Mum had been so tired and angry. And she was in bed with the wine.'

Becky blinks in shock.

'I wanted to . . .' Xander continues. 'I wanted to stop her crying.'

I realize at the exact moment Xander says it.

He leans forward in the little blue chair and puts his face into his pink hands. 'I think it was me.'

'You?'

'It was an accident – I was trying to help. I didn't realize until . . . after.'

There is complete silence in the courtroom. My ears shiver with it. I stare at Xander in shock.

The experts . . . they must've got the time wrong. But how could they? They did the nomogram test. They were so sure. How could it be wrong?

My baby. Layla. She *was* smothered. They were right, and they were wrong, all at once.

Xander is shaking in his chair. Somewhere, a switch is pressed, and the monitor is turned off.

The courtroom seems to hum around us. I look across at Becky. Her mouth is open, just slightly, her jaw slack. She brings a hand to her chin and stares at the blank monitor. Her eyes are wet.

'No further questions,' Ellen says faintly, to nobody.

64

Xander

1.30 a.m., Friday 27 October

He could hear the crying from his room right above Layla's. He wished he could switch it off, mute it, but he couldn't, and Mum was always talking about it, always looking at the baby. The baby that was always, always crying.

Mum had been weird lately. Like when Dad had left and they'd both been cross and short with him for months. That had got better, but now it had got worse again. It was his fault, he thought. Dad was always telling him off. Sudden shouts and door slams and fists thumped on tables, all because of Xander. He was bad. He was a bad boy.

No, he should be positive, like they'd learnt about in school just before the half term holidays. Maybe they'd do sports again at the weekend, he and Mum. He wanted to learn to play tennis, after watching this documentary about Andy Murray. Maybe she could help him? But she wouldn't; he knew why. They'd had a rubbish dinner the previous night. Beans on toast. He hated the way they made the bread soggy, had tried to tell her, but she hadn't listened.

He looked at the ceiling in his bedroom. He shouldn't be awake, but he couldn't sleep. He'd got back late, and he kept thinking about *The Shining*. It was horrible. Why would anybody watch that for fun?

He rolled on to his side and put a hand over his ear to block out the crying. He'd been playing the Xbox since midnight, but he'd be banned from it tomorrow if Mum caught him up much longer. If he could sleep, the morning would come sooner, and he would get to play.

The crying sounded like something else now. A squawking, like a bird. His hand over his ear didn't quieten the sound.

He got up to look out of his window, the highest window in the whole house. He could see his school right there across the road from his house. It looked like it was asleep. The art room had the blind drawn down but the window next to it didn't. He could see the rows of red chairs where he sat during the day and looked out at his house when he was supposed to be concentrating properly. He was rubbish at painting but he was better than Barnaby so he did both of theirs, usually, then got told off for taking ages, which he and Barnaby laughed at. 'You're welcome,' Xander would say to him, and feel so completely *adult*.

That crying. He turned his head to the door of his bedroom and clenched his fists. He ought to go down. Mum was asleep after her wine – she was so tired, her eyes looked dark and lined – and maybe he could help, anyway.

He ventured out of his room, over the little wooden lip of his door frame, and down one flight of stairs.

The crying was intense on the landing outside Layla's room. He waited, listening. Poor Layla. He shouldn't be angry with her: she was only sad, just like him. He stepped inside and picked up the blanket. He would swaddle her, just like Mum did sometimes. Wrap her up nice and tight and safe, but he didn't want her to be too hot, so he reached up, still holding the blanket, and opened the window. The cool night air came inside. It smelt delicious.

Carefully, he picked Layla up and began wrapping the blanket around her. Nice and tight. Safe. There: she wouldn't cry now. He held her to him. She was warm, and moving, her little fists coming out to clutch at him, but still he held on. He held her tight, so tight to him, his hand supporting her neck, his thumb right by her ear. As tight as can be, that's what Mum once said about swaddling. He held her tight, so tight and warm to his chest, and held and held and held until she stopped moving, and stilled, peacefully, in his safe arms.

Eventually, standing in the cold air coming in through the window, she cooled, too, and he placed her back in the Moses basket, completely, peacefully asleep.

65

Becky

Martha is leaving the courtroom and I should go to her – I know I should – but my body is turned, against my will, to my child, emerging from the stairs, his face blotchy and wet. Marc is right behind me.

Martha crosses in front of me and time seems to stand still, for just a moment. She stops, expecting something from me, but I don't give it to her.

Instead, I cross the foyer, continuing up the stairs to Xander.

I look behind me, just once. She's standing, in the centre of a forming crowd, microphones pointed at her. Her eyes are wide and wet. She has supported me here, every day of my trial for the killing of her daughter, hoping that I am innocent, looking at me encouragingly, sometimes, across the courtroom, but I can't do it. I have to go to him.

I choose him: that is motherhood. She would do the same.

'Xander,' I say to him.

We walk up the stairs. We will only have a few minutes, I am sure, before the authorities will want to speak to him. Marc and I go into a meeting room with him and close the door.

I sit down. I've got to play it carefully. It is the most important conversation of my life.

'Is it true?' Marc says gently. He reaches across the table to touch Xander's hand.

I take the other. It unfurls on the desk, on its back, like a creature, and I hold it. It's warm and clammy.

Xander nods. He looks at Marc, and then at me, and then down at his lap. He withdraws his hand from mine and wipes a tear from his cheek. My baby. Those little red cheeks. He used to smear Bourbon biscuits all over them when he was first feeding himself. The chocolate would get everywhere; I would find it in the folds of his ears at bath time, and laughingly wash it out.

'It's okay,' I say to him.

'I was trying to help – to do the, the swaddling thing like you did. I opened the window, in case she was too hot, and I wrapped her up tight . . . and I was too . . . I was too . . . I was too afraid to tell Dad.'

Marc closes his eyes, just briefly. Just once. His shouts at Xander. His door slamming. His masculine assertions, in the face of his infertility. They have all led us here. To our son making a terrible error, and not being able to tell the only parent he was regularly alone with. To keeping a terrible, terrible secret, out of fear, even though he knew I might go to prison for it.

Oh, Xander, oh, my baby Xander.

'I know. It's okay. We know.' I close my eyes.

All those experts' testimonies about the time of death were based on the temperature if the window had been closed the entire time, but it hadn't been. It had been open all night. And then I had closed it. How could I have forgotten something so crucial? I could have saved us all of this pain, this public unsheathing of the secret at our family's core.

'But I thought she was asleep, she was so still, and then I realized in the morning what I must have . . . that it must have been . . . that it was me.'

He looks at me. His face is creased up, his chin trembling, his eyes wet. I scoot my chair around to him and, wordlessly, he climbs – all five feet of him – into my lap, leans his head against my shoulder, and sobs.

66

Judge Christopher Matthews, QC

'Not guilty,' Christopher says to Rumpole as he lets himself in.

Rumpole tilts his head to the side.

'Her kid did it,' he adds.

Rumpole turns around and pads away.

Christopher sits down alone on the sofa. What would he say to Sadie, if she were here now? She always listened intently to debriefs about his cases.

'There had been an error with the forensics,' he would say. 'A window threw the time of death completely out. They thought the baby died at eight or nine, but she actually died at one thirty in the morning. Nobody even thought about the window. The defendant had forgotten she'd closed it. Even though the paramedic noted it in her evidence. What a comedy of errors.'

'Kind of crazy,' she would say, with a faint smile.

Christopher takes a deep, cleansing breath and thinks of Becky: *Well, look at that. She was innocent, after all.*

But now she will have to live with Xander having done it.

He shakes his head. He doesn't know which is worse.

He takes Rumpole's lead off the peg in the hallway and opens the door. Rumpole runs out ahead of him.

The Blackwaters left the courtroom together after

Xander's confession, their body language still close, despite everything. That was love.

He has lost his love, but he can find it again. He closes the door behind him.

It is time to get out into the world.

Epilogue

One year later

Becky

Xander is here with us as we walk along the country lanes, and so is Marc. Together again, the family unit. So different to last year.

It is exactly a year since the day I woke up and thought I would be receiving a verdict of guilty for something I didn't do. I had packed a bag containing items allowed in prisons – plain clothes, non-spray deodorant – and left Mum and Dad's for what I thought was the last time as me, innocent-until-proven-guilty Becky.

If I let myself – which I don't, often – I can still remember the smell of the courtroom. Recently hoovered carpets and old wood and dusty books. I can still feel the chill of the glass I stood behind like a goldfish, staring at the jury who were about to try me, staring at my childless sister as she wept in the public gallery. I can still conjure up the feeling I got as Xander appeared on the monitor. The rising horror that began in my gut and spread outwards, knowledge feeling like acid as it moved through my body.

Xander is out of counselling now. He seems okay. Happy, even, some days.

Martha has only said a handful of words to me since the trial ended. No, that's not fair: more than a handful. But nothing compared to how it used to be. She's never been angry with me. Just sad: quiet and sad.

The last time I saw her, we were outside. I was smoking.

She was sipping a takeaway coffee, outside my house. She had this expression on her face, worn permanently since the final day of the trial. Regret, I think.

'I didn't know,' I said. 'I never even considered it.'

'But it wasn't you,' Martha said, looking at me, a drop of milky coffee on her bottom lip. 'You knew it wasn't you. Therefore you must have suspected it was somebody else.'

'No, I didn't,' I said.

I went to add: *He's my child*. But I didn't. Couldn't. The truth was, you didn't suspect somebody you loved as much as I loved Xander. You just didn't. Or, at least, I didn't.

'I just . . . I just hoped it wasn't anyone. That it wasn't anything. The medical stuff wasn't *conclusive*. I hoped it was an accident. That she'd rolled over.'

Martha stared at me, saying nothing.

'You wanted the same,' I added simply.

'I did hope for that, for Layla, yes,' she said. She didn't say anything else.

She left her coffee cup on my garden wall and went home. Later, I cleared it up and found it was still half-full.

I turn to Marc, now, his hair glowing almost white in the sunlight. 'I don't want to think about it today,' I say to him. 'Just for one day.'

'Don't, then,' he says. 'It won't help.'

I swallow. He is still Marc. My simple Marc.

'Sammy,' he adds softly.

And there it is. A hint of something. What is it, after all this time? Laughter, happiness? Joy, maybe. There is still a little bit of joy in my world, against all the odds, like a summer flower pushing up through the barren winter earth. I can, almost – if I stretch my hands out to touch it – grasp it, and hold on.

I close my eyes and banish the thoughts from my mind. I replace them with others. It is hot; the sun is warm on my arms and face. Marc's hand is in mine. Our son is just in front of us. I think he might just be okay. I dare to hope it.

And now, just for this moment, I only think about Marc's hand. About our son. And for a second there is no guilt or shame. There is even joy.

I open my eyes and stare. Is that Martha in the distance?

Martha

I know Becky will be doing the school run at three thirty, so I make sure we're on her route on a sunny Friday afternoon. She arrives like clockwork, at quarter to four, with Xander and Marc.

She holds herself differently these days, I think, as we approach each other in the lane. More upright. Prouder, in a funny kind of way. Perhaps she is less cynical, these days. I don't know.

We don't speak. We couldn't talk during the trial, and we still don't, now. I know why, of course. Your children should come first. Mine should have. And Becky's does. That's the way of it, the natural order.

I look at her. She still has the same walk.

Marc is by her side. Their hands are entwined. They hold each other differently to the way Scott and I do. They tangle, always moving. Scott's is firm in mine. He removes it, just as I am thinking about it, and replaces his arm around my shoulder, solid as a rock. My Nice Guy. He reaches up to ruffle my hair. It is regrowing, slowly: a crown of unruly fuzz around my temples.

Xander is walking with her. He wasn't charged, in the end. And neither was she, for failing to protect. They said she couldn't have known; none of us could.

That much is true.

She's looking intently at me, just like she did for all those days when she was in the dock in the courtroom.

I still remember that morning we left the court. She wasn't guilty. We should have been relieved. Mum and Dad and Ethan and me. But nobody was. Later on, Ethan texted and told me he was glad we had both believed in her, but it felt too raw to respond to.

Scott and I are going out to Kos next week for a fortnight. We have found an Airbnb with mismatched duvets, old tiles on the floor, an avocado-coloured bath suite. It is perfect: unpretentiously perfect. It would have been Layla's second birthday.

Becky opens her mouth to say something, then closes it. Without thinking, I slow my pace. She stops, too. And now we are standing, all five of us, in the sunny lane, looking at each other.

An image flashes into my mind. Layla dying in Xander's arms. Not smothered, in anger, like the lawyers said, but held near to his warm body. Still gone, but ... loved. I close my eyes, then open them again and look at him. He's looking nervously up at me: my optimistic, caring, eleven-year-old nephew.

'You doing okay?' I say to Becky.

She nods, too enthusiastically. 'Yeah. Are you?' she says.

'We're fine,' I say.

She reaches a hand out to me, but I don't take it. Instead, I turn to Xander. 'How're you?' I say to him. 'Any progress on *Tomb Raider*?'

He doesn't say anything for a couple of seconds, and

then a wide smile spreads across his features. 'Location fourteen,' he says. 'One more to go.'

'That's great,' I say. I reach out and squeeze his shoulder, then look again at Becky. 'We should get a takeaway,' I say to her. 'Sometime.'

'I'd like that,' she says. 'Yes.'

Acknowledgements

Like all good authors, I must disclaim liability here for any legal error or artistic licence employed. The reality of a courtroom drama – which would be more than one week, and would have multiple adjournments, and many more witnesses! – is different to the reality, and there are so many things I have manipulated for pace and plot.

No author is much of anything without their agent, and mine is my linchpin. Clare Wallace at Darley Anderson plucked me off the slush pile, held my hand through initial rejections, and remains there most days of my literary career – even (I am ashamed to say) when she is supposed to be on maternity leave, which neither she nor I are especially good at. I couldn't be without her.

I am, too, nothing without my very incisive and kind editors at Michael Joseph, Penguin Books. I'm for ever in debt to Maxine Hitchcock, who launched and made my first *and second* books bestsellers, but who does so very much more than that behind the scenes: author guidance, hand holding, and so many updates I may as well be in the office with them all. Thanks to Eve Hall for her initial input into the script, and Matilda McDonald who is so organized it's unreal: her edits are also forensic in their detail. Thanks, as always, to my brilliant marketer, Katie Bowden, and my publicist, Jenny Platt. You should really check out my Facebook page, because they've made it look beyond awesome. Thanks, too, to my copy editor, Shân Morley Jones, who went beyond this time, and actually made a timeline in order to line edit this beast of a script. I couldn't have done it without her.

And thanks, too (I am delighted to write), to my US editor, Sally Kim, who just three days before the writing of these acknowledgements acquired this novel to publish Stateside. Thanks to Camilla Wray for brokering the deal during what was one of the strangest and loveliest weeks of my life. I didn't sleep for three whole nights – from the moment I learnt there was serious American interest – and basically existed on New York time the entire week, refreshing my inbox in the small hours and speaking to Camilla on my sofa at midnight while my boyfriend and cat slept upstairs. Once the deal was done, I ate my body weight in American-style burgers and s'mores and couldn't believe my luck. Sally, you've changed my life. You get this novel so *well*, and I'm so grateful. Thanks, too, to the Darley Anderson rights team. I had a Chinese takeaway when they sold my Chinese rights last week, so we are all winning here.

Never has a book been so research-heavy as this one. At the outset, I knew almost nothing about the medicine of smothered babies, nor how that would be explored in a court of law. And so it's thanks to the following people that this book exists.

The first and largest thanks go to Patrick Davies and Cathy Cobley, who both responded to my many hundreds of emails during summer 2017 about, variously, retinal haemorrhages, MRI scans, initial police interviews and more. The nomogram in this novel belongs entirely to Patrick: it was his idea and my entire plot turns on it.

Patrick also facilitated me attending a trial of this nature, which was instrumental in writing sensitively and credibly about it. It was the strangest two days up in Lincoln in a hotel, attending a court case with my father, and I will remember that for ever. I owe Patrick and Cathy both so much. I'm constantly surprised by how many experts will do so much for so little in return.

Second thanks to my garden-variety medics who are always on hand to describe horrendous A&E scenes to me and to answer my sociopathic questions: Sami and my sister, Suzanne. Thanks, too, to the crew of lawyers – Alison Hardy, Ian Peddie, QC, Imran Mahmood (whose own novel is simply perfection) and Neil White. Thank you for making this a 'real' courtroom drama with not a shouted 'Objection!' in sight.

Thanks also to my police – Phil and Marie Evison and Alice Vinten. You're always steering me away from hard-cop clichés and into reality, and I remain for ever grateful.

And now – if you will bear with me – on to my personal thanks. Thanks to those people who are always on the end of a phone and who are riding this rollercoaster with me. The people I tell about my foreign rights and press reviews know who they are, but Mum, Dad, Paul and Sarah Wade, G. X. Todd, Holly Seddon (afternoon!) and Lucy Blackburn – you're in the inner sanctum. Sorry I'm so annoying.

To Tom Davis, my old university professor, who taught me about free indirect speech, and then distinctive character voices, last summer: you saved my crazy multiple-narrator novel. I owe you my career.

Penultimate thanks, as ever, to my father. Last spring I

turned up at his house and said, 'I don't think I can do justice to all of the witness vignettes in this novel.' He said to me, 'Let's choose one witness per week, and we'll walk and talk about them, and sort it all out.' We talked about Bridget, the midwife, while walking around Sutton Park, and about Sophie Cole in a bluebell wood. Every time I left him, I knew my characters a little better. I mean, could you really ask for a better dad than that?

And finally, as ever, thanks go to David. I write about love, really, in all its forms, but for you it is the purest.

Read on for a sneak peek of
Gillian McAllister's stunning new book

THE
EVIDENCE
AGAINST
YOU

Coming Spring 2019

I

It was a wicked and depraved act, Izzy is thinking as she closes her curtains. That's what the judge said. She remembers his exact words from seventeen years ago. *It was a wicked and depraved act. You wanted Alexandra Harrison to die, and you made sure that she did.* Her father was standing in the dock, staring impassively at the judge, his gaze not faltering, his body completely still. He wouldn't even look across at her. Not as the guilty verdict was read out. Not as he was sentenced to life in prison. And not as he was taken away, either.

It's been an unusually cold spring. There was snow last weekend, at Easter. She bought Nick an Easter egg from Sainsbury's and by the time she had brought it in from the car it had a light dusting on the top of its box. It has felt unnatural, somehow, to see the April flowers trying to push up through frosts and snow. She has tried to air the bedroom this evening, but it's still too cold, and her hands chill as she draws the curtains.

Downstairs, she can hear Nick gathering up their mugs. He always does it right before bed. Always has, for their entire fourteen-year relationship.

Next he will methodically swill them, then up-end them in the dishwasher. She listens for it, an ear cocked. The tap. The chink of the china. The noise of the dishwasher drawer on the runners.

A tree seems to shift in the darkness outside their bedroom window. Izzy is used to the palm trees, but Nick couldn't believe it when he first moved across. 'It's not *that* south,' he kept saying. Izzy had shrugged. The Isle of Wight was special; everybody knew that. It was new to Nick, but she'd grown up here.

'It's tomorrow,' she says to Nick, still standing by the window, when he arrives upstairs. She likes to confront things in this way, head on, though it embarrasses Nick. Gentle, dithering Nick, her cousin Chris once called him.

'I know,' he says, his tone tentative. Neither of them has mentioned it this evening until now. What is there to say? Besides, Nick will only list each eventuality, and what they should do about it. Izzy would rather see what happens. In some ways, the worst has already happened.

'I can't believe he's out tomorrow,' she says anyway, unable to stop herself. She lets the curtain fall. She wonders again what her father will do – where he'll go – but she stops the thought before it can really begin.

Nick is looking at her from across the bedroom. She had always said she wanted a bedroom like a hotel room and, after a weekend away for her thirtieth, four years ago, she arrived home to a different bedroom, as though she had walked into the wrong house. A high bed with a dark suede headboard, six duck-feather pillows piled up. Aubergine-coloured walls, a deep carpet. Everything. He'd done it all for her. He'd bought copper lamps from HomeSense and scented pillow spray and a leather ottoman that he placed at the bottom of the bed.

She looks back at her husband. He is tall and pale, with dark hair and freckles. She thinks she sees pity cross his features as he hesitates, but she isn't sure in the dim lamp-light. He doesn't reassure her. Doesn't ask her how she's feeling. She no longer expects him to, not after so many years. It is enough that he comes and stands next to her and pulls the curtain properly shut. He's been at work, at the police station, and smells of stale coffee and biscuits.

'You'll tell me, if you hear anything,' she says to him. They ought to be practical, at least, and Nick will hear before she does. If her father does anything. If he causes any . . . trouble.

'Yes,' he replies softly, still looking at her. 'And you me.'

She squeezes past him to go downstairs. She could step into his arms. They would tighten around her, and keep her safe, but she won't let them, not right now. She might never leave his arms, and life goes on. It must go on.

She unlocks the front door and drags the bin across the back alleyway. It's Sunday, bin night. They live on the end of a set of four houses, isolated in Luccomb, only three miles from where Izzy grew up. The row of seventeenth-century cottages are set back from the road, and share a cobbled access way. Bin night went from friendly nods to protracted chats to something more formal, for Izzy's neighbours. A way to welcome the week, William said, when he rang her doorbell to ask her to join their barbecue one night. Nick was working, and she went alone. She met Thea and her dog Daniel, and now they speak every day.

She hears them now as she reaches her bin. They're laughing about something, a burst of noise in the quiet night. She nods to them as she wheels it past. They're in scarves, hats and gloves, exasperated with the cold spring, but outside anyway.

'Happy Sunday,' Thea says to her. Her cheeks are red with the cold, grey-streaked hair poking out from underneath a hat.

'And you,' Izzy says with a smile.

'Did you decide on the paint?'

'No – I've narrowed it to four,' Izzy answers. Last weekend they'd spread out ten Farrow & Ball samples on her kitchen table. 'Pavilion Grey will be too dark in here,' Thea had said, and Izzy had instantly discarded it.

She can't stay and speak, not this week. Not today. She'll only tell Thea everything. She continues to wheel the bin by the group quietly and leaves it at the end of the path with theirs. She pauses again, in the chilly night, listening to them.

'June – June, she'll be home,' Thea is saying. 'She's going to some Californian festival over Easter instead of revising.'

Imagine, just imagine. Izzy closes her eyes just briefly and stands shivering in the cold. It was warm, the April her father was convicted. 'It's a sweat box already,' she heard one of the prison van drivers say outside the courtroom as they led him away wearing a suit and handcuffs. She didn't try to speak to him.

When Izzy walks back to her house, Thea has turned to their other neighbour, William. He is holding a cup of tea and the vapour steams up his glasses as he sips. 'Anyway, she's graduating in three months and – not a clue,' Thea is saying.

William nods, his mouth turning down. 'Neil's the same.'

'So she'll be back here, I expect, at least for a few years.' Thea's smiling, her eyes crinkling, looking upwards at the sky as she thinks of her daughter coming home. 'I never knew what I wanted to do, either,' she adds. 'We can work it out. And in the meantime, she's the best company. We're both stupid at going to bed. We stay up together, buying rubbish on the internet.'

Izzy averts her eyes as she walks past. When she reaches the back door, her hand lingers on the doorknob. She takes a deep breath, and allows herself to imagine her own mother. Murdered by her father, when Izzy was just seventeen.

After a few seconds, she goes inside. She locks the door, then checks it, just to be sure.

BM